Forever, Lately

A Regency Time-Travel Romance

Linore Rose Burkard

LILLIPUT PRESS

OHIO

Cover Design by 100Covers.com

FOREVER, LATELY: A REGENCY TIME TRAVEL ROMANCE
Copyright ©2019 Linore Rose Burkard
Published by Lilliput Press, OH

Cataloging-in-Publication Data
Burkard, Linore Rose
Forever, Lately: A Regency Time Travel Romance
ISBN: 9781733311106 (ppb)
ISBN: 9781733311113 (ebk)

LCCN: 2019912372

1. Fiction—Romance, Time Travel   2. Romance, Historical, Regency

First Edition

Bulk Ordering Information: Available from Ingram

What Readers Are Saying About Forever, Lately

Move over, Poldark! Julian St. John is our new English heartthrob! The fun is on with Burkard's cast of mismatched, mischievous characters. I highly recommend this read!
Lisa K. Simonds, Author, *All In*

A delicious romp through time that will keep you on the edge of your seat! This was such a fun read. The plot moved quickly to the expected time-travel and then didn't stop! A hilarious mix of misunderstandings…combine into one nail-biting experience that doesn't hit the brakes until the final pages!
Nicole Sager, Author, *The Heart of Arcrea*

This is such a good book. Pure Magic. It's the best Regency novel I've ever read! I'm actually sorry it is over.
Kristen Malone, Historical Romance Writer

In *Forever, Lately*, Linore Rose Burkard has combined romance and time travel into a delightful roller coaster ride of a book! Had me reading non-stop. Highly recommended!
Donna J. Shepherd, Author, *Love Under the Bubble Wrap*

I would read anything Linore Burkard writes. It takes a great author to write so well in multiple genres, and this regency time travel is a great addition to Linore's other works, including a Christian Regency series and her heart stopping dystopian trilogy. This is an author you don't want to miss!
Jaimee Dinnison, Reader Reviewer

With eccentric characters, well-defined period details (have you been to 1816, Ms. Burkard?) and a rollicking plot, Linore Rose Burkard takes us on a fast-paced, unpredictable journey that leaves the reader breathless until the very end!
Janice Dick, Author, *Eye of the Storm*

This story is fantastic! Will leave you wishing you had your own portal to another time. I was completely enthralled. I highly recommend this book.
Deb Mitchell, Reader Reviewer

Can I just say I am in love with St. John? Thank you for such an amazing and fabulous story!
Hannah Q., Reader Reviewer

Such a fun read! I do believe it is my favorite of your books!
Debbie Lynne Costello, Author, *Sword of Forgiveness*

Forever, Lately **may turn out to be my fav read in the past decade!**
Judith Blevins, Writer

This time travel romance was a winner. The author's extensive research and excellent writing style created such a plausible story that I slipped in and out of the time-periods seamlessly.
Diane Hiller Engelhardt, Reader Reviewer

A delightful book that, chapter after chapter, kept me wanting to turn the pages!
Lisa G. Smith, Reader Reviewer

Loved this book! The opening threw me into a tailspin and I (thought) I had an idea of where the book was going but I was wrong! The pressures in each time period created lasting suspense. A really enjoyable read.
Fiona Rowe, Reader Reviewer

Research, research, research! Ms. Burkard shows her diligence. I'm a history buff and the first part of the 19th century is my favorite era. Plot twists will keep readers turning pages, (as well as) lively, often humorous transitions from one century to the other!
Peggy Lovelace Ellis, Writer, Freelance Editor

*To my agent and former Harvest House
editor, Nick Harrison, who said of this book,
"A masterful handling of a difficult genre."
And to my readers, who make it all
worthwhile.*

CHAPTER 1

March 1816

England

Julian St. John dug in his heels and spurred on Brutus, his thoroughbred of sixteen hands, as he approached the drive to his estate. A light rain was falling, obscuring the moonlight, and he wanted nothing more than to get home and return to his books and fireside. He'd been dragged off by a messenger who'd claimed that a "proper lady" was on the road and in need of assistance.

He'd ridden all the way into the village and found no lady in need of help. Neither did he see the boy who'd appeared at his door claiming there was one. He didn't mind an urgent gallop; he was born for speed, and thrived on racing, but it was a fool's errand and he was tired. He secured his hat and nudged on Brutus with his heels. As he neared the turnoff to his own drive, suddenly the lights of a coach against the side of the road about fifty feet ahead lit up, looking dully at him like two sleepy eyes.

St. John squinted and slowed Brutus. The coach hadn't moved, so he spurred the animal gently towards it, wondering if his assistance was needed after all. But the sound of a whip and a coachman's yell brought the idle vehicle to life, and it barreled down the road—straight towards him. He moved Brutus to the side but was astonished when the coach veered again in his direction. Was the coachman buffle-headed?

He spurred the animal's sides and maneuvered off the road and up a steep incline, and then turned to watch the vehicle. Unbelievably, it was still coming crazily at him, its lamplights brighter now, blazing like evil eyes. And closing in. This wasn't poor driving—the coach was *trying* to hit him! As it bowled towards him, the coachman's face materialised out of the haze, his eyes opened wide in terror.

A fence prevented St. John from vanishing into the trees that fronted his property, but just as the coach would have bowled into him, he shouted at Brutus, snapped his spurs, and cracked the reins—they missed a collision by inches as the sturdy animal lunged out of harm's way. The coach's horses hit the fence whinnying.

Turning Brutus around quickly, St. John patted his neck while surveying the vehicle as it came to a rollicking stop, balanced precariously on the incline. The messenger boy, he saw now, had fallen from the coach to his backside in the wet brush.

Taking a deep breath at the close call, St. John quietly reached into a coat pocket and pulled out a pistol. Good thing he rarely rode in the evenings without one. Good thing too, that he was an excellent horseman or that insane coachman might have caused his demise.

Brutus nickered nervously. "Good show, old boy," he said, never moving his eyes from the sleek black coach, silent and mysterious. Its horses stamped impatiently. There was no other sound as he approached and made his way past the closed door, but he found the coachman huddled on his perch.

"How the devil do you explain your driving? Are you hocused?" he asked, thinking the man was in his cups.

"Nay, guv'nor. Followin' me orders, that's what."

"Orders from whom?" St. John demanded. "Who do you have in there?"

"T'mistress an' 'er sister," he answered sullenly.

St. John's heart sank—two women—if the driver could be trusted. "And you drove like a madman with women aboard!"

The man shifted uneasily on his perch but muttered, "I follows me orders, guv'nor."

"And what were your orders, precisely?" he asked in a scathing tone.

Again the man shifted uneasily. "Ask t'mistress."

"Who is your mistress?"

The coachman gave him a guarded look. "Ask t'mistress," he repeated.

St. John turned away in disgust and urged his horse nearer the window of the equipage. He peered cautiously inside but saw only darkness. Dismounting, he kept the reins in one hand.

"Hello?" No answer. He readied his pistol. "If you do not answer, I warn you—I am armed." When still no sound came forth, he reached for the latch and turned it, eliciting a gentle click. Holding the pistol out, he swung the door open and peered inside. "Hello," he said again, wishing the clouds weren't obstructing the moon so well.

He heard movement and tensed. A muffled sob came from the far side of the coach. He shoved his pistol in a pocket—heavens, it *was* a woman—and was about to jump in when a female laugh, very close to his head, rang out, clear and distinct.

"Oh, Margaret," the voice scolded. "You've spoilt it! You needn't blubber; we are unharmed, are we not? And you can see St. John is equally unscathed."

Julian forced himself to take a deep breath before he spoke. "What the devil have you done?" he hissed at the speaker, who now pushed her face forward from the shadows, where the coach lamp illumined the lovely features of Clarissa Andrews in all her wicked, seductive beauty.

She smiled at him, turning her head demurely, only it wasn't an honest movement, for there was nothing demure about Miss Andrews. She was a vixen, a minx, a she-devil, and she'd been trying to get St. John beneath her power since the start of the season. She knew, as did all of London that St. John, after thirty-four years of bachelorhood, was in need of a wife. He'd made an oath to the Marquess of Worleydon, his deceased guardian, and he meant to keep it.

"Allow me to congratulate you, Julian, on the excellent handling of your horse," she purred. "I am infinitely relieved you have kept yourself in one piece, you must know. I should have been utterly cast down had you been harmed."

Steely blue eyes glinted at her.

He wished he could tell her to go to the devil, to plague *him* with her incessant fooleries, but he was too much a gentleman—by God, he would be a gentleman. So he said only, "You could have got someone killed."

"Yes, you," she agreed calmly. "But here you are, as handsome and alive as ever." She gave him a sweet smile, reminding him of what he found so vexatious in her. She had an innocent smile, delectable lips, but behind it all a black heart.

"Oh, come, Julian, you give me too much credit. No one was anything near being killed. You know it was naught but a lark, only a lark!"

"Only a lark?" His voice dripped ice. "Your coach came directly at me, and if I had been any less a rider, I'd have broken my neck. My horse might have died as well."

She was thoughtful a moment. "We were not supposed to drive quite so close to you, I own. And why do you insist upon riding such an immense animal? We should have fared the worst, not you; only it did not work out the way I planned." She spoke with barely a moment's stopping. "And I warrant you would have come to rescue me in a moment if Margaret had not spoilt everything." She pouted at him from within the reaches of a richly beribboned bonnet. "I was perfectly prepared to swoon for your benefit. You would have come to my aid, would you not?" She looked at him hopefully, but he made no answer. He directed his next words to the opposite wall of the coach.

"Are you all right, Miss Margaret?" He couldn't see Miss Andrews's younger sister, but a sniffle came from the darkness.

"I—I think so. Thank you, sir."

"Margaret's perfectly well!" Miss Andrews cried, moving forward so her ample bosom, half revealed in the formal dress of evening wear, was not only plainly in sight, but blocked any possible view behind her. St. John looked away, refusing to admire her.

Other men did admire her, for any wall in the kingdom would proudly boast her portrait. She had dark, lustrous hair, an ovaline face with a well-delineated nose, and dark, long-lashed eyes. She also had slim ankles and small feet, which he knew from attending many a ball or rout in town. But St. John could not admire Miss Andrews's face or slim ankles, for her brazen impudence gave him a disgust of her.

In the past he would have taken advantage of her, welcomed her when she teased him with her alluring countenance and everything beneath it. At times he wanted nothing more than to take hold of her and…He forced his mind to concentrate only on her irksome behaviour. Tonight's escapade, what she called a 'mere lark,' was the latest in a string of vexatious attempts by her to gain his attention. And it was merely a hoax, another of her tricks, to put him in her path.

As he considered how best to give her a set-down, the jarring sound of a ring tone, quite close, made St. John turn in amazement and look around, not understanding the sound or its source. It was unrecognizable. But Claire Channing, the author writing St. John's story, did. She shut her eyes with a low groan, while St. John and the coach, the dark road, all of it, vanished, and she was back, sitting before her laptop, waiting for the call to go to voice mail.

CHAPTER 2

Dove Cottage, Maine
Present Day

Note to self: Mute the cell phone before writing!

Claire didn't get many calls. She'd become downright reclusive as her career as an author took off. Her agent could be calling but that was doubtful. Her last two books were flops, and the one he was shopping around now had only garnered "mild interest" from publishers. He'd called it "promising," but Claire suspected he was only being nice.

She didn't recognize the number, so waited long enough for the caller to leave a message and then picked up. To her surprise, the caller was still on.

"Oh good, Claire, you're there! Adam Winthrop here."

Claire sighed and shut her eyes. "I'm not really here. Can you leave a message?"

Adam's family owned Bavarian Mountain Ski Lodge, a lucrative resort that surrounded Dove Cottage. He'd been pestering her since her arrival two weeks prior to sell them the little dwelling.

"I'll keep it short. It's important. But if you don't want to stay on, I can show up at your door in approximately…five minutes."

"No, no," said Claire. *Definitely not.* "I'm listening. Go." Twice before he'd offered to come to her door—or threatened to, depending on how she looked at it—and she'd put him off. Was he curious to meet the struggling author? Size up the opposition? Well, she wasn't about to indulge him. He just wanted an opportunity to pressure her about selling.

"Okay, look, I thought you should know," Adam said. "The old man's ready to up his offer."

Claire sighed. "How many times do I have to say this? I'm not selling. And I would never sell without Mrs. Grandison's signature even if I wanted to, which I don't." Charlotte Grandison was Claire's grandmother.

"But she's still MIA," he countered. "The town says the land's not deeded—it's up for grabs, Claire, and my father's already in the process of buying it. Once he owns it, he'll tear down your cottage. I'm doing you a favor by offering to take it off your hands now, while you can still make money on it."

Claire gripped the phone. This was the first she'd heard about tearing it down. "Your father will have to tear it down around me because I'll be here. Goodbye, Adam."

"Don't go; don't go!" His voice softened. "Look, I'm sorry about your grandmother. But you don't really have ties to the place. You just moved in."

"It was my grandmother's home, and I live here now. I'll find that deed."

"Face it, Claire. If there was a deed, the town would have a copy. Mrs. Grandison lived there as a squatter, I'm sorry to say. And that makes you one too."

"You're wrong," she said. She *hoped* he was wrong. "My family bought this land, fair and square."

"There's no record of a purchase."

"Goodbye, Adam!" Claire hung up, breathing hard. The Winthrops were going to play dirty, were they? What did they want Grandmother's measly two acres for, anyway? They owned scads of land all around the cottage and as Adam had pointedly told her, "in plenty of other places." She'd heard their ritzy lodge was booked year-round, even when skiing wasn't an option—the cottage wasn't infringing on their profits.

Her sheepdog Charlie got up and lazily sniffed around her feet, then settled in a hump at the floor. He seemed as weary of Adam's calls as Claire. She'd block the man in a heartbeat except she needed to know if the Winthrops were really going to snatch the cottage right out from under her.

When she first arrived, Adam called to invite her to a small mixer, a get-together of locals. Surely she wanted to know her new neighbors? Then it was to offer his assistance—did she need help with the woodstove? Or maybe she needed some wood chopped? When temperatures dipped into freezing single digits, he called to remind her not to let her pipes freeze. But something told her he wasn't just trying to be helpful. Sure enough, he soon revealed that his family wanted her cottage. To be exact, they wanted to tear it down for its land.

She *needed* the cottage. They only wanted it because it wasn't already theirs.

Claire had come from Connecticut to Dove Cottage in Maine out of desperation, and with one purpose: to churn out a masterpiece to save her writing career. She'd learned of Grandmother's disappearance months ago, but since she barely remembered the woman, she hadn't given it much thought. Not until Mother announced she planned on having Grandmother declared dead so she could sell the cottage, did Claire feel a sense of loss about the woman, accompanied by a sudden need to check out her home. She'd been there only once when Mother had reluctantly visited, bringing Claire, aged twelve, along. Apparently, Mrs. Grandison had nearly died after routine gallbladder surgery. But she didn't die, and Claire's mother had never seen the need to visit the matriarch again.

Mother and Grandmother had a long-standing feud. Claire was never able to get details about what started it. All Mother would say was that Grandmother had gone off the deep end; that living alone in the woods had made her crazy. She didn't want Claire picking up any of her craziness, and had severed ties completely with the old lady after that last visit.

She wasn't in favor of Claire's sudden wish to visit the place.

"You don't want to go up there," Mother said, during a rare phone call. Claire and Mother had seldom been in sync, and now spoke infrequently. Women in Claire's line, it seemed, were destined for frosty relationships.

"Why not?" Claire asked. "Grandmother can't influence me; I'm not a child, and besides, she isn't even there."

"Living there is what made her crazy. She's been missing for a year. I'm having it torn down."

Claire protested, "I remember it as a cozy little house. Just give me a few months—enough to finish my book. Besides, maybe I'll find something that will tell us where Grandmother disappeared to."

"I went up once and looked around and couldn't find anything," Mother said. "I don't know what's happened to her, but I don't think she's still alive."

Claire was sorry to think she'd never have a chance to know the old woman, but she was determined to get up to that quiet place in the pines. She'd started a new book that could be a game-changer for her, and Dove Cottage was just the place to get it finished. It lay off a quiet secondary road, an ideal writer's retreat.

She ought to have visited Grandmother before her mysterious disappearance, of course. Why had she let her mother deprive her of the relationship they might have had? Since it was too late, and with the Winthrops threatening the cottage, Claire felt the least she could do was hang on to the place. What if Grandmother Grandison returned? She deserved a home to come back to.

After the call with Mother, Claire hurried to get her ducks in a row in order to get to the cottage before Mother had it razed. What started as a vague longing to see it, to find a connection to the woman who was family, became a conviction. That cottage was not only a link to her lineage, but her best chance of producing a game-saving book.

And her career definitely needed saving. The bad reviews that followed her last two books, both Regency romances, were overpowering, each one an anchor, strapping her to a loser's plateau that now she must escape from. One reviewer wrote, "Ms. Channing's fans may keep her alive, but it certainly isn't this latest book doing so." And even her agent warned that if she didn't turn things around, she'd have to write with a pseudonym. Or self-publish. Claire wanted a contract and a big advance, not the responsibility and headaches of self-publishing. She wanted a blockbuster.

She'd terminated the lease on her apartment, grabbed Charlie and a few suitcases, and drove up in her silver Capri. She phoned ahead first since the cottage had been empty for so long, arranged for snow to be cleared, and hired a cleaning service, an electrician, and a repairman. Working appliances and an internet connection weren't optional. On the third day after her arrival with Charlie, Adam called.

His family was surprised to see someone living in the lonely cottage atop the hill; wouldn't she like to sell it, seeing as it was surrounded by property—their property? They'd give her more than a fair market price, and who else would ever buy it?

Claire had been adamant from the start about not selling. Grandmother could be abroad on some pilgrimage, for instance—the old lady did pilgrimages, according to Mother. But also the cottage had instantly felt welcoming and she was already getting in a lot of writing. It wasn't paradise, but had rustic charm. Inside a log-cabin exterior with a quaint red-metal roof was an old-fashioned kitchen that included an ironstone stove and a wide hearth. The cozy living room had a fireplace, as did the main bedroom, and the Winthrops' lodge was far enough away so she heard nothing of tourists and ski lifts. It was peaceful. It was perfect.

During her first walk-through, she'd found a cloth table runner in the bottom of a cedar chest. As she admired its lovely gold-and-mint embroidery, Claire had a sudden memory. It wasn't a runner; it was a shawl, a prayer shawl. Grandmother had found it in Israel on one of her pilgrimages. She called it by a special name which Claire couldn't remember. It was woven in sturdy white cotton, with a wide embroidered hem on all sides. The shorter ends were tasseled, and included two small doves—or were they lovebirds—meeting in a kiss.

The shawl had hung in a glass case on the wall like a museum tapestry on Claire's last visit. The glass must have broken, for the case was gone. She draped the fabric over the brow of the sofa where she'd see it as she worked at the kitchen table, and the memory bubbled up: a tallit, that's what Grandmother called it.

She added a log to the blaze in the fireplace. She'd need more logs eventually but Grandmother's front porch was stacked with two cribs of seasoned wood. If the old lady hadn't planned on being back for winter, she certainly had left enough firewood. She peeked out a window as she moved her laptop to the kitchen nook. Maine days were short in winter. She appreciated the falling snow, light as dust today, but sparkling upon the ground and trees in shafts of fading sunlight.

Well. St. John and Clarissa Andrews were waiting. It was time for Clarissa to apologize to St. John for the dangerous coach caper. Clarissa really was sorry and would begin to mend her ways. And St. John would have a change of heart towards her. By the end of the book he'd propose to Clarissa and they'd live happily ever after.

That was the plan, the outline she'd labored over for this new book which she called *Forever, Lately*. Later, when it all fell apart, Claire would wonder how she'd stumbled upon real people to inhabit her story. If she'd known they were real, she might have known, too, that they wouldn't ever do as she planned.

> But some characters in books are really real.
> Dodie Smith

CHAPTER 3

1816 London

St. John happened to be looking toward the entrance during a public ball the following week when Miss Clarissa Andrews appeared. Her daringly low décolletage emphasized an ample bosom and slim waist; any lower and it would be fit only for a Cyprian's ball. A Grecian headdress of net and olive leaves adorned her black locks, and around her neck lay a ponderous necklace with a large wooden cross against white flesh and cleavage.

Miss Margaret trailed in behind her, every bit the shy, awkward girl of fifteen. Where Clarissa was curvaceous, Margaret was straight; where Clarissa had mounds of allure, Margaret was flat. Though she received little attention, her saving grace was that she required none. As soon as the pair entered, Margaret scampered to a wall at the back of the room and took a seat. Her only ambition was to watch.

Clarissa was quickly taken in hand by a matronly dame who had an available first son. A baronet's daughter, Miss Andrews was known for a large dowry which made her of interest to mammas with sons to marry off.

Clarissa had little interest in the woman or her son, however. Instead, her gaze swept the room until it alighted upon St. John. She underwent a change in demeanour. First there was relief, but this was shortly followed by the insolent, confident look she wore whenever she felt challenged by anyone. And St. John was a prodigious challenge.

Despite many admirers, she wanted only him. And this season

she must win him, for he was finally wife-hunting. He was about to turn thirty-four and had apparently made a vow to some venerable deceased relation to be married by that age and see to the business of begetting an heir. Even better, St. John's rakish days were behind him. He used to be too dangerous for Clarissa. Though she wasn't entirely proper herself, she could scarcely afford a man who might not follow an impropriety with an offer. But St. John had changed, "got religion," so they said. He no longer went about using women—even those who wouldn't mind being used—but was every bit as good-looking and rich as when he did.

Julian turned away from Miss Andrews's gaze. What once might have appealed to him in her, the daring gowns and brazen manners, he now disliked. Even more, he despised her hoaxes, what she called larks. A woman wasn't supposed to chase a man, though the anger he'd felt last week when her coach had nearly run him down had dissipated into a feeling more akin to pity. St. John wasn't malicious. But he had no wish to fall into old temptations or to raise false hopes. When he saw her searching the room, he knew from experience she was seeking him out. She would dangle around him and plague him if he let her. He must not let her.

He'd been near ready to act the gentleman and ask a young woman, a noted wallflower, to stand up with him; but Miss Andrews gave him pause. Clarissa had the unfortunate habit of giving the cut direct to any lady he took to the floor. St. John had reprimanded her for this social injustice more than once, but Miss Andrews made it utterly clear that he was the cause of the lady's misfortune. If he had not insisted upon dancing, there would be no need for her to give the cut. This only deepened his conviction that she was a vixen of the first water, a female scoundrel, for she would snub an inferior and think nothing of it. *Woman, thy name is frailty.*

From the corner of his eye he saw her extricating herself from the clutches of the ambitious mamma, and making her way toward him.

Mr. Timbrell, an acquaintance he'd been speaking to, said, "Do not look now, but I believe 'tis my brother's keeper coming this way."

"Your brother may keep her," Julian answered smoothly, "for I never shall."

Mr. Timbrell smiled but said, "She is a most determined lady where you are concerned. I know it plagues you Julian, but I shouldn't complain if she were to set her cap at me."

"Only tell her your fortune has doubled, and I have no doubt she may."

"When she knows of your family obligation—that you must wed this year? If I were as rich as Croesus she'd not look away from you."

Clarissa arrived. The men bowed politely.

"Beware, Miss Andrews," Mr. Timbrell said, as she finished a curtsey. "St. John is in a nasty turn of temper; I warn you." He gave a mischievous grin to Julian and sauntered off.

Clarissa studied him. "Are you indeed in a nasty temper? May I know why?"

"Is not your presence enough to warrant it?" he asked in a low tone to spare her embarrassment. Clarissa produced a delicate ladies' fan with a hand-painted Chinese design on it, and started fanning herself.

"Dear me, do not say you are still cross over that lark the other night."

"Very well, I shall not say it."

She fanned more rapidly. "My dear sir, if you tire of my pranks, as you fashion my behaviour, then why not offer for me and settle it? I should obey you with all my heart as your wife. I will no longer endanger anyone's life, including yours, and I shall make a very proper wife to you."

St. John stared at her. He knew Clarissa was brazen, but—an outright offer! A woman, to a man! "Miss Andrews—for once you nearly render me speechless. I am too astonished, indeed, to make any reply at all. Excuse me."

Her countenance dropped at his last words, and with the merest hint of a bow, St. John turned and walked away.

A bonny lass I will confess, is pleasant to the e'e,
But without some better qualities she's no a lass for me.
Robert Burns

CHAPTER 4

Dove Cottage

Note to self: If characters are going to change from what the writer envisioned, they must do so early on in the writing.

"You are a terrible flirt, and you didn't say the right thing to St. John," Claire said to her laptop. Clarissa was supposed to apologize, not propose marriage. Claire felt as though she'd watched the scene unfold more than written it.

Charlie had been resting placidly at her feet, but he sat up, peered at Claire, and whimpered.

"You need to go out, don't you?" Claire asked, setting his tail wagging. By the time she got to the door, he was frantic with excitement. When she opened it, he whooshed out like a north wind.

Wrapped in coat, hat and gloves, she got ready to follow the dog but spied the tallit lying over the brow of the sofa. Why not? It would add some warmth. She circled it loosely around her shoulders as she stepped onto the porch. Then she trailed after Charlie who was scampering ahead, joyful as a child.

There was a frozen top layer to the snow, making it crunch with each step. She took in the beauty of snow-encased pines, the quiet of a world blanketed in white and felt deeply grateful to her grandmother. She hoped the old woman was off on one of her pilgrimages in some corner of the world, and that nothing dire had happened to her. For living in the cottage gave Claire no clues as to the mystery of where she'd gone off to. In fact, Claire found suitcases in the closet of the spare bedroom—surely if the old lady had planned on a sojourn she'd have needed her luggage! It troubled Claire.

Ahead, Charlie barked and took off around a bend in the trees as though chasing a bird. She went in his direction and soon heard him.

Growling. Her heart dropped as she wondered if he'd encountered a coyote. A bear wouldn't be around in midwinter, would it? She turned the bend and caught a flash of dark fur—or was it fabric?—behind a dense, bare bush. Her heart jumped into her throat. "Charlie!" she gasped.

But Charlie's tail now wagged furiously, but low, as though he was torn between being happy or suspicious of whatever it was beyond Claire's sight. He barked, then whimpered, then scampered around and returned to the spot. Claire stood there, half terrified, ready to turn and run, but feeling protective of her dog.

"C'mon, Charlie!" she called. And then a man stepped out from behind the bush as he stroked Charlie, now in full wag, behind the ears, with gloved hands. But not snow gloves. No, they were buff leather, perfectly in keeping with what a Regency gentleman might wear—as was the rest of his costume! Claire froze.

Was she seeing things? She shook her head and blinked, but he remained. From the side, as he seemed not to see her and gave his attention only to the dog, she suddenly realized it was St. John! Her idea of St. John, anyway. It couldn't be him, really; he was fictional! He wore hunting boots and pantaloons, a double-breasted coat and beaver hat. He held a riding whip in one hand, and a beautiful cravat peeked out above his coat. Claire's legs went weak. This had to be a joke. But why hadn't he seen her?

"Charlie!" Her voice sounded weak. St. John seemed oblivious to her presence. Charlie was too busy enjoying his attention to pay any heed to Claire, so she turned and hurried back to the house. She felt spooked and confused, and twice checked to see if the man was following, but he wasn't.

She rushed into the house, slammed the door behind her and locked it as fast as her fumbling hands could manage. Quickly she grabbed her cell phone and dialed 911. She heard Charlie yelp on the porch—she'd locked him out! She peeked out warily, but the dog was alone. Seeing nobody, she opened the door just enough to let him in and then hurried to lock it again. She stood behind a curtain at the window while waiting for 911 to answer, her heart still pounding in her throat.

Outside she saw only a wintry landscape, snowcapped trees and bushes, and a weak sun beginning to set. The man was nowhere in sight.

Imagination does not breed insanity.
What breeds insanity is reason.
G.K. Chesterton

CHAPTER 5

Adam Winthrop put his hands in his coat pockets and studied Claire. "You sure you want to stay alone out here? We have a great guest bedroom." Smiling, he added, "It'll give you a chance to meet the whole family—we are your neighbors, you know."

"I'll be fine," she said, her tone clipped. "I must have been imagining things." Claire was miffed that the local sheriff had called Adam of all people, to meet him at the cottage. Apparently, the Winthrops were tight with the sheriff, who knew they wanted to buy the place. Did he consider that justification to bring Adam along? Or was it that the Winthrops were rich and brought in the lion's share of tourist dollars to the area? Either way, it ruffled Claire that she had to meet her foe under this circumstance. Both men thought she'd imagined the incident.

They'd gone over the place slowly and carefully, especially around the bush where Claire had seen the man. She couldn't explain why there was nothing but paw prints in the snow: no footprints, and no fresh snow that might have covered them. She told how Charlie had reacted.

Sheriff Levin pushed his hat back. "Probably saw a rabbit, ma'am."

Claire had seen a man. And there weren't any rabbit tracks in the snow. *Note to self: Sheriff Levin is useless.*

With assurances that she could call anytime, and after exchanging a knowing nod at Adam, the officer was off.

Adam stuck his hand out. "I'm glad we finally got to meet. If I'd known how pretty you are, I wouldn't have waited this long."

Claire wasn't glad, but she shook his hand. With Adam's blonde hair, long, lean face, and blue eyes, he could have come from Norway, but she saw only one thing in those eyes: a determination to oust her from the cottage. And calling her pretty wasn't going to win him any favor, for the last thing Claire wanted was a relationship. If she'd learned anything from Mother, it was that men were not dependable. Career came first. Claire couldn't even remember her father, who had left before she was three.

Besides, she was in old clothes, her hair was untidy and her bangs overgrown, almost covering her eyes. She hadn't expected company, and when she was neck-deep in writing, rarely took pains over her appearance. Heck, she rarely took pains over her appearance at any time. She gave him her best, practiced, icy smile.

"I'd feel better if I knew you weren't alone," he said.

As if he cares. "I have Charlie," she responded, tightly.

He nodded. "OK. You have our number. But here," he walked over to a note pad Claire had near her phone and started writing, "is my cell number. I can get here a lot faster than the sheriff. Don't hesitate to call me if you see or hear anything unusual." He turned and grinned. "You know, like a Victorian man in costume."

"He wasn't Victorian. He was Regency."

"Oh, er...is there a difference?" He finished writing his number.

"Huge."

He turned, his face scrunched in thought. "Um, Regency...when was that?"

"Early nineteenth century," said Claire, who added her standard answer, "The time of Jane Austen."

"Ah." His face cleared as he came back toward her. "Well—whatever." At the door, he turned and gave her a lazy smile. "Hey, I read some of your book reviews."

"Yes?" she asked cautiously. She'd had more than her fair share of negative reviews in the past two years.

"That reporter from the *Tribune* said you need to live your own romance before you try writing another."

She crossed her arms.

He winked. "I'd be happy to help in any way I can—"

"Goodbye!" Claire urged him out the door and hurriedly shut and locked it.

"Just sayin,'" he called, after regaining his foothold. She watched furtively from a window as he shrugged, then shook his head, and tramped off the porch. It was growing dark, but she watched until his car disappeared in the gloom down the drive. *The nerve!* He'd read book reviews but hadn't even bothered to read one of her books.

She turned away, but now the awful truth hit her. She'd seen a man that had left no evidence of being real. Worse, he looked like St. John—her fictional hero.

She fed Charlie. "We know what we saw, don't we, Charlie?" It must have seemed like madness to Adam and the sheriff when she'd described the man's apparel, but what else could she do? It's what she'd seen. But no footprints! What did it mean?

Was her mother right about the cottage making her grandmother mad? Maybe it was happening to Claire, too. But every time she remembered how Charlie reacted, she knew it hadn't been just a vision, or solely her imagination—and definitely no rabbit.

After mulling it over, she called her mother. She'd be surprised to hear from Claire again so soon since they seldom spoke. If Mother showed any interest in Claire or her life, things might have been different. Talking to her was just a reminder of how that hurt. But curiosity about the cottage won out. As soon as uncomfortable pleasantries were over, she asked, "Can you tell me more about why you hate Dove Cottage? I need to know."

"Is everything all right?" her mother responded nervously. "Anything strange going on?"

"I thought I saw someone on the property today. But the sheriff couldn't find any sign of an intruder, not even a footprint."

"Are you sure you saw someone?"

"I'm totally sure! Charlie growled at first, but in a minute he was wagging his tail, and the man petted him."

"A man! Maybe it isn't safe up there."

"I'm okay. I have Charlie." She paused. "Can you just tell me what you've got against this place—or against Grandmother? I never understood that." She peeked out the window, holding the phone. But she couldn't have seen the man even if he was there, it was so dark. "What made you say she was nuts? And that you wished the cottage would be demolished?"

Her mother hesitated. "I don't want to talk about it."

Now Claire was really concerned. Her mother knew something! She went back to the kitchen and sat down. "I need answers."

"No, you need an alarm system. Or a husband. Someone to keep you company if you want to live in the woods."

"Mother, please!"

"Your grandmother had a lot of strange ideas, that's all. She swore she could see visions."

"Well, is that so strange?" Claire asked. "Maybe she was a Christian mystic or something."

"No, no, your grandmother was religious but her visions weren't." She paused, then added, "And she didn't have visions when she lived near us when you were a baby. They started when she moved there, into Dove Cottage."

"So Grandmother had visions; so what?"

"Well..." Her mother paused. "Okay, how's this? She believed she could see into other times of history. Is that weird enough for you?"

Claire was shocked. She'd never heard a word about this. "Did she really believe that?"

"That's why I kept you away from her. You thought I was just being mean, but I didn't want her giving you any wild ideas, filling your head with fantastic impossibilities. It's hard enough to raise children in today's world..." Her voice trailed off.

Claire frowned and rested her head on one hand. "Actually, what's so wrong with claiming to see visions of history? Even the Bible's full of visions."

"Of the future. Grandmother's were of the past. That's a big difference."

Claire sighed. She headed toward the only desk in the cottage, an old-fashioned roll-top in the living area and pulled open the file drawer. "Maybe she was just having memories and called them visions."

"Memories of things two hundred years before she was born?" her mother asked, sardonically.

Claire froze and her eyes bulged. "Two hundred years ago?" The Regency was approximately two hundred years ago, and Claire had seen St. John—a Regency gentleman!

"Your grandmother went off the deep end. After living there, she no longer had an orthodox bone in her body."

Claire was rifling through files Grandmother had left, not even sure what she was looking for. "So are you saying she was a heretic? Like, she believed in a past life?"

"No, not reincarnation. She was a Christian. But she went off the deep end at some point, and that cottage had everything to do with it. Her ideas got…frightening. That's all I can say about it."

Later, as Claire prepared dinner, she mulled over the conversation. Was Grandmother a visionary? Or had she really gone off the deep end, as her mother said? She hoped, if either were true, it didn't run in the family.

When she was back at the kitchen table ready to get in more writing, she said aloud to the *fictional* St. John, still in that ballroom, "I have forgotten to write in your costume tonight, sir. You must stand out from the crowd, and so—a scarlet, silver-threaded embroidered waistcoat, perhaps?" She quickly entered it to the page. But she felt cold—the fire was dying. She stirred the embers and added a few logs. Spying the tallit, she wrapped it tightly around her shoulders, crossing it over her chest.

And then chaos hit.

She heard a rushing sound, like a strong wind or waterfall—*or something*. And no longer was she in the cottage.

Logic will get you from A to B.
Imagination will take you everywhere.
Einstein

CHAPTER 6

The quiet of the room vanished, replaced by a hum of background voices and sounds such as one hears at a gathering. Claire blinked, as everything was fuzzy. What was happening? Still blinking, her surroundings came into focus. She swallowed—and thought her heart would stop. She was IN a Regency ballroom! She put out a hand to steady herself. And there—wasn't that St. John standing amongst a group of men? It was him, all right—the same man she'd seen on her property!

Was she going mad like her grandmother? Having visions of the past? But this wasn't the past—it was her book!

Despite her confusion, she noticed St. John's waistcoat wasn't scarlet and silver threaded as she'd just written it, but black with gold thread, visible beneath a lovely white cravat and the lapels of a twin-tailed topcoat. He wore beautifully fitted trousers, and—. Suddenly he squinted toward her. Their eyes locked, sending an electric current through her whole body. She was caught in his gaze like an embrace, captured by eyes that were curious, yet almost forbidding. He was *seeing* her! It wasn't just a story!

Get a hold of yourself. This can't be real. In fact, she refused to believe it. Aloud, she said, "It's just my wonderful writer's imagination." *She'd spoken with an English accent! How odd.* She tried to ignore her rising heart rate as she stared, fascinated, at the roomful of people in Regency attire. She looked down and nearly fainted. She wore a period correct Regency gown with a shawl. No, it was the tallit! And she wore satin ball slippers! What was happening? Could this be a lucid dream? It was *all so real*.

Claire peeked at St. John. He was still studying her! She was filled with awe and a surprising rush of sympathy for Clarissa. St. John was an imposingly masculine man, more muscular than Claire had realized. He had a strong nose and brow in addition to those arresting eyes. No wonder Clarissa would pine for him. Claire's heart pounded at how handsome a figure he was, in fact—but wait—hadn't she given him blue eyes? His, it appeared, were blue-grey, almost hazel, with the smallest hint of crow's feet at their edges. And his black hair had a light tinge of grey over his forehead and at his sideburns, which added to his distinguished good looks. He was a man aging well. Could he be older than she thought him?

Older than she'd thought? How could he be anything other than what she thought? Hadn't she invented him? She *was* losing her mind!

It was both strange and wonderful. She was like a character in her own book. Now St. John was looking, with an intrigued expression, back and forth at her and another lady. Claire followed his gaze and saw—Miss Andrews? She saw only her profile, but yes, it was Clarissa! Claire would know her anywhere! Miss Andrews was impressive in her revealing evening gown, Grecian-style headdress, and weighty jewellery. Her gown at least, Claire thought with satisfaction, fit the description she'd written earlier.

Claire turned and saw St. John heading her way. Was he going to speak to her? *This was too much!*

An imperious-looking woman stopped him. Claire sighed with relief. But chaos hit again as she heard that same rushing wind. Her head spun and everything grew fuzzy. When she opened her eyes, blinking, she was back at her laptop.

We never end up with the book we began writing.
Characters twist it and turn it
C.K. Webb

CHAPTER 7

Dove Cottage

With a gasp, Claire pulled her hands away from the keyboard and hurriedly shut it, not even bothering to save her work. *Note to self: Research lucid dreams—how real can they seem?* She stared at the laptop in alarm, and then, blinking, tried to assess what happened. She'd felt she was in a Regency ballroom, but how? How had she seen it all in living color as if she'd really been there? Even her own clothing had been Regency correct—that alone *had* to mean she'd dreamt it. Didn't it?

Such a thing couldn't happen.

She shivered. The tallit had fallen to the floor. She picked it up, draped it on her chair and stood to get a glass of water, but her legs almost gave way. She sat back down. *Her hands were shaking, too.* She'd been working too hard. But hadn't she worked hard on all her novels? She searched her brain for another explanation—it couldn't be that she was having visions like Grandmother! It was her own characters she'd seen.

Could she have fallen asleep? But such details she'd seen! Speaking of which—she opened the laptop again and brought up the character sheet for Julian St. John. She scrolled quickly down, shoving aside her bangs to read. *Blue eyes!*

She closed her eyes and saw St. John as he'd stood across from her. Her heart thumped at the memory of his dark good looks. But his eyes were not purely blue. She changed it to "blue-grey with hazel tints," on the character sheet. She'd have to do a "find and replace" in the manuscript, changing his eye color. Was it ludicrous to change a description based upon an imaginary encounter? But all her characters were imaginary, so it was no different, really, than changing her mind about any other of their traits—except this decision seemed to have been made *for* her!

She sternly reminded herself that blue or hazel, St. John's eyes were fictional. She hurriedly keyed in the clothing she'd seen on him and on Clarissa, and added all the rich details she could remember. Who could forget that black, thick hair, with its sideburns and hint of distinguished grey?

The idea that she might be following in Grandmother's footsteps bothered her. First, she'd seen St. John on her property, and then in the ballroom. Worse, she'd felt herself to be there, too. It was crazy, of course. But she didn't *feel* crazy.

What had Mother called it? *Visions from the past?* But it wasn't the past Claire had seen, was it? It may have been a kind of vision, but it was a fully immersive experience! She'd really felt she was *there,* in that Regency world. How? When she'd invented it?

She made a quick dinner of grilled cheese with ham while mulling over the experience. Slowly, she came to terms with it. She'd reached a realm of imagination that was like virtual reality. Maybe the cottage was magical and made it happen. Or maybe she'd always been capable of imagining so well, and just didn't know it. Nothing similar had happened for any previous book, though, so something must have changed. *Something like coming to Dove Cottage.*

So there *was* something strange about it! It magnified one's imagination. That's what Mother had been so afraid of, why she'd not encouraged Claire to visit Grandmother. But now Claire knew it wasn't something to be afraid of. It wasn't a curse, but a gift! She'd seen St. John in a way most writers never could see their characters— in the flesh, as if he were real. If it happened again, she'd not get alarmed. She'd savor the experience and try to record every detail for her book. She'd read once that the brain retains a great deal more than the conscious mind is aware of. Evidently, her researcher's brain was putting all that retained research to good use in this imaginary vision.

Her heart lightened. If it happened again, this *would* be the book to salvage her career!

Everything you can imagine is real.
Pablo Picasso

CHAPTER 8

1816
Earlier

Miss Andrews frowned. She'd been watching St. John furtively while keeping up a light banter with a peer by name of Earl Brest. Suddenly St. John came to attention. He seemed to be taking note of something with a great deal of intensity. She followed his gaze and found him staring at a woman whose face she could not see. The woman was well dressed and had a good figure, but who was it?

She managed to get the earl walking in the lady's direction so that when they reached her, Clarissa could finagle an introduction. She needed to know her competition. But a most unimaginable thing happened. The lady *vanished!* Just like that, she was gone, as though she'd never been there! Clarissa froze and gripped the earl's arm. She looked to see St. John's reaction, but he had turned to speak to Lady Merrilton.

"My dear Miss Andrews," said Earl Brest.

"Did you see?" Clarissa asked. "That woman! There was a woman—a moment ago!" Clarissa's legs went weak. What on earth was happening? She looked at St. John, but his face showed not the smallest surprise. He hadn't seen the woman vanish. Or had Clarissa been imagining things? Looking around helplessly, she saw her sister Margaret was staring just where the lady had vanished. She turned the earl in Margaret's direction. When they reached her, Clarissa asked, "Did you see her, Margaret?"

Margaret turned blank eyes to her sister. "See who?"

"A lady," Clarissa said meaningfully. "That lady who was standing over there—and went away, somehow?"

The earl said jovially, "There are ladies throughout the room, Miss Andrews. Perhaps Miss Margaret needs a description more explicit."

"Yes, I need a description more explicit," said Margaret, with large, innocent eyes.

"Never mind," said Clarissa. Margaret was a lackwit. Even if she'd seen the lady vanish, she'd no doubt take not the least note of it. Clarissa turned wistful eyes to see if St. John was looking at her, but he wasn't—he was watching the dancers. It gave her a small satisfaction that at least he hadn't stood up with any of the myriad young women lacking partners. He knew better than that. He knew she'd give the cut direct to any lady he went near.

But Clarissa wouldn't soon forget the way he'd turned his eyes upon that woman with intensity, such as she longed to have directed at herself. If only she'd caught a better look at the lady! She had almost been close enough and then, *poof!* The lady *had* vanished.

There was no explanation for such a thing, but Clarissa did not doubt her senses. She only hoped, whoever that woman had been, she would stay gone and *never return.*

You don't get explanations in real life. You just get moments that are
absolutely, utterly, inexplicably odd.
Neil Gaiman

CHAPTER 9

Note to self: This cottage is magical. Find the deed!

Claire pinned back her hair and scrolled to the ballroom scene
where she had seen St. John in astonishing clarity. Now that she
understood her experience was a gift of imagination, a help to her
writing, she could only hope it would happen again. If Grandmother
had seen visions, they too were simply imaginary pasts—things that
seemed real, but weren't. While Grandmother hadn't realized they
were only imaginary visions, Claire, as an author, did. She might not
understand how or why Dove Cottage heightened one's imagination,
but she could surely enjoy the benefit!

Ah. Now she could write in the apology scene and get the story
back on track according to the outline. She grabbed the tallit, wrapped
it around her shoulders, overlapping it across her chest, and put her
hands to the keyboard.

And a rushing wind surrounded her, leaving her breathless and
blinking—and in the ballroom.

What a scientist cannot account for is the
alteration of time and space and dimension that is God's.
Mary C. Neal

CHAPTER 10

1816, England

A corner of musicians began to play a tune and Claire watched in astonishment while a scene she had written many times for her stories came to life. Gentlemen were leading ladies to the dance floor where they lined up across from one another, bowed and curtseyed, and started the figures. Claire silently congratulated herself—her imagination was in full swing again! *Good thing she understood it wasn't happening, really!*

Glancing down, Claire noted she was still dressed in perfect Regency fashion. Somehow her imagination ingeniously supplied her with a lovely sprigged-muslin Empire dress with flounced, short sleeves and a matching hem. A shawl draped around her back and hung from her arms—the tallit again! She had on some kind of headdress; she could feel it, and even a little fabric purse—a reticule, it was called here—hung from her wrist.

Suddenly from across the room, Earl Brest called, "Smelling salts! Who has smelling salts? Miss Andrews has swooned!"

Claire gaped: her own Clarissa, who was nobody's fool, had fainted? This wasn't supposed to happen. It wasn't in the outline. And Clarissa was not the missish or swooning sort. But right now Claire was only an observer, not an author. She watched in fascinated silence.

The earl had caught Miss Andrews in his arms. While the dancers continued with the figures, oblivious to the disturbance, some of the older women rose from their seats against the walls and hurried to the area. Claire, with stark incredulity, went with them.

"What is your problem, Miss Andrews?" Claire asked aloud,

stopping about a foot away. She often spoke aloud to her characters when writing, and really did not understand why Clarissa, who never fainted, should be swooning at a mere ball. Only when she spoke this time, it was not to her keyboard, and everyone around her heard the question and looked at Claire interestedly. Miss Andrews cracked open an eye—*so she hadn't really swooned—Claire should have known!* But upon seeing Claire, she gasped. Claire, getting her first good look at Clarissa, gasped back at her. *Clarissa looked like her! Like a twin!*

While she stared in amazement, Clarissa's look became a glare. Claire stepped back from the sheer hatred in her eyes. *Ouch.*

A woman stepped forward from the crowd. In a commanding tone she said, "Take Miss Andrews to a side parlour where she may recline until we fetch a doctor." The earl made a valiant effort to lift the lady (whose eyes were again firmly shut) but he faltered. Looking around, he spied St. John and said, "I need a man stronger than myself, I'm afraid."

St. John's face went bland as he accepted the need for his assistance. But Mr. Timbrell stepped forward. "Allow me," he said. He bent, and with a grunt, lifted the lady into his arms and obediently followed the woman who motioned them away. Claire watched, still wondering why she was imagining a Clarissa look alike—and at the lady's evil eye toward her. And then St. John was there in front of her, in all his impressive manly bearing.

A shock ran through Claire—a delicious shiver—though it was tempered by alarm. *He's not real,* she reminded herself. This was her fictional hero.

He seemed as if he wished to speak, but looked around as if searching for someone. He turned back to her and bowed politely, yet as one resigned.

"I beg your pardon," he said. "I see no one from whom I may request an introduction. May I take the presumption of introducing myself?"

Claire belatedly remembered she was supposed to curtsey. She did so, awkwardly.

He bit his lip. "I have astonished you, no doubt." He eyed her uncertainly for a moment. "Do not hesitate to send me away if it pleases you."

"No!" she said finally, dry-mouthed. Her heart was pounding, but wasn't this fascinating! She was "meeting" a character she'd invented! He waited for the merest second to see if she wished to say more, but then bowed again. "Julian St. John, at your service."

"I know," she said breathlessly.

His face registered no surprise. "Ah. But you have me at a disadvantage." He smiled gently. Oh—he was waiting for her name!

"Channing. Claire Channing," she said, with a little curtsey which she hoped was less awkward than the first.

"Is that *Miss* Channing?" he asked, with a gleam of amusement in his eye.

What a dolt she was! "Yes! *Miss* Channing, I beg your pardon," she said, wide-eyed. This was incredible! She was getting to practice being a Regency miss. Thank goodness it was all imaginary!

"A pleasure," he said with a nod, looking at her with intense eyes, and making her blush like a schoolgirl. *He isn't real!* She scolded herself. Any moment and she'd wake up and find herself before the laptop in the cottage. She wasn't really in a nineteenth-century ballroom, no matter what her senses told her.

He gazed at her curiously. "I hope it is not impertinent to ask; are you a relation of Miss Andrews? I've wondered since I first saw you."

Claire stammered in response, for she was as surprised as anyone at their similarity. All she could say was, "Why—why do you ask, sir?"

He smiled gently. "You must allow the remarkable similarity of your features. You are almost her twin. I believe you look more like Clarissa than her sister, Miss Margaret."

Claire's brows furrowed. She'd written Miss Andrews to be a beauty, but never had she dreamed of herself as the model for the character. She'd spent her life hiding behind thick bangs and happy to be as little noticed as possible. Hairdressers begged her to get rid of the bangs, but she'd never agreed. The only way she'd striven for attention was through her writing. Clarissa had her features, though, and was undeniably attractive. It must have been the fashions of the day, and how her hair was off the face; it brought out a beauty Claire had never tried to emphasize. But now that she'd seen Clarissa, Claire knew she must be every bit as beautiful.

Nevertheless she said with a little smile, "I almost believe you are trying to flatter me, sir."

St. John's eyes narrowed. "I never give flummery. You resemble her remarkably, though I daresay that on you, Miss Andrews's features become...more respectable." He leaned in. "But pray, do not repeat that I said so. She'll seek revenge against you."

Claire felt her face turning crimson.

Returning to his full height, he said, "You blush; am I behaving like a boor? Flustering you with observations I ought to keep to myself, no doubt?"

She could find no response. He held out his arm. "May I escort you for some refreshment? Lemonade? Or ratafia might refresh you."

Claire stared at his arm. How many times had she written moments like this for heroines? She put her hand upon his arm gingerly, feeling amazed. He felt quite solid and real. Perhaps it wasn't a vision, but a dream. *But could she dream all this?*

As they walked, she saw curious faces looking at them; the old ladies began whispering.

"Which are your friends?" St. John asked as he glanced around them.

Claire swallowed. Of course. No young woman in the Regency simply showed up at a ball without connexions, without family or a sponsor. What could she say? And then suddenly she was saved from answering, as Miss Margaret appeared before them.

"Hello," she said, turning a gaze bright with curiosity upon Claire. St. John mistook her greeting as that of an acquaintance of Claire's, for he said with a smile, "Ah. You *are* relations. Just as I thought. How do you explain, Miss Margaret, why Miss Channing should look more like your sister than you do yourself?"

Miss Margaret studied Claire benignly. Claire was surprised to find the young lady did not look the part of a shy, retiring wallflower, as she was supposed to be. She was not attractive, but had an interesting face with intelligent, mischievous eyes. Claire met those eyes with a silent plea. Watching Claire, Miss Margaret said slowly, "We have always marvelled at that very thing, sir." She gave Claire a secret little smile.

Miss Andrews's excuse for fainting was that she had eaten but little that day. A maid had been sent with a tray of refreshments to revitalise Clarissa and keep a watchful eye upon the guest, but Miss Andrews was too vexed to eat. She could not erase the sight of that woman from her mind. A woman who had the audacity to look like her, like a twin!

It was this woman who had earlier seemed to vanish, though now Clarissa saw she hadn't vanished at all. *The interfering trollop!* She'd seen the way Julian looked at her. Whoever she was, she had better keep her claws off that man. Julian St. John belonged to *her.*

Mr. Timbrell came urgently up to St. John, and with barely a glance at the ladies said, "I say, Julian, but might I have a word with you?" He peeked at Claire sideways; and did a double take. He bowed hastily at her. "Miss—Miss Andrews?"

Julian said, "Miss Channing, may I have the honour of presenting Mr. Charles Timbrell to you?"

"Miss Channing," he said, slowly, taking in the sight of her, and giving another fine bow. Claire curtseyed. She was getting good at it, she thought. "A pleasure, sir."

"Why you look—you look remarkably like—"

Margaret smiled at the amazement upon Mr. Timbrell's face. "She is the perfect twin of my sister, is she not?"

Claire stared at them, still rather dumbfounded at this development. *Why was she dreaming such a thing? She'd never had the least wish to make Clarissa in her image!*

Mr. Timbrell smiled gently. "Indeed, she is."

"There is a difference," said St. John, studying her.

"There is" said Margaret. She looked about triumphantly. "I think she has none of my sister's cruel nature."

Claire looked at her helplessly.

"Lud, that's it!" cried Mr. Timbrell, gazing approvingly. "She radiates rather, a sort o' serenity, don't she?"

Claire could have laughed, for she felt anything but serene. Her heart was like to pound through her chest any moment.

Julian looked at his friend. "Did you say you wished to speak with me?"

Mr. Timbrell tore his eyes from Claire. "I did. But I daresay it can wait. I'd prefer to further my acquaintance with Miss Channing."

Julian put a hand possessively upon Claire's, which was all this time still upon his arm. "I'm afraid that will have to wait. We were on our way for refreshments."

Mr. Timbrell nodded a bow as Julian moved Claire off. As they went, Margaret smiled at her timidly—or was it mischievously?

Claire wondered how long this dream, or vision, could last. She looked about as they walked; astonished that everything still seemed real, just as real as anything else in life. St. John walked her past people whom she tried not to gawp at—but *real Regency people in their exquisite clothing! If only she had her cell phone for pictures! You must remember these details*, she told herself. Such as the lambent light from the candelabra overhead and against the walls—so much dimmer than modern lights. And her feet could practically feel the planking of the floor through the thin satin slippers. How did women dance away whole evenings in such flimsy footwear?

Why and how this was happening fled to the back of her mind as she scrambled to study everything. St. John stopped at a table sparkling with crystal bowls of liquid, allowed a servant to ladle out two glasses, and handed one to Claire. He led her then to a bench against a wall, and studied her a moment. Her heart skipped a beat.

She stared out at the room, too afraid to try more conversation. When she finally peeked up at him, he instantly met her gaze and offered a reassuring little smile. She flushed and looked away again— St. John was fictional but he was making her feel like a schoolgirl. He was too imposing for her to relax.

The master of ceremonies announced the last dance of the evening. St. John turned to her. "Do you dance, Miss Channing?" he asked.

Claire glanced at the dance floor. She'd once learned the steps of a simple Regency reel at a Jane Austen Society gala. But she dared not risk taking to the floor. There were any number of dances they might hold that she didn't know.

"I beg to be excused, sir," she said, amazed again to find herself speaking easily in the manner of the day. "I am not in mind to stand up tonight, I'm afraid."

"I understand you," he said, coming to his feet as if to leave. Claire realised he'd taken her answer as a dismissal! "My dear sir," she said hurriedly, stopping him. "I pray you to understand that on another occasion I should be delighted to stand up with you."

"I thank you." He paused, studying her. "I have not seen you in town before," he said.

She faltered for a reply. Raising a brow at her hesitation, he added, "I beg your pardon if I seem to stare, Miss Channing. I cannot stop marveling at how very much you *look* like Miss Andrews. The resemblance is remarkable. If you claimed to be a twin kept hidden all your life due to some dreadful misunderstanding, I would not doubt you!"

Claire smiled, but only shook her head. The very idea of her looking like Clarissa still astonished her.

"No iron mask or dungeons have been hiding you, then?" he continued.

"Nothing so dramatic," she answered, though it hit her as she spoke that visiting what she thought was a fictional world was highly dramatic.

"If you are long-separated twins," he said, "she is undoubtedly the evil one." He smiled; a frisson of pleasure ran through Claire. *She liked that smile.*

"We are not twins, I assure you." Suddenly, she realised she ought to put in a good word for Clarissa. Miss Andrews was supposed to have apologised and hadn't yet—she could do it for her. "I should tell you, Julian—" She stopped for he nearly gaped at her use of his first name. "I'm so sorry," she cried, feeling very stupid, very much like a twenty-first-century author, not at all like a Regency belle who would never make that mistake.

His gaze softened. "No matter. Proceed, please."

"I should tell you how very sorry Miss Andrews is about what happened last week."

"The coach," he answered, in a flat tone.

"Yes. She didn't mean to—"

"She lives to vex me, Miss Channing. If you don't mind, I'd much prefer to discuss anything else but Miss Andrews's sorrow. In fact," he continued, "apart from your similarity, there is nothing of Miss Andrews I am happy to discuss."

Claire stared at him in consternation. He and Clarissa were supposed to end up falling in love. "Do you mean to say, you would prefer a different love interest?" This would be disastrous to her novel.

He looked around quickly. "You astonish me," he said, trying to keep a straight face. "I'm afraid I underestimate our fairer sex these days."

Claire blushed.

He gave her an odd look. "She has never been that, but you intrigue me, Miss Channing."

Claire's face fell. "She has never been that? For you?"

He shook his head. "Never. If I gave the least impression—but no, I am sure I have not. Has she put ideas of such a thing into your head? ' Tis a delusion, I assure you."

Claire could not help being concerned at this admission. "But you *might* consider her, would you not, if she were more to your liking in her temperament?"

He looked suddenly serious and met her gaze evenly. He looked out at the room. "Why do you plead her case?"

Claire sighed. "I'm sorry. I'm afraid you wouldn't understand."

He looked back at her. "I think I do. *She* has put you up to it."

"No, I assure you!"

But he was unconvinced. Troubled, she continued, "I daresay that in your deepest heart of hearts you wish to approve of her, but she makes it impossible for you. I have tried to make her behave—"

He stood up and stared down at her with an inscrutable expression. Softly, he said, "Pray, do not presume to tell me what is in my deepest heart of hearts. We have only just met." He bowed and turned away. Claire watched him go, her heart filling with regret— and pounding in her ears.

Miss Margaret was suddenly by her side. "My sister will do all she can to crush you after today, you know."

Claire studied her a moment. "Because of St. John, you mean?"

She nodded. "Oh, yes. She thinks he belongs to her."

Claire nodded. In her heart, she agreed with Clarissa. Her novel depended on their getting together eventually. But she said, "Have no fear on my account. Your sister has no power over me. It is quite the opposite, I assure you."

Miss Margaret looked thoughtful. "Do you say that because you can vanish?"

Claire stared at her. "What—what do you mean?"

"I saw you earlier," Margaret said. "I saw you appear out of nowhere. And I saw you vanish as if you'd never been here. You're not from around here, are you?"

Claire was shaken. Really, this dream was too, too realistic! She wished she could awaken. But Margaret waited upon her for an answer, so she said. "No, I'm not. I believe I'm from another *time*."

Margaret's eyes widened, and she grew thoughtful. "You'd best come clean to St. John as soon as possible. He won't countenance being fooled with, you know."

Across the room, Lady Merrilton saw another chance to speak to St. John. She licked her lips, hoped her cheeks held colour, and approached him. "Good evening, Julian. Who is that charming creature you sat with just now? She appears to resemble our Miss Andrews."

"She does, indeed. She is Miss Channing. A relation of Clarissa's."

Lady Merrilton gave him a hollow smile. "And has she caught your eye, sir?"

He surveyed Claire, who was now speaking with Miss Margaret. "She is an innocent, my lady." He turned and gave her a look.

Hurriedly she said, "Oh, to be sure, I've no doubt. A proper young woman, and therefore a bore—to a man like you." She glanced at him and then back at Claire.

"On the contrary," he said. "I found her delightful. She is quite *un*like our Miss Andrews."

"Well, Julian," she said, before turning away, "I daresay you know where to find me. When your Miss Innocent bores you to distraction."

He made a small grimace, and nodding his goodbye, said softly, "You know better than to expect me."

Lady Merrilton was left looking after him, her gaze a mixture of wistfulness and resentment.

Claire sniffed and gave a little smile to Miss Margaret. "You seem awfully wise for a fifteen-year-old younger sister. I hadn't realised how wise you are."

Margaret beamed for a moment. "You have no idea, Miss Channing."

Claire looked struck. Could Miss Margaret be so different—even though Claire had invented her—that she could have no idea of her true character? The thought was preposterous! But she'd had enough of this dream for now. "Can you take me somewhere so I can be alone?"

Margaret's eyes lit up. "So you can vanish again?"

Claire let out a breath. "Well, I hope so. I think I'm dreaming, actually. So all I really need do is awaken."

Margaret took her hand. "Come along. You are not dreaming. But I'll show you the water closet."

Claire stopped. "Really?"

Miss Margaret giggled. "You said, *alone*."

They resumed walking. Claire realised it was actually a great opportunity to see an actual Regency water closet. She never mentioned them in her novels, for it wasn't fun reading, to her mind, to be reminded of the mundane details of existence. Novels were for exciting stuff—romance, adventure, mystery.

Ballrooms with handsome men.

After leaving the dance floor and following a narrow corridor for a short space, Claire saw a side room, closed with only a curtain. A woman was leaving as they passed, allowing her to glimpse a number of ladies in it. She stopped.

"What is this room?" she asked.

"The retiring room," Miss Margaret said. "Would you like to check your hair? Fix a loose stocking? 'Tis what we do here."

Claire said. "Ah. Please, just for a moment."

They went in.

Miss Margaret surveyed the ladies for a moment as if seeking an acquaintance, but finding none, motioned with her head toward a looking glass. There were a number of them, evenly spaced along the wall. Claire went to one. And gasped.

There, reflected back at her in the glass, was Miss Andrews! Only it wasn't Miss Andrews. It was Claire. She looked astonishingly different than her usual self.

Her hair was done up in Regency fashion, tightly pulled back, with curls allowed to hang down to frame the sides of her face. On her head, instead of the popular ostrich feathers, she wore a simple tiara, a beautiful little piece with sparkling gems—they looked real, like diamonds and pearls! Gracing her neck was a pearl necklace, and even her reticule had a little tassel containing tiny pearls in the strands. Her appearance was fascinating! Her dress had short, puffed sleeves and a square bodice. She wore perfect three-quarter length gloves on her arms, and the shawl around her was the tallit! How strange.

Even stranger, though, was how this style of hair and clothing brought out a beauty in Claire that her usual straight-hair and bangs utterly failed to. Her features looked delicate, her nose diminutive. Somehow Claire really was every bit as beautiful as Miss Andrews. They *could* be twins! She touched her own face in wonder.

"Are you different here?" Miss Margaret asked in a whisper. Another lady was mending a tear in her gown on a side bench, and one woman was applying some kind of rouge from a porcelain box to her cheeks, but neither paid any attention to them.

Claire turned to the girl. "Yes. Please, let's go." They turned back into the corridor and followed it farther down, until Miss Margaret turned off into a mostly empty room. On the far side of it was a wooden door. She stopped in front of it and motioned with her head. "This is it."

"Thank you," Claire said.

"May I watch?" Miss Margaret asked eagerly.

Claire looked at the door of the water closet, blushed, and then looked back at the girl.

Miss Margaret smiled. "I mean, watch you vanish."

Claire wasn't sure she would vanish, but she said, "Why not?"

She turned the handle and pushed open the door. Simultaneously, she heard the loud, rushing sound like a great wind—and found herself at the kitchen table before her laptop.

We are what we see. We are products of our surroundings.
Amber Valletta

CHAPTER 11

Dove Cottage

Damp with sweat, Claire gripped the table, her legs weak. *Note to self: Learn how to wake from a lucid dream!*

She took deep breaths while Charlie barked and came and sniffed her, wagging his tail. "Just as if I'd been gone," she murmured, reaching a hand to pat his shaggy mane.

When the weakness subsided, she took stock of herself. She had on her usual jeans and shirt. She thought back to the beautiful Regency gown she'd worn in the ballroom. How paltry her clothes were in comparison. She felt like Cinderella after midnight, as though she'd lost her own glass slipper. If only she could imagine such lovely things in the here and now. But wait—what was she thinking? She hadn't gone anywhere. It hadn't been real. She looked at the clock and saw that an hour had passed since she'd sat down to write. It felt as though she'd been in that ballroom for an hour.

She came slowly to her feet and stretched. She turned on the porch light and peeked out as best she could, mindful that St. John might show up again on her property. Seeing no one, she let the dog out, but again her hands shook. She poured a glass of wine, hoping to stop the shaking. Surely a vision shouldn't leave her sweating and shaking.

Surely a vision should not seem so very real.

She let the dog back in, locked up, and showered. In the bathroom mirror, she played with her hair, trying it up in various ways and looking at herself. To her amazement, with her hair up, she really did look like Clarissa. Unlike that lady, however, Claire's brows needed plucking, and her face could use a good rejuvenating mask.

As she plucked her long-neglected brows and reflected on her ballroom adventure, she decided that either she was having incredibly lucid dreams, or surely she was losing her mind.

If her mother was right, and her grandmother was nuts—so, now, was Claire.

CHAPTER 12

Miss Margaret gasped in delight. Miss Channing could indeed appear and disappear! She searched briefly to be sure Claire wasn't hiding behind the door, and then turned back toward the ballroom with a wide grin. She was fond of Mr. St. John and had no wish to see Clarissa win him—not that there seemed to be a danger of that, but Clarissa was a beautiful woman, and St. John a red-blooded man. Miss Channing's sudden appearance—a rival for Clarissa— filled Margaret with hope. Not only would Clarissa fail to get St. John, but she might have to stand by and suffer another woman to do so. It was the perfect revenge for the years of misery Margaret had endured at her sister's hands, who ruled their household with an iron fist since the death of their mother a decade ago.

Respect cannot be inherited; respect is the result of right actions.
Amit Kalantri

CHAPTER 13

While Claire's nerves settled and she got her bearings, her cell phone trilled. She didn't bother to reach for it until the call ended.

"Hey, it's Adam" said the message. "Just checking that you're okay."

Did he think she needed a babysitter?

"Uh, if you see any more strange men in strange clothes on your property...I'm here, babe. Ciao."

Claire shook her head. Was he for real? She'd call him as soon as volunteer for a root canal. Maybe she was being hard on the guy. But he wanted her cottage. She didn't trust him.

The phone trilled again, and it was Adam again. "Um. Just wanted to remind you about next week's mixer. The neighbors want to meet the new famous writer in town. If you need a ride, I'm your man."

She turned her phone off. The new famous writer? The new has-been, more like. And if she told anyone she'd felt as though she visited the world of her book? Infamous writer would be lucky. Insane would be more apt.

She went over her book's outline, printed and kept in a binder. She checked off scenes as she wrote them or added in new ones if they became necessary, but the checkmarks stopped at the scene when Clarissa should have apologized.

"Well, I tried doing that for you," Claire said aloud, "But St. John wasn't buying it. Today, my dear Clarissa, you need to do it yourself."

She studied the next few scenes and put the binder aside. Then she sat staring at her laptop. Earlier, the moment she'd put her hands on it, she'd been taken to the ballroom. She sort of hoped it would happen again, but also sort of didn't. It was stressful appearing in her book—it was too real. If only she could appear invisibly and just be an observer.

She took a breath, logged in and put her hands cautiously to the keyboard.

Nothing. Whew. So it really had been a mere flight of fancy. Otherwise, why wasn't it happening again?

She scrolled over yesterday's ballroom scene to edit. Housecleaning, she called it. Polish the grammar, discard extra words, stage important lines for the biggest impact. Claire lost track of how long she sat there until Charlie brought his leash in his mouth and dropped it at her feet. Claire hadn't used the leash since they'd come to Maine, but she got the message.

She let out the dog, shivering while waiting for him to return. Wait—shivering? The fire. Why couldn't she remember to keep it fed and stoked? The cottage had propane but she preferred to conserve it. After Charlie was back inside, she fed him and then added logs to the fire. After trying for minutes and minutes to get a good flame going only to watch it fizzle out, she called it quits and turned on the heat. If only she'd not let it go out in the first place.

She grabbed the tallit and went back to work. Charlie came and sat by her feet. When she looked down at him, he thumped his tail in appreciation of the attention. "OK, pal," she said. His tail thumped harder. "Let's blast out this book." She wrapped the tallit around her shoulders.

Oh my, it was happening! That sound of rushing water or wind…and, oh dear, she was back at the ballroom! Couldn't she be done with that scene?

My imagination functions much better
when I don't have to speak to people.
Patricia Highsmith

CHAPTER 14

Claire blinked and put a hand against a wall as the room came into
focus—thank goodness she materialised in the ballroom in an obscure
corner. Here she could be a silent observer—just what she wanted.
She looked out at the scene, not much varied from what she'd left.
Miss Andrews came out of the retiring room and searched the dance
floor. Her eyes lighted upon St. John striding toward the exit. Claire's
heart sank, though she didn't know why it should. If he was taking
himself off for the night, she wouldn't have to face more
conversation.

Clarissa hurried toward St. John, calling out to him.

He turned. His face registered dislike for the merest second, but
was swallowed by good breeding. He nodded curtly.

Clarissa curtseyed. "You were, I believe, speaking with a woman
a short time ago—do not ask me her name for I know her not—but I
wonder if you discovered it?"

He gave her an odd look. "Her name, as you well know, is Miss
Channing. Is she not your cousin or some such relation?"

"My cousin? That—imposter? No!"

St. John studied her. "I have no time for pranks, Miss Andrews,"
he said, and with another short bow would have turned away, but she
cried, "I do not comprehend you, sir!"

"Your sister spoke for her," he said derisively. "Good evening."

She almost called him back. How dare he accuse her of a prank
when she wasn't playing one! Whoever this woman was, Clarissa
would soon put her in her place. She'd seen the unmistakable

similarity in their appearance, but she would have known of a cousin. There was no cousin, certainly no female cousin that looked like her.

And no one else must turn St. John's head. She spun about at that moment and saw—the imposter! And headed in her direction.

Claire saw Clarissa coming and swallowed involuntarily. A quick glance at her clothing told her she was still dressed appropriately in the same gown, though it boggled her mind how it could be so. Hardly realizing it, she headed for St. John. He seemed the safest place to go. She might have invented Miss Andrews, but that lady was proving to be formidable. Just then, Clarissa put herself squarely in Claire's path.

"So," she said, looking at Claire with compressed lips, "we are cousins, you say?"

Claire stared at her. "I never made that claim."

"St. John said you did. You or Margaret—and Margaret is incapable of thinking for herself, so it must have been you." She took a breath and raised her head importantly. "If you think, Miss Channing, for a second, that I will let you turn his head—"

"I have no intention of doing any such thing," Claire interjected quickly. "In fact, Clarissa—"

"How dare you!"

Regency etiquette! How could she forget! "I beg your pardon; I simply want you to understand," she continued, but suddenly St. John was there. She'd been about to tell Clarissa she wanted nothing better than to see her and St. John get on, for they needed to be married, but she held the thought.

St. John turned to her. "Is Miss Andrews plaguing you?"

Claire wavered for one second. "No," she said.

Miss Andrews flicked out her fan. "This has nothing to do with you, Julian. Miss Channing and I were coming to an understanding."

"Indeed we were," agreed Claire, for she felt Clarissa would cease being antagonistic as soon as she understood Claire was not her rival.

St. John gave Clarissa a sour look and held out his arm to Claire. "May I, Miss Channing?" Claire eyed him uncertainly but then took his arm. How could she refuse such a man? As they walked off, she looked back. Miss Andrews's eyes blazed at them.

Claire turned her gaze to the distinguished profile beside her. "I was trying to tell Clar—Miss Andrews—that I am no threat to her."

He looked down at her with a small smile. "I think you may be, Miss Channing, whether you would, or not."

He walked her toward the exit. "Where shall I take you?" he asked. He looked around the room. "Did you come with the Andrews?"

"No." She studied him a minute, remembering Miss Margaret's warning to tell him the truth. "I must tell you; I am not—"

But waves of people were suddenly sweeping past, for the last dance had ended and everyone wished to return to their carriages and homes, and he moved her aside protectively. "Whom shall I bring you to?" he asked, over the din. "Who are your friends?"

She drew her hand from his arm and looked around helplessly. "I am sure to find them. Please do not concern yourself. Goodnight." She smiled, hoping to reassure him, though she felt utterly alarmed. Everyone was leaving, but she had nowhere to go. She suddenly thought of the water closet. She'd make her way to it, and hope the door was a portal again.

A half smile played around his mouth. "I believe I've just been politely dismissed." Claire could well understand his amusement. He wasn't a man used to being dismissed; most women coveted his attention, she knew that as his author.

Intrigued, he said, "As you won't volunteer who your friends are, I must know the mystery. I'll wait for them to claim you."

Claire's eyes widened, but she turned, hoping to hide her alarm. People going by hailed him, calling out greetings, and looked curiously at Claire. Mr. Timbrell stopped. "Are you in need of an escort home, Miss Channing?"

St. John listened for her answer. When she hesitated, he said, "Whatever makes you think so, Charles?" His tone and look were just

forbidding enough that Mr. Timbrell bowed his head. "My mistake."
He eyed St. John. "You don't escort ladies home these days, Julian.
How was I to know—"

"Good evening, Charles."

He bowed to Claire, who curtseyed. "Good evening." And he
walked off. St. John turned to Claire. "Am I to understand that you
are in need of an escort?"

Claire looked helplessly at him. Miss Margaret had said to tell
him the truth as soon as possible, and indeed, she had no wish to
bamboozle him. "In all honesty, sir, I don't believe you can help me
get home, though I thank you."

He gave her a quizzical look. "You are concerned about propriety.
I am a gentleman, Miss Channing. If you've heard otherwise, I assure
you, those days are all in the past. I guarantee you shall be safe."

She almost smiled, as she knew he meant those words. She'd
given him a rakish past which he'd turned from completely. But her
problem was not one of distrust. She opened her mouth to explain,
but he offered his arm, stifling a smile. "Come," he said. "Unless
someone else claims you, I must be of service to you." Claire, feeling
hopeless, went along with him. He did not understand; how could he?
She tried frantically to think of a way to excuse him without injuring
his feelings, but nothing came to mind.

There were only stragglers left. Miss Andrews and Miss Margaret
had gone already, Clarissa staring icily at Claire as she passed, and
Miss Margaret, with an impish wink.

Claire thought hard. Ought she to run to the water closet? It had
somehow ended this illusion of being in the Regency. What if she left
this place with St. John and had no way of getting home again? She'd
be as good as a ghost—a homeless wanderer, without an identity or
friend in the world. But then, the water closet had not been her portal
for getting there, so why should it be her only means of escape? It
was all so befuddling!

Meanwhile, her escort stopped at the cloak room. A servant,
seeing Claire, went and retrieved a shawl which St. John draped
loosely about her arms. While he turned away to speak to another

gentleman, she stared at it in consternation, thinking she must be stealing some lady's wrap. But she gasped. It was the tallit again! Earlier, she'd been wearing it. How had it got to the coat room? And why was it continually showing up in her dream—or vision—or whatever this was? The servant proceeded to give her a bonnet. When she looked at it wonderingly, the man said, "In't it yers, mum? 'Twas with the shawl." He motioned behind him. "All the other ladies 'as got their bonnets, mum."

She saw it bore a design that was identical to the embroidered pattern on the tallit. It had the two doves in gold-and-mint thread. She put it on, not surprised that it fit exactly right over the tiara. Somehow her dreaming—or imagining—took perfect care of such things. Now if only she could imagine herself home again!

St. John turned back to her just then and held out his arm. His eyes took in her bonnet, and then the shawl, draped behind her and across her arms. The approval in his gaze lightened her heart. If only that gaze would remain approving when she would soon be forced to explain her predicament! She really shouldn't leave the building with him, but what could she say?

She had nowhere else to go.

I believe in the power of the imagination to remake the world.
J.G.Ballard

CHAPTER 15

St. John led her out of doors where they waited momentarily as numerous coaches lumbered past. He left her, strode to the curb, and whistled loudly. He gave three long whistles followed by three short trills. Soon a small black coach from down the street headed their way.

"Does everyone call their coachman with a particular call?" she asked. This was news to her, and useful to know for a Regency romance writer.

He studied her. "Not everyone. But my man knows my whistle."

The polished black carriage rolled to a stop before her, and from that moment, the magic of the night bore in on Claire, erasing her worries momentarily. She stared as a liveried footman jumped off the back and let down the steps for them. She marvelled as St. John took her hand to help her into the coach. She was ultra-aware of every sensation, every inch of the carriage. Inside it—how small and intimate it seemed—she studied everything. He watched from the door with a curious expression.

"What is your direction, Miss Channing?" he asked with a little smile. "My coachman is no mind reader." Claire stared at him helplessly.

When she hesitated, he climbed in and sat across from her, studying the look of adorable confusion on her face.

"Perhaps you ought to leave me here," she said, moving to exit the coach.

But he put out a hand to stop her, regarding her curiously. His eyes were soft. "No doubt your brother or cousin has abandoned you in pursuit of gaming or some such thing, and you are loath to reveal his negligence. 'Tis indulgent of you. But I shan't leave you here."

She shook her head, frowning, to show him he was wrong.

Gently, he said, "Have no fear; I will take you anywhere in London. You needn't be afraid."

She sat forward in concern. "I am afraid, sir—" She stared at him, troubled.

"Yes?" He sat forward also. Their knees touched. "I beg your pardon," he said, moving over slightly so each had more space. "I brought my smallest coach, as I did not anticipate taking a lady home." He levelled his gaze on her. "What are you afraid of?"

She said, "I am afraid I cannot—that is, I cannot supply you with a direction." She looked away in embarrassment, for she knew how perfectly inane such a statement must sound.

He sat back and regarded her with some puzzlement. He knocked a hand lazily against the wall, and the carriage began rolling with a slight jolt.

Claire looked at the street, clinging to the cushion, but fascinated with the thought that nineteenth-century London was slowly rolling past. The occasional lamp posts were ineffectual, illuminating only the smallest halo of hazy light. She craned her neck to get a good look. They were still candlelit, she realised! He noticed the direction of her gaze, and said, "Our gas lit streets are brighter, are they not? They should get around to this street soon, from what I'm told."

After travelling a few blocks, St. John sat forward and said, "Now then. No one will hear where you live but me. What is your direction?"

Her mouth dropped open slightly in realization. "You are very kind. You thought I was afraid to say where I live. You are thinking I live somewhere that is not fashionable."

He nodded. "Perfectly understandable. We have our fair share of gossips and highbrows." He gave her a mild look. "I assure you, your secret is safe with me."

She sat forward again. "You are too kind; only it is not that. I am not ashamed of where I live." She hesitated. "You see, I do not live in London. You really cannot take me home. 'Tis…unreachable by coach. I should not have come with you."

He sat back again and gave her an inscrutable look. When he lit the interior lamp, she watched in rapt fascination. He caught her gaze, and looked mildly puzzled.

"I must say, you have me perplexed," he began. "I am not certain what to make of you. A young woman without friends, who now claims to have no home." He looked up suddenly. "Miss Margaret knew you. I'll take you to the Andrews's on Red Lion Square."

"Oh, please, do not!" Her cry startled him. "Miss Andrews loathes me! She will turn me out on the street!"

He rubbed his chin in thought. "You put me in a difficult position, Miss Channing. If I take you there, you are distressed. But if I do not, what am I do to with you? A gentleman—an honourable gentleman, that is—does not take a young woman to his home. If I had a sister or an aunt at my house, perhaps—but I am quite alone. I daresay you and Miss Andrews have had a falling out; nevertheless, I must return you to your friends."

"But they are not my friends. Miss Margaret was mistaken, St. John."

He stared at her.

"I beg your pardon, *Mr.* St. John." Then, as if trying to commit it to memory, which she was because she always thought of him by last name only, she said it again. "*Mr.* St. John."

His eyes narrowed. "You are the strangest creature. Er, how was she mistaken?"

Claire did not want to call Margaret a liar. "She pretended to know me, in order to help me. Because I did not know a soul in that ballroom."

He frowned. "You begin to put me in mind of Clarissa. This is some kind of lark, is it not?"

Claire fell back against her seat.

"You had to come from a home somewhere," he said, with renewed patience. "What is the direction?"

She stared at him. "212 Timber Tree Drive."

He gave her a blank stare. "What part of town is that? I've not heard of—"

"'Tisn't in London."

"Where, then? How far do you live?"

She sighed. She recalled the earnest words of Miss Margaret: *You'd best come clean to St. John as soon as possible. He won't countenance being fooled with, you know.* "I live in America."

"You tax my patience, Miss Channing." His jaw hardened. "WHERE are you stopping in London?"

She fell silent, thinking how to answer. She shook her head helplessly.

He looked out the window, his lips compressed. When he looked back, it was with disdain. "I thought you an agreeable woman. I see now I misjudged you." He gave her a cutting look. "I am no longer the type of man to keep a woman; if that is in your mind, you are quite mistaken."

"No, no, of course you're not!" she cried.

He added, "I endeavour now to live a proper life. I am become a man of some religion, if you must know. But you force my hand. If you persist in this—" He thought for a moment. "I shall take you to an inn and leave you there."

"I couldn't pay my shot!" She gave him a wide-eyed, frightened look.

"I warn you, Miss Channing. I am not to be trifled with. I am endeavouring, as I said, to act the gentleman, but as such, I cannot take a lady into my home." In an acid tone, he added, "An upright woman would little desire it. If you force me to take you in like a street waif, I will have no choice but to call a magistrate."

"Return me to the ballroom, then!"

"'Tis no doubt locked up by now."

She looked forlorn, and closed her eyes and moaned, "Oh, why did I come with you?" Opening her eyes again, she found him watching her disapprovingly. "I am terribly sorry I accompanied you. But you must have a guest bedroom, er, bedchamber. Can you not consider me your cousin?"

He squinted at her. "You astonish me. I think even Clarissa is not your equal in depravity."

"No, no, you misunderstand me!" she cried, blushing. "Consider me like a sister, then!" Suddenly, it seemed hopeless and ridiculous—her position *was* unthinkable! What else could he think except that she was an *impure*? "I cannot—account—for being here. Or explain to you why I am, because I do not understand the mechanism of how it happened myself!" She went on hurriedly. "I wish I could tell you—"

"Tell me what?" The carriage pulled to the kerb. He glanced outside.

"Is this where you live?" she asked, looking interestedly at the street. St. John lived on South Audley Street, a respectable typical ritzy street in Mayfair, lined with stolid Regency town houses. Amazing!

"You wish to tell me what, madam?"

Oh dear. The cold, 'madam.' He had thoroughly lost patience with her! "That—I am a writer. I was merely writing a novel. You and Miss Andrews are characters in my book."

He frowned. "No flummery, if you please."

She looked stricken. "No—I am telling you the truth."

He looked outside again. "I am going into my home. You may direct my coachman to take you wherever you like. I no longer care to know your direction. Good night." He rose and left the coach. Claire began to cry.

St. John heard her as he stood on the pavement. He closed his eyes with a sigh. For a moment he deliberated. This woman was no better than Miss Andrews with her tricks. But Miss Andrews never shed tears—not real ones, anyway. These sounded real.

Finally he turned back, opened the door, and poked his head in. Claire looked at him, hardly daring to hope. What was there to hope for? Even if he were to welcome her into his home wholeheartedly, she was still stuck in a world that was not her own, to which she did not belong. She would never, ever, be able to explain her presence in a way that wasn't demeaning to St. John.

"Miss Channing, what would you have me do with you?"

She stared at him hopelessly. Suddenly, she remembered that

she'd returned home from the ballroom after Miss Margaret had shown her to the water closet. "Do you have—do you have a water closet?"

His brows rose, and he looked at her doubtfully. "You are finagling a means of entrance into my house."

"No! I—I need—I *need to visit a water closet*," she said firmly. She bit her lip, watching him. What would he say? "No one will know," she added weakly, hoping that might help.

He stared at her. "I will know. My servants will know. God will know."

Claire blinked back tears. He saw her face and seemed moved. He took a deep breath. To the footman waiting beside the coach, he said, "Fetch Mrs. DeWitt." To Claire, he said, "My housekeeper will see to you. I'll get to the bottom of this. You can't keep this up, you know."

She allowed him to hand her down, though her relief was tempered by the thought that the water closet might not be a portal. He did not offer his arm as they approached the door. Claire's heart was in her shoes. But what could she do?

They entered the well-appointed town house, striding past a butler holding the door for them. Claire thought he had the perfect servant's bland expression until St. John said, "Don't gape, Grey. Yes, I've brought a woman, and 'tisn't at all what you think."

"No, sir," said the man, bowing as if he were apologizing. Claire could not help looking about in awe at her surroundings. She was inside a Regency home! She needed to memorise everything she saw. At the water closet, she would disappear, and it all would be a memory, like waking from a dream.

She hoped.

It's better to be absolutely ridiculous than absolutely boring.
Marilyn Monroe

CHAPTER 16

Grey took St. John's coat and hat, and waited until Claire handed over her bonnet and gloves. She held onto the tallit, reluctant to part with it—a token of home. She marvelled again that somehow it had come through with her to the world of her book. As she gave up her things, she wondered, come through what? A portal of some kind? A dimension? If it hadn't been the world of her novel, she'd have thought it was time travel. It certainly looked and felt thoroughly real.

While St. John watched warily, the housekeeper arrived and curtseyed. "Show Miss Channing to a water closet, if you would, Mrs. DeWitt."

A water closet—the house had more than one, then! Claire was surprised by this. Many Regency homes still used an attached or detached privy. St. John's house was evidently outfitted with the latest conveniences.

If the housekeeper felt any surprise at bringing a lady visitor to the water closet, she hid it. "This way, please, ma'am." But she hesitated and turned to her master. "The first floor, sir?"

He took a breath, studying Claire. "Yes. Then bring her to the library. A small teaboard, also." His tone was of one resigned to something unpleasant.

"I'll see to it directly, sir."

"I'll see to the fire, sir," Grey said.

Claire followed the lady, very aware that St. John climbed the stairs behind them. She didn't dare turn or try to speak to him, though she was tempted to— in case she was about to disappear back to her own world and might never see him again—it would be goodbye for good. But a relief. She had no place in this world!

She followed the lady along a corridor lit by only a few candle-lamps, giving the home a mysterious air. *Regency lighting*, she thought. But she could tell there were interesting paintings on the walls and, pausing before a landscape said, "Oh, please stop a moment!" Mrs. DeWitt held up her candlestick and told Claire as much as she knew about the painting. When they passed others, the lady began to stop and talk even before Claire asked; she seemed pleased at such interest. Claire learned with some amazement that each was an original.

When they reached a certain door, the housekeeper said, "Here you are, ma'am. I'll wait for you."

Claire looked at her curiously. She added, "To show you to the library, ma'am." Her words ended with a little disapproving frown. Claire realised with a start that she probably thought Claire was not respectable! A respectable woman did not go to the home of a gentleman unchaperoned—if at all.

She hesitated, wondering if poor Mrs. DeWitt would be frightened out of her wits when Claire disappeared. Well, there was nothing else for it. She turned, opened the door and went inside.

She waited. No rushing wind. Neither was she back at her laptop. Instead, she was in a very upper-class Regency loo, about twice the size of an outhouse. A mahogany bench with a round opening was inlaid to a wall of mahogany. There was a chain attached to a pipe that disappeared beneath the wood. Surprisingly, there was little odor. It was all very interesting, but Claire sighed—she had not escaped her present difficulty. The water closet hadn't worked as a portal.

Note to self: Do not allow a gentleman—or anyone else—to take you away from a known portal.

Afterward, the housekeeper escorted her to a beautiful, oblong, book-lined room. Longer than wide, it had two fireplaces, one of which had a cozy fire shooting out shadows that lent warmth and an intimate feeling to the room. The floor was tiled but with lovely Oriental style carpets. Detailed plasterwork graced the ceiling with evenly spaced roundels. The central roundel was a painting, a classical scene with angels and shepherds. So lovely, Claire thought, staring up at it in admiration.

Seeing no sign of St. John, she wandered along the room, marvelling at the beauty of the architectural details, the elegance. The section with the bright hearth also had a double-branched candelabrum on a table, illuminating the area well, though shadows jumped around the far reaches of the room. She moved to a wall of books and ran her hand along a row of real leather spines. The jumping light of the flames flickered along the books and wall.

She peered closer to read the spines. One row was biblical commentaries; another church history; the next, sermons. St. John really had become a man of some religion, as he'd said. She heard a polite cough behind her. She spun around and saw him. He was standing before a small settee—evidently he'd been there all along—watching her.

"Do you read, Miss Channing?"

"I do, with great pleasure." She looked around appreciatively. "What treasures you must have here!"

His brows went up. "Well." He motioned her to a twin settee opposite where he stood. Claire draped her shawl over the brow and took her seat, while a maid came in accompanied by Mrs. DeWitt and laid out a tea service under that lady's eye. Claire watched the servant closely, studying how she did it for details—something she might put in a novel. The dishes seemed to be of an expensive Staffordshire. She looked up and saw St. John watching her, and studiously ignored the maid from then on. After the servants curtseyed and left, he said, "May I ask why you are enraptured of a tea service?"

Blushing, she hesitated. "I try to learn what I can, wherever I am."

"You wish to learn from a housemaid how to pour tea?" She said nothing, just looked away in consternation.

He came and took a teacup, and stood holding it, before sitting down at the end of her settee. He motioned to the teaboard. "Please."

She stared at the spread before her, determined to remember every last thing so she could repeat it exactly in her book. There was the expected fruit and nuts, but also biscuits, cheese, soup, seed cake (she guessed) and what looked like bread pudding. And St. John had ordered a "small" tea board! She sipped the tea first. It was good and strong.

"Very nice!" she said approvingly.

St. John's brows came together.

Claire tasted the soup. It had a strong, gamey flavour. The biscuits were even-textured, but not as sweet as modern cookies; the seedcake was on the heavy side, and also less sweet than she expected. The fruit? Grapes and apples, which looked exactly the same as modern varieties, though the apples were small, and the grapes had seeds!

"Is this bread pudding?" she asked, taking a delicate forkful to sample.

He glanced at the dish. "'Tis called tansy, I believe." He watched while she tried it.

"The cinnamon is quite strong," she pronounced.

He said, "Have you never tasted of a teaboard before?"

She looked at him plaintively. "Not—not from this year. What year is it?"

Now he stood and began to circle the settee, hands behind his back as if he needed to study her from all angles. When he was back before her, he stopped.

There was something so manly about tight-fitting pantaloons, a waistcoat and a spotless cravat, she thought. She said, "Judging by your clothing, and the elaborate embroidery on the hem and sleeves of my gown, I would guess we are somewhere about 1816—is that right?"

He put his hands on his hips. "What are you about? No more Banbury tales, if you please."

Claire put down her fork. The time had come—St. John deserved a full explanation. She twisted her hands together and apart, then came nervously to her feet. "You will not understand," she said, going toward him, making him take a step backwards. He looked down at her with surprise. She stopped, struck again by his Regency finery. St. John was so handsome. "You are…real!" she said softly.

His eyes held a mixture of annoyance and amusement. "Do not tempt me to show you how real I am," he said dryly. Then he shook his head. "How is one to answer such a statement?"

With a curious look, she tentatively reached out her hand—his eyes followed her movement—until it rested upon the lapel of his jacket, making him stiffen with surprise. She felt the fabric as though daring it to disintegrate with her touch. It was thick but soft—and very convincing. How could she possibly imagine such texture?

"What material is this?" she asked, distracted by her researcher's brain.

He took her hand in his, and removed it from his coat. "'Tis superfine," he said in a strange slow answer as if realizing that Claire really was behaving like someone unused to the normal things of life.

St. John in fact was astounded that she had placed her hand upon him, for only a child could be so bold and get away with it—or a Cyprian. And yet Miss Channing had nothing of the minx about her; her action did, in fact, remind him of a child's, for there was much innocence about it.

He led her to resume her seat, and sat a foot away on the same settee, facing her. She was like a softer version of Miss Andrews—far more appealing—except she must be up to some trick.

"What is it you want, Miss Channing? Be plain with me."

She met his piercing gaze and searched for the right words. "Only to finish writing my book. You see, my last two books were not well received." A frown flitted across her face. "The fact is, they hardly sold at all," she said in a subdued tone. "If I am to continue writing, I must write a very special book." Her face brightened. "And being here is certainly a great help. I'm sure to get a great deal of money for it, considering the authenticity of this research!"

"You, a woman, expect to be paid a great deal of money for a book? A book you haven't finished writing?" He gave a stark look of disbelief. "This may be your worst invention, yet."

"It happens all the time," she returned, "where I come from."

"What kind of book?" His tone of forced patience intimated that he was appeasing her, nothing more.

"Historical romance."

"Romance!"

Claire stiffened, thinking his tone was one of disdain. "'Tis perfectly respectable! I include good history, I'll have you know."

"What part of history?"

She didn't blink. "Your part. The Regency."

His gaze pinned her. "The Regency of Prince George?"

"Yes."

He gave something of a snort. "'Tisn't history. 'Tis contemporaneous."

"Not to me. I live—that is, I usually live—in another time. As I've been trying to tell you!" A coal in the grate hissed, making Claire stare at it. She'd never thought of putting a hissing coal in her books.

He gave her an inscrutable look and sighed, as though burdened. "Very well, I shall play your game. What time period do you live in?"

"The 21st century."

"The 21st century?"

"Yes."

Still facing her, he put his head to one side, as though weighing her words. "Yet you wear contemporary fashion. Do you care to tell me what fashion women are wearing in..ah...the 21st century?"

"There is no single fashion," she said, fingering her teacup nervously. "Women wear dresses or slacks."

"Slacks?"

"They're like trousers," she said, but he laughed. "Now I know your story is an invention! Women in pantaloons! How indelicate."

"We do not think it indelicate. Though I admit that the clothing of this day, at least for your class, is finer. You see, we have mass merchandizing—"

He held up a hand. "We have discussed fashion sufficiently. Tell me what your true purpose is here."

Claire's face fell. "I have told you as much as I know, but you do not believe me."

"Tell me again." He moved an inch closer, with one arm stretched along the back of the settee. "I begin to enjoy the fantastic nature of your tale."

Claire swallowed and eyed him with wide, earnest eyes. "I know it sounds fantastic! But I beg you to take it very, very seriously!"

He nodded. His eyes roamed over her but were indecipherable.

Shaking her head she said, "I have no idea how I came here." Her face scrunched in thought. "Except that I was wearing this shawl," she motioned at the tallit. "I think 'tis magical."

He barely glanced at it. "It grows late, Miss Channing. May I ask if you've remembered where you belong?"

She looked at him sideways, trying not to panic. "I haven't forgotten, I assure you, but I seem to be stuck here for the time being! You are very kind in giving me shelter."

"You must have someone," he persisted.

"If I were from this time, I would, would I not? But I have no one!"

He gazed at her quizzically. "You play your part well."

"I am not playacting! I live in America, as I said before!" It was hopeless! He'd never believe her.

His gaze never wavered. "You are aware that you speak like an Englishwoman? You dress like an Englishwoman?" Claire stared at him. She *was* aware, and it flummoxed her completely. How could it be? "I—I...Only when I'm here!" she said weakly. With eyes full of earnestness, she turned to face him fully. "And that's just the thing I'm trying to make you understand! I live in another *time*!" She stared at him, wide-eyed.

"And you have no doubts regarding this? That you live in another time?" He moved closer.

"None whatsoever. All of this," she stopped and looked around. "Is happening because of my book, somehow."

"Oh, yes—your *historical* romance novel." He came an inch closer.

"Yes, and you...well, I thought you and Miss Andrews and Miss Margaret were characters in my book. Only now I'm in it, too!" She shook her head and looked around. "And it is all very real!"

When she stopped looking around, St. John was almost beside her. He stared into her eyes. "You seem quite real to me too, Miss Channing. In fact, you are the most outrageous, lying, beguiling woman I think I've ever met. Your prank differs somehow from Miss Andrews's, though perhaps 'tis only that you are a superior actress."

"Do not say that! I am telling you an extraordinary truth, I realise, but—"

"Why are you here, Miss Channing?" He slid right next to her, and his eyes blazed intently into hers. "Why are you in my library? Alone? At night? Unless 'tis to beguile me?"

Claire was struck by the strong, handsome face so near her own. A man she thought she had invented. She cried, "As I said—I—I cannot account for it! But I depend upon you to behave as a gentleman! You are a—a Regency gentleman, you said yourself, remember."

His eyes sparkled. "You realise that were I to believe you, I should be a simpleton." Claire went to protest, but he put a finger on her lips and then took her chin in his hand. "And since your claim is not to be credited, it means you must needs be lying." Again she went to open her mouth, but he stopped her. "Which follows then, that you are not only lying, but are a disrespectable woman, for you fashion yourself to be without friends, relations, or indeed any protection whatsoever. As such, you put yourself entirely in my power."

She tore her head away and looked aside. "It appears that way, I grant." She looked warily at him again. "But I am respectable in my day!" Feeling helpless to convince him she added, "I'm a virgin!"

He froze. "And would a respectable woman say such a thing?"

"A woman from my time would." They stared at each other, their faces only inches apart. His proximity was rather exciting, but also threatening.

"Has someone put you up to this? I suppose they've got wagers on it at White's."

She shook her head, puzzled. "No! Nothing like that!"

"I think so. You are sent here to bedevil me; to see if I won't return to my old ways; is that it?"

"Your old ways," Claire repeated, dazed. "But—but you are a *good* man, St. John."

He seemed struck by that. "I have seldom been that. Had you appeared in this manner only a short time ago, I assure you, my behaviour would have been quite different. And, I must say, you are appealing to the worst side of my nature now. You are very like Miss Andrews; the both of you with pranks."

She turned on him. "I do not play pranks or larks like Miss Andrews. I am very sorry if you think I would do that to you."

"What you are doing is nothing, Miss Channing; 'tis what you are undoing that should concern you." His gaze fell to her mouth, and with a gasp Claire realized he was going to kiss her! She shot up from the settee—or wanted to—but St. John was faster and caught her before she could. In seconds she was wrapped in strong arms. She froze as his mouth found hers and she was caught in a passionate kiss.

When you are imagining, you might as well imagine something worthwhile.
Lucy Maud Montgomery

CHAPTER 17

Claire hadn't been kissed in years. St. John's kiss, moreover, was warm and somehow quite lovely. Though his arms held her fast, his lips were soft.

He closed the kiss and said, "I offer you congratulations. You have succeeded where Clarissa failed. You have beguiled me out of my reserve, out of my better judgment, out of my resolve to behave."

Staring at him with the astounding realisation that somehow she truly was in an alternate reality—for she could never imagine such a kiss!—she was momentarily bereft of speech. She wriggled to get free, but when he refused to release her, she stared at him and murmured, "You are mistaken."

"How am I mistaken?" he asked.

"You're mistaken about me. I have not tried to beguile you. I only want you to believe me!"

"And you beguile me yet more." He bent his head towards her, but this time Claire freed her arms and quickly put her hands about his face to stop him. Eye to eye they stared at each other with her hands cradling his head. Claire's eyes swept over his face. She was in the arms of a man whose arms she should never, rightly, be in. Not if time was behaving and had kept her in her own world. But she was suddenly Claire the author, and said, "My, you really are a beautiful man, St. John! No wonder—"

She was going to say, No wonder you're the hero of my novel, but he swept her hands aside and pulled her up against him and kissed her soundly. When she could speak again, she gasped, "You mustn't—I do not belong—in your world!"

"Agreed. You are otherworldly. You put yourself here, though."

He moved as if to kiss her but she blocked him by holding his head again. "I am certain I do not belong in your arms. Miss Andrews does."

He drew his head back. "Miss Andrews? My dear Miss Channing, you must realise, I am rendered helpless to resist *your* charms."

He started to remove her hands from his face, but she cried, "You are the hero of my novel! You must behave! You're supposed to be scandalised at improprieties! It's how I wrote you!"

Suddenly St. John seemed struck. He released her, looking at her thoughtfully. He stood and went before the fire, and gazed into the glowing coals. He turned to her. "I thought you were trying to bamboozle me. I begin to believe you are in earnest."

"I am! Oh, I am! You believe me, then?" Her hopes rose.

With gentle eyes he said, "Someone is missing a sister, a daughter, a cousin—or wife?"

"I am no man's wife."

"In the morning, I'll summon my best physician for you. I believe they can treat cases such as yours. A strong delusion brought on by some shock or disturbance, no doubt."

Claire's heart sank. St. John didn't believe her. He thought she was mad.

And the worst of it was, Claire was beginning to think so, too.

What is life? A madness…An illusion, a shadow, a story…
for all life is a dream.
Pedro Calderon de la Barca

CHAPTER 18

There was a scratch at the door, and the butler entered the library.
"Sir," he said, and with wide eyes, nodded behind him. "Lady
Ashworth, sir," he said meaningfully.

"Thank you, Grey," said St. John. He glanced at a clock on the
mantel and then turned to face the visitor at her entrance.

An older woman dressed in high Regency style strode confidently
into the room. She was followed by a footman in livery who went and
stood against the wall. She stopped and surveyed first St. John, then
Claire. Her brows were raised in an expectant posture, but at the sight
of Claire, she smiled. She held out her hands, and St. John went to
her, bowed, and took both her hands in his for a moment before
letting them drop.

"A pleasure, ma'am," he said. "And a surprise," he added,
pointedly.

"At this hour, I daresay, 'tis," she replied, in a strong, throaty
tone. "But all in good time." She beamed at Claire, who sat fixated at
the lady's attitude, for she was positively glowing. "I must say, I am
infinitely relieved, and proud of you, sir," she said. Her voice was
commanding, like her presence.

He surveyed her calmly. "I suppose I've done something to
deserve that? Would you join me and my guest for tea? You can tell
us all about it."

The woman turned, still smiling, and looked at Claire. "My dear
sir, allow me to inform you—for I know it has escaped your notice—
that Miss Channing is my granddaughter!"

Claire gasped; her mouth hung open. St. John's expression also
changed, going swiftly from surprise to caution. He levelled an

accusatory glare at Claire. His mouth hardened.

Claire sat forward in astonishment and could not find her voice. This woman—Lady Ashworth, the butler called her—was her missing grandmother?

Her Ladyship moved towards the circle of furniture, but stopped to allow the perplexed butler to finally take her cloak. She saw St. John's expression. "You must not be hard on her, sir," Her Ladyship said, as she came and stood in front of Claire. "She suffers from a malady. Let's see...what did the doctor call it?"

Claire stared hard at the lady.

"Ah!" She smiled. "Amnesia."

St. John saw Claire's frowning expression, but now his became disarmed. "I've heard of that," he said, rubbing his chin. "Forgetfulness?"

"A severe case, I'm afraid," said the lady.

Claire frowned at them both as he went and helped Her Ladyship to a seat facing Claire. Amnesia? A severe case? How mortifying for anyone to think so!

The older woman smiled at her. "You did not expect to see me here, I daresay?"

"I cannot say I know you, ma'am," Claire said slowly, trying to reconcile this fashionable lady with the woman she remembered. *Note to self: Ask Mother for family photos.* The photos of Grandmother at the cottage were old, and in them she was dressed in regular clothing. This woman was tall and stately, clothed in the Empire style. She wore a grey figured silk dress with a turbaned headdress, and carried herself as a regal lady of means, with self-assurance and grace. Could it really be—her own grandmother?

Lady Ashworth seemed not the least put out. "Of course not; you have amnesia."

Claire looked in consternation to St. John, who eyed her with a mild look. She shook her head at him to signify that she didn't know Lady Ashworth. He only nodded reassuringly.

"I will be honest with you, sir," the lady continued, while helping herself to a tidbit from the teaboard. "I had half a fright when I learned that you had escorted my granddaughter. I knew at once what the situation was, you see, for if she had known herself, she would have come to me."

He listened, nodding. "And so you worried that I might have ravished her."

She stopped and gave him a shrewd look. "Exactly." She popped a grape in her mouth.

Claire looked in astonishment from one to the other. Lady Ashworth saw her face and said, "Oh, Julian and I understand one another; he was my husband's favorite ward, you know."

"Really?" Claire was honestly surprised. She'd never read a single Regency in which the ward of some wealthy patron wasn't a woman. "Men can be wards, then?"

"Oh, they often are!" exclaimed the lady, with a wave of a hand. "Julian's father was great friends with the marquess, and entrusted his entire fortune to his keeping before he died. The marquess took perfect care of it, but of course it has long been in Julian's hands entirely. I keep a keen interest in him, however, you see." She glanced affectionately at St. John. "He is almost the son I never had!" Returning her gaze to Claire, she added, "And we are nothing if not frank with each other."

"You—you are a marchioness?" asked Claire, in awe.

Lady Ashworth smiled. "Of course, my dear. And you are a marchioness's granddaughter." Her Ladyship gazed back at St. John, took a bite of seed cake, and said, "Where was I? Oh, yes. I hurried here the moment I got word from Mr. Timbrell of Claire's being at the ball. As I said, I had a few frightful minutes, but I remembered"— and she smiled again at St. John—"that you found religion. I felt much assured."

Claire eyed St. John with an accusing look.

He said, "You shouldn't have. I daresay your granddaughter nearly beguiled me out of it. I was just in the process of ravishing her."

Lady Ashworth let out a delighted laugh. "I stopped you in time, though." Turning to Claire she gushed, "Oh, my dear, I am enormously pleased to have you in town! You are just the thing for Julian, you know. I daresay you are the first lady to make him misbehave since he was reformed."

"Matchmaking for me, now?" he asked, leaning against the mantel with a casual air.

"Surely you will allow she has a bewitching beauty," said Lady Ashworth. "And if you marry her, you shall be more like my own son than ever!"

"A bewitching beauty that has amnesia," he said.

"I do not!" cried Claire.

They ignored her.

"And were you really going to—going to—ravish—"

"Shhh!" Julian put a finger over his lips. "No such thing, I assure you. I hadn't forgotten myself that much, and I wasn't about to." He turned to her grandmother. "She has an amazing likeness to Miss Andrews. How do you account for it?"

She paused and surveyed Claire a moment and then turned back to him, pointing a little piece of seedcake at him as she spoke. "Because Clarissa, too—surely you have not forgot—is my relation."

"How is it I have never heard of Miss Channing until tonight?"

"She has only arrived, sir, from—the country."

"From another country," put in Claire. She could not erase a feeling of indignation despite Lady Ashworth's accounting for her presence there in the most propitious manner possible. Her explanation whitewashed all the outlandish—though true—answers Claire had given St. John, as though a load of dirty laundry was now cleaned, folded, and put away.

"What part of the country?" St. John asked.

Lady Ashworth wiped her mouth with a napkin and stood. "I am in a hurry, sir, if you must know."

"Fine. I should be pleased to have this young woman off my hands." But he studied Claire and said to Lady Ashworth, "How long has she been afflicted?"

"It comes and goes, sir. I suppose that is why her family kept her squirrelled away in Lincolnshire."

"Lincolnshire?" asked Claire. "Do I have family there?"

"Of course, my dear." She looked at St. John. "She'll come out of it soon and be in her right mind. Just as if it never happened."

"She is a danger to herself. You ought never leave her alone. She quite insisted upon having no protection whatsoever in all of England."

"She claimed to be from America?"

"That's it."

"Because I am!" cried Claire.

"You, er, brought the shawl?" asked Lady Ashworth, looking keenly at Claire.

"You mean the tallit!" cried Claire. "It shows up whenever I'm here!" She turned and took it from the brow of the settee. Lady Ashworth gazed at it like it was a Crown Jewel. "Does it have something to do with my being here?" Claire asked.

St. John looked at a loss. Her Ladyship stood up. "I'll take her from here, sir. And perhaps you may call upon her soon to see how she gets on. When she is in her right mind, she is a charming creature, I assure you."

"She is charming already," he said quietly, gazing at Claire. "How is it you never mentioned her to me?"

"But I am in my right mind!" Claire cried.

Lady Ashworth gave her a warning look, but said, "A grave failing, on my part, Julian. I beg your pardon; I suppose I was waiting for her mother to give her leave to stay with me." Her face brightened. "And she has, just at the right time! For now you are ready for a wife. I call that providential!"

Claire blushed pink at that, but was still smarting from her grandmother's words, "when she is in her right mind." Lady Ashworth motioned for Claire to follow her. But Claire felt a sudden suspicion towards the lady. She really looked nothing like the grandmother she remembered, or the one in the photos at the cottage. Alarmed, she hurried to stand behind St. John. What if this woman wasn't really her grandmother? He turned in surprise and she hissed, "I do not have amnesia! And I am not certain this woman is my grandmother!"

He took her hands. All of his annoyance had vanished now he understood her malady. In fact, Miss Channing now made him feel only protective. She was attractive to him before, but the revelation of her innocence—she was afflicted, not lying and deceptive—made her seem twice as beautiful. "You have nothing to fear, Miss Channing. Her Ladyship would hardly claim to know you if she wasn't your relation."

"Indeed, not," said the lady, smiling at her.

"But I tell you, I do not know her," she insisted softly.

"Which adds credence to her claims," he said, looking down gently into her eyes. "Only think for a moment—how else could you be here? Dressed properly? Speaking proper English? How could you really have come from America, which is an ocean away?"

It did sound impossible, but Claire knew that somehow it was not. She sniffled.

He dropped one of her hands to pull a starched white handkerchief from a waistcoat pocket and handed it to her. "Now be a good girl and go with Grandmamma. I'll call upon you tomorrow."

She looked up at him. "Will you?"

"I shall." Keeping one of Claire's hands in his own, he drew her with him as he went for the bell pull. When Grey appeared, he said, "Have the ladies' things ready."

He walked them to the entrance hall, keeping one of his own hands gently upon Claire's, where it rested upon his arm.

Lady Ashworth saw his manner towards Claire, and couldn't remove a small smile from her face. St. John took Claire's bonnet and gloves from Grey and helped her into them while the butler helped Her Ladyship. Seeing the tallit upon Claire, Lady Ashworth stared as if mesmerised. Her eyes met Claire's. They were heavy with unspoken words.

It's delightful when your imaginations come true, isn't it?
L.M. Montgomery

CHAPTER 19

As soon as they were off in Her Ladyship's shiny black coach, the door of which was emblazoned with the marquess's seal, her grandmamma folded her hands upon her lap and surveyed Claire with an inquisitive look.

"How is your mother?" she asked.

"So you really are my grandmother? And you know I do not have amnesia?"

"Yes, on both counts. But we could hardly explain to St. John, how things stand."

"I tried," Claire said.

The woman nodded. "You see what came of it." She gazed fondly at Claire and leaned forward to exclaim, "How delighted I was to learn of your being here! I always thought the tallit must have gone back to the cottage, but I never dreamt of it bringing my own granddaughter to me!" She paused and frowned. "Your mother certainly never did. I saw you as a child only a few times."

Claire nodded. "Why is it you and she don't get along?"

Lady Ashworth waved a hand dismissively. "Your mother is a cold woman. She never needed me like other children need their mother."

Claire said, "She never loved me like other mothers love their children. We rarely even talk."

Lady Ashworth nodded understandingly. "Precisely. She's an odd fish. And when I tried to tell her about the shawl bringing me here, she wouldn't believe me. She cut me off, as you probably know."

Claire nodded with sympathetic eyes. "How does the shawl work? Why did it bring me to a ballroom?"

The lady gazed at her and gave a slow smile. "It brought you to

St. John!"

Claire wasn't prepared to believe in a matchmaking shawl, but she thought back to that amazing, surprising kiss and said, "He wasn't joking; he kissed me, you know! Though I did all I could to dissuade him."

"He took to you!" she said, smiling. "But he was naughty. I ought to have given him a great combing over it."

Claire stared at the marchioness. "You look healthier and happier than your photos."

The marchioness patted her bandeau and smiled again. "Happiness, I daresay, does wonders for the complexion." She gave Claire a wide-eyed look. "You will be happy here, too, my dear." Claire was about to say that she couldn't possibly stay there, but the woman continued, "And I am in raptures to have you—my own flesh and blood!"

"Why do I look like Clarissa? We are two hundred years apart!"

"'Tis in the genes, I suppose. These things happen."

"Are you saying she is my—my relative? I'm an author—I made her up! I made all of this up!"

Lady Ashworth shook her head slowly back and forth. "She is in your family tree."

Claire gasped. A flash of memory shot at her—she used many sources to collect names to use for characters in her books. She'd taken Clarissa and Miss Margaret's names from a family history!

"So it's true," she said, sitting back in a daze. "I really am not in the world of my novel?"

"Not at all. These are your forebears."

Claire looked struck. "St. John, too?"

"No." She leaned forward in her seat towards Claire. "And this, my dear, is why I thank God you showed up just now, of all times. If we don't do something speedily, St. John will not live out the year. Clarissa will kill him!"

"Kill him?"

"I'll explain it to you later," Her Ladyship said. The carriage pulled up in front of a large town mansion on Berkeley Square.

A footman lowered the steps and assisted the ladies down. Once in the house, a butler took their things. Lady Ashworth told a servant to prepare a bedchamber for Claire, adding that Miss Channing was her honoured granddaughter. The butler looked faintly amazed, to which she said, "Surely I've spoken of her to you, Yates; you must have forgot."

"Yes, ma'am," he said, with a nod. But Claire caught him stealing a curious glance at her. She tried not to gawp at the rich rooms her grandmother led her through. Despite very poor lighting, she could see ornate gold frames which housed enormous portraits and landscapes along a wide corridor lined with a patterned red-and-gold carpet. But Claire could scarcely pay heed. Her head was reeling with the thought that she wasn't in her book. She really was in the past!

"But—but," she said. "St. John was also a character in my book. How could I have got his name right, if not from the family tree?"

"From an old newspaper report, no doubt," put in the lady. She turned and gave Claire a grave look. "Of his untimely death, perhaps."

"How do you know? Have you been here in different times, then?"

Lady Ashworth stopped. She looked about to see that there were no footmen or other servants about. When she saw none, she answered, "After my first visit, I looked up everyone I'd met. To see what their end was, you know. I read about St. John's demise." She motioned Claire to follow her as she opened a double door. They entered a grand bedchamber, where two maids were already busily building up a fire.

Lady Ashworth signalled Claire to sit by her on the bed. She leaned in and said confidentially, "He has only two weeks left. You are here just in time to prevent a calamity!"

Claire's eyes widened. "Two weeks! Oh dear! But how am *I* to prevent it?"

With a care to keep her voice low, the lady continued, "Miss Andrews went scot-free after the so-called 'accident,' claiming that her coachman lost control of her vehicle, which barrelled into

Julian's. Everyone else was hurt—but he alone, unfortunately, was killed from a broken neck. They hung the coachman, who I've no doubt was merely following orders." She paused and added, "Well, they will hang him, that is, unless we prevent the accident."

"I'm sure he was following orders!" put in Claire strongly, whose first chapter had portrayed just such a thing. She looked struck. "So Miss Andrews really does pull larks like that?"

"That is precisely what she called it, now I think on it. A lark!" whispered her grandmother fiercely. She touched Claire's arm. "But now you're here, you can put an end to Miss Andrews's interest in him."

The two maids had finished their duties. As they were leaving, Lady Ashworth called, "Send Marie." They curtseyed and were off.

"How could I put an end to her interest in him?" Claire asked.

"By marrying him. She will hardly pursue a married man."

Claire smiled, despite herself. St. John had been kind to her—before he got naughty, that was. His handsome face loomed before her. She thought of the kiss, and being in his strong arms—a blush crept across her cheeks. But then she frowned. "Are you not forgetting, dear Grandmother—"

"Call me Grandmamma," the lady said. "'Tis what they do in the upper class."

"Are you not afraid of changing history?" Claire asked. "And I have so many questions about why I'm here and how it happens. And St. John may not wish to marry me!"

"One thing at a time, my love," said the lady. "As for history, after I married the marquess, I returned one last time to the cottage. I looked up the history of our family—the marquess's family, you know—and there was my name, Charlotte Grandison, listed as his wife! And then, when I came back, well—I never returned."

"Have you tried?"

Lady Ashworth gave her a guarded look. "Do you understand how you got here?"

"No," Claire paused. "Is it the tallit? I thought it had something to do with the cottage."

She looked relieved. "Yes, the cottage! But 'tis quite the mystery how or why it happens."

"Do you mean you do not understand what brought you here? Or how you got back?"

"Not precisely," said the woman. "I think—I've thought long and hard on this you know—I think, once you come through a few times, you create a pathway. But the coming pathway—to the past—gets stronger, while the going back pathway—to the future—gets weaker. I say this because it got easier for me to come back, and more and more difficult to return. Finally, I could no longer return at all. I wore out my going back pathway."

"Oh!" Claire put a hand on her heart. She'd best not make the trip too often!

"But I have no wish to go back, my dear." She surveyed Claire. "Your mother and I hardly spoke for decades; and she denied me opportunity to know *you*. So in the future I am a lonely old woman. Here, I am a marchioness. Lady Ashworth. Here is where my friends and family are."

"Do I really have ancestors in Lincolnshire?"

"Yes. That is Clarissa's family seat; as I said, they are in our tree."

"Clarissa loathes me! Her family will never own me."

"They will now, because I have. 'Tis poor form to deny what a marchioness allows."

"But how did they come to accept you?"

She regarded Claire thoughtfully. "Get some rest. We'll talk more tomorrow."

Claire's eyes widened. "I cannot stay, Grandmamma! I must return tonight! I have a dog. He'll need attention."

A scratch at the door revealed a woman, probably the housekeeper. She curtseyed and said, "Miss Channing's chamber is ready, ma'am." Lady Ashworth's lady's maid breezed in around the housekeeper. "*La! Madame!* How late you are up tonight!"

"Nonsense, Marie, I am often out later than this." Turning back to Claire, she whispered, "I am sorry, my dear! I cannot tell you how to return! The tallit has a mind of its own." Claire's heart sank. But she figured she'd been gone no longer than three hours—Charlie would be okay for a few more.

Lady Ashworth instructed the servant to provide Claire with nightclothes, and then stood and took Claire by the shoulders.

"My dear—I cannot tell you what a comfort 'tis to have you here. And you looking so beautiful! You are just the thing to save him!" She leaned over and kissed Claire on the cheek. Marie scooted over and began undoing the older woman's gown from behind.

"Thank you, Grandmamma. You are a comfort to me as well." And she certainly was. Claire had gone from homelessness and dubious respectability to being the granddaughter of a marchioness! Now if she could just make her visit last long enough so she could nose out something no other Regency researcher had found. Her career would be set. She would like to save St. John's life, but really, if he fell in love with Miss Andrews she wouldn't have to pull any larks to get his attention, and his life wouldn't be in danger.

Suddenly, the thought of that—of St. John falling in love with Miss Andrews—did not seem like a happy thought. Her story was flawed. She might have to discard her outline. But she couldn't stay here in the past like Grandmother. She was going to use everything she'd learned in her book. It would be a blockbuster and make her name household words, like J.K. Rowling.

Claire's room was Regency luxury itself. Besides an ample four-poster bed and side table, there was an elegant satinwood escritoire, large dresser and wardrobe, and off to one side, a sitting area. A fireplace crackled with a flickering fire, sending warm shadows to the ceiling. An exotic rug graced most of the floor. Still, the air felt cold to Claire's modern sensibilities, but she allowed a maid—by the name of Mary, she was told—to help her out of her gown and into a clean chemise and robe. She was given heated bricks wrapped in wool for her feet, and a bedwarmer had been applied to the rest of her mattress, making it comfortable from the moment she rested her head.

"Will there be anything else, mum?" asked Mary, with a curtsey.

Claire thought for a moment. "Is there paper and ink in the desk?"

Mary smiled. "O'course, mum."

"Then that is all, thank you, Mary."

"Goodnight, mum."

Claire hated to leave the warmed sheets, but she hurried to the escritoire. After rummaging in a number of drawers out of sheer curiosity—most were empty—she took a few sheets of paper, a quill and ink bottle. She had visions of Catherine in *Northanger Abbey* searching the old desk in her room, and realised the book might not have been published yet! St. John never did tell her what year it was, and she'd forgotten to ask Grandmother.

She wanted to curl up in bed and write her notes from the day, but looking at the quill pen and ink bottle, realised she'd be bound to cause ink splotches. But there were so many things to write down! Why, she might already have enough details to be the best Regency writer ever—for who else could describe anything near what she'd seen and touched and tasted? That publisher who had shown "promising interest" would be drooling to get their hands on her book! She sat on the rug beside the fire and began to jot her impressions.

Where to begin? And to think—she'd found her own grandmother! It would be lovely to really know Grandmamma, but the older woman was staying here, in the past. Claire couldn't do that. If her grandmother was right and St. John's life was in danger, she'd try to help, of course. But there had to be a less drastic way than marriage. And if she went back and finished her book, who knew if she could return? She had no power over when she came to the past or went back to the future. Each time had been different. She couldn't control it.

After filling only two pages with exquisite impressions of things she'd seen, of St. John, of Clarissa, of St. John's carriage, the water closet, and the library, a deep exhaustion fell upon her. She recalled that, when she had appeared back in the cottage, she was covered in sweat. Somehow this time traveling took its toll on her, even if it accented beauty in her that went unnoticed before. It was taking that toll on her, now.

She crawled between the sheets—the bricks still had faint warmth—and tried to sleep. But despite her exhaustion, she couldn't stop peeking at the cozy flickering lights of the fire as it bounced off the walls, and she loved the thought that there was no cell phone, no tablet, TV, or other device—nothing at all to ring or claim her attention. It was peaceful. It was amazing.

She fell asleep.

Lady Ashworth dismissed Marie, and though ready for bed, summoned the butler, Mr. Yates.

"Find the shawl that Miss Channing came with and dispose of it."

"Dispose of it, ma'am?"

"Yes. And do not give it to someone you know. It must go in the *fire,* she said sharply."

"Yes, ma'am." Mr. Yates blinked at his mistress in surprise. But, like the well-trained butler he was, found the offending shawl, brought it to the kitchen and threw it on the flames. None of the other servants were about, fortunately, for they'd surely try to prevent him from burning a perfectly fine shawl. Servants often supplemented their incomes with cast-offs from their betters. He waited only until the shawl picked up a curl of flame, then turned and left the room. He'd seen enough things burn to know it would soon be engulfed.

As Yates walked away from the fire and out of the large kitchen, the flame in the shawl flickered out. There were flames still behind and around it, but the tallit did not burn. And then suddenly it disappeared from the grate altogether.

It appeared upon Claire, asleep upstairs.

Two things never mix: one is enchantments
and the other is meddling with them.
Lloyd Alexander

CHAPTER 20

The next morning the servants at the home of the marchioness were in a tizzy. The young miss had vanished and no one had a clue as to how, when, why, or where she'd gone.

Even the marchioness, a woman of rare affability, was in high dudgeon. She demanded to see where the butler had burned the shawl, and even poked about in the grate. Upon learning that a maid had already cleaned out yesterday's ashes—including those of last night—she sent the poor girl to the ash pile and told her to check it for the slightest remnant of a shawl. Nothing was found.

In her heart, Lady Ashworth knew it was hopeless. Somehow that tallit had survived. Claire had returned to the future! If only she could get there herself to bring her back. She remained in a brown study all morning. When St. John called as promised, she told him her granddaughter had taken a sudden ill. She bade him call again on the morrow, hoping against hope that Claire would return.

She hadn't explained the power of the tallit to her grandchild. She didn't want Claire to know that she might control her path through time with it—until that time ran out, as it had for her, Lady Ashworth, and the tallit had disappeared on her. She'd been left in the past, and was happy to be there. But she had to ensure Claire stayed there, too. Lady Ashworth's best chance of keeping a young woman in a society that had died out generations ago, and had none of the modern advances of medicine or technology, she felt, was to make her stay. If she could get Claire back and destroy the shawl—that would do it.

Next time, she'd burn it herself.

St. John was both relieved and disappointed not to see Miss Channing again. Disappointed because he had been looking forward to seeing that beautiful, maddening girl, though she was half out of her mind. And relieved for the very same reason. She was a beautiful, maddening girl half out of her mind.

A person needs a little madness.
Nikos Kazantzakis

CHAPTER 21

Claire awoke in the cottage. She opened one eye lazily, then shot up in bed when she saw where she was. From across the house, she heard Charlie bark and scramble to his feet. He came bounding in, tail wagging, and exuberantly jumped on the bed.

"No, down!" she said. "You know you're not allowed up here."

Charlie was behaving as though she'd been gone for a day—of course. She had. He began whimpering. "You poor thing!" she said. "You need to go out. And you're probably hungry and thirsty!"

She threw off the covers, including the tallit—huh! It had come through with her again! And discovered she was in the clothing she'd had on before going back in time—jeans and a shirt. She grabbed socks, donned boots, and quickly went for her coat. She checked Charlie's bowls as she headed for the door. He still had some water and a little dry food—good. At least she hadn't left him to starve. But the poor animal hadn't been walked—for how long? Claire didn't know.

He was all over the door before she had it open, and then into the yard in bounding leaps. He stopped at the closest bush to do his business. Claire breathed in the cold Maine air, sweeping her gaze over the pretty, snowy landscape. Such a change it was, from Mayfair!

How had she returned? And why? Her grandmother would be so disappointed! But Claire had a lot of writing to do. Unfortunately, the pages of notes she'd written at the marchioness's house hadn't come along for the ride, but she still had things fresh in her mind.

After waiting while Charlie relieved himself of a day's worth of endless pee, she let him romp around. She followed him for a ways, enjoying the wintry beauty. And then, there he was! St. John—on her property—again!

Now, why was it that when she appeared in the Regency, she was dressed appropriately for the day? But here he was in the twenty-first century and still dressed like a Regencian. She cautiously approached. Her pulse picked up, but this time she felt excitement. St. John was dreamy, after all. He had a big heart, too, for he might have "taken a disgust" of her and simply kicked her out of his coach on a dark London street. But he'd gone against his better judgment and allowed her into his home. And he'd kissed her passionately, twice—also against his better judgment.

"Mr. St. John?" He was bending to scratch Charlie around the ears, but he ignored her. "St. John," she said again, getting closer. He still ignored her! How odd. Finally she went right up to him. "St. John!" When he continued to scratch Charlie around the ears, saying "There's a good boy," she put out a hand to touch him—and he was no longer there. He'd vanished!

Claire gasped and nearly fell back. Charlie shook out his coat and licked Claire's boot. He didn't seem disturbed in the least by the man's disappearance. But he was only a dog.

Note to self: When St. John appears, take his picture!

This time traveling was getting out of hand. Not only couldn't she control which time she was in, she was seeing St. John in her time when he apparently wasn't really there! But Charlie had behaved as though he was. What could it mean?

She remembered her grandmother's words. He has two weeks left. Was St. John appearing in her time as a kind of SOS? To remind her that he needed help?

Back in the cottage, she made a quick egg omelet with cheddar, and got online. She needed to see Julian's fate for herself. She entered his name over and over with different keywords, history of, genealogy of, and other searches. Nothing went back as far as the Regency. Finally, she came across a parish record that said it had information about a Julian St. John—at a price. Before paying it, she tried another link. And found an article with St. John's name highlighted. Her breath caught at the simple headline:

"Fatal Accident."

"Last night occurred one of those dreadful catastrophes, the result of which has so stunned the country with horror that sober people will, we trust, not engage in that madness called racing, which we fear led to this terrible and melancholy event. On Saturday afternoon a coach belonging to Julian St. John, a respected member of our gentry, met with disaster on the road to Wembley, about three miles below Harrow, owing principally to the recklessness of his coachman. Coming to a precipitate turn, he dashed around the bend at full gallop. The velocity was so great his horses could not clear a turnpike post. In an instant the carriage was split in two. By the tremendous shock, Mr. St. John was dashed from the coach and instantly expired. A companion, Mr. Timbrell, was conveyed away in a chaise for surgical aid, but in the greatest agony with fractured limbs. A second equipage (belonging to Sir Cecil Andrews, of London) nearly partook of the same fate, but managed, by a narrow hair, to escape the calamity. Miss Clarissa Andrews, the amiable daughter of Sir Cecil, was its sole occupant and, though she suffered no harm, witnessed the horrible end of her friend.

Claire stopped and huffed, "So she *is* responsible! And 'amiable?' They got *that* wrong!" The article continued:

The coachman, Will Smithton, claimed he was following orders to outrun the Andrews's coach, but Miss Andrews vehemently denied the accusation, backed by the word of her driver, who also witnessed the unspeakable horror. "Was it not a race?" she was asked; but at this the fair damsel nearly swooned, exclaiming upon the strongest terms that she disavowed racing of any kind, detested, even, the thought of it, and could only thank Providence that her own carriage did not collide with that fatal post. Her horses, she said, had taken up the reckless pace of St. John's coach, owing to that mad, drunken coachman, putting her in the gravest danger. It is with inexpressible grief that the *Chronicle* notes that Mr. St. John himself was a noted whip, a respected member of the Four-in-Hand Club, and an undoubted horseman. We express our deepest sorrow HE was not atop the board on Saturday, and our purest hope that justice will prevail against his reckless and mad coachman.

Indignation rose in Claire. Anyone who knew Clarissa could see, from this article, that she had certainly been badgering St. John, chasing him in her carriage, and that he had tried to escape her. Poor St. John!

She shouldn't have proceeded to find and read his obituary, but couldn't help herself. She wanted to know all there was to know. She read of a "stately and frigid show of solemn mourning" in a "long, gloomy parade" with "mourning carriages, and mourning horses, and mourning plumes." The casket was strewn with "chaplets of flowers," and when a light rain began, it was "as if heaven cried," said the *Chronicle*. The hyperbole ought to have undercut the solemnity but a tear escaped her eye as she closed the browser window.

That Clarissa! She really would kill St. John if someone didn't stop her! Surely that must be the reason why he was appearing in her world! He needed her help. And if she could save him from this end—well, she had to try.

She'd write up the exquisite details of her last visit to the Regency and incorporate what she could into her book, for she must keep working on it. Then she'd risk returning to the past. And it was a risk, if Lady Ashton was right about one's return path drying up. But Her Ladyship, er, Grandmamma, had made many trips before her return was blocked. Surely Claire could safely make another. Grandmamma's idea of Claire marrying St. John seemed unlikely, even extreme, but there must be something she could do! She had to try.

Destiny is not a matter of chance; it is a matter of choice.
William Jennings Bryan

CHAPTER 22

Clarissa Andrews stepped daintily from her coach, dropping the hand of the groom assisting her. She surveyed the town mansion that belonged to her great aunt, Lady Ashworth. She'd learned an hour ago on a morning call that Miss Channing had been claimed by Her Ladyship as her granddaughter! How could it be that Clarissa and her family had never known of her? She studied Debrett's, the society book, as much as anyone—possibly more than most.

The butler informed her that the mistress was out.

"Is Miss Channing at home?" asked Miss Andrews. She had little hope of it, but wanted to question that woman.

"No, ma'am." Yates gazed at her doubtfully. He was under no obligation to inform her that the young woman had vanished. Yates despised gossip. He said nothing more.

"I'll wait, Yates."

"As you wish, ma'am. I cannot say when Her Ladyship will return."

Clarissa entered importantly, handing the butler her things with an impatient air.

Meddling is the evil, not indifference.
Marty Rubin

CHAPTER 23

When Claire sat at the laptop to record her notes from visiting the Regency, she was half prepared to disappear into the past. She'd draped the tallit across her lap, as even Lady Ashworth seemed to afford it special reverence. And each time she'd gone back, she'd been at her laptop, just like today. But it didn't happen. If only she knew what the mechanism was. But at least she was able to write up everything she could remember from the visit. She described jewelry, Chinese-style wallpaper, the tea board, and her own gown and tiara.

Most of it was what she'd written at Grandmamma's house, but which hadn't come through with her. If only the tallit had a pocket—she might be able to sneak such small things to the present. She pictured everything, the sights and smells and tastes of the Regency, and wrote as much as she could. It wasn't exactly progress on her novel, but it would all come in handy in one scene or another. For now she was satisfied just to record it.

As she described St. John's masculine presence, Claire stopped writing, hardly realizing it. She saw him in her mind's eye, bending that handsome head in for a kiss. She remembered with guilty pleasure his lips meeting hers, and his strong arms around her. Even now, she felt a delicious shiver go through her.

What was she doing? She mustn't let St. John go to her head. Though he wasn't fictional, he fully deserved a woman of his own time. If only Claire really could induce Clarissa to change her tactics. That was the key to this whole mess. If Clarissa had hopes of St. John—real hopes—she wouldn't have to resort to foolish and dangerous larks to win his attention. She wouldn't chase him to his death on that fateful day.

Claire suddenly realized what she needed to do when she got back in time. She wouldn't try to win St. John's hand in marriage. That was a longshot at best, and ingenuous, for she would have to return to the present. She'd finish her book and become a celebrated author. With her firsthand knowledge from the past, wasn't it almost guaranteed? But she couldn't leave St. John to die such a death. She'd have to win over Clarissa and convince her to play nice—be more missish. Wasn't that what he wanted?

Her phone rang. Adam. That man needed a life. Just in case there was good news—maybe the town had found the deed proving her grandmother's ownership—she picked up.

"Claire—I was thinking we ought to call a truce."

Smirking, she replied, "Does that mean you'll let a day go by without pestering me?" She wandered into the living room to check the fireplace.

"What? I'm sorry. I'm not trying to pester you."

"But that's what you're doing." She stirred the ashes. Not a bit of fire was left.

"I just want you to know I'm here if you need anything."

Claire's gaze fell to Charlie. "Really? Do you mean that?"

"I do. Anything."

The offer gave her an idea. If she returned to the past and got held up, what would happen to Charlie? She took a breath and figuratively crossed her fingers. "I need a dog sitter. Can you...watch my dog?"

"That sheepdog?"

"His name's Charlie." Charlie's tail thumped when he heard his name. Claire bent down to stroke his head.

"You goin' somewhere?" Adam asked.

"A research trip," she said, hoping he wouldn't ask for details. She certainly couldn't give them.

"When d'you want me to watch him?"

Claire swallowed. "Today would be perfect."

"Until?"

"Until I call you." She kept expecting him to flat-out refuse, but so far Adam was being surprisingly open to the idea. He'd fallen quiet, though. Claire felt sure he was about to turn her down. Only he didn't.

"Fine. I can be there in…five minutes. Is that too soon?"

"That's perfect! And thank you! Now I won't have to find a kennel." As soon as she hung up, she felt badly. She knelt down by Charlie. "I'm sorry, old boy. But if I disappear like Grandmamma— what if I can't get back? I couldn't bear to think what would happen to you alone here." Charlie's large trusting eyes brought tears to hers, so she added, "I wouldn't be going back except he'll die if I don't! You see? I have no choice."

She gathered Charlie's things and put them into a tote bag. It occurred to her that she might not be able to return to the past. It wasn't as if she controlled it. Well, if she didn't, she'd get Charlie back sooner rather than later. She felt better at the thought.

When Adam arrived, she greeted him with a smile.

"Now, that's an improvement," he said, coming in with earnest eyes.

"What is?"

"That smile. It's the first one you've ever given me." He gave her an impish grin. "I like it." Then his eyes grew more serious. "You're really pretty when you smile."

Ignoring the remark, she picked up the tote and handed it to him. "Thank you very much. Everything you'll need is in there. He's fed twice a day, and walked three times. He doesn't bite, and he loves company. I put a few of his toys in there, and his favorite treats."

Charlie sniffed Adam interestedly. Adam scratched his head, and frowned. "Wait a minute. It sounds like you're planning a long trip. May I ask where you're going?"

Claire stared at him. "No. But I'll try to call."

"I hope so. " He nodded. "So how long will you be gone?"

"I'm—not sure. Book research is unpredictable."

"And where did you say you're going?"

She stared again. "A research library. Perhaps a few."

Adam took a breath. He gazed at her and bit his lip. His tone went down a notch. "Will you be back before the deadline? You do remember what's going down with the cottage?"

"How could I forget? That's why I have to finish this research as soon as possible. I'll need a great book contract to buy a new house." If Adam had a conscience, that ought to give it a good nudge, she thought.

He cleared his throat, not meeting her eyes. "I spoke to Dad about that…" He peeked at Claire. "We're happy to offer you a small suite at the lodge. It was scheduled for renovations, so we didn't book it for the summer. If you want it, it's yours. Gratis. All you need do is vacate this place before demolition day."

Claire folded her arms. The lodge was ritzy and expensive, making the offer seem suspicious. "Why would your family be willing to let me have a suite all summer for free?"

Adam rubbed his neck and looked around the cottage, then back at Claire. "It makes things easier for us. We don't want a mess. We don't want it to get drawn out."

"You mean you don't want me to cause trouble. It's a bribe."

Adam let out a heavy breath. "It's not like we haven't made you solid offers on this place, Claire. We're not unreasonable. We'd much rather you sold it to us than pull it out from under you." He looked troubled. "You can still sell it to us."

When she said nothing, he studied her and moved a step closer. "Look, even if we buy it from you, the suite is still yours. We, uh, could get to know each other better…"

She looked up at Adam. And thought of St. John. Somehow, Adam's Nordic good looks paled, literally, next to St. John's rugged Regency masculinity, refined by his period manners.

"I'll call you when I get back," was all she said.

He frowned and petted Charlie and then looked back at Claire. He cocked his head to one side. "When you get back, I hope I've earned the right to at least have dinner with you?"

Claire crossed her arms. "I can do better than that."

Adam's eyes lit with curiosity. He slowly smiled. "Is that so?" He looked at her suggestively.

Claire smiled. "I'll think about selling the cottage." Since now she knew Grandmamma no longer wished to return, Claire felt she could safely offer that option.

"Oh. Well, that's good, too." He gave her a husky look and winked. "Not quite as good, but my father will be happy."

She smiled sweetly. "Thank you, Adam. I'll be in touch." She gave Charlie another hug and then motioned Adam toward the door, but he stood his ground.

"That's it? Don't I get a little gratitude?" His gaze fell to her mouth.

She turned him toward the door. "You get Charlie. Thank you and good bye!" *Note to self: Adam is relentless!*

When he'd gone, she surveyed the room and felt lonely. She'd miss Charlie. And Adam had let in a lot of cold air. She kicked herself for not asking him to get the fire going. She grabbed the tallit and was about to throw it around her shoulders when it hit her. Each time she'd gone to the Regency, it had been around her shoulders and crossing her chest! Yes, she'd been at her laptop, but she'd also been wearing it! Laying it across her lap hadn't done anything, but the tallit was the mechanism. It had to be. How slow she'd been to realize it!

No wonder Grandmamma had asked if she'd brought it with her. The old lady knew. But she hadn't wanted Claire to know. Why?

She sat at her laptop and studied the shawl. "Here goes nothing," she murmured.

She took a breath and settled it around her shoulders, and carefully drew it together across her chest. The rushing wind made her grimace, and forced her eyes shut. It felt stronger this time.

And she was back in the Regency.

She always wanted to believe in things.
Kazuo Ishiguro

CHAPTER 24

Adam came to a stop under the portico of the front entrance of the lodge. A valet hurried out. As he handed the man his keys, Adam said, "There's a dog in the backseat. Name's Charlie. Take him to the kennels."

"Wait!" A young girl in a wheelchair was in front of the large automatic doors to the lodge's entrance. She frowned at Adam. "I told you I want to see the dog!" Blond-haired like her big brother, Adele Winthrop might have been only twelve years old and disabled, but she was no pushover. "You promised I could take care of him if I wanted to."

Adam grimaced. "I didn't think you meant it. Why not let the kennel look after him?" He'd planned on taking Charlie to the kennel from the moment Claire asked him to dog-sit. She probably didn't know the lodge had its own pampered pet kennel for their rich clients who didn't want a ski vacation without their pet. They'd take fine care of Charlie—and Claire would never know her dog wasn't getting his personal attention.

Adele wheeled forward to the edge of the curb. "Let me see him."

Adam looked at the valet. "Wait a sec. I don't think she'll really want him." He opened the door and Charlie came bounding out, heading straight toward Adele. She shrieked in excitement. When the animal put his large paws on her legs and reached up to lick her face, she smiled and laughed.

"What's his name?" she asked her brother. When he told her, she said, "Charlie's mine, now." It was in the decided tone of voice she used when something was nonnegotiable. Adam retrieved the tote bag with Charlie's things from the car and followed his sister wheeling ahead of him into the lodge. He felt heavyhearted. It wouldn't be fun when he had to return the dog to Claire. Because of her disability, Adele was treated with kid gloves—spoiled as rotten as they came.

He hoped she'd tire of the animal by then.

CHAPTER 25

Claire found herself in a water closet. Again! So it *was* a portal! She thought of Superman changing in phone booths and wondered if a water closet was the time-travel equivalent of a phone booth for her. She peeked out into a corridor, but it wasn't the ballroom. Was it Grandmamma's house? She moved along it, thinking it was somehow familiar, and suddenly saw—St. John! Her heart did an unexpected flip.

He wore a dark blue double-breasted coat over pantaloons and hunting boots. He held a whip in one hand, his hat in the other. His dark good looks almost took her breath away. He spied Claire and stopped short. His head went back.

"Miss Channing?" he asked in surprise.

"Hello." She smiled weakly. How on earth was she going to explain her presence in his house?

He looked around, as though to see who else was in his corridor. "When did you arrive? No one informed me."

"Just now."

"Is Lady Ashworth here?"

"I–no."

Now he looked at her sideways. "How did you get here?"

Claire looked at him helplessly.

Instead of the annoyance he'd felt on the last occasion when she'd been unable to supply answers, St. John was filled with an uncustomary tenderness. In fact, the more he'd thought of Miss Channing, the better he liked her. And seeing her now filled him with a sudden and surprising wish that she might be often near.

Just then behind him came running two dalmatians, who stopped momentarily at his feet in greeting. He instantly grasped their collars.

When, upon spying Claire they let out low, rumbling growls, she saw why he had. A groom was at their heels.

"Sorry, sir, I didn't mean to let them loose." He attached leashes to the animals' collars, who were now whimpering to run at Claire.

Looking at her, St. John said, "Return them to the kennels, Ewen." He handed the man the whip. As the groom turned to lead them away, Claire said, "Oh, wait! May I pet them?"

St. John gave her a curious look. "These aren't my friendliest animals. They're good- natured but protective."

Perhaps because she'd just given up Charlie, Claire said, "Let them smell me, then." She went towards him. "They'll not be as wary of me next time they see me." She knew that with dogs familiarity did not breed contempt, unless one treated them cruelly. She was unconscious of having implied that they surely would see her again. St. John's eyes sparkled as he nodded his permission.

The dogs growled again at her approach, but St. John reprimanded them, and she cautiously held out a hand for them to sniff. Both dogs did, and then kept sniffing her, first her feet and then her gown. The groom pulled them back speedily, but Claire giggled and leaned in to them, and when one approached her face with his inquisitive nose, she fell to one knee and stroked him. Soon she was smiling and petting both animals. When one tried to lick her face, she turned her head but chuckled again.

"What are their names?" she asked.

"Apollo and Zeus," he said, now leaning back against the wall with his arms folded, wearing a little smile. "I believe you can beguile anything living," he murmured, while exchanging a look of surprise with Ewen who affirmed that thought with an instant, "Indeed, sir!"

"Oh, but anyone could," she returned, now scratching the dogs behind the ears. "When they're this good-natured." Above her head the groom and St. John exchanged another look. St. John came to his full height. He nodded at Ewen. "Take them," he said.

Claire stood up. "Do you have other dogs?"

"I do," he said, gazing at her.

Her face scrunched in thought. "If I don't misremember my research, you keep the dalmatians to accompany your coach on long journeys, is that right?"

He responded with a slow smile. "Research. For your, eh, historical novels, of course?"

She smiled. "You remember."

He offered his arm, and then patted her hand when she took it. "Come. We'll get to the bottom of this."

"The bottom of what?" she asked, as they moved down the corridor.

"Of how you showed up in my corridor just now, unannounced. And with your bonnet, shawl and gloves. My butler has been remiss."

"Oh, no. I can explain all that, but you won't believe me," she said hurriedly, pulling them to a stop in front of one of the paintings that lined the walls of the corridor.

St. John wore a look of patient amusement, while Claire studied the artwork. It was a beautiful rural landscape with a coach and two dalmatians, one running alongside it, and one just visible beneath the rear axles.

"Are these your dogs?" she asked, pleased, but amazed.

"They were," he said. "One is their mother."

She turned to him. "Oh, I'm sorry."

He shook his head as if to say, it was no matter.

"I remember this from last time," she said, turning back to it. "I can see it better now in daylight." She turned to him. "Though corridors here are very dim."

His brows furrowed, but he said nothing. Dim? Compared to what, was his instant thought, but he was loath to plague this woman. She was like Miss Andrews without the devilry—only infinitely more pleasing.

He moved her on, bringing her to the library and then rang for the butler. When he appeared, he said, "Grey, when Miss Channing arrived, she was alone?"

Grey looked in surprise at Claire. He seemed bereft of words for a moment. "I could not say, sir."

"Eh? Did you not open the door to her?"

"No, sir. Though I have been at the door most all morning." He gave Claire a strange look.

Julian rubbed his chin, the ghost of a smile about his lips. "Am I to understand that Miss Channing gained entry without your knowledge, Grey?"

The butler swallowed. "I am afraid, sir—I don't see *how*, sir."

Claire sat by guiltily.

"Take her things. And find out who let her in."

Claire removed her bonnet and handed it to him—after staring at it appreciatively for it was a dashing little thing with a small feather, trimmed in lace. St. John caught her look of surprised admiration, and looked away quickly, stifling a smile.

Claire kept the tallit, not surprised to find it hanging from her elbows like a shawl. She might need its warmth, for her gown was of the popular thin muslin of the day over an equally light chemise, and the large room lacked the central heat she was used to. Even the cottage was warmer with its single fireplace, for its rooms were small, unlike the high-ceilinged, long library.

The butler accepted her articles and left. When the door shut behind him, Claire said, "Do not fault the man. Nobody let me in. I just showed up in your water closet. I don't know why—except this shawl has something do with it."

His brows furrowed, and his mouth wavered. "The shawl?" he said, looking at her interestedly.

She nodded with large-eyed earnestness. "Yes, I just figured it out!" She was going to explain further but fell silent as he returned to the bell pull and rang again. A footman appeared almost at once.

"Send a messenger to Lady Ashworth." He moved to a desk and took a stationer's notebook, opened an inkpot and dipped a quill. After scribbling a message, he folded it and gave it to the footman. "No one but Her Ladyship is to see that."

"Aye, sir."

"And send a maid in here immediately."

"Aye, sir." The footman took off.

St. John turned to her with his hands folded behind his back. "That will stop Grandmamma worrying about you. I shouldn't like to take you from here in broad daylight, or I'd deliver you to her. She'll have to come and collect you." He studied her. "What made you come here again?"

She looked at him with wide eyes, wondering how to explain. Why had she come there, indeed? To save his life? She couldn't say that. "I do not control where I show up—but I suppose I was concerned about you."

"Concerned about me?" He gazed at her with surprise. "On what account?"

Claire wavered. She couldn't tell him what she knew; that a carriage accident involving Clarissa would cause his death. Looking at him, she felt very sorrowful about it, though. She bit her lip.

Watching her keenly, he gave a little smile. "Never mind," he said, coming and sitting across from her, "but I should like to know how you got by Grey." He grinned. "The old boy prides himself on being up on all the comings and goings of this establishment."

Claire sighed. "I told you, I just showed up in the water closet." She paused, gazing at him helplessly. Why couldn't she make up a good lie? Of course he couldn't believe a word of her story for even she wouldn't believe it if she hadn't experienced it herself. It was mortifying, but Claire felt compelled, for some reason, to be wholly truthful with St. John—no matter how outrageous or foolish the truth sounded. The coaching accident was the only thing she would not speak of. Why should she? She was there to ensure it never happened.

Blushing, she added, "It sounds absurd, I know it; you must think me a simpleton. And you shan't believe me, no matter how many times I explain." Where had those words come from? "You shan't believe me." Once again she was speaking effortlessly in period correct speech—as if she was born for it. How could a shawl account for that?

He gave her an affectionate look. "I suppose you're having an episode. I should put you straight to bed." His eyes came alight. "Do you know, that's what I'll do."

Claire gaped at him. "What do you mean by that?"

He smiled. "Nothing sinister, Miss Channing. You are Lady Ashworth's granddaughter, and I am a gentleman. I merely mean to take care of you. In truth, I should enjoy doing so."

"Well, I thank you for the kind thought, but I am not tired, and there is no need for that, I assure you."

Not all of us dream awake. But those of us who do have no choice.
Patricia A. McKillip

CHAPTER 26

Miss Andrews grew weary of waiting for Great-Aunt Lady Ashworth. She summoned a maid and told her she'd pay well to be shown to Miss Channing's bedchamber. After pressing some coins into the abigail's hand, the maid brought her to the room and left. Miss Andrews surveyed it carefully, hands on her hips. She went to look at the lady's wardrobe. She opened a trunk at the foot of the bed but found only a chemise and stockings. The rest of the room was equally devoid of clothing. The maid must have brought her to the wrong chamber. But if not, perhaps Miss Channing had already ended her visit! Wouldn't that be lovely?

She continued looking around, saw the notepapers on the bedside table and snatched them. As she read, her brows came together. It was all scribbled descriptions—including what Clarissa had worn to the ball the other night! There were other mundane details, such as wallpaper and glassware and food. What was Miss Channing up to? Clarissa folded the papers and stuck them in her reticule.

Claire Channing was a mystery. But Clarissa would get to the bottom of it.

For some women finding real love seems to be
something that will never happen.
Taisen Deshimaru

CHAPTER 27

When the maid entered the library where Claire and St. John
were, she curtseyed, and then looked curiously at her employer. St.
John said, "Stay in the room. You're to accompany Miss Channing
when she is in this house."

"Yes, sir," the girl said. She went and stood against a wall where
she could see Claire, who smiled at her.

Claire turned to her host. "Is that my chaperon?"

"Housekeeper's day off," he said. "I'm afraid she'll have to do."

"Thank you."

He gave her an inscrutable look and rang the bell pull. When a
footman arrived, he said, "A decanter of negus." He then went and
said something into the man's ear which Claire couldn't hear. The
footman looked as if he'd smiled, though, upon receiving the
mysterious order.

"At once, sir," the servant said. He left the room.

Claire said, "Negus! Yes, I'd love to try that! It's very popular
now, is it not?"

He suppressed another smile. "You enchant me, Miss
Channing." His eyes sparkled. "Of course! Miss Channing is Miss
Enchanting." He folded his arms across his chest and again sat
across from her, watching her.

She saw now that he was dressed to leave the house,
remembered the dogs at his heels earlier, and frowned. "I've
interrupted your day," she said. "I do apologise."

He shook his head. "No need. 'Tis a pleasant interruption."

Her breath caught at the warmth in his blue-grey eyes. She
looked away, but murmured, "Thank you." Aware her heart was

beating strongly, she looked around the room for a diversion. She'd only looked closely at one bookshelf on her last visit. Surely there were books here she'd never have access to in the future. "May I look at your books?"

"Be my guest. What subjects interest you?"

She came to her feet. "Many." He stood also and motioned her to start wherever she liked. As she went up to one wall of books, he accompanied her.

While she read the titles, he asked, "Do you read the same book more than once? Due to forgetting that you read it?"

She gave him a frowning sideways glance, pursing her lips.

He stifled a smile.

She took a book from the shelf and began leafing through it. "If you are referring to whether or not amnesia affects my recollection of what I've read, the answer is no. I maintain, sir"—she replaced the book and turned and faced him—"that I do not suffer from that affliction."

He looked amused, pursed his lips, but said, "I should not have asked. 'Twas ill-mannered of me."

Standing so close to him, the sudden memory of being in his arms sent colour into her cheeks. She turned hastily away and moved along the wall of books, hardly seeing the titles. He followed. "You will agree today, however, that you indeed belong to Lady Ashworth?"

Claire stared at the books. This section was comprised of travel literature, with spines showing such places as *AFRICA: The Dark Continent*, and, *The Exotic Far East*. Without turning to face him, she answered slowly, "I do, indeed." She turned and met his eyes. "My mother has no use for me, you see." She'd done it again—told him the truth! Why had she? He didn't need to know that she had a distant mother whom she barely ever heard from.

"I regret that it must distress you, but I count myself fortunate that she hasn't," he said. "Or perchance you would not be stopping with your grandmamma."

His gentle gaze scaled the walls of her heart and filled Claire with a rush of warmth, more than she wished to feel for him. "You are kind," she said, keeping her voice even. She turned away again uneasily. Being around St. John was becoming intoxicating. He thought she was addle-brained, and yet he cared for her! She really needed to settle whether she wanted to stay in the past or not. But what was she thinking? She couldn't possibly stay. Not when she had such an edge on her competition! No author would be able to match the research of her first-hand experience. She had to make St. John understand how unsuitable she was, coming from the future.

She spun about to face him and nearly lost her footing, for he was right next to her. He steadied her with a hand upon her arm and one about her waist—which he removed shortly. Her head reached the height of his cravat, and she studied it now.

"Is something amiss?" he asked, seeing the direction of her gaze.

"No. It's beautiful. Such a shame men stopped wearing these. May I?" And she reached up to touch the snowy fabric and examine how it was tied, exactly. She'd never have a better opportunity. The knot of a cravat was considered an art. His, not meant to make a wave at a ball or some evening affair, was small and neat, but nicely done.

St. John bit his lip.

She smoothed it down. "Thank you. What do you call that knot?"

He took her hands in his.

"You are mystifying, Miss Channing." He was looking at her with an interest, an appreciation in his eyes that brought a blush to her cheeks. A distinct feeling of weakness in the knees wobbled through her—my goodness, was she truly feeling weak-kneed on account of a handsome face and well-mannered attention? Only fictional heroines reacted thus! But there was something undeniably fairy-tale-ish about the man. She let out an unconscious sigh and was suddenly clinging to him for support—her legs were giving way! What was happening?

"I'm sorry!" she exclaimed in surprise as her legs buckled.

With a look of concern he swept her into his arms. "I believe you must be overwrought," he said. He turned and strode towards the double doors of the room, motioning with his head for the maid to follow them. He stopped only to grab Claire's shawl, which she'd left on the settee, and then passed a footman in the corridor holding the negus. "Not now," he told him, adding, "I want a fire going in the first guest bedchamber; have Grey call for Mr. Wickford, and I must be notified the moment Lady Ashworth arrives."

There are people who think that things that happen
in fiction do not really happen. These people are wrong.
Neil Gaiman

CHAPTER 28

As St. John carried Claire along the corridor towards the bedchambers, she didn't know whether to laugh or cry. She was behaving like a frail heroine from a 1970s dime-store romance—swooning into the arms of the hero! But she was also sweating, and now started trembling. And then she understood what was happening. Usually this weakness and trembling occurred after she returned to the cottage from the past. But it was happening already—and she hadn't even got back, yet!

"Please—I only need a moment. I'll be fine. I would still like to look at your books."

"You're in no condition for that right now," he said gently.

She found herself staring at the square-jawed, handsome face, now so near her own. He carried her with little effort. She couldn't have written a more romantic scene.

When St. John reached the guest bedchamber, he managed the door with one hand while still holding her. Mary the maid scurried in behind them. He said, "Pull down the bed-covers." When she did, he placed Claire gently down, pulled up the covers, and surveyed her a moment. He took a handkerchief from an inner pocket and wiped her brow. "You tremble!" he said in concern. He took her shawl and added it atop the blanket, tucking it beneath her chin. He sat beside her, took a hand and kissed it, then took the other and kissed it. She smiled faintly each time though her eyes were dazed, for she was trying not to fall in love with him.

"See to the fire," he said to the maid.

A footman appeared at the door. "Sir, Lady Ashworth is here."

"Bring her up."

Claire started to sit up, but he said, "You need to rest." He spoke so earnestly that she lay back obediently. As he left to meet Her Ladyship, Claire watched him, still in a daze. He was a wonderful man, St. John. If only— No, she mustn't even think about staying in the past. She had no right to him—she was not of this time—he deserved a woman of his own day.

And Claire surely was poised to write the best book of her life when this was over. A book that would far exceed anything she might otherwise have written. The blockbuster she'd dreamt of! Her career would be salvaged, her future, secure. She had no choice. As wonderful as St. John was, she was from a different world and must return to it.

St. John met Her Ladyship in the corridor. "She's weak. I've sent for Mr. Wickford."

"Surely you don't mean to keep her here?"

"She's resting comfortably," he replied.

She gazed at him with an inscrutable expression.

"Well?" he asked.

"You need a wife, sir, and an heir," she said.

He chuckled. "I thought you might bring that up."

"Miss Channing is everything you could want in both. She'd be a marvellous mother to children. And she'll rid you of the unwanted attentions of Clarissa." She paused and opened her arms to him. "Furthermore, you'll be my grandson-in-law!" She said this as if it was the biggest prize yet for which the long-standing bachelor should consider marriage.

St. John grinned. "Your encouragement is wasted upon me—"

Lady Ashworth's face fell. "Oh, Julian! How can you be so cold-hearted?"

"You misunderstand me, dear lady. I need no encouragement. I am already in grave danger of being fast in love with your Miss Channing."

Lady Ashworth gasped and smiled. "Indeed?"

"Somehow even her delusions delight me. Do not ask why, for I'm sure I don't know." He thought for a moment. "Perhaps 'tis the way she so tries to make me believe them. She is adorably earnest."

Lady Ashworth levelled a strong gaze upon him. "But if she were telling the truth, would you not find her adorable, then?"

He thought about Claire. "I should find her delightful either way." But then he raised an eyebrow. "My only worry is, how do I know she won't forget who I am after the wedding? This amnesia has her treating everyday stuff like it's utterly new to her. She stared at her own bonnet as if she'd never seen a bonnet before."

Her Ladyship grew thoughtful. "She mostly only forgets where she's from," she said, though her tone was weak.

"She also forgets *when* she is from; she thinks she's from the future."

"Oh, you must forgive her that, sir;" Lady Ashworth waved a hand. "'Twill pass in time, I've no doubt."

"I was about to ply her with some strong negus, to see how long she would maintain her illusions. Or witness them fall, rather."

"Naughty boy! Happy I arrived before you could do that!"

"I may do it, yet. Once she's well."

"In that case, I'll remove her to my home." She lifted her eyebrows at him in challenge.

"Not today, you won't. Let her rest."

Don't worry if people think you're crazy. You are crazy.
Jennifer Elisabeth

CHAPTER 29

A few moments later Her Ladyship entered Claire's bedchamber and said breezily to the maid, "Give us a few minutes." The maid left.

"Here you are, my darling!" she said, coming and giving Claire a peck on the cheek. "You gave Grandmamma such a fright." She looked back to see if anyone had entered the room and then turned to Claire with a serious expression. In a lower voice she added, "I was in dread that you wouldn't return. I do hope you'll stay this time."

"I never meant to leave," Claire said. "I do like it here," she added. "St. John is all politeness, now. But my book will be stunningly realistic."

"Is that all you can think of, still?" asked Her Ladyship. "A book? When I've told you what may happen to—" Her face wrinkled in worry.

Claire played with the fabric of the sheet. "I am sorry; I do wish to save him from such a fate! But—don't you think—he deserves a woman of his own day?" She peeked up at her relation.

"Certainly not! Need you ask that, when I married the marquess?"

"But there is no certainty that I can save him. And the longer I'm here—well, he is not a man to dismiss lightly. I'll fall in love and then he'll be gone and break my heart!" Her mouth compressed. "And I'll be stuck here." Claire looked miserable.

Lady Ashworth clucked her tongue. "Nonsense. You'll prevent the tragedy. And do you not see? You are meant to be here. That's why the tallit brings you."

Claire gave an agonized look at her grandmamma. "But I can't give up my career now! I feel sure this book will set all to rights. 'Twill make me famous!"

"All the success in the world won't hold you at night, or give you children, or fulfill your life." Her grandmamma's face was stern.

Claire glanced at the door to be sure they were still alone. She whispered fiercely, "There is no guarantee that St. John will do any of those things either! He thinks me utterly pigeon-headed. I showed up here, and had no explanation, of course. Why could I not appear at your house?" she asked.

Lady Ashworth shook her head. "The tallit seems to obey a divine directive that we have no control over. But I think you must admit, it proves you belong with St. John. I used to show up at the marquess's estate in Gloucestershire!"

Claire studied her grandmamma. She saw a faint resemblance to herself in the older lady. She really was the granddaughter of a marchioness! It was still amazing.

"I cannot control when I come or go," Claire said. "Except when I'm home, all I need do is put on the tallit. Here, it just happens, whether I'm wearing it or not."

"I comprehend that, my dear; 'twas the same way for me." She looked thoughtful of a sudden. "Speaking of which, in case you find yourself back again…" She paused. "There is a safety deposit box I need you to empty. The key is beneath a floorboard in the bedroom. You'll have to lift the area rug to find it. The box is in a credit union building whose direction, er, address, is with the key."

Claire nodded.

"I want you to empty the box," Lady Ashworth said, "and take what's in it. There's jewellery that would look divine with our fashions today! I believe if you wear them when you put on the shawl, they will come through with you."

Lady Ashworth would have preferred that Claire stay in the past without ever returning again to the future—she'd happily forget the jewellery—but she'd been unable to destroy the tallit. At the right time, it would no longer work for Claire, just as her own time travelling days came to an end. Claire's return path to the future would dry up. She would have to wait for it—but in the meantime she saw no reason why Claire might not retrieve a few valuables for her.

Claire was reminded of something. "Grandmamma—I forgot to

tell you last time; the Winthrops want to tear down the cottage!"

"My cottage?"

"Yes. Some technicality, apparently you don't own the land it's on."

Her grandmother looked faintly amazed. "That is a strong technicality."

"Do you have a deed to the land?"

The old lady thought for a moment. "I cannot recall. I'm afraid I never gave it a thought. Your grandfather would have known, but he is long gone." She frowned. "There may be papers in that box, come to think of it." She levelled her gaze at Claire. "My dear, you really must stay with us. Forget the jewellery. The tallit brought you here for a reason—to save Julian!" She shook her head and blinked back a tear. "And I would adore your staying. You would be the only person who really understands me. And above all this, you must know, St. John has taken a fancy to you!"

"He thinks I'm addle-brained; he merely feels sorry for me."

"No, 'tis more than that."

Claire looked at her relative plaintively. "I'll stay at some other time; but I have to finish the book. I can't drop it, now."

Grandmamma sniffed. "If they destroy the cottage, you can't come back."

Claire sat up in consternation. "But I have the shawl. I thought it was the tallit that brought me here."

"It's the combination. The tallit only works from the future through that cottage. Here, it seems not to matter where one is. It takes you back, regardless. But if the cottage is demolished, and you're not here already—there's no coming back. What's a book when you might have a man who loves you? And such a man! Many of our sex secretly swoon for him. And with St. John's standing in society as well as mine, you will be a star in our little world—you'll have all the fame you desire."

"But—St. John doesn't love me."

"He told me he's very much in danger of doing so."

"He said that?" Claire thought for a moment, remembering how it felt to be swept into his arms, earlier. He'd lifted her with such a concerned expression. She thought of how he'd kissed her. It seemed heavenly, now. And he was a kind, intelligent man, someone she could engage in meaningful conversation with.

She smiled. "He makes me blush like a schoolgirl, not at all the way I feel when I'm home. I may be a mid-list writer, but I know who I am. When I'm with St. John, I feel like a scatterbrain!"

"But you are a smart woman, and somehow he knows it." She paused, studying Claire. "I've known him a long time, Claire. I've never seen him with serious intentions before. And he's ready for a wife. Don't throw it away." She looked behind her to make sure St. John hadn't entered the room. "And don't forget—only twelve days now! Surely you can stay that long. You must save his life!"

"Grandmamma—when I return, I'm usually sweating and weak. But this time it happened here. Why?"

The older woman stared at her, thinking. "Your pathway is shrinking. The two realities are merging. Your return path may be gone already. You may as well accept it." She went on to detail how wonderful Claire's life would be if she stayed. She would have the finest England had to offer, the use of servants and a fine wardrobe. She would have the love of an intelligent and kind man. "You will enjoy all the entertainments of the season; meet the royal family— and more." Claire listened but with a heart that still wanted to be a successful and famous writer. She'd worked so hard at her craft, and for many long years. How could she give it up?

"We'll speak more tomorrow when I come back for you. Julian insists upon your staying here to rest, but I'll send one of my servants so there will be no question of impropriety."

After she'd gone, Claire was troubled by the idea that her return pathway was shrinking, or worse, might be gone! She'd only been back and forth a few times. Could it happen that quickly? Why, it would make more sense, she thought, if the pathways grew stronger over time, not weaker. Stronger by reason of use.

The maid came back in, followed by St. John. Claire tried to rise when she saw him, but he admonished her not to in gentle tones. "A day's rest will restore you. The library will await your pleasure." He gave a small smile.

"Do you get the papers?"

"The *Morning Chronicle* and The *Times*. Do you wish to see them?"

"Yes, please." He turned and gave the maid a look. She took off at once to fetch them.

"I feel much improved," said Claire, sitting up again. "I do not need to stay abed."

"I just sent off your Grandmamma, insisting that you do. You'll need to humour me, I'm afraid."

Claire said, "I can recline on the settee in your library. We can both read, and I will still be resting."

He seemed to consider her proposal. "If Mr. Wickford approves, so be it."

"Mr. Wickford?"

"My personal physician. He's en route as we speak."

When Mr. Wickford had examined the patient's pulse, listened to her heart and lungs, checked her eyes and complexion, he pronounced her well enough to remove to the library. St. John took him aside and said something in low tones. The physician looked at Claire with interest and returned to the bedside. "Miss Channing," he said, "Will you be so good as to answer a few questions for me, ma'am?"

"Certainly," she said.

"What year are we in, ma'am?"

Claire didn't blink. "Do you not know the year, sir?" St. John chuckled but put a hand to his chin and stifled it.

The physician frowned. "I do, ma'am, but I ascertain to know if you do."

The maid dropped the newspapers upon Claire's bed at just that moment, and one glance was all she needed. "'Tis 1816," she said. She looked at Julian and whispered fiercely, "I was right!"

Mr. Wickford eyed the papers and sighed. "Who is our king, ma'am?"

"King George, of course!"

"And how does our king at present, ma'am?"

Claire gazed at him. Modern medicine had debunked the theory that madness was the ailment afflicting the king, for now many believed it was porphyria. She said, "You consider him to have gone mad." To the physician's look of perplexity, she added, almost to herself, "Oh, I know what you want to hear." Louder, she said, "He's quite mad."

Julian came and whispered something to the man, who looked back at Claire with understanding. "Ah," he said. "Where do you live, Miss Channing?"

"On Berkeley Square with the marchioness. My Grandmamma Ashworth!" She said, as if any dolt should know it. She glared at Julian for a split second, though, for she realised why the physician was questioning her. Happily, she had no problem answering to his satisfaction. When Julian questioned her, she was somehow compelled to tell only the truth—but not for this man.

Mr. Wickford cleared his throat. "What year were you born, ma'am?"

Claire looked away. She'd have to think about that one. Math was never her strong point. If it was 1816 and she was—

Mr. Wickford pounced on her hesitation. "What year, ma'am? You shouldn't need to think on it. Everyone knows the year they were born."

"I cannot recall," she admitted with reluctance—and another sidelong glance at Julian, who was studying her intently. Mr. Wickford turned and looked at St. John, his brows raised as if to say, "Ah, now we're getting somewhere."

"What is your father's name, ma'am?"

Claire stared at him.

"Ma'am? Do you know your father's name?"

Claire turned to St. John. "May I have a word with you, please?"

He motioned to the physician that he would speak with her. With a frown, Mr. Wickford obediently turned to leave. "I'll be right in the corridor, sir," he said. "Call me when I may return. I like to study cases like this."

St. John came to the bedside, looking expectantly at her.

"Why are you subjecting me to this? If you wish to know anything about me, all you need do is ask!"

"I do wish to know more about you," he said with a sparkle in his eye.

"Like what?"

"What year were you born?"

"Nineteen ninety-five."

He compressed his lips. "Why didn't you say so to Wickford?"

Claire felt equally cross. "I don't have to tell him the truth. Only you."

One thick brow went up on the masculine face. "Only me? And why am I to be favored with the 'truth' if no one else is?"

She gazed at him. Her expression lost its anger. Earnestly she admitted, "Because I shan't trifle with you. I must be honest with you."

He crossed his arms and put one hand on his chin. "You may tell Mr. Wickford anything you would tell me. I told him of your malady."

"And let him put me in a madhouse? In this day and age? I'd rather die!" To herself she added, "I think I would die."

"Of course not."

She sat forward. "Can you guarantee it? If I told him the truth?" Their eyes met.

"I would never allow it," he said softly. But his resolve seemed to waver.

She lay back down. Looking up at him she added, "Please get rid of him?"

He put his head back, surveying her thoughtfully. "As you wish."

You need to be a little bit crazy.
Crazy is the price you pay for having an imagination.
Ruth Ozeki

CHAPTER 30

After watching St. John leave to dismiss the doctor, Claire sighed, resting her head against the pillow. She pulled up the blanket, realised it was the tallit, and examined it. Why should a mere shawl be magical? It looked ordinary enough, and fit the Regency fashion admirably. Staring at the doves, she had the strangest thought. That this magical shawl was made to bring people together—like its love birds suggested. Hadn't her grandmamma said she had been thrown into the marquesses's path by the shawl? And hadn't Claire been thrown into St. John's path by it? Oh, what could it all mean?

She sighed and held it to her chest. A loud noise suddenly drowned out all else and the room grew dim. She blinked to get her bearings.

She was back home, in the cottage.

> Very often the protagonists happen upon time travel against their will.
> Rudyard J. Alcocer

CHAPTER 31

St. John bade the doctor off after ascertaining that whatever malady was afflicting Miss Channing, she was otherwise hale in body. With that assurance, if she felt perfectly well, he'd return to his scheme of plying her with a small amount of negus. The beverage could be made very weak such as for a public ball, or with more spirits. He had instructed it be made with a middling amount of alcohol. He didn't wish to undo Claire in any manner—but to get at the truth. He felt sure she wasn't intentionally dishonest, but wondered if she might know more than her sober mind could access. With Her Ladyship gone, he had the opportunity to test his theory.

He had a tray brought to the library and went to fetch Claire. He arrived at her chamber and found the bed empty. He turned to the maid, who sat sleepily in a chair against a window. "Where is Miss Channing?" he asked.

She came alert, blinking. "In't she in bed, sir?"

"She's not."

The maid stared at the bed in astonishment. "Bless me, sir, I saw her there, only a few moments since!"

With a frown, he turned and left the room. That wayward girl had no doubt tried to find her own way to the library.

Soon, every servant in the house was scurrying about searching for the lady. With dismay, Grey had to inform him that Miss Channing's bonnet and gloves were also gone.

Fifteen minutes later, St. John had to draw an infuriating conclusion. Miss Channing had vanished.

What is a Wanderess? Bound by no boundaries,
contained by no countries, tamed by no time...
Roman Payne

CHAPTER 32

Note to self: Don't play with that tallit! Claire looked around at the cottage in surprise. The tallit was at her feet. She picked it up and draped it across the brow of a chair. Everything looked so normal and just the same as ever. But Claire wasn't the same. She thought of St. John; he'd be angry at her disappearance. She ought to go right back—perhaps he hadn't discovered her absence, yet. She caught a glimpse of her cell phone on the counter attached to the charger. Perhaps her agent left a message. Perhaps that publisher, the one he'd said was "somewhat interested," had asked for the complete manuscript.

She didn't have a complete manuscript yet, but felt confident they'd love whatever she gave them. How could they not? With the details she had now to plug into the book, it was bound to ring with an authenticity that would wow anyone.

But her only message was from Adam. He'd left two words: "Twelve days." Claire's first thought was of St. John. Grandmamma had said there were twelve days left before the accident. How ironic that her cottage was slated to be destroyed on that very same date—two hundred years later. But it wasn't two hundred years later, because in the past—the past she visited—it was yet to happen!

She checked Facebook and email. By the time she returned the phone to its charger and plugged it in, twenty minutes had passed! Oh dear. She rushed for the tallit.

⚜

When Claire stepped out of the water closet into the corridor of

St. John's town house, a maid scurrying by halted with a look of shock. She stared at Claire, her eyes wide as saucers. She swallowed. "The master's lookin' for ye, mum," she said with a curtsey. "He be lookin' all over for ye!"

"Oh, please tell him I'm—I'm—"

"That ye'r 'ere, mum?"

"Yes! Thank you."

As the maid scurried off, Claire realised she was wearing her bonnet, shawl and gloves again. Normally, her clothing magically fit the occasion of wherever she appeared, but twice now she'd arrived at St. John's home dressed for the outdoors. How would she explain it, when he'd left her abed? Why hadn't she simply appeared properly dressed, such as when she was at the ball? She would be forced to admit having left—or at least, having been prepared to. She undid the strings of her bonnet, removed it, and after admiring it once again (for it was just so pretty and lined with silk) placed her gloves inside it.

She headed to the guest bedchamber where St. John had left her.

Julian was at the front door, whip in hand, when the maid caught him.

"Oh, sir! Miss Channing—she's 'ere, sir!"

He turned and stared at her. "Are you certain?"

"Aye, sir! I just seen 'er! In the corridar, sir!"

Grey's hands were already out, and St. John had merely to quickly place his whip, hat, and gloves into them. He hurriedly undid the buttons of a beautiful twin-tailed topcoat and the servant just as speedily helped him out of it. "Have Brutus returned to the mews," he said, and without another word, St. John hastened to the stairs and took them—two at a time.

Claire heard him coming just as she neared the bedchamber door.

She turned guiltily. His mouth was set in a firm line—his eyes, not promising.

He stopped abreast of her, glancing at the bonnet in her hands and asked, "Where were you?" His blue-grey eyes pierced hers.

"I—I'm sorry," she said. "I didn't mean to flummox you. I—"

"But you did, Miss Channing," he said, leaning closer. "In fact, you quite begin to plague me, if you must know."

"Oh dear!" Claire swallowed, rather in awe of the strong, disapproving gaze. "I didn't mean to—to plague you, sir, you must know—!"

"What did you mean to do?" he asked, coming closer yet. His eyes were veiled and dark, his tone grave. Keeping his eyes glued to hers, he wrested the bonnet from her hand—and let it fall to the floor. Claire stared at it, dumb with surprise. St. John was different. He seemed odd. She glanced up at him, almost afraid of the stern, handsome face.

"Why did you mean to leave?" he asked, his face rigid. He moved right up next to her. And then what Claire saw in his eyes set her heart pounding. His head drew closer; his lips were perilously close.

"I tried to explain," she said, as his mouth came towards hers, "how I do not control it—when I come or go."

He hesitated. "So you have. To no purpose, as yet it explains nothing." His mouth almost grazed hers. But suddenly he pulled back and his eyes blazed. He turned her about to face the bedchamber and with one hand about her waist, ushered her in.

"I believe I must put a guard at your door," he said, sounding annoyed.

She turned to him suddenly—once again their faces were only an inch apart. "I should leave!" she blurted.

"No, Miss Channing. You should stay." He took her about the waist. "You must."

She looked up in surprise at him.

"I am sorry I kissed you that night in my library," he said, "for if I had not, I could resist you better now." He lowered his head. Claire knew she was about to be kissed. She knew she could not let him kiss her, for she had no intention of staying in the Regency. It would be wrong to lead him on.

He placed his mouth gently upon hers. *Now*, Claire thought. Now I should stop this!

But he deepened the kiss and picked her up so their heads were at the same height, pulling her tightly up against him. Claire circled her arms around his neck. It felt wonderful—goodness, she cared for St. John! She didn't wish to care for him—she wanted to think only of her book. But she returned his embrace, and her lips were just as eager as his. He gently closed the kiss, but continued to hold her, nuzzling her face and brow.

Claire felt something she'd never experienced before: it was like coming home, it was like Christmas, it was belonging. A thousand lights flicked on inside her soul. He wanted her, and she belonged there, in his arms! When they came apart, her breathing was quickened, as was his.

He put her gently upon her feet and said, "Miss Channing—Claire." He stared deeply into her eyes. "There is nothing for it except for you to become my wife. Say that you will."

Love is a lot of magic and madness followed by marriage.
Sriti Jha

CHAPTER 33

Miss Andrews hadn't waited for her great-aunt Lady Ashworth to return the last time she called at Berkeley Square. Thus, the following morning when she appeared at the town mansion, she was determined to see her relation. Miss Margaret had clamored to come along—an annoyance to her elder sister—but Clarissa gave in. Miss Margaret's whinging could be burdensome if she did not get her way.

Yates showed them to the yellow saloon, where Her Ladyship set aside the morning paper and waited with a small, polite smile of greeting.

"Dear Aunt Ashworth," Clarissa said with outstretched hands and a cloying smile, as she crossed the room to her relation.

"Dear Clarissa," returned Lady Ashworth, with a nod. She smiled with real pleasure when she said, "And Miss Margaret." Lady Ashworth had never found Miss Margaret trying.

Clarissa clasped her relation's hands a moment and then sat down near her. Miss Margaret quietly took a seat on a facing sofa. Lady Ashworth gazed at Clarissa, wondering what she was about.

"My dear Aunt, is your—eh—granddaughter not joining us?"

"She is not home at present."

Clarissa waited, hoping for more information, but as none was forthcoming, she said, speaking brightly, "Do you know—'tis the oddest thing—I can find no mention of her at all in the society book."

"You must look again," said Lady Ashworth. "I am sure you missed it."

"How could I miss it, ma'am?" asked Clarissa, wide-eyed. "I am sure I did not miss it."

"Look again," said Her Ladyship blithely. She recalled how, once her presence in the Regency became stabilized by the marquess's offer of marriage, her own name had suddenly appeared in the historical record as his wife. It was one of the last things she'd ever looked up before leaving the future for good. She had no doubt at all, now that St. John would be offering for Claire, that her name would similarly be added to record books, including Debrett's, known as the society book.

Clarissa cleared her throat and gave her great-aunt a wary look. "If she is not in the book, there is bound to be talk." The words were spoken like a veiled threat, and Lady Ashworth bristled inwardly.

"The only talk, my dear Clarissa, which is likely to occur, is that Claire is soon to become Mrs. Julian St. John."

Clarissa gasped. She stared at Lady Ashworth. Her face grew white.

Lady Ashworth felt a pang of sympathy for her.

Miss Margaret's eyes came alight; her lips pursed as if suppressing a laugh.

Clarissa's face wrinkled into a frown. "Why do you say that? Has he made an offer?"

"I have his assurance on the matter," said Her Ladyship. "Which is the same thing."

Clarissa looked down. But she said, "No, no, 'tis not the same." She looked up. Her face wore an injured expression. "I will not believe it until I see it in the *Times*! How could she—how could he—they have only just met!"

Lady Ashworth nodded. "It does seem rather extraordinary, except that Julian must be married by his next birthday, and he is in need of an heir. And he took an instant liking to my granddaughter, you must know."

Clarissa swallowed. "And when is this match to take place?" she asked quietly.

"Soon," said Her Ladyship. "I suppose as soon as the banns can be published and all that."

Clarissa shook her head again. "I tell you, I do not understand. St. John's been in no great hurry to marry—if anything, he has avoided getting leg-shackled with amazing determination!"

Lady Ashworth saw how difficult this was for Clarissa, and her heart softened. She was not fond of the young woman, for she did not approve of her seductive manner with the gentlemen, or of her thoughtless "larks" against Julian. Also, she knew, unless Claire succeeded in intervening, what Clarissa would do to him! Accident or not, it would be her fault if Julian was killed in eleven days! She had ever struggled to feel any warmth for the woman since learning of that. And she was only a great-niece, after all. Nothing so close as to make it incumbent upon her to love the girl.

Miss Margaret said, "So is Miss Channing staying, then, ma'am?"

Clarissa looked at her sister in annoyance. "Of course she's staying! What woman in her right mind would not stay if she is to marry Julian?"

Miss Margaret ignored her sister and watched Lady Ashworth with a knowing look. Her Ladyship thought, *she knows!* Upon my word, she knows. But all she said was, "I agree with your sister. She must stay, for she is head over heels in love."

Lady Ashworth didn't really think Claire was head over heels in love, but she wanted to make certain that Clarissa understood Julian was a lost cause. She must not attempt any of her larks, and particularly not one using her coach and four. She said, "Clarissa, dear, I know this is hard for you. I have a small supper planned for you, to which I'll invite Earl Brest. He is in need of a wife, you know."

"I have no wish to dine with Earl Brest!" shot out Clarissa. She looked wide-eyed at her great-aunt. "The only reason St. John could like Miss Channing so well, and so soon, is because she looks like me! 'Tisn't fair! 'Tis me he really wants!"

Lady Ashworth frowned. "Now there I know for a fact you are wrong. He likes her despite her looking like you." Lady Ashworth did not really know this to be a fact, but she would say almost anything to put Clarissa off the scent. She must learn to forget St. John!

"Oh!" Clarissa stood up. "How can you say that? St. John and I are—well, we have an understanding. I must say your granddaughter has stolen him! He really belongs to me!" She was getting rather hysterical. "His feelings are really for me!"

"My dear, you are distraught," said Lady Ashworth, staring at her with large eyes. She stood and rang the bell pull. She hadn't known until this moment how fiercely unreasonable Clarissa was with regard to Julian. She suddenly felt cross with her great niece. No wonder she will hound him to death! Claire must prevent her from doing it!

Miss Margaret was evidently not surprised by her sister's vehemence. Her eyes sparkled as though the entire conversation was highly entertaining. She said, "'Tis no use, Your Ladyship. There is no reasoning with my sister when it comes to St. John."

Lady Ashworth turned on Clarissa. "Is there no reasoning with you? Let me try. If I hear of your doing anything to undermine the coming marriage of my granddaughter to St. John, I'll ruin you, do you understand? You must not interfere, Clarissa."

Clarissa's eyes clouded but then understanding dawned, and they came alight. "You fear me! You DO think I can ruin it. Because you know St. John really has feelings for me!"

"No such thing!" thundered Lady Ashworth. "You are incorrigible, Clarissa! I advise you to study the society book again and chuse any other man who is unmarried. If you do, I'll lend my support and help you get him. But you must keep your distance from St. John—and from my granddaughter."

Miss Margaret stared at Clarissa as if waiting to see what rejoinder she would give, but Clarissa only grabbed her reticule and said, "Come, Margaret! I can see we are not welcome here!" She stopped at the doorway just as the butler arrived at the door.

"See the ladies out, Yates," said Her Ladyship.

"No need for that," said Clarissa. We can find our way, I'm sure." She levelled a mean gaze at her great-aunt. "I was good enough for you before she showed up. Why have you let her replace me?"

Lady Ashworth slowly shook her head. "No, my dear Clarissa. I'm sorry to say, but no. You were never good, my dear."

Clarissa turned with compressed lips and stormed from the room. Miss Margaret stopped to shoot a small curtsey at Lady Ashworth. "Thank you, ma'am," she said. As she was about to leave, she stopped and turned back and added, "And yes. I understand, you know." She leaned in and whispered, "I saw her vanish twice." She paused and added, "And I notice she always wears that same shawl. Is it magical?"

Lady Ashworth just stared at the girl, too surprised and alarmed to form an answer.

Miss Margaret saw her hesitation. "Are you sure you can make her stay?"

"She loves St. John," Lady Ashworth said, hoping it was true.

"But is that enough to make it stop happening?" Miss Margaret asked.

"I believe it is," said Her Ladyship. After all, she fell in love with the marquess and suddenly she could no longer return to the future. She was a widow now, but still she hadn't been transported from the past. Falling in love is what seemed to seal her presence there. It was sure to happen for Claire, too.

Hurrying from the room with a look of triumph, Miss Margaret nearly collided into her sister, wearing a dark countenance, in the corridor. Had she overheard her conversation with their great aunt?

"Come, Margaret dear," said Clarissa, in honeyed tones. "Let's you and I have a nice little talk," she added with musical sweetness, grasping Margaret's arm tightly, and turning toward the front of the house and the street. Miss Margaret surveyed her cautiously.

"Talk about what?" she asked, dreading the reply.

Clarissa was silent until they climbed into their carriage. Then she turned with glaring eyes and said, "About a certain lady appearing and vanishing. I knew I saw it! And I knew you did, too! Why did you not admit it to me, then?"

Miss Margaret shrugged. "What difference does it make? She's here now, Clarissa, and she won't go back, as you well know."

"Back to where, is what I want to know," Clarissa said. "And 'tis what I shall find out."

Remember, curiosity killed the cat.
Anonymous

CHAPTER 34

Claire stared at St. John. She was almost tempted to believe it was all a delusion, as he called it. For how could he offer for her so soon? She must be dreaming!

But he was looking at her earnestly, awaiting a reply. "I—I don't know what to say," she faltered.

"Say that you'll be my wife." He stroked the side of her face.

She stared at him, and loved him, and it broke her heart. "Oh, Julian! If I could—!"

"Of course you can."

"But you don't realise—what I've tried to tell you—about where I'm from!"

"Is that what worries you? I promise you it makes no difference to me whatsoever, where or *when* you are from."

Claire was stunned. "Really? You mean you believe me, now?"

"I believe you are entirely in earnest," he said.

She frowned. "But I really am from the future, and I go back without meaning to! I cannot control it. If I agree to marry you and then disappear—what if I cannot get back to you?"

He took a breath and leaned his head down so that their foreheads were touching. Then, moving back enough to see into her eyes, he said, "I will not lose you. I promise you."

Instead of reassuring her, this sweet, heartfelt promise ratcheted up Claire's worst fears. "Have you never lost something you did not wish to lose?" she asked desperately. But she was suddenly wishing very much to marry St. John, and it terrified her to no end.

At that moment, there was a scratch at the door. It opened and a maid walked in.

"Who are you?" St. John asked, in a tone that said he did not relish being interrupted. Claire was still in his arms.

"Mary!" said Claire. "She's from Grandmamma."

St. John looked at the abigail. "Go to the kitchens and eat something."

Mary curtseyed. "I'm not hungry, if you please, sir." She looked wide-eyed at Claire and swallowed. She evidently thought Claire was in need of her protection.

"Go anyway," St. John said. He stared at the maid, who looked uncertainly at Claire. Claire nodded at her. "It's all right, Mary. I'll be fine."

"Wait," St. John ordered. He turned to Claire. "You haven't yet said you'll marry me."

She opened her mouth—she shut it.

"As I thought," he said. He turned to the abigail. "Mary, are you watching?"

She nodded at him, wide-eyed.

"Good." He drew Claire to him in one swift movement and kissed her, a good, long kiss. When he drew apart, she gasped, "What are you about?"

"About making it impossible for you to refuse me." He checked that Mary was still watching, and then lifted Claire, and, holding her up against him, planted little kisses on her face, her nose, her cheeks, and then her neck. Giggling, Claire said, "Stop. You must behave!"

He only smiled roguishly. He moved them to the bed where he planted her upon his lap, and continued to shower her with small kisses. He spoke to her, too, murmuring how she had undone him, disarmed him, destroyed his bachelorhood. In between kisses he purred that he wanted to marry her, take care of her, have children with her. Somewhere during his sweet nothings Claire stopped giggling. He drew his head up when he kissed a tear on her cheek.

"My sweet!" he said. "Do I distress you?"

"You do indeed," she said pitifully. "You break my heart!"

He lifted her chin to look into her eyes. "I want you to be my wife. How is that heartbreaking?"

"Be-because! How can I?"

"Shhh." He touched a finger lightly to her lips. "I've been thoughtless. You aren't completely well. You must rest now."

She said, "That is the last thing I can do right now. But—but—let me sit in your library and I'll find some light reading to calm my mind."

He surveyed her. "I have a better idea. Join me for dinner." Claire couldn't help but feel a small thrill at the thought of an actual, real live Regency repast. And with St. John! But her eyes clouded. "I have no evening gown here."

"I can send to Lady Ashworth if you like, but there will be no other company, just the two of us. No reason for you to worry over costume."

She said, touching his cravat, "But you will look very smart, as you always do, in your evening wear—"

He took her hand. "I need not dress for dinner unless I have guests, or will be leaving the house afterwards."

She smiled and then impulsively rested her face against his. He closed his arms around her and she breathed in deeply of his scent— he evidently had superior standards of hygiene for a Regency gentleman, for all she discerned was soap and linen, and perhaps a faint hint of port.

A surprising feeling of contentment swept through her. From across the room, she met Mary's eyes, but there was no censure in them; the maid tried not to grin.

Claire closed her eyes to concentrate on the sweetness of being held by Julian—she could stay in his arms forever! He was any woman's dream! How could she even think of returning to the cottage? He was thoughtful and kind—and didn't care that she might be delusional! It was maddening not to be taken seriously, but she couldn't blame him for not believing the unbelievable. How she wished, suddenly, that she had been born in this day and time! That she wouldn't have to worry about disappearing or not being able to get back!

And then, suddenly, it was ridiculously clear: she wouldn't go back. She'd stay, just as Grandmamma had stayed. She would marry

Julian and be Mrs. St. John! The very idea of returning for the sake of writing a book, just for fame and fortune? Pah! Who needed it?

Meanwhile, the cottage would be destroyed, and then she'd truly be safe here in the past. And yes, she'd keep Julian from that coaching accident! Tears filled her eyes at the mere thought of losing him.

He kissed the side of her face and lifted her off his lap, landing her feet gently upon the floor. As they headed to the door, he motioned for Mary to follow. She wore an indulgent little smile as she did. What a tale she had to tell the other servants when she got back to Berkeley Square!

In the corridor, a footman was at the ready. He said, "Tell Mrs. DeWitt I have a dinner guest."

"Cook's been instructed as to that already, sir," he returned.

"Good," St. John said. He led Claire on.

She was still sniffling when they reached an elegant dining room. As they entered, he put a hand over hers, which rested upon his arm. "Had I known my offer would send you into the doldrums, I would have held off. Forgive me."

She looked at him with large eyes. "Oh, Julian! If only there was something to forgive! You are—you are perfectly—wonderful!"

It took all his restraint not to take her right back into his arms. "Persist in this manner," he said with a glint in his eye, "and I'll take you directly to Gretna Green."

Servants filtered into the room, carrying covers. He led her to a seat adjacent to his own at one end of the table. She noted the beautiful place settings and lovely muted light of the candles. "Shall we light more about the room, sir?" asked a footman.

"This will do," he said.

Claire agreed, smiling. "'Tis lovely," she said.

He looked at her with a soft gaze. "You are the loveliest thing in this room." Claire sighed—and felt utterly content. A footman came and filled her glass. Mary had sidled in and stood against a wall. St. John turned to her. "Go to the kitchens. Eat with my servants."

She curtseyed and left.

Claire took a sip of her drink and then looked at the liquid, for she didn't recognise the sweet, pungent taste, rather like a strong mulled wine.

Watching her he said, "Negus. I recall you wished to have it."

"I wondered!" she replied. "Thank you." She took another sip. It was stronger than she'd expected, somehow. Regency misses drank this at balls? Surprising!

While Mr. Yates came and watched as two footmen served the dishes, Claire and St. John said little. She was unable to stop herself from watching everything the servants did, though, as well as looking interestedly at every last bit of what was before her. From the gleaming silverware and crystal, to the folded linen napkins, she was fascinated.

The food! The first course had three different meats—fowl, venison and pig. They didn't call it pork, Claire noted, simply "pig." She was always asked first by the liveried footman whether she'd like to try a dish, before St. John. She wished it had been the other way around, for she would have followed his lead, as she forgot that Regency meals were lavish for the upper class. St. John looked faintly amazed when she allowed the servant to fill her plate during the first course.

During an interval when the servants were absent, he said, "Tell me all there is to know about you."

She smiled, but said, "After you. I want to know everything you can tell me." He seemed amused, but said, since he'd asked her to spend her life with him, she deserved to know. He told her he owned an estate in Gloucestershire with many tenants where he grew crops and leased land to farmers. He was a shareholder in the East India Trading Company but a supporter of abolition. When at his estate, he was often called upon to act as magistrate, but it was not his favourite occupation.

"And what is your favourite occupation, then?" she asked. She expected an answer that many a Regency gentleman might give, such as hunting or fencing—she hoped it wouldn't be gaming—but he said, "Driving. Hands down."

"Ah, yes," Claire said, recalling the words of the article in the *Chronicle*. "You're a 'noted whip.'" He chuckled.

"And—and you're in a club, are you not? The, er, Four-in-Hand, is it?"

He nodded. "And the Four Horse Club." He paused and sipped from his glass. "I am seldom averse to a good race, but I find greater pleasure in a fast drive—as fast as the horses are capable of—on my own, rather than in competition with the members."

Claire put her fork down and leaned toward him with a serious expression. She couldn't help but feel that Julian's love of speed might have been—or would be, that is—a contributing factor to the fatal coaching accident. "What is it about driving fast that enthralls you?"

He put his head back, gazing at her while considering the question. His eyes roamed the room. Finally his gaze swivelled back to her and he said quietly, "Freedom. And the sheer pleasure of the wind in my face. I never feel so appreciative of God's creation as when I'm atop the board. I love an open road surrounded by country." He paused and added, "I was born for speed, you know."

Claire gave a reluctant smile. "Then it seems you must indeed be forgiven for risking life and limb." She didn't wish to approve of his speeding but his answer was beyond reproof. She couldn't help but to add, though, "Yet all I see while you speak is how dangerous it must be, what with the frailty of carriages, wooden wheels, and dangerous turnpike gates and posts—"

He wiped his mouth with a napkin, his eyes sparkling at her. "There are risks to any worthwhile endeavour. I have an excellent carriage maker, and my plan is to improve upon those 'frail wooden wheels,' if you must know."

A footman came and whisked away their plates, putting new ones in their place. Claire glanced stupidly at her plate and remembered instantly that there would be more courses. St. John dined like the wealthy upperclassman he was. Now she saw her mistake in accepting a full plate and glanced uneasily at him.

Nevertheless, she would study each course—already she'd

learned much. Then she remembered—she didn't need to study, she was no longer storing details for a book. She could simply live and enjoy it all. But she allowed only the smallest servings upon her plate after that, nodding only to let her glass be refilled.

"A few of my equipages are in the mews here," St. John said, while nodding that he would accept a ladle of asparagus in sauce. "Though I had to let space elsewhere in order to keep as many as I like when I'm in town."

She smiled. "Do you have so many?" Keeping coaches wasn't inexpensive. He might not have meant it as such, but this told her more about the state of his finances than any amount of land, tenants, and shares of stock could. St. John had blunt to spare—in spades.

He gave her a little sideways smile. "I believe only the Regent and two dukes own more in this country."

"My goodness! I should enjoy seeing your collection."

He looked at her appreciatively. "And so you shall."

"Will you take me for a drive? I may find that I like speed as much as you do."

Something flitted across his face. "I would never attain top speed in your company," he said gently.

Claire blushed. "Oh—my presence would slow you down, you mean?"

"Not at all," he said. "I wouldn't risk your safety in such a manner. But I would be delighted to take you for a leisurely drive."

Claire ate little after that, but took bites of nearly everything that looked appealing for the novelty of it. He noticed, of course.

"Are some of these dishes new to you?" he asked.

Instantly she said, "Nearly all of them."

His hand, holding a fork, froze in the air. Then he smiled and said, "Of course"—as he resumed eating.

Oh dear, Claire thought. He thinks I'm pigeon-headed again. Why must I always tell him the truth?

He gave her a sideways glance. "How do you find the negus?"

Claire looked at her glass. It was a brownish liquid and rather less sweet than she expected, but not unpleasant. "Interesting," she said.

The glass had been kept full, and Claire really had no idea how much she'd drunk. She could tell there was alcohol in the negus, for her head grew light—as did her heart.

Dessert arrived in the form of sugared fruit and cake, but Claire had no appetite left. When he saw she would not eat, he came to his feet and held out an arm for her. A footman she hadn't even known was behind her pulled back her chair. St. John took her glass and handed it to the servant, along with his own, saying, "To the parlour."

"The parlour?" she asked, surprised, coming to her feet. "Isn't the library your favourite room?" She tottered a little when they started off, to her great surprise. A giggle escaped her. "Oh dear!" Claire exclaimed. "I seldom drink alcoholic beverages," she explained, while he put an arm around her waist to steady her. "I'm afraid that negus is—is—a bit more than I'm accustomed to."

He turned his head to speak to the footman. "Send Miss Channing's maid to us."

The parlour was a gorgeous display of Regency style with its mix of Georgian restraint and exotic trinkets, Grecian pilasters and rich carpet, symmetry and exuberance. A small table beside a sofa sported glowing candelabra, beside which St. John sat them. The fire was being built up by two maids.

The footman gave St. John Claire's glass, which he in turn handed to her. When he'd got his own glass, he put it on the table. He turned back to her.

"This negus is the exact recipe the Regent serves his guests."

Claire's eyes widened. "Indeed!" She took another sip, enthralled at the idea of tasting an "exact recipe" of the Prince Regent's household. She wanted to remember it always, so she took more sips, letting them linger over her tongue.

"Do you know the recipe?" she asked.

"We haven't spoken more about you, yet. I've told you a good deal about myself—"

"Not about your family. I've heard nothing at all of them."

"I'm the last of the line," he said simply. "I lost my parents when I was quite young, hardly knew them, in fact. I spent my days, like many children, in the nursery and then was sent off to school. That's why I became a ward of the marquess. My father, fortunately, arranged it before he died."

"How did they die?" she asked softly.

He paused. "A carriage accident."

To her look of horror—for she knew too well that St. John might have died the same way, had she not come to save him—he added, "They're not uncommon."

"No; I'm so sorry." Claire's eyes were large in her face.

"As I said, I hardly ever saw my parents." He put an arm along the back of the sofa and said, "Now let us speak of you."

Claire felt alarmed, for she had little to say that he would not doubt entirely. She took a swig of her drink. Mary entered the room and went and stood against a far wall.

"Where were you born?" he asked.

Claire studied the intense blue-grey eyes looking into her soul. She swallowed. "In Maine."

The brows furrowed. "Main?"

"The state of Maine. In the United States," she added, while lifting her glass. She took a good sip. Somehow the negus was getting tastier with each one.

"There is no such state," he said softly.

Claire stared at him stupidly for a moment. She sputtered a laugh. "Oh! There will be—in 1820!" She giggled again. "But we're not there, yet, are we?" She lifted the glass to her lips, but St. John took hold of it.

"I think you've had enough," he said.

But she was feeling splendid—so light-hearted. She felt divine, in fact, and pulled the glass away from him. 'I'm almos' done!" she objected. "And the Prince Regen' serves this to his guests." He watched while she drained her glass.

"Go on. Are you certain you were born in Main?"

"Yesh, yesh, yesh." She popped her head up and declared, "My grandmother used to live there!" She'd suddenly realised he ought to know that.

"Lady Ashworth?"

"Uh-hum. Only she wasn't Lady Ashworth, then." She turned to him with one finger raised in the air. "She was Mrs. Grandison!" She said the words with great emphasis, missing the fact that they were beginning to slur.

Leaning back, Claire felt amazingly relaxed. And Julian was so easy to talk to. And he seemed to finally believe her! She went on. "My mother and grandmother didn't see eye to eye. My mother only let me visit her twice." She paused and turned to him. "Whish is why I didn' know her!" Claire swayed in her seat. "You remember? I didn' know her?" She looked at him to see if he did.

He nodded. He remembered.

"And my shawl—well, it was Grandmother's shawl."

"Is this another woman, another relation, or do you mean Lady Ashworth, your grandmamma?"

"OH, yes! That's what you say, here. Grandma-MA. I mean her. Grandmamma." Claire was having a marvellous time. How nice it was to tell St. John all about herself without a care in the world!

"Yes?" he waited, half smiling.

"Grandmamma had the shawl in a glass case; it was in glass! Hanging on the wall. I remember that."

"On the wall, like a tapestry?" He seemed surprised.

"Yesh!" Claire paused. "But in glass." Her face puckered in concentration. "I should've known then that it was special." Her voice became sad. "But we moved to Connecticut, and I didn' know. I didn' know about the shawl and I didn' know Grandmamma. And my mother"—she turned to be sure she hadn't lost her audience, but he was listening—"my mother," she continued, "said Grandmamma was nuts."

"Nuts?" His eyes narrowed.

"Loco!" She waved a hand around in circles, near her head.

"Are we speaking the same language?" he asked, repressing a grin.

"Mad! She meant, she was mad!" Claire cried. She went to take a sip from her glass, saw it was empty, and looking disappointed, put it down unsteadily on the table. She spied St. John's glass, grabbed it and quickly took a sip. She swallowed and said, "Oh, isn't this nice!"

He leaned over and gently removed the glass from her hands.

"I was enjoying that!" she cried.

He looked to the maid, who came to attention. "Take this. Bring coffee." She came and took his glass and left the room. He turned back to Claire. "You were telling me how your grandmamma was mad," he said.

"I never said that!" Claire cried. She stared at him, blinking.

"But you did—loco, remember?" He took her hands to help settle her, for Claire was growing fidgety.

"Oh! That was my mother!"

"Your mother was loco?" He was almost sorry he'd started this conversation.

"No!" She looked pained. "My gran'mother—Gran'mamma— was loco! That's wha' my mother said. I didn' know whyyyy she said that. But now I know." She stopped and pointed a finger at him. "NOW I know, all right! Because she visited the past! Just as I am! But my mother didn' believe her." She moved right up to St. John to look closely into his face. "Jus' like you don' believe me." She moved away again, and sat back against the cushion, closing her eyes. "You see, 'tis all very true!"

Claire's feeling of great contentment was turning into a strong urge to sleep. She moved towards him and snuggled into his chest. St. John seemed surprised at first, and almost reluctant to slowly encircle her with one arm.

His experiment was an utter failure. He had hoped to discover the truth about Claire's past, but had heard only more delusions and confusion. She was adorably confused; he'd have to grant her that.

But desperately deluded.

The first draught serveth for health, the second for pleasure,
the third for shame, and the fourth for madness.
Anacharsis

CHAPTER 35

"Come," Julian said gently. He tried to help Claire up, but she collapsed against him. He took her into his arms. "Time to get you to bed." Mary had returned with coffee on a tray. He motioned for her to follow as he carried Claire for the second time to the guest bedchamber. She stirred sleepily in his arms, blinked and then focused her eyes on him. She gasped as if she was surprised to see him.

"Julian! Hullo! I'm so glad I moved into gran'mother's cottage!" She threw an arm about his neck. "It brought me to you!"

"It did," he said. He kissed her forehead and, entering the room, placed her gently upon a wing chair near the fire. He motioned to Mary, who brought the tray with coffee. She poured a cup, which St. John offered to Claire.

Claire looked at it dubiously. "I won' drink that," she said heavily.

"Why not?" he asked. "'Twill help you."

"'Tis black!" she cried. Mary hurriedly added cream, stirred it, and gave it back to St. John. He again offered it to Claire. "Come, be a good girl. Take a sip."

She did as he bade. He spoke to the maid. "See that she finishes this. I'll be back in a few minutes." Claire's eyes were closed, but she murmured, "Goodnight, Julian!"

"See that she finishes it," he repeated.

He waited nearly an hour, giving her time to sober up. He felt badly for having plied her with negus. Whatever the cause of her delusions, they were stronger than he'd realised. For some reason, this was no deterrent to his growing assurance that Claire was the woman he would marry. She might be deluded in some respects, but she was delightful in others. She was surprising and beautiful and earnest. He felt restless until he finally returned to her chamber. He knocked lightly, and Mary opened the door.

"How is she?" he asked.

"More herself, sir." She opened the door wider for him to enter. Claire was already ensconced in bed with blankets pulled up over her chest. She wore a chemise—which had been beneath her gown—and a light white cap, supplied by a maid. She looked, he thought, charming.

She smiled as he came towards her. "Hello," she said. "I am quite recovered from the Regent's negus, I think."

"I am glad of it," he said lightly. His eyes darkened. "I should not have allowed you to drink so much."

"Allowed me to, or engineered that I would?" she asked with a smile.

He let out a breath of a laugh. "Little gets by you. I beg your pardon, then, for 'engineering' it."

She played with the edge of the blanket. "I daresay I was remiss in it. I made it easy for you—"

"Not at all." He came a step closer. "I'll see you in the morning. If you need anything, Mary will ring for it."

"I hope I'm here in the morning," she answered forlornly.

In reply, he took her hand and kissed it. Then, with a small bow, he was off. As he left, Claire's eyes searched the room and landed upon the tallit. That horrible shawl! It would take her away from him.

"Julian!" she called. He heard her from the corridor and came instantly back. "Mary," she said, "Give Mr. St. John my shawl."

"Your shawl, ma'am?"

"Yes, the shawl."

Julian received it and looked at Claire questioningly.

Claire motioned him to approach her, which he did. Keeping her voice low, she said very seriously, "You must destroy this!"

Julian looked at the shawl, and he looked back at Claire. He tilted his head at her, as though trying to figure something out; he looked suspiciously as though he might smile.

"This shawl," she said earnestly, "is magical! It takes me away and then it brings me back. But one day it might not bring me back!"

He remembered what she'd said about the shawl earlier— evidently it was part of her delusion. "If you wish," he said. He couldn't help it and gave a wry grin.

Claire shook her head. "I know, it sounds mad! But every time I wear it—every time, mind you—is when I travel from one time to another!" To his look of gentle disbelief, she said sadly, "I am not mad, sir."

He leaned over and kissed her forehead. "I am the one who is mad. About you. I will rid you of the offending shawl."

"Thank you! If you do, I *shall* see you in the morning!"

"I look forward to it," he said.

A strong wave of affection for him overcame Claire of a sudden, and she grasped his hand as he went to straighten up. The depth of feeling she suddenly had was almost alarming. In fact, it was so strong it made her nearly sad with the weight of it. But he'd offered for her. He must love her. It gave her courage. "Julian," she said in a low voice. She was dead sober.

"Yes?" He was listening intently.

"I've just realized—I'm afraid, that is—that I'm...I'm in love with you!" She kissed his hand. He sent a quick look at the maid, who hurriedly stared into the fire and pretended not to be listening. He leaned down again. "But you still haven't said it. That you'll marry me."

She stared at him with large eyes. Julian St. John was the best thing she'd ever seen, the best human being she'd ever known. If she agreed to marry him, there would no longer be any choice in the matter. She must stay in his world. For the last time, she thought of the book she would never write. The success and acclaim that could never be hers. But if she did not marry him—the only alternative was to lose him. As she thought all this, he waited with great patience.

She took his hand and kissed it again. "Of course I will."

The feeble, fluttering, thrilling—oh, how thrilling!—pressure of the hand!
Washington Irving

CHAPTER 36

St. John returned to the library, his favourite room for contemplation before the fire. Though it was going on eleven, like most of the *ton*, he was used to keeping late hours. He gazed at the sofa where he'd once kissed Miss Channing—Claire—and felt warmth about his heart. In fact, he was filled with a sense of well-being, of having done the right thing in offering her marriage. Their acquaintance was short, but somehow he felt he understood her deeply. He glanced at the shawl, wondering if he should indeed destroy it. But Claire wasn't in a sound state of mind. He'd best check with Lady Ashworth about it. If he remembered correctly, Her Ladyship had shown an interest in the shawl when she'd first come to claim Claire.

A scratch at the door revealed Grey, with a face that looked foreboding—for a butler trained not to show emotion, that is. St. John was too familiar with his long-time servant not to catch the hesitation on his features.

"Sir, a Miss Andrews and her sister Miss Margaret, await your pleasure. I have kept them in the entrance hall for now, allowing that you may not be at home."

St. John felt a frisson of annoyance. How like Miss Andrews to call upon him, when it wasn't done for ladies to call upon gentlemen not of their kin. And at such an hour! She was too brazen. All he had to do was have Grey insist he wasn't home. But a sudden curiosity got the better of him.

"Good show, Grey, but I suppose we can admit them. I may as well know what she breaks all propriety to see me about."

Grey nodded and left to admit the ladies, who entered shortly.

Miss Andrews was all alight with triumph. That St. John had

received her was proof to her mind that he was not averse to her. Miss Margaret curtseyed apologetically with regretful eyes, and took a seat near the fire. Miss Andrews held out her hand, but St. John merely nodded at her and said, "Have a seat."

"I know you find it irregular, sir," she began, sitting at the edge of her seat with her reticule upon her lap, "for me to call upon you, but you see, I brought Margaret; she is enough to ensure there will be no impropriety."

"If you mean, that she will force me to behave to you, she is entirely unnecessary; there is nothing that could induce me to misbehave with you, Clarissa."

Miss Margaret turned her head in astonished delight, which she tried to keep from her features, though her sister was not watching her.

"If you mean, however," St. John continued, "that Margaret's presence will prevent the gossips from sending a new *on-dit* into town, then I applaud your foresight. But I must ask why you are here?" He was standing politely to one side with his hands behind his back. For some reason, now that he loved Claire, his dislike of Clarissa was stronger than ever. That she looked like his love was now an affront.

Clarissa's lips compressed, and she shifted uncomfortably on her seat. But Miss Andrews wasn't one to be put off easily. "Julian," she said, "I have heard a rumour of a most dreadful nature. I needed to check with you to determine if 'tis true."

"And what rumour might that be?"

Clarissa shifted again and didn't meet his eyes. "That you are to marry Miss Channing." She now looked up at him.

St. John was much surprised, but quickly deduced whom the source must have been. "You have spoken with Lady Ashworth."

"No, sir," said Clarissa innocently. "I received a note from Miss Channing; she warns me away from you and says it is her great design to ensnare you for herself." To St. John's look of doubt, she added, "Those were her exact words, sir—to ensnare you." She paused and added, "I thought I should warn you."

St. John folded his arms across his chest and leaned back against the mantel of the fireplace as though he hadn't a care in the world. "Did you bring the note?"

"Happily, I did." Clarissa fumbled in her reticule and brought forth a folded sheet of foolscap. She handed it to him.

Miss Margaret was staring at the fire, but with a stony expression. If only she had the courage to expose her sister. It was a falsehood, this tale about a letter from Miss Channing! But if she dared tell St. John, Clarissa would make her life miserable. She'd already threatened to send Margaret off to a school for young ladies. A school, moreover, that had the reputation of being severe in its treatment of pupils—frugal with regard to food and good things—and in short no place Margaret ever wished to see. To her mind, it was only a step above a workhouse. She said nothing.

St. John perused the note, which Clarissa painstakingly had written out in Claire's handwriting, using the notes she'd found in Claire's bedchamber for her guide. He handed it back to her, but Clarissa said, "Oh, keep it! It concerns you more than I, and you must surely confront the lady with it."

He tucked it into a pocket of his waistcoat, but said, "Thank you for your concern. If you will excuse me now, I have business to attend to." He hadn't confirmed the rumour—though he did indeed intend to marry Claire—because Miss Andrews did not deserve to know his business. She would discover the truth along with the rest of London, in time.

But Miss Andrews's eyes lit up. "Am I to understand, then, that you are not to be married?" She stood and motioned for Margaret to follow. But she stopped in front of St. John, who had still not confirmed the matter. "It quite fills me with hope." She smiled beguilingly and moved on. But suddenly Clarissa stopped in shock, staring at something draped upon the sofa. "That shawl!" she cried. "I know that shawl. It belongs to—her. She has been here?"

"I will not answer that question, as it is not your concern."

Clarissa picked up the shawl. For a moment St. John almost told her to take it, to keep it. Claire wanted to be rid of it, didn't she? But to his surprise, Clarissa suddenly tore at it as though trying to cause a tear. He took it from her—or would have, except she refused to let go.

"If you please," he said, in a near growl, pulling the shawl. But still Clarissa hung on and tried pulling it from him. Suddenly, with a sound almost like a human gasp, it tore. The release nearly sent Clarissa to the floor, but she recovered enough to regain her footing. The shawl, however, was now in two pieces, so that each held one half of it.

He looked at the torn item, folded his arms, and frowned. Though Claire had told him to destroy it, it was another thing to have it ruined by Clarissa. "What on earth made you do that?"

She raised her chin impudently. "I will not answer that question, as it is not your concern."

He held out his hand. "It belongs to Miss Channing. If you please."

Clarissa gazed at him defiantly. "She will little want it, now. It is useless to her."

"And to you. Give it to me."

When Clarissa made no move to comply, St. John took a step toward her. She immediately wadded up the fabric and shoved it down her bosom. She eyed him suggestively. "Will you take it now, Julian?"

His eyes were daggers. "You are a vixen, Miss Andrews. Do not call upon me again."

As she walked out, Miss Margaret stopped to drop a quick curtsey in front of him. She gave him a frantic look, shaking her head in the negative. He noted her gestures with a nod, but, unsure of what she was trying to tell him, said only, "Good night, Miss Margaret."

As for the note being from Claire, St. John knew she would never write any such thing. If she were capable of that, he'd been wholly misled about her character, and if there was one thing he felt sure of, it was Miss Channing's character.

He never dreamt he could so quickly make an offer to a woman, but when he'd told Claire she had beguiled him, he meant it with every fiber of his being. Since Lady Ashworth claimed her as a granddaughter, any doubts he may have formed regarding her character instantly cleared. He could hardly understand himself how he'd moved quickly from attraction to something much deeper. But he now felt a need to have Claire beneath his roof, and by his side. He wanted more of her. He needed an heir. Marriage answered every purpose.

His biggest conundrum, as Fletch, his valet, shortly assisted him to prepare for a night's sleep, was whether he ought to get a special licence or not. Claire would no doubt want to go the traditional route and publish banns, or Lady Ashworth might insist upon it. He'd never thought he would do otherwise, if and when he found a woman he wished to marry. But with a special licence, they could be married in two days. He thought again of Lady Ashworth. If she would allow him to get it, and he thought she would, for the old dame was inordinately fond of him and in favor of the union, then he would go that route.

Having Claire in his house made him anxious to keep her there.

It was a pleasant prospect to sleep upon.

Before drifting off that night, Claire decided to leave Julian a note. Just in case she was to disappear again, she couldn't bear the thought that he'd think she willingly left. She must make him realise that she had no control over it—even more, that she loved him terribly and still wanted to be his wife, even if she was gone come morning.

She had Mary bring her the supplies and then wrote a heartfelt letter. Tears fell as she wrote, and painstaking efforts to be neat were in vain. Handwriting in the past was far prettier than anything she could accomplish, which meant that to his eyes, hers would not be to her credit. But she did her best.

She told him how it had all begun when she moved into the cottage. She gave more details, now. How the tallit was central to the time travelling and why he must destroy it! She even admitted that she'd fought against her feelings for him, for all she'd wanted to do was gather data to write a tour-de-force Regency romance. It would make her a celebrity author in her day. But she'd fallen in love with him. Now she wished only to stay in 1816.

She left the note upon the little table beside her bed, blew out the candle and went to sleep. At least, if the worst were to happen, St. John would know she hadn't wanted to disappear. He would know that she truly loved him, and had been telling him the truth all along.

By the time you read this letter, these words will be those of the past. The me of now is gone.
Fennel Hudson

CHAPTER 37

Claire awoke in her own room at the cottage. With a groan, she looked about the bed for the tallit, but didn't see it. She wanted to put it on and get right back to Julian without delay. Where could it be? It always accompanied her through time, whether going back or coming forward. She must find it and return! Like Grandmamma, she would stay for the rest of her days—but where was it? After searching all over the cottage, Claire had to accept that it hadn't come through. Why had she been able to, without it? If only she understood how it worked, this time travel!

She thought of St. John. She thought of his sweet declarations of love. He was ready to marry her! And then she had a terrible thought. Grandmamma had said her going-back path was shrinking. Claire thought she'd meant her going-back path to the future. But it seemed it was her going-back-to-the-past path that had shrunk! Not only shrunk, but vanished, vanished with the tallit.

Claire lay down again, feeling thoroughly shattered.

Her sobs, had anyone been about, would have been heard outside.

CHAPTER 38

St. John could hardly rise and get dressed fast enough in anticipation of seeing Claire at breakfast. When the maid came to the morning room with the news of her absence, his face darkened. He put down his newspaper and quietly rose and made his way to the guest bedchamber. A maid was already changing the sheets, but she handed him the note left by Claire. He read it with a sinking heart. He interviewed Mary: hadn't she seen or heard Miss Channing leave? He gave her a thorough scolding for being remiss in her duties when she had to allow that she hadn't seen or heard anything.

Somehow Claire had slipped out during the night, though it boggled his mind and perturbed him to think of her unprotected on the streets of London. But then it no longer mattered. Though the note was less neat than the one Clarissa had given him, there was one thing he could not deny about it. The handwriting matched. It was a poor hand, to begin with, and despite an eloquent plea, and all the nonsense she still seemed to believe—or at least wanted him to think she did—Claire was no less a she-devil than Clarissa. To think, he'd been willing to marry her! In a fit of anger, he ordered his carriage. She must have gone to the marchioness. He'd find and confront her there.

The pursuit of truth will set you free;
even if you never catch up with it.
Clarence Darrow

CHAPTER 39

When three days passed and Claire was still unable to return to the Regency, she felt at her wit's end. She'd lost St. John! He had said he would not lose her, but he had. And if she didn't take her mind off him, of wondering how he was, what he must be thinking and feeling, or of how she must have hurt him—oh! It was enough to drive her mad.

There was no way to get in touch. She couldn't call someone who lived two hundred years ago, and she had no way without the tallit to get back. She'd sat at her laptop hoping it would transport her as had happened in the past, but without the shawl, she stayed put. Oh! Why had she been able to return to the cottage without it, but not get back? Why had her path closed up so quickly and suddenly?

She saw a note on the floor which someone had evidently slipped under the door without her noticing. She picked it up and read, in a choppy handwriting, a request from Adam for his younger sister Adele, a special-needs child who was wheelchair bound had bonded instantly with Charlie. Could they keep the dog awhile longer? And if she accepted their offer to move into the lodge, his sister would be able to have Charlie nearby indefinitely. Wouldn't that be nice?

Claire missed her shaggy friend, but hadn't taken him back because she hoped not to be staying in the present. Now it seemed Charlie was all she had. But how could she deny a wheelchair-bound child? And, if she ever did get back to the Regency, it was safer for Charlie to be with them, wasn't it?

Only she could not get back. She struggled with whether or not to claim her dog, but decided Adele should have him—at least for now. She called Adam to let him know. He expressed real gratitude, pointing out how convenient it would be for Claire to move into the lodge whenever she was ready. Did she remember she only had eight more days until a demolition crew showed up? How could she forget, she'd pointed out, with Adam constantly reminding her?

But only eight days! And then the cottage would be gone—the final nail in the coffin for any chance of returning to Julian! He'd be lost to her forever! It was enough to drive a person to drink. She thought of Grandmamma and felt a wild hope that Her Ladyship would locate the shawl and bring it forward in time to Claire. If only there was a way—if only!

Suddenly, she remembered the safety deposit box. She moved the area rug aside in the bedroom and tried various floorboards, looking for one that was loose. When she finally found one that seemed different, she used a kitchen knife to pry it up—and there it was. A key with a tag attached. The box number was on the key, and the tag held the name and address of the credit union which housed it.

It was a good excuse to leave the cottage and perhaps get her mind off Julian. On an impulse, she gathered a leather portfolio that held all her most important documents: diplomas, awards, her birth certificate and the like, and brought them with her to put in the box. Whether she returned to the past or not, her documents would be safer there than at a cottage poised to be demolished.

Forty minutes later she was sorting through the box. The jewelry was a lovely matched set of diamonds and sapphires set in white gold—maybe it was sterling silver, but Claire guessed not. There was a necklace, earrings, and brooch. She skimmed through the rest but saw only old letters and cards. Claire read one. It was a love letter to Grandmamma from her grandfather, deceased for over two decades. Normally her history-loving brain would have devoured such things, but she was too heartsick over having lost her own love to enjoy them. Flipping through the stack and seeing only dozens more such letters, she hurriedly put them back. She couldn't stop thinking of Julian and was ready to burst into tears. She took out the necklace and earrings of the set, leaving the brooch for now. She put her leather portfolio of documents on top, and locked the box. Someday, if she never did get back to St. John (perish the thought!) she'd return and read every single letter.

Back at the cottage, it was all Claire could do not to give in to despair. She mentally rehearsed every episode of time travel. There had to be a clue, something that would point the way for her return. Had she done anything different before going back? Had some action on her part opened a time portal? Was there something, some way, to open it again without the prayer shawl? But every memory pointed only to the tallit. Without it she was stuck in the present, the same way her grandmother had become stuck in the past.

There was nothing she could do.

The specter of the coming demolition of the cottage grew in scope with each passing day. It wasn't just a building that would collapse— it was her whole life. The last possible connection to Julian would disappear when the walls fell. She hadn't even achieved her main purpose in coming to Dove Cottage, which was to write her book. And then it hit her. The only way not to lose her mind with grief and regret was to write.

With grim determination, she set her mind to completing the book. She'd already changed the names of the characters; it brought back too much grief to use them. And she wouldn't use Julian's name anyway much less have him fall in love with another woman—even in fiction. With bitter irony, she made the story a tragic time travel. Weren't authors always told to write what they know?

Claire worked like one possessed, for she was, by desperation. She wrote all day and far into the night. If she stopped to eat or rest, she continued brainstorming and had the whole story worked out, so that each day it was only a matter of getting it on paper. She had to keep working frenetically, for if she didn't, St. John was before her. The thought of him was as someone who had died—and he had died, hadn't he? In 1816. And yet she couldn't forget that back in the past it was still to happen! As if her life hadn't become crazy enough with time traveling, she'd go truly insane if she dwelt upon Julian, for he was doubly lost to her. Separated by 200 years, and lost to an impending tragedy that she ought to have prevented.

More days passed, and Claire continued to write like a madwoman in order not to become one. She took breaks only to eat or shower. Writing at such a pitch, she was amazed to find that her brain got on board with the urgency; she switched into a gear of creativity she'd seldom felt before, and the words flowed as if fueled by some inner power she hadn't known she possessed. When she reviewed her work, it was good—really good. At times she wrote with tears flowing, but she knew her readers would cry too, and love the book for making them do it.

When the new first draft was finished—the book was shorter than any of her previous novels, at only 160 pages—she put together a proposal and emailed it to her agent, along with the first three chapters. Normally, she'd put aside a manuscript for a few weeks or even months before taking a fresh look and deciding if it was agent ready. But she didn't have a few weeks or months.

The very next day, to her surprise, her agent called. He loved the story idea and felt optimistic about selling it. He asked for the full manuscript, which Claire sent. She was pleased, but there was a wall around her heart. All the excitement of writing the story of her life had disappeared. Her time in 1816 had indeed given the perfect fodder for a great historical romance, a groundbreaking book, but it was all too true what Grandmamma had said: what was a book compared to a man who loved her? And whom she loved! A book, even if it became a blockbuster, was small comfort next to losing Julian.

There's just something obvious about emptiness,
even when you try to convince yourself otherwise.
Sarah Dessen

CHAPTER 40

St. John had been three times to Lady Ashworth's home since Claire's disappearance from his house, and each time had been prevented from seeing her. Lady Ashworth was now refusing to see him. When he'd stormed over on the morning after he'd read the note from Claire and discovered her deception, Lady Ashworth seemed quite speechless at first, except to insist Claire was not well and could not be expected to face him. She utterly decried the note, saying she was sure Claire had not written one to Clarissa. As for the other note, with the elaborate explanation about time travel, Her Ladyship merely said, "You see, she is not well."

All of this would have been frustrating enough on its own, but today a new development would have made Julian challenge the marchioness, had she been a man, to a duel! One of his servants had found through the servant-grapevine that Miss Channing was not in residence at the marchioness's house. Not only that, but she hadn't been seen there since before her appearance at St. John's house. Which meant that Her Ladyship had been lying to him all along about Claire being indisposed.

He went once more to the mansion on Berkeley Square, prepared to end ties with Her Ladyship if she did not come clean about whatever she was hiding concerning Claire. And where was that deuced woman, if not with the marchioness?

Another frustration was that Miss Andrews still clung to her obsession about him. Whenever he went out in his carriage, another coach would shortly appear behind his, which his footman recognised as belonging to Miss Andrews. He considered confronting Clarissa but decided to ignore her instead. However, it was irksome. What did she hope to gain by watching his comings and goings?

When he arrived at Berkeley Square, Clarissa's coach likewise stopped at the kerb, not too distant from his equipage. Ignoring it, he handed the reins to a servant and went into the house. Yates insisted that his mistress was indisposed, but St. John said, "I'll be in the yellow saloon. Tell Her Ladyship that she must see me, or—" He thought for a moment."Or I will marry Clarissa." He had no intention of marrying Clarissa, but Lady Ashworth wouldn't know that.

Yates nodded. "Yes, sir."

In less than five minutes, Claire's grandmamma entered the yellow saloon, her face a picture of alarm. St. John was leaning against the mantel with his arms folded, but he came to attention and gave her a pointedly brief bow.

"What is this fustian I hear about you marrying Clarissa?" she said, without preamble. "Did you not tell me yourself that you made an offer to my granddaughter, sir?" She hadn't even taken a seat.

"As a matter of fact," said St. John, coming and standing abreast of the woman, his hands tightly closed behind his back, "I did. And she accepted. But speaking of fustian," he added, "I happen to know that your granddaughter is not here. In fact," he went on, while a guarded look crept onto the woman's face, "she has not been here since before she came to my home." He paused, searching the marchioness's face. Hardly able to keep his anger in check, he asked, "*Where* is she?" He crossed his arms and narrowed his eyes at her.

Lady Ashworth looked supremely uncomfortable but made no reply.

"You have deceived me in this. What are you hiding? I cannot fathom it." He stared at her with a piercing eye, one brow raised.

Lady Ashworth started pacing, looking at St. John now and then with a vastly troubled expression.

"My lady," he said, through gritted teeth. "Your explanation, if you please."

Lady Ashworth took a seat and motioned for St. John to do likewise. Reluctantly he sat across from her, but leaned forward impatiently. She produced a handkerchief from a pocket of a gown and wrung it in one hand. "Julian, I never meant to deceive you, truly!"

"But you have. Where is she?"

Lady Ashworth hesitated. She looked at him regretfully. "Everything you need to know is in that note she left you."

He stared. "There is nothing in that note except her delusions. Are you suggesting the explanation is that she is not in her right mind?"

Her Ladyship shifted on her seat, coming to the edge of it. She looked apologetically at him. "They aren't delusions. You see. I, too…" Her voice trailed off for a moment, and she licked her lips. "Came here from the future."

Julian shot to his feet. "You must think me a simpleton—no, a fool! Who else would believe such an outlandish claim?" He paced a few feet and then turned on her. "What is there to gain in this? If Claire wishes to cry off, she might do so without the elaborate deception. I fail utterly to comprehend the meaning of this."

"I kept expecting her to reappear," said Her Ladyship, wringing one hand. "She did the last time she vanished. She had the tallit—she ought to have returned. I thought if she loved you, surely she would."

"She had what?"

"The tallit. Her shawl. I bought it in Israel; it is a Hebrew prayer shawl. But it wasn't ordinary. When I wore it, I would suddenly find myself here. In the Regency."

He turned with a look on his face of incredulity. In a tone edged with derision, he demanded, "Are you telling me—that story she wrote—that wearing the shawl could actually transport someone from one time to another? Like some kind of—of—magic carpet? That it's true?"

"Not like a magic carpet," said Her Ladyship, blinking back tears. "But the shawl is indeed magical. Claire moved into my home, the cottage I left behind. The shawl had vanished from my hands after I married the marquess and evidently returned there. She must have put it on, and she wound up in that ballroom. She tried to tell you all of this, Julian. She never wished to deceive you!"

He stood up and began pacing. He went to the window and peered out. With his back turned, he said, "She disappeared without the shawl. If it is supposedly the means of transport, then how could she go back without it?"

Lady Ashworth shook her head. "When I came here for good, the shawl went back without me. That's why Claire found it in my house. And now she's gone back without it!"

"And the amnesia?" he said, his voice clipped.

"An explanation to satisfy you at the moment. I knew I should face—well, this very scene were I to try and tell you the truth."

He spun around. His eyes glinted dangerously at her.

Lady Ashworth said, "How do you know she went back without her shawl?"

"She gave it to me. She asked me to destroy it."

Her Ladyship gasped. "And you did! That's why she hasn't returned! She cannot!"

He surveyed her calmly. "I did not destroy it. But Clarissa almost did. She fought me for it and it tore in two."

Lady Ashworth's eyes bulged. "Do you have both pieces?" She sounded as if she dreaded the answer.

"I have only the one half. I'm afraid Miss Andrews has the other." He looked coldly at Her Ladyship. "But I'm also afraid I cannot believe this elaborate deception."

"Julian! I love you like a son! Why would I make up something so preposterous? And Claire loves you! Why wouldn't she be here if she could?"

He let out a derisive breath. "She loved me enough to warn Clarissa that she would ensnare me."

"You still maintain that she wrote that Banbury tale?" Her Ladyship shifted on her seat.

"The handwriting matched. There is no other answer for it." He was slowly approaching her. His face still wore the look of an animal preparing to pounce. Julian could be vastly intimidating, but Lady Ashworth loved him too well to fear him. In fact, she felt suddenly impatient with his stubbornness.

"Go home and examine both notes again, minutely. I'm sure

you'll find one is a forgery. I know my granddaughter. She could not have written that note, and the fact that it came from Clarissa should be enough to convince you likewise."

He paced back to the window, and stood with his hands behind his back. He turned and looked squarely at her. "My lady, it was delightful to know you. Until now. I am sorry for it, but this must be our last interview—"

"Julian! Don't be pigeon-headed! You must know, there is nothing I want more than for you to marry Claire!" In exasperation she ventured, "Why do you not bring me the shawl—the half you have? I'll get the other from Clarissa. And mayhap I will be able to reach Claire, as once I was able to."

"In the future, you mean?" His gaze was veiled.

She nodded.

He bowed. "Good bye, Lady Ashworth."

The marchioness covered her mouth with a hand. Tears pooled in her eyes as he strode purposefully from the room.

He left shaking his head, more frustrated than ever. "My coach," he said curtly to Yates, when he saw the butler. He felt ready to push his coachman aside, snap the reins and leave town for a good rollick on the road. But he was too upset to wait in the dwelling and went out to the street. When he saw Clarissa's coach, anger welled up in him. He stalked to the vehicle. She opened the door before he could.

To her coy smile, he said, "If there is one more occasion of your coach following mine, I'll take you to the magistrate and press charges."

She turned to push out her bosom in his direction. "What charges might that be?" she asked, innocently.

"Vexation, if nothing else," he said.

"What you call vexation, I will call coincidence. There is no law against being on the road the same time as you, Julian."

He put his head back. "If you were a man, I'd see you on the field for that."

"Sir!" It was Miss Margaret, who now leaned forward around Clarissa. With a look of alarm she cried, "My sister does not mean to harass you! She thinks she loves you and is slightly brain addled! Surely you can forgive her!" To St. John's consternation, she started crying. "She does not mean to—to plague you! Please promise you won't press—press charges, or meet—meet her on the field!"

Clarissa blinked at her sister, surprised by this show of affection.

St. John was equally surprised. He said, "Miss Margaret—"

But the girl cried, "She cannot help following you—or watching you—she loves you so well, you see! She only wrote that false note in Miss Channing's hand because—!"

"Margaret!" Clarissa cried. "Whatever are you talking about? I did no such thing!"

"I'm too worried about you!" Margaret cried earnestly. "I must make St. John understand that you only mean to love him! Else you would never have been so deceptive!"

"Margaret, you lack wit!" cried Clarissa. "Do be quiet!"

St. John heard enough. He stepped back but caught a last look at Clarissa's sister, whose tears had magically disappeared. She seemed, in fact, to be wearing a secretive little smile as she looked at St. John. He winked at her, with a little nod of thanks.

Clarissa, looking thunderously upset, hit the wall of the coach with her parasol. "Move on!" she cried, without once looking back at St. John. But she turned to her sister with a look of rage. Suddenly tears returned to Margaret's face. "Did I do something wrong, Clarissa? I'm sorry. I was so frightened for you when St. John said he'd meet you on the field! I—I wanted to protect you!"

Clarissa frowned mightily at her sister. "He said, if I were a man, he'd meet me on the field, you foolish chit!"

"But—I was frightened for you!" Margaret dabbed her eye with a handkerchief. "I don't know half what I said to him! I just wanted him to forgive you!"

"Oh, Margaret, you are a lack wit!"

But that was all she said. And when Miss Margaret turned her head away and faced the window on her side of the coach, dabbing at her eyes with a handkerchief, she was smiling.

   St. John told his coachman to get him home as fast as a coach and six. When he blasted through the front door, he flew past Grey without a word and bounded up the steps two at a time. He made his way hastily to the library, hurried to a desk and pulled out a drawer. He drew forth the folded notes; the one from Claire and the other, Clarissa.

   He went by a window and opened both sheets of writing. He compared them again, this time closely. And suddenly it was absurdly clear that the handwriting was not identical. One looked as if pains had been taken to be neat, the other as if pains had been taken to form letters a certain way. To copy a style. He sat back and stared ahead, at nothing. Claire wasn't like Clarissa. He'd been wrong, utterly wrong about that.

The truth is incontrovertible.
Malice may attack it, ignorance may deride it, but in the end, there it is.
Winston Churchill

CHAPTER 41

With only two days before Claire's heart would explode, for Julian would be lost forever—dead in the past, irretrievably lost with the cottage's demise in the present—Claire's agent called again. He'd sold the story! And not only that, but to a top publisher. "Hold onto your hat," he said. "You're getting a six-figure deal." He'd gotten an extra $50,000 simply by hinting he might shop it around to compare offers. Six figures! She'd get half when the contract was signed, and the second half after the book went into production.

Her agent gushed on, saying the editor hadn't seen such a heroine as Miss Gladstone—the new name for the villainess based on Clarissa—since Scarlett O'Hara. Readers would love and hate her, just like the owner of Tara.

When the call ended, Claire sat there trying to let it all sink in. Everything she'd ever wanted professionally—a six-figure contract, an enormous advance, a major New York publisher, was hers. And she felt empty.

How unfair! If she'd never met St. John, she would be ecstatic. Of course, if she'd never met him, never gone to 1816, she couldn't have written the same book. It seemed she couldn't have success without the heartbreak. Now, her career would be set. She'd be wined and dined, toasted, and treated like a celebrity when the book launched. What more could she want?

Julian.

She hated to think that now Clarissa would be putting all her diabolical efforts into plaguing him. In only two days she was going to instigate a hare-brained carriage chase that would kill him! The irony hit her afresh—the same day Julian would be killed was the day the cottage would be razed. Her hope of him in either world, simultaneously demolished at once.

She tried convincing herself that Julian's life—and death—had already happened; it was all in the past. But she'd visited that past. She could have changed that past. She might have saved his life.

Note to self: Never pass a chance to save a soul. The one you lose is your own.

She went out and did something she'd never thought to find herself doing: she bought a bottle of blackberry brandy and gave herself a chaser before bed. She had to drown out her sorrows somehow, for she felt little better than a murderer. Clarissa might be the one who caused the accident, but Claire had been given a chance to prevent it, and hadn't. Her failure had killed Julian—or would kill him. Which was it? She didn't know.

And what did it matter? He was lost to her forever.

You cry and you scream and you stomp your feet and you shout.
You say, 'You know what? I'm giving up.'
Nicole Scherzinger

CHAPTER 42

St. John dropped Clarissa's forgery back on the tabletop in disdain. The note from Claire he read again, very slowly. After the morning of her disappearance, he couldn't bear to look at it; he was too filled with disgust at what he thought was her deception. Now he read it, and read it again. With a troubled visage, he folded and tucked it inside a waistcoat pocket.

He walked as in a daze to his bedchamber. Fletch was putting away neckcloths, and looked at his master in surprise. "Can I help ye, sir?"

"That shawl," he said in a heavy, subdued tone. "The one that was torn. Where did we put it?"

"I know exactly where 'tis, sir." Fletch took off and in a few minutes returned with the damaged garment and gave it to his employer.

St. John thanked him and returned to the library. Distraught, he paced the room, clutching the shawl. Finally he sat down and examined it. "It passes all reason," he whispered. "Forgive me, Claire! Are you truly caught elsewhere in time? God help us both!" He held it against his chest.

And with that, a loud rushing sound filled his ears.

The moment when you feel like giving up
is right before your breakthrough.
Victoria Arlen

CHAPTER 43

Adam Winthrop, dressed in dark clothing, stood near Dove Cottage trying to decide what to do. His father had lost patience with Claire. They'd sent numerous eviction notices, but she hadn't left. They'd sent warnings of the demolition scheduled to take place in only two days. But still Claire hadn't budged. Adam had even showed up at her doorstep, but Claire wouldn't open the door.

Old man Winthrop feared things could get drawn out and ugly, as eviction proceedings were slow. He was determined to go through with the razing of the cottage, and he had big money deep in the pockets of the law to make sure it would happen. He'd had plans drawn up for a perfect beginner's hill on the site where the cottage sat. It was long overdue for their lodge to cater to the novice skier as well as the experienced ones. The cottage's smaller hill would add nicely to the lodge's list of features—and prevent them from losing that segment of clients to a competing ski lodge to the north.

He'd told Adam they needed to try a new tactic. If Claire couldn't be bought out, coaxed out, or romanced out by Adam, they must try scaring her out. Adam's job was to somehow create a noise or disturbance that would frighten a woman living alone.

Adam didn't relish the job. He liked Claire. He didn't need his father's encouragement to wish to get closer to her. If she would only have been friendly, things could have been different. He could see himself getting serious with a woman like Claire. But she hadn't ever been friendly. Even after he'd watched her darned dog without any notice, she still hadn't agreed to see him—or to sell. And now they were past trying to negotiate. They wanted Claire out.

He approached the front of the house, glad to remember that

Charlie wasn't there to bark and alert her to his presence. He quietly climbed the three steps to the porch, and just as quietly removed a light log from the wood crib. He'd hit it against the house a few times and then run, leaving a frightened woman behind. Suddenly, he heard a thump behind him and spun around. To his shock, in the weak light from a solar lamp at the foot of the steps, he saw only the shape of a person—a man! He hadn't been there a moment ago! Without another thought he lifted the log and slammed it down on the intruder's head.

The porch light came on. Instead of running, Adam stood there, stunned, staring at the oddly dressed man on the porch floor, out cold. Claire's face appeared as the drape moved aside. She saw Adam and her eyes widened. In a moment the door opened and she said, standing there holding it open, "What is it?" Adam looked down at the man just as Claire saw him. She gasped and came out and fell to her knees beside him.

"Julian!" His name left her lips in something akin to a sob. "Oh, my word! Julian!" She blinked back tears of joy mixed with concern.

"You know this man?" Adam asked, feeling guilty now. He dropped the log.

"What did you do to him?" she cried. But she didn't wait for an answer, and turned back to Julian, shaking him gently and calling his name. When he didn't respond, she cried, "Help me get him inside! Grab his hat."

Together she and Adam carried him in—no small feat for St. John was a tall, muscular man—and put him on the sofa. As they carried him, Adam said, "Why is he dressed like that? Does he actually wear that hat?"

It was a beautiful beaver top hat and quite dashing for a Regency gentleman. "Don't worry about it," Claire murmured. She was far more concerned with Julian than with explaining anything to Adam. She stroked his face. "Julian!" she said softly. "Please, wake up!" She turned accusing eyes to Adam.

"Why did you hit him?"

"I—I didn't mean to knock him out," Adam said. "He showed up out of nowhere! I never heard him coming. I'm sorry—it was a knee-jerk reaction."

Claire stared at him. "Why were you on my porch?"

Adam grasped for words. "I—uh—was just—I wanted to make sure you were okay."

"Why wouldn't I be okay?" She stood up. "I'm calling an EMT." But just as she said that, a low moan came from the sofa. She rushed back to Julian's side, dropping again to her knees beside the couch. Julian blinked at her.

"Julian!" she cried. He blinked again, but said nothing.

Adam said, "I'm glad he's waking up. Do you want me to call an ambulance?"

Claire said, "I don't think so." She couldn't imagine trying to explain his lack of identification to medical personnel. And he was coming out of it. But she turned and glared at Adam. "I think you've done enough tonight. I don't know why you were on my porch, but I don't want you to check on me again."

Adam nodded. "I'll get going." He motioned at Julian. "Tell him I'm sorry. I didn't mean—"

"Good night, Adam."

Adam hesitated. "Claire—you've only got two days—"

"That's really why you came here, isn't it? To harass me. Good bye!"

As Adam left, she turned back to Julian, who was just now starting to rise. Concerned that he was in no condition to do so, she pressed his shoulders back so he was lying down again, though he seemed to be blinking at her strangely.

"Hi!" she said softly, sniffling back tears of joy. "Are you all right?" Her heart was soaring! Although she couldn't return to him, somehow, somehow, Julian had come to her! It seemed a miracle! She stroked his hair and impulsively kissed him on the mouth.

This seemed to pull him from his stupor. He sat up on one elbow, looking frowningly at Claire. "What on earth are you about? I will overlook that impropriety. Do not attempt it again."

Claire blinked at him in surprise, but then realized he was joking. She threw her arms around his neck. "I am so happy to see you!" She went to kiss him, only he removed her arms with strong hands and forced her away. With a disturbed look, he said, "Miss Andrews, you astonish me."

Rough diamonds may sometimes be mistaken for worthless pebbles.
Thomas Browne

CHAPTER 44

"I'm Claire!" she cried. "Miss Channing!" She pulled her arms free and threw her hands around his neck again, only he said gruffly, "I beg your pardon!" And forced her arms down. He sat up fully, but winced and put a hand to his head.

Claire's heart sank to the floor. She was so horrified she could hardly speak. "You don't know me?"

He gazed at her warily. "You are Miss Andrews," he said in an irked tone. His gaze roamed over her nightdress and hair.

"She is my relation, but I am not Clarissa Andrews. It's me, Claire!" She couldn't believe he didn't know her!

He rubbed his head again.

"You're hurt," she said. "Let me look at it." She moved to touch him, but he pulled his head back and gave her an odd look.

"Let me just take a look," she said, moving a hand again to touch him, but this time he stopped her with a crushing grasp of his hand.

"Oh-ow!" She stared at him indignantly.

He let her go and started to get up.

"Wait," she said. "You've been hurt. You need to rest."

He gave her another strange look, but after sitting up, remained seated. He stretched his neck and put a hand again to where Adam had whacked him.

In consternation, Claire said, "You must let me take a look!" She pushed away his hand and examined the spot that hurt, just above his forehead.

"Oh, my! You've got a huge lump." She rose and said, "I'll get ice."

"How did I get hurt?" Julian asked, when she returned. He had been looking around the cottage in perplexity.

"My neighbor—for some reason—was on my porch when you appeared from the past. He didn't know where you came from; he was startled and so he hit you."

"He did this—with his fist?" he asked doubtfully, rubbing the swollen lump.

"No. A log. A small log. I'm sorry."

She held the cloth with ice to his head, but he took over holding it. He said, looking at her strangely, "You happen to have ice on hand? In this small box?"

Claire nodded. She wouldn't bother trying to explain.

"You said, 'when I appeared from the past.' What did you mean by that?"

Claire stared at him for a moment. He had no clue what had happened! How much of his memory was affected, she wondered. Getting closer to him, she asked, "Do you remember me, yet?"

He gazed at her. "You speak differently, but you are surely Miss Andrews."

"I'm not Miss Andrews. I'm Miss Channing!"

His gaze flicked over her, and Claire felt suddenly exposed, despite her nightgown being about as modest as they came. It reached her ankles at bottom and almost her neck, at top. Maine winters did not encourage the use of teddies. But she stood and went for her robe, feeling a strange mix of elation and despair. St. John had appeared, and she hadn't lost him! Clarissa hadn't done him in! But he didn't remember her.

When she came back, he was no longer sitting, but examining a floor lamp. He was squinting at the bulb, and tentatively putting a finger up to touch it. He spied the little cord and pulled it, turning the light off. He pulled it again. When he'd done this three or four times, Claire cleared her throat.

He said, "There is no flame, but 'tis hot. And quite bright. Rather ingenious. Where did you get this?" He looked down and saw the cord and now began to follow it. When he got near the outlet, Claire said, "You mustn't touch that!"

He looked up at her and then back at the outlet. "The cord

supplies a heating element?"

Claire's lips compressed. "Julian. I know you have questions, and you're bound to have many more unless we can figure out a way to get back to your time." She frowned. "But we must go together. I couldn't stand to lose you again." He took a final look at the outlet and came to his full height to give her a curious look. Then he winced, retrieved the cold cloth, and applied it to his head.

"Please lie down and rest. Your head will feel better."

He sat down and looked at her. "Nearly every word you've uttered makes no sense to me whatsoever. You use my Christian name, but if you are not Miss Andrews, I do not recognize you."

Claire turned away for a moment while she stifled tears. She turned back, blinking hard. "I am Lady Ashworth's granddaughter. Do you truly not remember me?"

He gave her a reproving look, though his tone, when he spoke, was soft. "Lady Ashworth has no granddaughter." He suddenly sat forward, looking at her closer.

She brightened. "You remember me?"

"You are indeed Miss Andrews, and this is another of your larks."

Claire pursed her lips. "I resemble Miss Andrews, but I am not her. I am Miss Channing. Have you really forgotten me? You offered for me!"

He stared at her, but shook his head. "I made no offer for you."

"You did. You most certainly did. That blow to your head has affected your memory!"

He gazed at her again but then shook his head. He knew for a fact that Lady Ashworth had no granddaughter; therefore, it stood to reason that he should believe nothing else this woman claimed. "If you don't mind, I must be off. Summon a servant to fetch my coach, please."

"Off to where, Julian? You're not in London."

He stared at her a moment. "I do not recall leaving town. How far away are we?"

She frowned. "Very far. What do you remember happening last to you?"

He thought for a moment. He looked puzzled. He closed his eyes. "I cannot—seem—to recall today at all." He took a breath. "Very well, Miss Andrews—"

"Miss Channing! You called me Miss—" Her voice almost broke here and she compressed her lips while gathering herself. "Miss Enchanting."

He looked at her thoughtfully. "Miss Channing, if you insist. Pray, remind me. Why am I here, and where is here?"

She tried to think how best to answer. She remembered how difficult it was to convince St. John of anything. "You came here...because you love me—"

He let out a snort of derision. "You are indeed Miss Andrews."

"I am Miss Channing! And the very fact that you must ask such questions, proves that you have forgotten quite a lot; including me!" She turned agonized eyes up to his.

He regarded her; the disdain in his eyes softened. "If I have distressed you, I beg your pardon."

"Stop!" she cried. "Do not be kind! You can't be kind while you don't know me! It's just more cruelty!" She bit her lip and searched his face. She would revert to Regency-style speech. She'd done it in the past without trying. In fact, she'd had no choice, for it just happened. But she could try to speak in a manner he'd recognize as normal, couldn't she?

"Cannot you recall me, really?" She asked softly.

He studied her, his eyes more gentle than she'd yet seen them. But he showed no recognition. Claire said, "Let me show you to the guest bedchamber. 'Tis very late. In the morning, you may ask questions to your satisfaction."

"I'm afraid that won't answer. I must be off tonight."

"But that's not possible. There is no coach, and as I said, you are very far from London."

"How far?"

She stared. If she said America or Maine he would no doubt laugh or grow angry. He wouldn't believe her. She said, "Very far. The farthest you've ever been, I daresay."

"Where exactly are we, Miss—Channing? Pray, do not trifle with me." He was losing patience. Just what she hadn't wanted.

She took a deep breath. "You're not going to like this, Julian."

"If you please—Mr. St. John will do."

She stifled a pang of hurt.

He crossed his arms. "So?" he said expectantly.

"You won't believe me!" Claire looked tragical.

"Where, madam?"

Oh dear. It was 'madam' again! "Very well! You are in America. The state of Maine. It's part of New England. You came here from the past, the same way I was able to visit you in your time."

He stood up. "This is madness. Good evening." He went toward the door.

"Julian—I'm sorry, St. John—" She shook her head. "*Mr.* St. John—it's freezing out! You'll die of exposure!"

He turned and gave her a look of disdain and went to the door. He had trouble opening the strange lock, but finally managed. Without another glance, he left the house. She went to the door, opened it and watched. Where could he go? As an icy wind blew and made her shiver, and as she watched the dark figure of St. John disappear around the side of the house—he'd be looking for mews, of course—a bitter irony occurred to Claire. When she'd been in his time, Lady Ashworth had said she suffered from amnesia, though she didn't really. And now Julian was in her time and did have amnesia.

If only it were funny.

Love is suffering. One side always loves more.
Catherine Deneuve

CHAPTER 45

Clarissa cornered Miss Margaret shortly after they arrived home. "You must think me a fool, Margaret. I've thought about your little scene in the carriage. I understand what you did earlier to alert St. John. As if you cared for me!"

"I would be very happy to care for you, Clarissa, if you would allow it."

"What flummery. You ought to know, I've written to the School for Young Ladies in Cheapside, and told my father you shall be sent there as soon as they allow."

Margaret stared at Clarissa. "I shan't go. If you try to force me, I'll tell St. John! And Lady Ashworth. One of them will stop you."

Clarissa laughed. "You cannot think they care a fig what happens to you, Margaret. Even you must have enough sense to know you matter not at all."

Margaret stood up to leave the room, but Clarissa said, "There is one thing you may do that will induce me to change my mind about the school."

Margaret stared. "Well?"

"You must explain to me how the shawl made Miss Channing vanish."

Margaret shook her head. "Ask Lady Ashworth! I only guessed that it did."

"But what made you suspect a mere shawl?"

Margaret thought for a moment. "Because twice she had it about her shoulders, and once, it was incorporated into her gown, like an embellished hem! And then, there it was again at St. John's house. I deduced it must be magical."

"If I discover you are correct, you shan't be sent to the school."

"So, where is the shawl?" asked Margaret.

"My half of it," said Clarissa, "is in my chamber. Shall we take a look?"

The ladies moved together from the parlour to the corridor and then on to Clarissa's bedchamber, which was the grandest in the house. Clarissa took the torn half of the shawl from a chest and held it up.

Margaret took it and examined it closely, wishing it would do something magical, give a sign so that Clarissa would believe it was.

Clarissa took it back, and held it out before her. "'Tis an ordinary shawl but useless, being torn."

"May I keep it, then?" asked Margaret. She intended to examine it again. She must find something to convince her sister it was special in some way. She must not go to that school for young ladies!

But Clarissa reacted by holding the shawl protectively against her chest. "'Tis mine, now. I'll let you know if I see anything in it that is out of the ordinary."

And with those words, suddenly Clarissa's eyes opened wide, for she could hear nothing but a rushing wind. And then she vanished, right in front of Miss Margaret. Margaret stood there in shock, staring at the space which so recently her sister had occupied, her mouth opened.

As she returned to the parlour, Margaret wondered where in the world the shawl had taken her sister. Despite Clarissa's cruelty, she felt a sense of loss. But at heart she mostly hoped that, wherever Clarissa had gone, she would stay there a good long time.

Some people are like clouds. When they go away, it's a beautiful day.
Bill Murray

CHAPTER 46

After thirty-five minutes had passed, Claire had no choice but to get dressed and follow St. John. He'd freeze to death before returning to her, she was sure. He was that stubborn—or proud. She hurriedly changed into jeans and a shirt, boots, gloves, coat and hat, and went to the door and opened it—and there he stood, suave and handsome and dressed to the nines in a dark jacket and waistcoat and spotless cravat—perfect for the Regency, but not for Maine winter weather.

She moved aside, and he stepped in, frowning. "How far is it to the nearest inn or coaching house?" His gaze swept over her—a look of disdain.

"There are none within walking distance," Claire said as she removed her gloves, coat and hat.

He folded his arms across his chest. "Perhaps you will allow me the use of your carriage."

"I haven't got one."

"A horse, then?"

"Sorry."

His jaw hardened. "I am forced, then, to stop here for the night. In the morning, I will find my way." He watched as she removed her outerwear and put it away. "I suppose you've no butler?" he asked.

"No. May I take your jacket?"

He didn't answer, but just stood there surveying her and the room. She felt a wave of affection for him and wished she could throw herself into his arms. But his gaze moved over her, and he put his hands on his hips. He looked, if anything, disapproving. She shut the door of the coat closet.

"Why do you wear men's clothing?" he asked.

Claire, unaccountably, blushed. "These are women's clothes;

they're not for a man."

He stared at her pants, then swept his gaze over her, toe to head. "Are you a servant?"

She sighed. "No. I have dresses, but they would scandalise you. I wish I had a proper gown—"

"You haven't a single gown? What manner of woman are you?"

She looked heavily at him. "A modern woman."

"An exasperating woman."

Claire's lips compressed. "The thing is, you are no longer in London, and you are no longer in your time." Claire turned, heading for the kitchen.

He followed her. "What do you mean by that? No longer in my time?"

"You're in the 21st century now."

He stared at her. "Do you think I am a fool that I could for one moment consider that claim?" She switched on the lights and went to fill a teapot. The lights began to flick on and off; she saw that St. John was playing with the switch.

"I told you it's not 1816. We have plenty of new things you haven't dreamed of!" She leaned against the counter and folded her arms. "May I offer you a cup of tea?"

"Is there no maid to do that?"

"No. Here's a major difference between your time and this. You depend upon servants and horses. We depend upon technology and electricity. Most people do not keep servants anymore."

He looked scandalised. "Impossible."

"We hire help for certain things, but no one keeps maids or butlers, except the fabulously wealthy, or royalty, I suppose." Looking at St. John, she felt an incredible sadness. It wasn't wonderful having him here after all. He didn't know her. She moved toward him. He watched her warily. His eyebrows rose as she went right up to him.

"You must be Miss Andrews," he said. "Though your hair is in desperate need of style, and your clothing is equally dismal."

She swallowed. "Yes, yes, by Regency standards." She stopped and surveyed him. "Yours is beautiful." His eyes narrowed and he put his head back as if to see her better. She said, "When I was in your time, I appeared in perfect Regency style. I cannot understand why you aren't in twenty-first century style."

"Only a fairy tale could work like that, Miss—"

"Channing." She sighed. The electric kettle was boiling and would turn off, soon. She went and got two teacups and teabags and poured the water. She almost knocked into him when she reached for a spoon because he had come to watch the proceedings. He first picked up a tea bag and let it dangle, dripping, into the cup. "Hmmm," he said (approvingly, Claire thought). Then he picked up the kettle and examined it.

"This, too, is wired to a heating element?" he asked.

"Yes." She took a breath. "I never succeeded in convincing you that I was not from your time, but now that you're here, can you at least concede you are in the future?" When he made no answer, she said "Look"—and brought him to the toaster. She gave a quick demonstration while he watched closely, peering into the slots as they turned red with heat.

"I grant that you have…interesting devices," he said. "Contrived somehow to support your outrageous claim."

She handed him his tea and said, "I'll get milk." She opened the door of the refrigerator and found him peering in beside her. He put his tea down and stuck an arm in the refrigerator. A brow went up.

"This, too, is wired?" he asked. "But not to a heating element. A—a cooling element?"

"Very good, sir," she said, turning to him with a little smile. He examined some of the contents of the refrigerator, reading labels, but his brows furrowed, and he shut the door.

She added milk to his tea, and handed him the cup, only when he took it, she did not release it. She looked up at him plaintively. "Can you not try to remember? You offered for me!"

He almost laughed, but St. John had breeding, and he merely stared down at her. "I grant that you don't speak like Miss Andrews, and your manner is quite different, but this ploy is in keeping with what I expect from her."

Claire frowned.

He glanced over her clothing again. "And I am certain that I could never have made an offer to you; I am sorry to say it plainly."

She stared up at him sadly. "There must be a way to jog your memory."

He moved away from her, took the teacup and began circling the kitchen, sipping it at intervals, looking at appliances. Claire realised that the old-fashioned kitchen was possibly not different enough to impress him with the vast changes in kitchens since his day, despite the refrigerator and toaster. But she had to keep trying to prove to him that he knew her. "Grandmamma said you were the favorite ward of the marquess."

He glanced at her. "Anyone may know that. 'Twas no secret."

"My grandmamma loves you like a son."

"The whole world knows that, madam." He was examining a hand mixer.

"The whole world of today doesn't know it!"

He gazed at her dubiously.

"What about this? I happen to know you are a reformed rake. And I was the first woman, according to Lady Ashworth, that made you— well, misbehave since you were reformed."

He gazed at her interestedly. "I misbehaved—with you?" He put the mixer down and picked up his tea.

Claire blushed. "Not so very terribly."

He came toward her. "How exactly, may I ask?"

She blushed again. "You kissed me. Numerous times."

Gazing at her, he said, "I should think I would remember kissing a woman. Even you. Unless I was hocused?"

"Not at all!" *Even you.* She felt very hurt but tried to shrug it off. After all, St. John had fallen in love with her once. She said, "And why should you remember kissing me when you cannot recall offering for me? Or telling me you adored me? Or insisting I stay in your guest bedchamber in order to rest? You sent for Mr. Wickford on my account!" Tears were in her voice and eyes.

He gave her a quizzical look, put his tea down, folded his arms across his chest, and leaned back against the counter. "You said you happen to know I am a reformed rake." He paused and added, "I have been called a rake, I own. More often, a libertine or a scoundrel, which I believe is the preferred term the ladies use." He looked at her squarely. "But I have not been called reformed."

Claire gasped. "But you were reformed! You had shelves of books about religion in your library!"

"Everyone does, Miss Channing. I have the books; they were part of my inheritance." Softly, he added, "But I do not read them."

"But you did! We talked about Martin Luther! And—and other theological things." An idea occurred to Claire. "You aren't reformed yet, because you've forgotten you are! But I have to tell you, sir, you do become reformed. You are quite the gentleman."

His eyes roamed over her from head to toe. "And you are not Miss Andrews?"

"I'm Miss Channing. Claire Channing."

"And I'm not reformed, yet," he said softly, with a half smile.

Claire's eyes widened. "Don't get any ideas! I only knew you as a proper gentleman, an upright man. And you were wonderfully good at it, very kind to me—except for those few small indiscretions." She blushed.

He looked at her with interest, and started toward her, his hands behind his back. "Indiscretions, you say?"

Her gaze became wary. "Merely a few kisses, as I mentioned." She added, "You offered for me, too, remember!"

He stopped in front of her. "We indeed kissed?" His gaze fell to her mouth. "How many times?"

Claire had the distinct impression he was toying with her. "Ohhhhhh, you are being the old St. John, aren't you? The man without a conscience!" She moved away from him.

"I have always had a finely developed conscience." He slowly followed her.

"But you admit to being a rake! A man who—who—no doubt ruined women!" She leaned with her back against the counter, folded her arms and surveyed him.

"I never ruined a woman." He came and stood in front of her. "I only trifle with women who have already ruined themselves."

She stared at him, wide-eyed. "Well, I'm not ruined. I'm respectable!"

"Are you indeed? You threw yourself at me earlier." He moved closer to Claire, making her come to her full height, up against the counter. "If I hadn't mistaken you for Miss Andrews," he said, putting his hands upon the counter so that she was closed in, "I would have been more welcoming, I assure you. Would you care to try that again?"

Claire gave him an indignant look, and pushed one of his arms out of her way in order to sidle past. "If you remembered me, you would know that we are—" She stopped and glanced back at him. "We were in love. I only expressed my joy at seeing you again. A man who loves me."

He gazed at her thoughtfully, made a face as if to say, "Well, that's that"—and moved away, again putting his hands behind his back. She looked after him with mixed feelings. She had seen a side of him she hadn't known before. A side she did not relish.

As he continued looking around, stopping now to examine a wall thermostat, she reflected that time traveling—until now—had worked like a fairy tale. When in the past, she appeared in perfect Regency attire, spoke properly, and even had a marchioness as a grandmother. Why couldn't the fairy tale aspect of her relationship with St. John continue here and now?

Then it occurred to her that fairy tale magic often involved a kiss. A magical kiss. One that would revive someone or restore them to former memories. And this St. John would be willing to let her jog his memory, the scoundrel! It was terrible to have him here when he didn't know her. How she longed to be held in his strong arms, to hear his voice speaking affectionately to her, and to have his eyes gazing at her with love, as in the past. If she could only make him remember! A kiss might do it!

But first, because it might further help his memory, she must look more like the Claire he had known. She hurried to her bedroom and put up her hair. She let some tendrils hang around her face, and found a wide headband to approximate a Regency bandeau. Though she usually downplayed her bust size—for she never had romance on her mind except for her novels—she had one bra that emphasized lift as the Empire style required. She put it on. She checked her closet—yes! She had a maxi dress. It wasn't the fashionable evening gown of the Regency, but it would have to do. She put on the sapphire necklace from the safety deposit box—bless you, Grandmamma!—and took a deep breath and returned to the living area.

"Julian," she said softly, going toward him. He was in front of the mantel now, and had one hand on it as he gazed into the fire, but he turned and surveyed her. His head came up abruptly and he stood up straight. His eyes swept over her.

"Charming, Miss Channing."

Without moving a muscle, Julian reminded Claire of a crouching tiger. Not that he was necessarily ready to pounce, but the sheer strength of the man said that he could. Nevertheless, she recalled when the tiger was tame—and she wanted him back.

She came up to him. She cleared her throat. "Please understand. I am not granting you permission to—to do anything like ruin me."

A brow went up on the handsome face. "Yes?"

"But if you will allow it, I can try to jog your memory. Perhaps you will remember me if—" She blushed but her gaze fell to his mouth.

Enlightenment cleared his countenance. "I understand you!" he said, taking one of Claire's hands gently and turning her toward the sofa.

"Do you understand? I only wish to know if—if you might remember me—if we—"

"I understand you completely," he said, drawing her to the sofa and then taking his seat beside her. He turned to her and suddenly all the charm of Julian St. John the rake was on full display. His eyes were only for her; his hands held hers as if she were made of porcelain; he spoke soothing words of comfort and admiration for her; he stroked her cheek and moved a stray lock of hair off her face.

"Do not be insincere," she said earnestly.

"I almost begin to think I remember already," he said softly, for reply.

Claire's eyes filled with hope. "Truly?" She felt a rush of gladness. The kiss would be magical, she just knew it!

He nodded, and then all the while gently drawing her to him, kissed her forehead lightly. He kissed the side of her face. He kissed her chin and then placed his lips gently upon hers and softly deepened the kiss.

Claire was touched. He was so tender. She felt fresh hope that she had done exactly the right thing. He was surely remembering her! Like so many other aspects of her experience since she first visited his world, this kiss, too, would work like a charm.

As he gently deepened his kiss, Claire threw her arms around his neck, loving that she was in his arms again. She kissed him passionately. Oh! If he were to remember how she loved him! She was right where she belonged—with Julian! She pulled apart and searched his eyes but could not read what was in their husky depths. She kissed him again, and laced her fingers into his hair. There was a sudden change in St. John. The arms circling her tightened, and he lifted her smoothly onto his lap, and now kissed her with passion, drawing her up against him.

She remembered this Julian, how his love for her had fueled just such a passionate kiss! She was so happy she could almost cry.

He drew his mouth apart to say, "How could any man forget you—the beautiful Miss Channing." His eyes were husky and intent.

Claire realized he was merely bamboozling her! He had never before called her "the beautiful Miss Channing." He lowered his head for another kiss, but Claire drew back. She took his arms and tried to push them off, but he resisted. She stared at him accusingly. "I thought you meant it! I believed you—the way you kissed me just now!"

Slowly he said, "I meant exactly what I said. You are beautiful, Miss Channing."

Again she pushed his arms off, and he let her scramble off his lap. She moved away, her arms crossed. When she finally peeked at him, he was watching her but with a look of slight impatience.

"I took you for a gentleman!" In a voice to mimic his, she said, "'I will overlook that impropriety.' Indeed!"

He chuckled. "Now there, I was behaving myself."

She turned on him. "Only because you thought I was Miss Andrews! And, if you dislike her so, why do you respect her more than you do, me? You behave yourself for her, though I've given you no cause for dislike." Before he could answer, she cried, "You are a dangerous man! I should throw you out into the snow!"

His head went back. "I only did what you asked."

Claire bit her lip and turned away from him. He was right—she'd asked for it!

"And, if you must know," he continued, "'twasn't out of disrespect for you or dislike, but I accommodate a woman's wishes if I can—with the exception of Miss Andrews. I would not have been accommodating for her."

Tears filled her eyes. She turned back to him. "But you kissed me just the way you used to!"

He took a breath. "You mustn't approach me like that again. A gentleman can be expected to withstand only so much."

She pursed her lips, hovering between anger and hurt—and concern. Perhaps she ought to call the EMT after all. St. John really had amnesia—probably a concussion. But her resentment spoke first. "It isn't fair! To you, I'm just a female. But you are the man I love! I thought there was meaning in your kiss—feeling. But there was none on your part!" Utterly disappointed, she added, "Do not trifle with me again!"

To her satisfaction, he looked almost contrite. He took a deep breath and came to his feet. He bowed. "I beg your pardon. I will endeavour to be on my best behaviour."

Claire turned in disappointment to retreat to her bedroom. *I don't like this St. John,* she thought. And then she spied it—the tallit! It was on the sofa where St. John had rested before coming to. She went and picked it up.

"My shawl!" she said. "Or part of it. You must have brought it. How did it tear?"

He came and looked at it and shook his head as though he'd never seen it before.

"You brought it with you," she said. "It wasn't here before, or I would have returned to you. Think, Julian!"

He gave a polite cough. "Since we are to be on our best behaviour with one another, 'tis Mister St. John, if you please. It is quite disconcerting to have you using my Christian name." He gave her a level stare.

Claire was still miffed at what had just happened and huffed, "I don't see anything Christian about you or your name. But how did it get torn, *Mister* St. John?"

He stifled a smile but obediently turned his attention to the shawl. He slowly shook his head. "I did not bring that item with me."

"You did." She paused. "I asked you to destroy it the last time I saw you. But if you had—" She stopped, considering. "You wouldn't be here, I suppose."

He gave her a quizzical look. "Are you suggesting this rag has something to do with my being here? Wherever this is?"

She put it down. "I told you where we are. And yes, it does." She headed to her bedroom. She would not stay in a dress to make that—that—chameleon happy; far better not to be attractive to him since he refused to remember her.

When she returned, his gaze followed her. "I must say, those pantaloons are not altogether unseemly on a woman. Although your frock was more pleasing."

She looked at him and sighed. "And you are infinitely more pleasing when you are your reformed self. I think it's well that you showed up here—now I see who you really are! You stand upon points when it pleases you, and discard them just as quickly if it suits the moment." He listened to her with interest, as if he enjoyed her disapprobation.

"Bravo, Miss Channing! You read my character well. And now,

perhaps, if you have a sufficient disgust of me, you will show me how to leave this shabby place."

"I will show you—in the morning," she said, with blazing eyes. As she headed back to her room, she realized that with the tallit back, there actually was a way for him to return! But wait—she couldn't show Julian how to leave. It was unthinkable to let him go without her. And she had no way of knowing if they could go back together.

If only he would remember her and return to his old self! Or should she call it his newer self? Nothing concerning time was simple, anymore! But still there was the problem of how to get back to the Regency together. If they could somehow return, surely he would remember her and everything would be wonderful again.

And then Claire realized that if they did not return, Clarissa could not kill him in a coach accident. That was it! Despite the threat to the cottage, and despite her dislike of St. John the rake, she had to remember the man she loved and keep him in the here and now. Two more days was all it needed. He'd be safe here. All she had to do was bear with him that long.

Forget? Forget? And can it be?
And is there aught beneath the sun
Can wean my constant heart from thee,
Thou lovely and beloved one?
Monos

CHAPTER 47

No sooner did Claire reach her bedroom door—longing to escape and wallow in the solitary misery of having St. John here only as a stranger—than she realized she needed to install him in the spare bedroom for the night.

When she returned, he was at her laptop at the kitchen table, examining it. She almost smiled. There was something incongruous about a man in a waistcoat and cravat sitting at a laptop. But she was still too angry to enjoy the sight. He'd apparently removed his twin-tailed coat and—amazingly—even hung it in the closet himself, for it wasn't in sight. Sensing her presence, he asked, "What is this contrivance?"

She came over and pulled her chair beside his. "A computer. Ada Lovelace, that is Lord Byron's daughter—"

"Byron's daughter is an infant. Her name isn't Lovelace."

"Her married name will be."

He stared at Claire. "What has Byron's daughter to do with this contriv—er computer?"

"Well, she becomes a mathematician. And she designed one of the earliest prototypes for a computer; I believe she called it an analytical engine—though it had nothing at all like the capacity of this one."

"What is the capacity of this one?"

She frowned. "It grows late, and I came to show you to the spare bedchamber. I will be happy to explain what this does for you, tomorrow."

He touched the lump on his head. "I rarely sleep with a headache, and this is a prodigious one."

"Oh! We can take care of that," Claire said.

He looked interested. "Not port, I hope. Brandy, perhaps?"

Claire said, "I do have brandy, but I have something much more to the point. It will erase the worst of your pain if not all of it." He watched as she went to a cabinet and came back shortly with a glass of water and two naproxen.

He took the little blue pills and studied them. Then the water, but looked doubtful. "Is this plain water?"

"Do you prefer milk?"

"I prefer anything but water. 'Tis seldom without noxious elements. If you threw a swig of your finest whiskey in it, I might consider it."

"This is clean water, I promise you." Her grandmother had left a "House" file in her little desk, and Claire had gone through it hoping to find a deed to the property. She hadn't found one, but she did read the results of the water test on the cottage's well from only two years ago. The water was pristine. If she were a businesswoman, she could bottle and sell it.

He still looked uneasy, so she said "Trust me, sir." Knowing he was in pain, her anger began to dissipate. Suddenly he was only the man she loved, so she added, with a great deal of affection, "You are the last person in the world I would wish harm to!"

He studied her in surprise. His gaze softened. "You are too kind, Miss Channing."

"Take the medicine," she urged. He looked at the pills again. "Don't chew them," she said. "They must be swallowed whole."

"What exactly are they?"

"I'll get the container—wait, let's look it up on my 'analytical engine,' she said playfully. He'd already powered it up, but hadn't been able to log on. Claire did so, and found a page explaining what naproxen was.

St. John began reading with avid interest, but he said, "The analytical engine is a compressed library?"

Surprised, Claire murmured, "Yes, I suppose it is," but added,

"But also much more than that."

"Fascinating," he murmured as he continued reading. She showed him how to scroll down. When he reached "Side Effects," Claire closed the page. She didn't want him to refuse to take it.

He turned to her. "Return the information. It said, "Side Effects. What does that mean?"

"Nothing important in this case. I take these all the time." She looked at him squarely. "Do you want to be rid of that headache or not?"

He looked again at the pills. "The contrivance said they must be taken with food or milk."

Claire nodded. "That's right! I forgot, I'm sorry. What can I get you?"

He frowned. "Do you do your own cooking?"

She took a breath. "Of course. Everyone does."

"I find that difficult to fathom. Is there no longer an upper class?"

She went and brought back a glass of milk. "Just drink this and take them." She wasn't about to try and explain how different things were now from his time.

He took the pills with one gulp.

"Drink all of it," she said.

He smirked, but did so.

"Come," she said. "You must lie down, and I'll get a cloth with fresh ice, until the pain subsides." Unthinkingly, Claire put out a hand to bring him along. Rising from the chair, he looked at her hand with a small smile. She was about to take it back, embarrassed, but he took her hand and raised it to his lips. He kissed it lingeringly, sending a delicious shiver up her arm. She pulled it back.

"You promised to be on your best behavior."

"You offered me your lovely hand," he returned, innocently. "What else could a gentleman do?"

"I didn't offer it for a kiss," said Claire irritably, motioning him to follow her.

He studied her as they walked. He cleared his throat. "So we are here alone, with no chaperon, no servants?"

Claire felt a small alarm, but turned forbidding eyes on him. "Of course we are! This is the twenty-first century and men are expected to behave themselves without a chaperon to ensure it." It was a bald-faced lie, but he wouldn't know it.

"Indeed? Am I to believe human nature has changed, then?"

Oh dear. St. John was too smart. She had already given him one whopper, however, so she tried another. "Men go to prison for misusing women." She motioned him into the bedroom. He was still watching her and when she glanced at him, he smiled.

"I believe you are lying to me, Miss Channing."

She bit her lip and thought about how to refute his suspicion, but her cheeks flushed red.

He considered whether to tease her for it, but instead said softly, "I've given you my word to behave. Have no fear."

She met his clear blue-grey eyes. She saw only the man she loved. Her heart swelled. "In that case, I trust you of course." With her heart in her eyes she added earnestly, "I'd trust my life to you, Julian."

He said nothing about her use of his name, but instead looked uncomfortable. He turned to the room. "So this tiny box is my chamber?"

She nodded. "I'm afraid so."

"No fireplace," he said, surveying the room.

"There's central heat." She went to the thermostat and turned it up. "You don't need a fireplace." She pointed out the register on the floor where the heat entered the room, and he went and felt above it just as the furnace kicked in and sent up a wave of warm air. He raised a brow.

She motioned to the furniture in the room and said, "I'm sorry; there's nothing as nice as what you're used to, and not even a desk." She smiled, remembering his town house. "I especially liked the mahogany escritoire in your guest bedchamber. I enjoyed using quill and ink, too," she said, as she turned down the blanket and then fluffed the pillow for him. She turned and smiled sadly. "Though, if you recall, my handwriting was atrocious. Nowadays, there is far less emphasis on a good hand, because of the—er, the analytical engines."

She met his gaze. "But you don't recall," she said sadly.

He'd been listening with an odd expression and now slowly reached a hand into his waistcoat pocket. He pulled out Claire's note, but looked at it with confusion.

She stared at it. "Is that my note? You still have it! You remembered!" A streak of joy ran through Claire. She watched him with breathless hope.

He looked at it; he looked at her. He opened the letter and looked at her again. "An atrocious hand, indeed." She waited while he read it, staring at him, hoping for some sign of recognition, something to show he'd remembered her. But his look was veiled. He said, "You might have put this in my pocket after I received that blow to my head."

She put her hands on her hips and pursed her lips. "And how do you account for knowing it was there?" With his intent eyes upon her, she blinked back tears. "I must tell you. I love you! Though you don't remember me. You are not, lately, the man I knew. But I love you, and I always will. I will love you forever!" She rushed to her bedroom and shut the door behind her. He was so buffle-headed! Crawling into bed, she cried in earnest. It was no use. He'd never remember her, now. A kiss hadn't done it. And if that letter didn't jog his brain, what could?

———⚜———

Standing in the doorway to his room, Julian listened to the weeping woman. He felt very concerned. Miss Channing was a mystery, but she evidently did care for him. He wished she wasn't crying. But what could he do?

The presence of that letter did trouble him. And the fact that he apparently was not in 1816 was even more troubling. He wouldn't begin to believe such an outrageous thought if it weren't for the ingenious contrivances in this hunting box, or, as he strongly suspected, a tenant's cottage, despite Miss Channing's denial. It made no sense, however, that such devices would be in a shabby box like this.

He removed his boots, cravat and waistcoat, and tried to sleep, but mulled over the letter. He thought about Claire's manner, her earnest protestations of love, and of how disappointed she'd been when he kissed her without remembering her from the past. He thought about the lighting, the refrigerator, heat coming from beneath the floor, and the amazing analytical engine.

Unable to sleep, he wandered out to the small parlour with the fireplace and sofa. The fire was low; he added a few logs, marveling that there wasn't even coal, here. So many advances, but they still burned wood!

He sat on the sofa and spied the shawl. Miss Channing had said he'd brought it with him? He picked it up and felt the fabric with his fingers, willing it to be familiar—only it wasn't.

And then, suddenly, as he fingered the fabric, a series of images ran through his mind. Claire at the ballroom. Claire in his coach. Claire in his house. Claire in his arms! Lady Ashworth claiming her. Miss Andrews tugging on the shawl until it ripped in half. He stood up and stared at Claire's bedchamber door. His face went through a series of contortions as he struggled with his emotions. He'd been willing to toy with her earlier, but—he loved this woman! What a scoundrel he was! He walked to the door. He hesitated. He walked away. He went back again. Suddenly, from inside, he heard a sob.

He listened to be sure. When he heard another, he knocked twice but then impulsively threw open the door. Claire had been on her side crying, but she turned in surprise and sat up. At first, she wasn't sure whether or not to be frightened, for the look on his face was unfamiliar.

"Claire!" he said, with eyes full of intensity. And a second later, he rounded the bed and pulled her out of it and into his arms. "Claire," he said again. "Forgive me!"

"Do you know me?" she gasped.

"I do. The enchanting Miss Channing." He placed his forehead against hers.

But Claire had learned not to trust this St. John, and she pulled back, looking uncertain.

He saw her face and added earnestly, "I remember it all!" Smiling, he said, "I did offer for you. I want to marry you. But you disappeared!" She threw her arms around his neck, smiling through tears of joy.

"I came here! I didn't want to," she said into his ear.

"I know. The letter."

He kissed her mouth, and kissed her again, and then kissed her cheeks, and her forehead.

Still blinking back happy tears, she gazed into his eyes. "I love you!" she said earnestly.

"And I love you!" They kissed again, a long, deep kiss. Claire thought her heart would burst for joy. She snuggled into him. He murmured into her hair. "I'll get a special license. We can be married in two days' time."

She pulled apart and looked up at him. "If we can return."

He said, "Do they not get married now?"

She smiled. "We can be married here, but—it might be tricky. You'll need papers that we don't have."

"What sort of papers?"

"A birth certificate, for one thing."

"Do you actually certify each and every birth?"

"We do. Big Brother. Oh, scratch that. It won't mean anything to you." She stared up at him and then wrapped her arms again around his neck. Looking up at him she said, "I can't tell you what torture it's been, you not knowing me. I missed you terribly! I so wanted to be right here, in your arms."

"You're here, now," he said.

He sat down, putting her on his lap, for all this time Claire was in his arms. She snuggled against him again. "I don't ever want to leave your arms," she said into his chest.

He gazed at the bed. He compressed his lips. He gently extricated her hands from around his neck. But she was still on his lap, and he lightly moved a stray curl off her face.

"I apologize for what happened earlier. I am a scoundrel!"

She smiled. "You mean, you were. But I have you back, now. The real you."

He frowned. "Unfortunately, that was also the real me."

"But not anymore." She ran her fingers through the thick hair on either side of his face.

He swallowed. "I'll leave you to your rest. Tomorrow we can work on the problem of getting home."

Home. The word had never sounded lovelier.

"And then we'll be married," he finished.

Another lovely thought! She hugged him tightly, kissed the side of his face and then his mouth. But afterward, his gaze suddenly darkened. "You won't disappear on me again?"

"I don't think so. But that reminds me, please don't touch that shawl."

He looked surprised. "It was the means of gaining my memory." But then he looked concerned. "You once asked me to destroy it. Shall I?"

"No! It may be our only means of getting back. But don't touch it unless I'm with you. I couldn't bear to lose you again."

In response, he held her up against him and kissed her forehead. "Nor I, you."

There is only one happiness in this life,
to love and be loved.
George Sand

CHAPTER 48

Miss Margaret called upon Lady Ashworth two days after her sister vanished. Unfortunately, St. John had missed an appointment with an important member of the *ton,* causing talk that perhaps the two had eloped. Miss Margaret had no standing in society, or she would have tried to put a quick stop to such speculation; but her great-aunt could do it.

Lady Ashworth dismissed the servants, made sure the door was shut, and then spoke with Miss Margaret. When she learned what had happened to Clarissa, she was uncertain what to make of it. On the one hand, it was good to be rid of Clarissa, at least temporarily, but it meant she knew their secret regarding the tallit and time travelling. And Claire had not returned, and she wasn't sure where St. John was keeping himself. Was Clarissa now with Claire in the future? It was all rather befuddling. She hoped for Claire's return, but dreaded Clarissa's.

"If I can find St. John," said Her Ladyship, "we could put an end to the speculation." She sighed. "He wouldn't believe me, you know, about why Claire disappeared. And he has the other half of the tallit." To Miss Margaret's questioning look, she said, "The shawl, my dear." Her Ladyship's face brightened. "If Clarissa could vanish with only half the tallit, I don't see why, if I can get it from Julian, that I couldn't also. I can find out what's happening with Claire and your sister."

"Aunt Ashworth," said Miss Margaret—finally sure enough of herself to use the term of a relation to the marchioness rather than the more formal "my lady"—"if St. John has half the tallit, what is to prevent him from vanishing? Perhaps that is why he has gone missing, also!"

Lady Ashworth put a hand to her chin. "Oh dear. I hadn't thought of that. I supp ose he may have." Her face crumpled into a frown. But then her countenance lightened. "Well! If he did, he'll believe me, now. Our relationship will be restored. The boy quite broke my heart when he last walked out of this establishment."

"Is there no danger of their not coming back, then, ma'am?" asked Miss Margaret.

Lady Ashworth stared at Miss Margaret as she considered that question. Finally she answered, "I'm afraid that is a danger. There is no telling whether we shall ever see either of them again." She looked worriedly off into the air, reflecting on that sad possibility. Even Miss Margaret seemed sufficiently struck by the thought of never seeing her sister again.

After the younger woman had taken her leave, Lady Ashworth reflected upon everything that had happened. If Clarissa was in the future, it would mean that Julian was safe from that coach accident—that was a good thing, providential! But if Julian was also in the future, who knew what devilry Miss Andrews might conjure there?

Lady Ashworth could almost wish that Claire had never discovered the tallit. Almost. But if St. John survived and they returned and were married, she could never rue that day. How she wished it could happen! In the meantime, she must discover if Julian had taken a journey in time. If he was still here in 1816, she could get the shawl from him and try to fetch Claire.

If not? If he had indeed gone to the future with Clarissa there as well? Then Claire must keep them apart. Surely she would realise that—wouldn't she?

Lady Ashworth called for her coach.

It is difficult, when faced with a situation you cannot control,
to admit you can do nothing.
Lemony Snicket

CHAPTER 49

Julian gently moved Claire off his lap and stood up. The best way for him to guard Claire's honour and his own sanity was to exit the bedchamber. Now.

"I am only just accepting the enormity of being in your time," he said, looking down at her. "And I am utterly wide awake with the implications of it."

Claire rose and slipped into her robe. "Come. Let's eat something." But he suddenly peered into the little bathroom off to one side. Soon he was examining the fixtures. He admired the "standing bath," and admitted that getting water warm from the tap was a marvelous invention. She showed him how the standing bath worked, which he declared "infinitely superior" to any he had seen, including one at Carlton House. "You must try it," Claire said. "It may help you sleep."

Though he had no change of clothing, Claire found a spare robe in her grandmother's closet and left it with him. After demonstrating how to use the shower, she left him to it and decided to catch a few minutes of rest—she wouldn't sleep, but rest while planning what their next move should be. It was past two a.m.

When Claire blinked sleepily awake, the clock said five a.m. St. John! She shot out of bed. She found him standing at the stove before a frying pan, cooking bacon. She suppressed a grin. He wore his tight-fitted trousers and shirt, though no waistcoat. His cravat hung around his neck, still to be tied. He sported a "five-o'clock shadow" and looked amazing, Claire thought.

"Shall I finish that for you?" she asked, coming beside him.

He glanced down at her with a small smile. "You ought to sleep longer. I seem to be getting along. I must say, this instant flame is a fine advance in a stove."

Smiling, she removed the fork he held and put it down. She got a spatula, and brandished it. She saw he had already found the eggs, but also on the counter was an assortment of condiments. Ketchup, barbecue sauce, soy sauce, and mayonnaise. Avocado oil and olive oil stood beside Worcestershire. She looked at him with faint amazement. He shrugged. "Thought I may as well be adventurous."

When they sat to eat at the small kitchen table, Claire was hardly able to keep her eyes off him. Julian's hair was no longer damp, but it looked different; curlier. When they'd finished and he'd helped her clean up—a lovely surprise—he then took one of her hands and covered it inside his two. "I should like to understand that fascinating analytical engine more; after that, if you can get us back home, I should terribly enjoy relieving you of kitchen duties, among other things."

She smiled with sparkling eyes. She got the laptop and powered it as he watched keenly, reading the screen. "Password. Is that a code?"

"I suppose it is," Claire said with a smile.

"What is your code?" he asked.

Claire was surprised to find herself hesitating. Why shouldn't she tell him? "Regency1814."

"Indeed. Why 1814?" He waited for her to meet his eyes. "For me, that was only two years ago."

Claire gazed at him with wonder. "Despite having been in your time, I can hardly fathom that." Looking back at the screen, she asked, "What would you like to know?"

"I'd like to know why 1814 is your code."

She suppressed a smile. "Because of the fashions. There are loads of illustrations from magazines of your day that I can find through this," she said, nodding at the computer. "And out of all the years of the Regency, I like 1814 fashions best. Not to mention all the fascinating world events going on for England."

"Out of all the years of the Regency," he repeated, looking at her. "That begs the question, dearest," he said. "How many years is the Regency?"

"Oh dear," Claire murmured. "Now we're getting into a new difficulty. Do we explore things you shouldn't know?" Her wide blue eyes surveyed him questioningly.

"Knowing you and being here makes that a moot question," he returned. "If you please, when does the Regent become king?"

Claire sighed. "Very well; 1820."

"For how long?"

"Ten years. He dies in 1830, I'm sorry to say."

Julian looked thoughtful. "I am sorry for him, though most of England will not be, for then Charlotte will reign."

She said nothing, but looked hastily away.

He gazed at her with concern. "The Princess does reign after her father?"

Claire's lips pursed. "I don't think we need talk about that."

His eyes narrowed. "How long does she reign?"

"There are other things that will interest you more," she said, looking back to the screen. "In fact"—she stood up—"I have other devices that will fascinate you." She thought of showing him a movie—anything to get his mind off the subject of Princess Charlotte. But he caught her about the waist and gently led her to sit again. He looked at her expectantly.

Frowning, she admitted, "She does not live beyond her father. I'm sorry."

He stared at her, as thoughts roiled behind his eyes. "What happens?"

"I'd rather not talk about it. You must love your princess."

"Of course; she is shamefully abused by her father. Tell me why she doesn't outlive him."

Claire looked troubled. "She—she dies in childbirth, I'm afraid."

He shot up out of his chair and began to pace.

Claire felt terrible. The British feeling of affection for their royalty ran deep. Even she considered Princess Charlotte's death a tragic, wasted loss. She wouldn't dare tell him that it was because of nineteenth century medical ignorance, one mistake upon another. Or that, had it been today, the Princess would have done just fine; that her stillborn son might even have lived.

"Her marriage is only just approaching," he said. "We can attend the wedding, if you like."

Claire's breath caught. The very idea! Of seeing Princess Charlotte wed! A woman, to her mind, who had died tragically so long ago! It was a thought both breathtaking and terrible. This is what awaited Claire in the past—a life of knowing much about the future before it happened. She wondered if that knowing would make life harder, or easier to bear.

He stopped and pointed at the laptop. "You didn't once use your—your analytical engine."

"I've studied your period extensively for my novels."

He stared at her. "I'd forgotten about that. I thought it was part of your delusion, your being a writer of novels." They smiled at each other. "You write books like Mrs. Radcliffe, I suppose?"

Claire smirked. "I hope not." Anne Radcliffe wrote Gothic novels such as *The Mysteries of Udolpho*, filled with long descriptions of scenery, fainting heroines, mysterious castles and dark dungeons. Claire had no ambition to write in that vein.

"Like Mrs. Burney, then?"

"Something like that," Claire hedged. Just then her cell phone rang. St. John looked around in surprise as Claire rose to grab the phone, which she'd left charging on a kitchen counter. She stopped and said hurriedly to him, "People can talk this way today." It was a pathetic explanation of the telephone, but she had to give him some warning. When she picked it up, Adam spoke.

"Claire. I see you're still at the cottage."

"Are you aware that it's only"—she glanced at the clock on the stove—"six o'clock in the morning?"

He cleared his throat. "I saw the lights. I could tell you were up."

"How could you tell?"

He cleared his throat again. "I have binoculars."

Claire felt her blood pressure go up. "That's spying! Now you're a peeping Tom?"

"Look, I didn't expect you to be there. I'm concerned about you. I thought you had more sense than to still be there. It's Thursday and you only have until tomorrow. You know my father means business."

Claire came slowly back toward St. John, who was on his feet, watching and listening keenly. "Give me a few more days and I promise you, I'll be out of here," she said.

"The old man won't negotiate anymore. You lost your chance for that."

St. John's eyes narrowed. Claire knew he could easily hear Adam's loud voice.

"Just tell him I said I'll go willingly if he'll give me a few more days." Claire thought ruefully that the days would come in awfully handy if they had any trouble getting back to the past together. Even a single extra day could be vital! If the cottage was demolished while St. John was still here, he'd be stuck in the present. "You can't raze the cottage when I'm in it. You have my word I can be out of here—in less than a week."

Adam took a breath. "You said a few days—now it's almost a week? Look—I'll tell him. But don't expect a miracle. The equipment's scheduled to show up bright and early tomorrow morning. If you're not out"—he lowered his voice confidentially—"the sheriff will serve a warrant and haul you out of there, Claire. You've gotta be out."

"I'll call the papers and local TV," Claire said, "and tell them I'll be in residence. Don't make it get ugly. I'll be out in less than a week if you'll just wait."

To her surprise, Julian motioned that he wanted the phone. She didn't have time to consider what he would say or how he would use this new "contrivance," but he took the phone and said into it, "This is Julian St. John. To whom am I speaking?"

Claire tried not to smile.

"Excuse me?" Adam asked.

"Who are you?" Julian repeated, while Claire stifled a titter.

"Adam Winthrop. Who are you?" she heard.

"Mr. Winthrop," Julian said, in an acid tone, "Am I to understand that you are pressuring an unmarried woman without protection to remove from her home? Are you utterly heartless?"

"Who is this?" she heard. "Claire, are you there?"

"You will speak through me, sir, if you wish to say anything more to Miss Channing."

Adam hung up. Claire laughed out loud. She turned to Julian and gave him a hug. "Do you know, I've never managed to get him to hang up before? I've always had to end our conversations!"

"He is a scurrilous cove," Julian said, but he couldn't be impervious to her proximity, and he took and kissed her. Inwardly, Claire had to shake her head. Julian had no problem getting romantic without a shred of feeling behind it—she'd experienced that—but apparently, evicting a woman from her home, no matter how humble, was against his idea of decency.

When he released her, the phone was still in one hand. He shut it, looking at it keenly. "What do you call this?"

"A cell phone. It works via…er…airwaves." He turned his head and gave her a quizzical look. "Well, invisible waves that go through the air," she amended. He still looked flummoxed, so she said, "I don't know! I can barely understand how these things work, I'm sorry."

"What about your analytical engine? Can it tell me?"

"Good idea!" They went back to the laptop. Claire was relieved that he'd asked no more questions about Princess Charlotte's death.

She did a search for "How do cell phones work?" and left Julian to read while she got changed.

As she dressed, she considered their options. They would of course try to return together using the tallit. If only one of them went back, she'd be stuck without him again—that was unthinkable! But then she realized she had to consider letting him return without her. She ought to send him back, in fact. It was safest with the demolition scheduled for the following day, as his return path would close! She couldn't risk having him stuck in the present. He belonged in his own time. But then she remembered Miss Andrews's threat was still very real in 1816. If she sent him back, it would be to his death!

All of this ran through her head as she dressed. If only the Winthrops would give her more time! She decided to say nothing as yet to Julian about the urgency. If he left and she lost him again—oh! There had to be a way for both of them to return—and she must think of it! Returning together wouldn't erase Clarissa's threat, but if Claire was with Julian, she could prevent the tragedy.

She thought it through. Julian would want to get a special license, as he said. But Miss Andrews might follow in her coach as he went for the license, or as they left to get married! In fact, their wedding could serve to drive Clarissa to hound him to death! Claire wouldn't put anything past that woman.

No, it was safer for Julian to be right here in the present. Two hundred years away from Miss Andrews. There was really no choice in the matter. Claire had to make him stay until just before the demolition began. His life depended on it.

Still thou art blest, compared wi' me!
The present only toucheth thee.
Robert Burns

CHAPTER 50

Claire put her hair up for Julian's sake—he liked it that way—and donned a skirt and blouse. She didn't want to wear the maxi dress again, so the knee-length skirt was the only alternative other than jeans or slacks. As she brushed her hair, it occurred to her that Julian might be looking up things he ought not to know on the laptop—such as his own death! She adjusted her blouse before the mirror and hurried out to join him.

When she peered at the screen over his shoulder, she was relieved to find him reading a history of inventions. She left to make a pot of coffee. When she returned and sat beside him, he had opened a page about cars. Of course he'd be fascinated with the modern car, she thought. What man wouldn't?

He glanced at her and did a double take, staring at her legs. His gaze traveled from her legs to her face. His demeanor wasn't promising.

"What are you about?" he said.

"This is perfectly normal today," she assured him. "This is how women dress." He looked again at her legs.

"'Tisn't normal to me, and if you do not cover"—he bent his head down to get a better view—"your beautiful legs, I will not be able to remove my gaze from them."

She pursed her lips. "This skirt is modest by today's standards."

"Then today's standards are depraved."

"They are, no doubt, but it's all I have." She gave him a look of indignation.

"Put on the frock you wore last night."

Shaking her head, Claire rose to do so. For some reason she

glanced back as she left. He was staring at her legs.

When she returned in the maxi dress, he looked her over and nodded. "I thank you." As he turned back to the screen, he asked, "Do you have a car? I would have called it a horseless carriage, but I've discovered the new nomenclature," he said. "I particularly like…this one." He scrolled down to a black Mercedes Benz.

"You would," Claire said. "My car isn't nearly that nice."

"But you have one?" he asked eagerly. And with that, Claire realized he'd just given her the way to keep him in the 21st century for another day.

"Would you like to go for a spin?" she asked, and was rewarded with a full, handsome smile she seldom saw.

"If you mean a ride in your carriage, indeed I would."

Her carriage. Smiling, Claire found a thermal barn jacket in the spare bedroom closet which she gave St. John. He held it up and said, "Surely you don't expect me to wear this monstrosity. It looks fit for a farmer."

"This is New England. It's probably about twenty degrees today—if we're lucky.

He studied her, thinking. "I'll bring it with me. To be worn only if wholly necessary." He paused, rubbing his chin. "I have a problem." To her questioning look, he said, "I need Fletch."

"Your valet!"

"Yes. He shaves me."

Claire approached him and ran her hand along his chin and face. "I rather like it," she said. He caught her hand and turned it palm up and kissed it. Trying to ignore the lovely sensation of his mouth on her skin, she said, "If you can wait a day to shave, when we go out I'll buy you an electric razor."

He looked mildly alarmed. "An electric razor?"

"They're very safe! You guide it; it's nothing like the razors you're thinking of."

But he shook his head. "A gentleman does not leave the house unshaven."

"Now sit still."

"Fletch shaves me daily—do you think I cannot sit still?"

Claire had St. John positioned in front of her bathroom mirror. She'd found a canister of shaving cream next to a few disposable razors and sprayed some into her hand. She carefully covered St. John's face and chin.

"This is fun," she said.

"Have a care with the razor," he replied.

Minutes later, as she toweled off his face, she stopped in front of him and said, "I rather envy Fletch his job." He caught her about the waist, and drew her up to him. Claire's heart thumped. He kissed her shortly upon the mouth, then did so again.

Claire looked dreamily up at him.

"We'd best go," he said.

There was a small garage adjacent to the cottage that housed Claire's ten-year-old silver Chevy Capri, a mid-size four-door she'd bought used. When St. John saw it, his eyes lit up as though it was a limousine.

"Fantastic!" he murmured, going about the outside, and running his hands along the doors and hood. He looked over at her. "Imagine it—a mechanical engine that will propel it forward!"

Claire smiled at his boyish excitement. He squatted by a front tire and felt the rubber and the rim. She opened the passenger door and motioned for him to get in. As he started in, he saw the wheel and said, "I'd like to sit by the helm, if you don't mind."

"The steering wheel, and you can't sit there. I have to drive, because I have a license."

"You need a license to drive?"

"There's a learning curve," she said. "A license is issued after you learn how to drive." She turned to him. "Watch me buckle up; you have to do it, also." He watched her, found his seat belt and closed it.

"Ingenious," he murmured.

He watched keenly as she put the key in the ignition. "The carriage must be unlocked?"

"Car. Call it a car." She'd never thought of the ignition key as "unlocking the carriage," but she supposed in a way it did.

When she turned the key and the engine revved to life, he stared in delight. He watched as she put the car in reverse and pressed on the gas.

"Foot pedals, too," he said, and then watched in fascinated silence as they backed out of the garage. "Backwards!"

Claire smiled. "Yes."

As she navigated out of the drive over light snow cover, he was touching the dashboard, the door, the glove compartment, and then the control panel and CD player. "What material is this?" he asked, after removing a glove to feel the dashboard.

"Some kind of plastic," Claire said. She tried to describe how plastic was made, but admitted, "I don't know, exactly."

"What makes the mechanical engine run?"

"Gasoline."

"A gas!"

"No, it's a liquid." Claire was beginning to feel like a kindergarten teacher. She thought of how she'd marveled at mundane things in his world; now it was his turn.

She turned from the drive onto the main road, which was lined with large blue spruce, heavy with snow. She said, "Now we can go a little faster." With the bright blue sky above the trees, it was a beautiful day. A black truck moved off the side of the road behind them, but Claire barely noticed. St. John had been raising and lowering his window with a look of concentration, but he glanced ahead and cried, "You're on the wrong side of the road!"

"No, this isn't England. We drive like the French, on the right."

As she picked up speed, St. John seemed energized, even delighted. He stared out his window, then the front; he spied the speedometer.

"MPH. Do these numbers signify miles...per...hour?" he asked, in amazement.

"Very good! Right now we're at forty...now fifty.

"Fifty!" he said, in wonder.

"I can't go any faster on this road. There's a speed limit by law, but it changes according to where we're driving."

He stared ahead, saw a car approaching and watched it with rapt attention. He turned swiftly as it roared by to watch it disappear behind them, at the same time noting a black box-like carriage coming up on their rear.

"How fast can this carriage go?"

Claire glanced at the speedometer. "Car. Theoretically, up to a hundred and twenty miles per hour." To his look of stunned excitement, she added, "I would never go that fast. I'd lose control of the car if I tried."

St. John glanced in his side mirror and said, "Well, you may need to go faster than you are now; there is a black equipage coming up fast to our rear."

Claire nodded, glancing at the rear-view. "It's a truck. I see it." When the truck did indeed get very close to their car, she sped up by another five miles an hour, but they did the same. "Tailgaters!" Claire said. St. John smiled at the term.

"We'll part ways soon," Claire said. "I'm getting on I-95." Smiling, she added, "Solely for your benefit, because you like speed. But they probably won't follow us onto it."

In a few minutes she was on the entrance ramp to I-95, which was Maine Turnpike. Behind them, the black truck followed closely.

"Well!" said Claire. "Now they can pass us and we'll be rid of them. I hate a tailgater!"

As she eased onto the turnpike, the black truck followed. The road wasn't busy, so Claire signaled and moved into the middle lane, and then into the left. She was creeped out when the black truck did the same.

"They're still with you," St. John said, watching the progress from his side mirror. He turned in his seat to try and see the driver, and saw a big, dark man with a stony visage who would not meet his eyes.

Claire frowned and looked in the rear-view. "I don't know what their problem is—" But suddenly her eyes widened, and her heart rate jumped into hyperdrive. She returned her gaze to the road, reeling inside. In the passenger seat of the black truck Claire had seen a sight that was as unsettling as it could possibly be. She wouldn't tell St. John.

It was Clarissa.

You often meet your fate on the road you take to avoid it.
Goldie Hawn

CHAPTER 51

One Day Earlier

Miss Andrews blinked and tried to assess her surroundings. Margaret was gone; her home was gone! She was standing on a wooden balcony of some sort, which was attached to an inn or lodge. There was a great wall of windows before her through which she saw people—strangely dressed people. They were mingling and holding drinks in their hands. She shivered—her legs and feet were cold. In fact, the air was cold! Far colder than it had been of late.

She looked at herself and saw she wasn't clothed properly! Her shoes had heels that were too high, and her legs were showing! She had a thick, heavy coat on of an unknown fabric, and a shawl about her neck. She carried something on her shoulder—a stiff pouch of some sort. Could it be a reticule? And beside her was a large container—a type of portmanteau, she guessed. As she tried to take in the strangeness of it all, a door opened and a man stepped out, smiling. He was tall and good-looking with very light hair, although utterly ill-dressed for an evening party; but so, Clarissa realized, was she.

"Claire!" he said. "I'm so glad you've come!"

An American! Who thinks I'm Miss Channing!

He held out a hand, and Clarissa automatically went forward. "Come in, come in," he said. "You look frozen." He grabbed the large portmanteau with one hand and ushered her in with his other arm around her waist. "Are you all right?"

Before Clarissa could answer, another man was suddenly there, an older man. "Look, Dad, it's Miss Channing," the first man said. "She's come to our mixer—and with luggage—she's accepting the suite."

"Miss Channing. I'm delighted," said the old man. "You won't regret cooperating with us. We'll make sure of that."

Having no idea what this meant, Clarissa merely nodded mutely. He stepped forward and reached for her hand, but Clarissa saw with horror that she was wearing thick, fat, ugly gloves such as she'd never seen before.

"Here, let me take those," the younger man said. He reached for her gloves, those horrid thick things, though Clarissa had to admit they'd kept her hands warm. He proceeded to take them, then the stiff reticule. He helped her out of her coat and shawl. Clarissa stared. Her shawl—it was Claire's, the magical shawl!

"Your scarf is torn," he said, holding it up. "We'll get you a new one. The lodge has a great gift shop." But Clarissa grabbed it from him, as well as the strange, hard reticule and shoved the scarf in it. "No need; I'm fond of this one." To her shock, she sounded utterly American!

The old man said to the younger one, "It has sentimental value. She must keep it, then. She's losing enough with the cottage, eh?"

Clarissa nervously glanced at her dress and straightened it, trying to pull it down lower, as it ended—shockingly—above her knees. Meanwhile, the older man was saying something about it was high time to bury the hatchet, and how delighted they were to have Claire as their guest. He congratulated her for having the sense to vacate the cottage in time.

Clarissa had no clue what most of his speech meant, but she did understand that both men took her to be Miss Channing. She bristled at the mistake, though she realized it was propitious in that she would learn all about that Channing creature now. The younger man handed Clarissa's coat and portmanteau—luggage, he'd called it—to a person she guessed was a servant, though he was dressed much like his betters. He gave the man a room number. Then a young girl in a wheelchair came rolling up to them. "This is Adele, my little sister," he said.

"Thank you for letting me keep Charlie," Adele said to her. Clarissa smiled, wondering what kind of servant Charlie was, and why Miss Channing had let this child keep him. "I adore him!" Adele added. At that moment a big shaggy dog came bounding toward them. "Oh, here he is!" she said.

Charlie was a dog? Clarissa was not fond of dogs and steeled herself as she saw it coming. Charlie, fortunately, was fond of all human beings, and came, tail wagging, and even jumped up at her—almost as if she had been his former owner, Clarissa hoped. She smiled and patted him, but he started whimpering, and jumped down. Adele wheeled closer and took him by the collar. "C'mon, boy," she said, pulling him away. She looked back at Clarissa. "I think he's forgotten you."

Clarissa saw the man was staring at her curiously. "You're awfully quiet, Claire," he said. "You miss your dog, I suppose." His gaze swept over her. "But you look stunning. I'm really glad you came." He took a step closer. "You know I've always wanted us to be better friends."

She looked uncertain for a moment, for she felt anything but stunning—yet Clarissa was well versed in recognizing male admiration and could see it was genuine. She smiled. "Thank you." The man returned a bigger smile.

"I like it when you smile," he said. He took her hand. "C'mon, I'll introduce you around. We'll talk about the cottage later," he added. Clarissa went along with him, walking carefully on the high heeled shoes, and feeling better about her legs showing because, to her astonishment, all the women she saw also had their legs revealed. She had no idea what "talking about the cottage later," referred to, but she'd worry about that when it came up.

During introductions—which were wholly confusing—Clarissa could find neither rhyme nor reason to them, for older people were introduced to her as if she were the superior, and other times she was introduced to younger people, as if they were! It made no sense. But she learned a great deal quickly. The man's name, for instance, was Adam, and she—Claire Channing, they thought—an author living in a cottage on land belonging to Adam's family, the Winthrops. So this is where she came from! Clarissa thought. An author! She recalled the pages of notes Claire had left behind at Lady Ashworth's. Notes about mundane stuff—now it made sense. At the same time, she realized it was no longer 1816—a magical shawl, indeed!

She slowly ascertained that she—Claire, rather—had apparently been asked to vacate the cottage but had held out until now. Her arrival tonight signaled to the Winthrops that she was ready to accept their terms, that, in exchange for leaving the cottage voluntarily, they would furnish her with an excellent suite right in this very lodge for as long as she needed it or until the end of the year.

As people politely inquired about her books, Clarissa smiled and insisted she never spoke about her work. How did she feel about losing her grandmother's cottage? She would shrug and say, "Some things can't be helped." And then, while marveling still at her own Americanized speech, she would swiftly turn the conversation around. Now and then she would chance to see Adam—always his eyes were upon her, with a pensive and admiring look.

She studied him in return, trying to imagine how he would look in a proper outfit of breeches and stockings with a shirt and cravat. When he came back to her—as she knew he would—he said, "There's one more neighbor you need to meet." He took her to a tan-skinned man named Omar with very thick, black hair, and an intense facial expression that made him look perpetually angry. But he smiled upon the introduction. Omar, she learned, was a "contractor," a man who hired himself out for any need imaginable. He'd escorted people across deserts and mountains, but he'd also run grocery calls, purchasing and delivering food items. There wasn't a job on the planet, Adam said with a wink, that Omar wouldn't do.

"I may have work for you," Clarissa said. "If we can agree upon a price." As soon as she spoke, she realized she had no money in this world. Or did she? She found a water closet, and gawked at the gleaming fixtures and then at herself in the mirror—for she looked so different! Her gown was totally without style, though it displayed her figure admirably enough and her hair was in a plain chignon without any adornments whatsoever. She opened the stiff reticule. She had money! American dollars. And lots of them. How propitious.

When she left the water closet, Adam was there. He came up close. "Claire."

"Call me Clarissa, if you would. It's my full name."

"Claire's a pen name, then?"

Clarissa nodded.

"Clarissa," he said, taking her arms, "I want to apologize once more, for hitting that man, Julian. Was he okay?"

Clarissa gaped at him, and forgot herself. "Was Julian here?"

"With you at the cottage," he said, with surprise.

"Oh, yes. And you hit him?"

He blinked at her. "Don't you remember? It was an accident. He startled me, came out of nowhere. On your porch. Did you forget?" He chuckled. "Well, I guess that answers my question. If he was hurt badly, I don't think you'd have forgotten already. " He went on. "And I take it that means he isn't important to you, since you forgot so quickly. That's a relief," he added with a smile. His look became more serious. "I honestly didn't think you'd come tonight. I can't tell you how glad I am that you did. You can stay here as long as you need to." He moved closer to her and, impertinently, put his arms about her waist.

It was a serious breach of manners, but Clarissa also found it rather fascinating. No man of her day would have dared. With a quickened pulse, she said nothing but simply stared up at him. Adam gazed at her with surprise—and longing. He kissed her, a short, tentative kiss. When she still said nothing, he said, "Claire! I mean, Clarissa!" And he pulled her up against him and kissed her again, much longer this time. Clarissa enjoyed every second.

"Be with me," he said, softly. He added, "I'll make sure you have everything you could ever need."

"Will you?" she said.

"Yes! Name it, beautiful lady," he answered, smiling.

She smiled back sweetly, but said, "I need Omar."

———✦———

Adam required knowing only that Omar was not a love interest of Clarissa's before leading her back to the gathering and to the man. Clarissa motioned Omar aside and said she wished to hire him, that his work for her must be a secret, and that she needed him immediately.

He asked for details; they spoke at length. Adam kept sending worried glances in their direction, but Clarissa was focused only on her business.

"I'll need a retainer of $1,000 upfront, and $5,000 afterward," Omar decided.

Clarissa checked her reticule and gave him the stack of bills.

In a moment he looked up. "That's a lot of cash to have on hand, but only half the retainer."

She frowned. "It's all I have at the moment."

"Let's go," he said.

When she gazed at him questioningly, he added, "I'll take you to your bank."

She licked her lips. "Banks aren't open, now."

He stared at her a moment. "Your ATM won't give out that much at once?"

Cautiously, she said, "No." Knowing she had no more money, she swallowed her pride and added, "There are other things I can give. If you're interested." She looked at him innocently. Only an iron-hot determination to have his help getting Julian—or at least keeping him from Claire—gave her the boldness to make such an offer. She must find him, and she needed Omar to do it.

Surprised, Omar cleared his throat. He looked her up and down. "Okaaaay," he said, with a little smile. "Let's go."

"But only afterward," she added.

He stopped. "Deal's off."

"If we do this before, then I want my $500 back."

"That's an expensive proposition," he said, looking at her. But suddenly he smiled. "You're on."

Adam hurried over when he saw them preparing to leave. "Clarissa!"

Omar looked confused. "I thought your name was Claire."

"Clarissa's her full name," Adam said. He looked at Clarissa. "Leaving? Together?"

She said, "We have business." In a lower voice, she said, "I'll be back. You said I have a room here?" He reached in a pocket and drew out a key. "Here's your key. Will you need help moving out of the cottage? Need to put anything in storage? Remember, the equipment will be there in two days to start razing the place."

Clarissa hesitated. "I'll let you know; thank you, Adam." She smiled.

"I'll see you later," he said unhappily. He watched her leave with Omar.

———✦———

"My place or yours?" Omar asked, once they were seated in his black Chevy Trailblazer.

Clarissa was all agog when he had opened the door for her. "This is your carriage?" she asked wonderingly.

"My carriage?" He chuckled. "Ah, yes, your chariot, my lady."

Clarissa knew she'd said something wrong. "I'd like to go by the cottage," she said slowly, "and then we'll go to 'your place.'" Omar knew where the cottage was and took her only far enough up the drive to where they could see the dwelling, for Clarissa cried sharply, "Stop here!"

Omar did so. As he glanced out at the little house, he said, "You left the lights on."

"I have houseguests," she said. "The man I told you about, whom we must follow. And a woman," she added, with compressed lips.

"Oh!" He drummed the wheel with his fingers. "Do you need anything? Are you going in?"

"No. Let's move on."

"These are the people you want me to follow tomorrow, though, right?"

Clarissa nodded.

"Hold on a sec," he said. Omar left the car and sprinted up to Claire's garage. It wasn't locked. He went in the side door. A minute later he came out and sprinted back to his truck and Clarissa. They left.

———————✦———————

When they were at Omar's house, a sizable condo in a newer development, and after Clarissa had been offered a drink—which she refused—she looked at him plaintively.

He took her hand and started leading her to the bedroom.

"Omar," she said nervously.

He looked her way. "Yes?"

"I should tell you—I—I've never done this, before."

He stopped. He stared at her a moment. "Never?" His tone was of real curiosity.

She shook her head. "Never."

"A beautiful lady like you?" It seemed as though he had trouble believing it.

Again she shook her head.

He took a breath, looked around thinking, and then leveled his gaze upon her. "And you're sure you want to do this? Instead of paying me?"

She sighed. "The truth is, I haven't got the money to pay you. What choice do I have?"

His brows furrowed. "What did you do with all your money?"

Clarissa stared at him uncomprehendingly.

"I saw it in the papers, that six-figure deal you got for your book. Did you really spend it all, already?"

She swallowed. "Six figures? Oh, yes. No, I didn't spend it. I just don't have it, yet."

"Look, the article said the contract was signed. That means you're getting the money." He looked thoughtful a moment, his lips pursed. "I'll let you pay me when you get it."

Clarissa gazed at him in surprise. "You would do that? And you'll still work for me, tomorrow?"

He turned her around, heading back to the living area. He gave her a sideways smile. "Astounding, I know, right? I'm a devil with men; I don't give them an inch. But you? You're a lady. I can respect that."

Clarissa felt as though a load of bricks had just been lifted off her. She gazed at Omar with real appreciation. "You, sir," she said, "are a true gentleman."

He smiled as they sat down before a large-screen TV. While Clarissa watched in fascinated silence, he picked up the remote and pointed it at the screen. When it sprang to life, she jumped, but Omar, watching the screen, missed it. "Clarissa," he said, clicking the remote to change channels, "I think this is the start of a beautiful friendship."

A complete stranger has the capacity
to alter the life of another irrevocably.
J.D.Stroube

CHAPTER 52

Claire was horrified to see Clarissa. She'd thought Julian would be safe from her in the present! But Miss Andrews was here! That meant she was still a threat, right in the here and now.

Claire's foot hit the gas to put space between them, while her mind raced with what Clarissa's presence meant. How could she have gotten there? Julian had the tallit—and then she remembered. He only had half of it.

"How did the shawl get torn?" she asked, trying to sound nonchalant.

"I apologize about that—"

"No, I don't mind; it got you here," she said, darting a little smile at him between keeping her eyes fixed on the road and the truck at their rear. "But what happened?"

"It was Clarissa, I'm afraid."

So that explained it!

Julian shifted in his seat, removing his attention from the dashboard to look at Claire. She felt his gaze but kept her eyes on the road.

"How did she know about the shawl, I wonder?" Claire asked.

"If she did know, she beat me to it," he said. "I never suspected there was any truth to your delusions until just before I arrived here."

"How did it happen for you?" Claire asked.

He took a breath, but never had time to answer. Behind them, the truck had inched precariously close. "My word!" Claire cried. She almost laughed at her exclamation for sounding so…Regency, but there was no time for that. Any second and the truck could hit them! Claire was already at 75 mph, but she hit the gas again—the turnpike was straight at the moment—but she'd never driven above 80 in her life and didn't want to now.

She swerved into the middle lane. When they immediately followed, she veered farther into the right lane. They did the same.

"Never a police car around when you need one!" Claire griped, while veering back into the center lane. The truck followed. Claire glimpsed the driver's intense face—he looked mean. Who was he, she wondered? Clarissa couldn't possibly have known anyone in this time, which meant that somehow she'd worked her manipulative magic on the poor guy driving the truck, getting his cooperation in her insane pursuit of St. John.

She changed lanes again, her heart in her throat. She'd never driven so wildly. Julian seemed utterly immune to worries about their speed or a possible crash. He'd discovered the car's owner's manual in the glove compartment and was reading with great interest. Now and then he'd pop his head up and watch the world whizzing by with a short grin or look of appreciation. Knowing how much slower travel was in his day, Claire was amazed that he didn't find the speed daunting. Of course he didn't know about Clarissa, yet. She didn't want him to, either.

Claire continued to weave in and out of traffic, but however she maneuvered, the truck stayed with them like a fly at a picnic. If she went to the middle lane, it did too. If she returned to the left, it followed. It was so close now she could see the driver's face clearly. He looked Middle Eastern, with narrowed eyes focused like magnets on her car, his expression stony. Claire's gaze returned to the road, but then she took a quick peek at Clarissa in the mirror. Miss Andrews wore a smirk.

The next exit sign revealed they were approaching South Portland; traffic picked up. Claire was glad. It might be possible to lose them in thick traffic.

She tried not to show her perturbation, but the truck was still riding precariously close to their rear. It could ram them! It would be an instant wreck.

St. John glanced at the speedometer. "Eighty? In one hour? I can hardly fathom it!" he cried excitedly, turning his attention to the passing road. "In my day if you do fifty miles in six, 'tis newsworthy—and you'd likely kill a horse doing it." He turned to her. "Do you often drive this fast?"

Claire was watching for a break in the next traffic lane—a break that wouldn't be large enough for the truck to follow her. Not taking her eyes off the road, she said, "No." She was gripping the steering wheel so hard her fingers were getting numb. Julian must have noticed. Gently he said, "Do not let her presence flummox you. Our best response is to give her the cut."

Claire glanced at him in surprise. "How long have you known?"

"Almost since we got on the road," he said, "I didn't want it to concern you."

Claire let out a breath of frustration. "My concern is for you." She glanced in the mirror again. This time, Clarissa followed a smirk with a wave.

"You needn't fret on my account," he said. "But I think that woman is brain-addled," he murmured, looking in the mirror at Clarissa. "Imagine her dangling after me even into the future!" He turned to Claire. "Do not go faster than is comfortable for you on her account. She is a vexation but nothing more."

"If they hit us, we could all be killed!"

He turned to look behind him and shook his head back and forth at Clarissa, with a quelling look. Claire was surprised at his calm. "Doesn't it bother you that she's come all this way—to the present—to vex you still?"

He said, "To no purpose; she is wasting her time, utterly."

Claire took a sudden swing into the middle lane without having used a directional. The car coming up behind them beeped its horn, but she was satisfied to see that Clarissa's vehicle could not follow them—yet. The exit ramp was in sight. If she could keep them from following behind her and then move right and exit swiftly, the black truck would have to keep going. It would be a chance to escape.

The little white car now behind Claire was another tailgater, but Claire welcomed it. Clarissa's truck couldn't squeeze in. As they neared the exit ramp, Claire saw her opportunity. Again without using a directional, she darted to the right lane at the last moment and swerved onto the exit ramp, bouncing and braking at the same time. The black truck hit its brakes, but they were already past the exit.

St. John smiled at Claire's maneuvering. "Well done, Miss Channing!" They shared a quick smile. She had to tear her eyes away to watch the road, but she felt his gaze upon her as he added, "There is something pleasing about a beautiful woman handling an equipage with aplomb." Claire blushed like a teenager. He chuckled.

She eased onto U.S. Route 1 and turned back off at the first exit. She made a right at the light and began meandering around the outskirts of South Portland. St. John was mesmerized by what he saw. He stared at storefronts, people, and signs. Claire saw people gawking at him and reached over and removed his hat. He turned to her and she said, "No one here has ever seen a beaver hat except in old movies—er, moving pictures."

"Moving pictures?" He looked intrigued. "I should like to see moving pictures."

With wonder, Claire said, "You've never even seen a photograph, have you?"

He said, "I have."

As she made a smooth right onto a side street filled with shops, she said, smiling, "You couldn't have."

"But I have." He grinned. "On your analytical engine."

Claire had to laugh. Wait until he saw a movie. He'd not yet examined the television at the cottage since it was in her bedroom. She'd have him carry it out so they could set it up in the living room. She'd find something that wouldn't horrify him. Something rated G.

As they continued down a strip with increasing density of stores and pedestrians, Claire saw a mall up ahead, visible by the huge Reny's department store sign, and headed for it. The parking lot was a small sea of cars. Claire felt they'd be virtually invisible even if Clarissa did somehow manage to come down this same street. She found a spot and parked.

She glanced at St. John. She had money in the bank now—or

would very shortly. That advance from the publisher would be deposited electronically, directly to her account. Even if she returned to the past by some miracle, she could spend money today. She'd earned it fair and square.

When Julian got out, his eyes practically glazed over at the rows and rows of vehicles: cars, vans, and trucks of all shapes and sizes. He shook his head. "Amazing."

She took his arm, but then stopped and removed his hat again, though he frowned. She put it back in the car, at the same time grabbing the barn jacket.

He retrieved the hat, looked at the jacket and then at the entrance to the mall. "I will not wear that monstrosity, even for so short a walk."

"If you don't wear it, everyone will stare at you."

"And do you imagine that concerns me?"

She gazed at him and had to smile. He looked magnificent in Regency finery, after all. "Fine. But we must leave the hat."

When she went to take it from him, he didn't let go. He winked at her. "A gentleman isn't dressed properly without his hat."

Smiling, she returned, "But today's gentlemen don't wear hats." She pulled on the hat again, but he resisted. "Julian—no one today is properly dressed." He finally released the headwear and gave a sigh.

He offered his arm. But instead of placing her hand upon it like a Regency miss, she wrapped his arm around her and snuggled against him. Julian stared at her in amazement, so she said, "If I merely take your arm, we'd only get more stares, I assure you."

Just as they neared the entrance, St. John looked up at the sound of a jet. Claire followed his gaze and said, "Oh! We're near Portland Airport. That's a plane, an airplane. People can fly in planes, now."

"Are you suggesting there are people in that thing?"

She smiled. "Yes, dozens and dozens." To his look of disbelief, she added, "A plane is like a car, sort of, but it takes off at a very high speed and then flies, like a bird." She noticed at that moment a man and a woman had stopped behind them, and were staring at them in consternation. Claire said, "Oh—he's um—he's had—brain damage."

She took his arm and hurried him into the mall.

"Brain damage?" he said with a scowl. "Was that the best you could do?"

Claire giggled. "Sorry."

He dipped his head. "I'd prefer amnesia, thank you."

Once past the entrance corridor, Claire made a beeline for the mall directory. People did stare, some yanking on a companion's or parent's sleeve to point out the oddly dressed man. Teens pulled out their cell phones and snapped photos. St. John made things worse by walking in slow motion, or so it seemed to Claire, for he stopped to examine store windows, the ceiling, other people, everything. While he surveyed the architecture, or wares in a booth, others stopped to stare at him as if he were a mall exhibit. Claire tried to be as patient as possible, but ended up hurrying him along.

She located the store she was hoping to find and headed up the escalator—another marvel to St. John, who had to hop on and then hop off at the end, turning to look back at it. A young girl walked up to him. "Are you an actor?"

He peered at her a moment with narrowed eyes. "No." He turned to Claire. "An actor, indeed!"

"No one knows what to make of you," she said.

"They've no doubt never seen a properly dressed gentleman in all their pitiful lives," he responded, looking disdainfully at two young men in baggy jeans, sneakers, and long tees. A girl with multicolored streaks in her hair went by—he stared, frowning. "Is she a gipsie?" he asked. "They've been a plague for ages."

Claire tried not to chuckle. "No."

A minute later, another child cried, "Look, Mommy! A man in a costume!" St. John's eyes narrowed; he raised an indignant brow at the brat, making the mother hurry her little girl away. Claire quickened her pace, saying, "Let's get you some new clothes."

His look of distaste increased as he surveyed people as they walked. Some wore puffy coats over jeans and boots, but others were carrying coats, revealing oversized sweatshirts, layered tees, hoodies and other like shirts. "Surely you don't expect me to wear such ill-looking apparel as I see on these creatures?" A passerby heard him and stopped to stare, openmouthed.

Claire hurried him on. "We'll get you quality clothing," she said, and walked him into Brooks Brothers.

"Is this a tailor's?" he asked.

"Something like that." Gazing at St. John, Claire had to admit the idea of dressing him differently was not abhorrent. Despite her admiration of his Regency duds, she brimmed with anticipation at the thought of seeing him in contemporary styles.

The clerk took one look at St. John and, without a blink, hurried toward them as though they were the president and first lady. Amazing, Claire thought, how people can smell money—no matter what century it's from.

In minutes St. John was being measured and sized. They took their fittings seriously here, and Claire was thankful for it. It would seem almost normal to Julian. She found a place to sit, and waited.

Inside the dressing room, the clerk helped St. John from his jacket and waistcoat, without a word about them. When he held up a yellow-checked sport shirt, St. John looked at the tag and said, "Irish linen? Do you have only Irish linen?"

"It's very good quality, sir," said the clerk.

"I don't want very good quality," returned St. John. "I want your best."

"I see," said the clerk appreciatively. "I'll be right back, sir."

When Claire looked up, St. John was before her in a blue-checked sports shirt, a merino wool cardigan in denim blue, brown herringbone sport coat, and dark brown merino wool pants. He wore classic leather brown penny loafers on his feet. She hadn't expected the sheer muscular strength of St. John to translate so well in contemporary clothing, and just gazed at him admiringly for a moment. "You look wonderful," she said.

"Doesn't he?" agreed the clerk.

Julian's lips curved into a reluctant smile, but he pulled at the shirt's standing collar. It looked nice, but somehow wasn't right. Was it too tight? Claire cocked her head to one side, trying to pinpoint the problem.

The clerk walked up to St. John and started opening the top button of the shirt. "I tried to convince him to keep this top button opened," he said, as he undid it. But no sooner had he done so, than St. John, now frowning, began to close it.

"No, leave it!" Claire cried, jumping to her feet. He dropped his hand. She went to him and smoothed down the shirt. There was just the smallest hint of a dark blue T-shirt showing; and the open button transformed his look from one of mild discomfort to that of casual suavity. He looked ready to board a yacht or meet a friend for lunch at an exclusive private club.

The clerk was as admiring as Claire. While another clerk talked with St. John about the sport jacket, the first one came and sidled by Claire, stopping by her ear.

"I had to work on him to give up the neck cloth," he whispered, holding a hand over his mouth. Then, standing up again to his full height, added, "But I do think it was a worthwhile effort."

But St. John was unconvinced. He thanked the second clerk, but motioned to Claire and then leaned in to her. "Much of my neck is showing, you realize." He looked down at himself. "And more." He went to close the button again, but Claire stopped him.

"Every man's neck is showing. It's perfectly acceptable." He looked doubtful, so she added, "It's expected!" She smiled at his still doubtful expression. "You look exceedingly handsome, if you must know," she assured him.

CHAPTER 53

Outside the mall, Clarissa Andrews and Omar were just pulling into a parking space.

"I must say, your locating device is ingenious!" Clarissa said. She gazed admiringly at Omar, but when he saw her expression, he cracked a smile.

"You mean the tracker? I didn't invent it," he said. Studying her a moment, he added, "But I'm glad you approve." They made their way to the entrance, stopping people for questioning as they went.

Clarissa wore jeans and a blouse under her warm L.L. Bean coat, a hat, gloves and thermal-lined boots. Unlike St. John, she'd not had to buy anything, for like Claire in the Regency, all the right clothing was magically provided. After watching a movie that mesmerized her at Omar's house, she'd slept in a spare bedroom. In the morning, she'd found today's outfit in her giant (to her) reticule. Only the boots hadn't been in the bag, but were on the floor in place of yesterday's high heels.

When she came out dressed differently, Omar hadn't said a word. He must have thought women always carried extra clothing with them.

If it kept up, this magical supply of clothing, Clarissa saw a good reason for not returning to the past. Even St. John was here! And so many magical devices!

"Have you seen a man in costume?" she asked everyone they stopped. So far, they'd all shaken their heads; no, they had not. But a mother with a young child just leaving the mall overheard Clarissa as she passed. Holding the hand of the little girl, she stopped and turned back.

"What sort of costume?" she asked.

"I saw an actor!" cried the child.

Clarissa ignored the child but answered the mother, "Old-fashioned, nineteenth century."

"Yes—like Charles Dickens!" cried the woman. Clarissa had never heard of Charles Dickens and just looked at her blankly.

"But you were with him," said the little girl, staring up at Clarissa. Clarissa's eyes came alight, for she knew this meant they'd seen St. John, who was with Claire, who looked like her.

"No, dear, she couldn't have been," said the mother. She turned back to Clarissa. "He had on a strange jacket—and a vest, and—and—something around his neck."

"That's him!" Clarissa cried. She motioned to the mall entrance. "Was he in there?"

"Yes," the lady said. "Only minutes ago."

Clarissa and Omar rushed into the mall. The little girl watched them go. "But she was with him, Mommy," the girl repeated. "I saw what she looked like."

The mother looked down at her daughter and just shook her head.

"C'mon," she said, moving them into the parking lot.

My sole delight the headlong race
And frantic hurry of the chase.
Walter Scott

CHAPTER 54

Claire turned to the Brooks Brothers clerk. "We'll need another shirt. And a pullover sweater. Something in an argyle pattern."

"Very good, ma'am. Will he try them on?" the clerk asked.

"No. Just add them to the other purchases." With Clarissa in the present, it occurred to Claire that now Julian should be safe in 1816. But she was filled with the fear of losing him, for she had no certainty that two people could time travel together. She had to keep him with her for as long as possible.

That coaching accident had taken place north of London—a continent away, two hundred years away—surely he was safe here. And they'd managed to lose Clarissa, so she posed no immediate threat. She'd keep Julian for this one last night until the wrecking crew began their horrid work in the morning. Then she'd send him back, though it would break her heart, to where he belonged.

The clerk returned. "Ah, I see no winter coat," he said, looking at St. John. Claire thought of the cost. This was, after all, Brooks Brothers. She said, "I think I'll try Old Navy for that, or Macy's."

The clerk looked at St. John and then back at Claire. "For a man of such distinction?" He leaned in toward Claire. "We're running a sale on a line of excellent coats," he said.

Twenty minutes later St. John looked cozy in his new wool knit topcoat, which had cost only $598 instead of its original $998. The clerk handed her a shopping bag with St. John's Regency clothing. "Allow me to remove the tags from what you're wearing," he said to St. John. He circled him with a small pair of scissors, removing the product description tags, which he handed to Claire, before going off to the register with the price tags and other purchases.

As St. John watched keenly, Claire paid with a credit card. The bill came to $3248.85. Must have been the sport jacket and top coat, she thought. St. John raised a brow, but Claire acted as though it was perfectly ordinary to spend a small fortune on clothing—reminding herself this was, after all, Brooks Brothers, and it was only a tiny bit of the large advance coming her way. And Julian, besides, was used to wearing the best. She wanted him to be comfortable. She felt quite happy, in fact, to take care of him in style. In the Regency, she was totally dependent upon his generosity—at least, until Grandmamma showed up. Here, she had a chance to be generous to him.

Thinking of Grandmamma gave her a pang. She hoped she would be able to return to her, to that world, to that time. St. John unquestionably had to return. Here he was without an identity, without his home, his family respectability, his fortune. If he remained, Claire had earned enough to keep them going for some time, but she doubted he would be happy living off a woman. In his day, men sometimes lived off a woman's fortune by marrying her. But it wouldn't be the same, now.

When they'd left the store and were in the mall, he said, "Are all prices that shockingly high?" But there was no time to answer. Claire saw something that had her turning him around and hurrying in the opposite direction. Clarissa and that man! Again!

How had they been found? Claire hurried Julian around a store directory so they weren't in Clarissa's line of sight.

Sporting Brooks Brothers clothes, St. John no longer garnered curious stares, but did catch the eye of two young women for quite another reason. Both wore heavy makeup.

"Hello," one murmured with a little smile, as she passed.

Claire looked after them with an indignant expression. "I think I updated you a little too well," she said.

"Not to worry," he answered. "Such face paint strikes me as disrespectable. And I've seen nothing in modern clothing that is attractive." He gazed at her, and his voice softened. "With the exception of you."

She smiled. And remembered that Clarissa could be approaching.

After checking the directory to be sure they would not walk past any lingerie stores—for that would give St. John a conniption, Claire was sure—she located a restaurant and headed for it. He continued to people watch, and saw two couples walking along, their arms entwined around each other. Claire saw, too, and turned to him. "Put your arm around me like that," she said, "We'll look normal."

St. John hesitated. He saw yet another couple walking that way and shrugged. "As St. Ambrose said, 'When in Rome, do as the Romans,'" he said, circling his free arm around Claire. She snuggled against him, sure that Clarissa would never recognize them as the two people she was searching for, especially with St. John in his new clothing and from behind.

She hurried Julian into a restaurant, and asked the maître d' for a booth in the back. She hoped Clarissa and her henchman would never think to search there.

St. John read the menu cover to cover. "Shrimp?" he asked.

"They're like prawns," she said. She wondered if she ought to order for him, but he settled upon New York strip steak with shrimp, salad, and hot rolls. When the waitress turned to Claire and said, "And you, ma'am?" St. John looked at her and with mild irritation said, "You will serve this lady exactly what I ordered."

Claire found it amusing, the way he assumed it was his part to order for her. She was about to make a snide remark when he asked the waitress what kinds of ale they had. He shot her a look of disdain when he was told she wasn't sure. "I'm new," the waitress explained.

"Make it Madeira," he said, as if he was settling.

The waitress stared. "Uh...I don't think we have that," she said. Julian's lips compressed. "What do you have?" The woman hurriedly produced a bar menu.

He searched it for a moment but Claire said, "Just give us a bottle of red wine."

The waitress said, "We only sell wine by the glass."

Julian said, "Do you have good wine?"

The waitress looked to Claire in consternation. Claire had been reading the menu and said, "Bring us the Merlot." When she left,

Julian gazed after her a moment. He leaned toward Claire. "Why is her hair sticking out like a tail?"

Claire glanced at the waitress, who was taking an order at a nearby table. "Amazing, you described it that way!" she said. "It's called a ponytail."

"Do you mean to say, 'tis a fashion?"

Claire looked back at the woman. "A casual fashion."

At his frowning countenance, Claire said, "You'll feel better once we eat." She smiled, still admiring his new look in modern clothing. The waitress brought the wine and moved off.

He looked around the restaurant and then settled his gaze on a couple seated across the aisle in another booth. Claire noticed him staring at the pair, who were young. The girl wore a nose ring, lip ring, and eyebrow rings, besides numerous earrings. The man also had earrings and one eyebrow ring.

St. John leaned forward again. "Are they slaves?"

Embarrassed, Claire hissed, "No! We don't have slavery today, not in this country, anyway." She could hardly bring herself to raise her head she was so mortified that they might have heard him.

"Does England?"

She shook her head.

"None?" he asked, with real curiosity. "Not even in the shipping trade?"

"Slavery was abolished in England in 1829," she told him. "Thanks in large part to Wilberforce."

He sat back with a smile. "Fantastic! I must tell William not to despair. His day is coming."

Claire was in awe. "Do you actually know William Wilberforce?"

"We are recently become friends. Before I was, eh, reformed, we had little sympathy for one another." He smiled.

"What is he like?" Claire asked, rather fascinated.

"He's a good fellow. Intense...you might say, about his convictions. A Christian man."

Claire savored every moment of their meal. In the back of her mind the thought hovered that it could be her last dinner with Julian, filling her with an aching regret. She watched him closely, trying to memorize every nuance of his expressions, every look, every shade of change in his voice. Now and then he would level his gaze at her and it would soften before her eyes, and he would reach for her hand across the table. Such moments were precious to Claire. Soon she would have to tell Julian that the shawl only worked in conjunction with the cottage, and that he must be gone before they razed it tomorrow, or he'd lose his home and life in 1816 England. She'd also have to tell him that one half a shawl might not be enough to take them both back. But not now—it could wait until they were at the cottage.

Before they left, he looked once more at the metallically adorned couple across from them. "If they are not slaves, why do they wear face rings?"

St. John hadn't spoken loudly, but the young man heard something. He stood up in a huff. Coming to face St. John, he demanded, "What did I hear you say?" He sized up St. John and lost some of the bravado in his eyes, but Claire said hurriedly, "He's never seen jewelry like yours, that's all," she said.

"Indeed I have," Julian responded, nonplussed, keeping his eyes steadily upon the young man as though daring him to make more of it. "On slaves."

The young man's eyes widened. He looked ready to pop a gasket.

"He's from another country," Claire said hurriedly. The young man stared at St. John as though considering what to do next, and let out a few choice oaths.

"Hold your tongue in the presence of ladies!" St. John growled. "If you wish to meet me on the field, so be it, but do not forget yourself in mixed company, sir." His words were ground out in silky venom.

There was stunned silence on the young man's part. His companion said, "C'mon, Tino, sit down! Sit down. Just ignore him!"

"Where are you from, man?" asked the boy.

"From very far away," Claire said, apologetically, as she pressed Julian to move on. "Trust me. Very far. I'm sorry."

She urged him toward the exit, and hissed, "Do not make any assumptions about people based on their appearance."

He gazed at her with surprise. "That is the best way to ascertain anything about people," he returned. "By their attire and speech. One can tell instantly what class a person is by such things."

"Not today," she said. "Not like in your day."

After a young woman thanked them for coming, he said, in Claire's ear, "Have many women all but shaved off their eyebrows in this century?"

Claire gave him a sideways smile. "You evidently haven't seen Brooke Shields."

Back in the mall, Claire stopped and looked warily around.

"You are concerned that Miss Andrews is here?"

She nodded. "One never knows with that woman."

"Do not even think of it," he replied. To Claire's delight, he circled an arm around her waist and drew her closer to his side with a little smile. "Not all customs of today are disagreeable."

Claire took them to the nearest mall exit, but remained guarded. She wouldn't relax until they'd arrived safely back at the cottage. It niggled at her that Clarissa knew the cottage's location. She'd been waiting on the main road with her driver to follow them. But once they were home tonight it wouldn't matter. There was nothing Clarissa could do to Julian there, and Claire would send him home to 1816 come morning. Clarissa didn't know that. She'd stay in the present and Julian would be safe.

They stopped at the entranceway to put on their coats. Outdoors, Claire got her bearings—they were on the opposite side of the mall from where she'd parked. But she wouldn't dare go back inside though it offered a shortcut. "We'll have to walk around," she said. St. John didn't mind the extra time in the parking lot, looking keenly at the cars they strode past in the weak late-afternoon winter sun. He gazed admiringly in all directions.

He stopped by a Mercedes Benz that resembled one he'd seen online. Claire had to tug at his arm to move him on. Then they came across a forest green Jaguar, and he came to a decided stop. He stared at it. When he continued to stare but said nothing, Claire asked softly, "You like this one?"

He went up to it and looked it over, peering in the window. "Like it? I cannot think of anything I've seen that is quite as beautiful as this." He came back to his full height and turned to her. "Aside from you, that is."

Claire smiled, but pulled him along. "No wonder they put women in car commercials," she murmured. "Two things men love to admire."

"Car commericals?" he asked, while giving a last, sidelong look at the car. Claire pulled him along.

"I'll explain it later," she said, looking around nervously for the black truck, but there were similar models all over the parking lot. She hadn't studied the license plate and wouldn't know even if they passed it. She was relieved when they were back in her car.

St. John buckled up like a pro and turned to her with an expectant smile.

"What is it?" Claire asked, smiling. She backed out of the spot.

He shook his head. "I am anticipating the ride. I find the speed utterly exhilarating, if you must know."

She grinned, edging the car to the parking lot's exit. "I thought it might be unpleasant—or frightening, for someone unused to it."

He surveyed her. "I've always enjoyed a good pace." He went back to playing with the dashboard controls, turning the heat up and down, as Claire wondered, not for the first time, if Julian's liking for speed contributed to the accident that would take his life. Except, thank God, it couldn't take his life now, for he wasn't in 1816. Good thing!

"Do you have inns that offer good ale?" he asked.

"We have bars; I'll find one," Claire said. But she dreaded taking him into one. He might say something that would start a brawl! "I'll only take you if you promise not to say a word about anything that strikes you as unusual."

He grinned. "Agreed."

They passed a bar here or there, but somehow the atmosphere

didn't look beckoning to Claire. She realized she might be able to get him decent ale at a grocery store, and pulled into one that was open. In the back of her mind she worried that Clarissa might still be on the lookout for them, but really—that woman needed a life! When they reached the store, she turned to him. "I'll only be a minute. Wait here?"

"And not see"—he surveyed the storefront—"a market in the twenty-first century?"

They went in together.

After twenty minutes they walked back out. St. John held two bags, one with items Claire had picked because now she could afford them; smoked salmon, a large chunk of Jarlsberg, artisan crackers, and an olive bar container filled to the brim. She'd also grabbed toiletries for Julian just because he needed them; a toothbrush, comb, and mouthwash—what the heck, he was a man. And since it might be their last night together, she bought an outrageously expensive bottle of Dom Pérignon. They'd share a glass of the champagne before the fire, before she had to send him home in the morning, never to see him again.

The other bag held a six-pack of ale, and an assortment of junk food. Never had a supermarket's hopes of capturing impulse buys been so successful, Claire thought, as she watched with a smile while Julian added one of every kind of chocolate bar and bagged chips near the checkout, to their purchases.

But thinking of the future clouded her mirth. She tried to stay hopeful. The tallit had taken her to St. John. And didn't the embroidered lovebirds prove that its job was to bring true love together? But she couldn't escape a nagging sense of doom. It had left her in the future without Julian once before. It could happen again— only this time, with the cottage destroyed, it would mean forever!

At the car, St. John took her arm and looked at the driver's seat. He motioned with his head. "Will you do me the honour of allowing me to try my hand at this?"

Her eyes widened. "Not in a parking lot! These places are like the wild west—even for experienced drivers."

He looked intrigued. "Is the American West still untamed?"

She smiled but gently urged him, pressing against him, to go around to the passenger seat. "No. It's just a saying." When they were settled in the car she had a sudden hope that perhaps, if the Winthrops had granted her request for more time, there might be a message from Adam. She rummaged in her bag for her cell phone, but realized she'd left it in its charger at the cottage.

Evil itself may be relentless. I will grant you that,
but love is relentless too…and the human heart outlasts
- and can defeat - even the most relentless force of all, which is time.
Dean Koontz

CHAPTER 55

Claire's cell phone, on the kitchen counter in the cottage, played its little jingo tune.

In the lodge, Adam listened to her recorded message for the umpteenth time, sighed, and snapped his phone shut.

Adele was playing fetch with Charlie, but she looked up from her wheelchair and asked, "Still trying to reach Claire?"

"Her name's Clarissa," he said.

"She'll get back to you," Adele said.

"How do you know?" Adam's gaze was doubtful.

She shrugged. "Because tomorrow the cottage will be razed and she'll be homeless. She'll come crawling," she said, and smiled.

Adam gazed at her. "She doesn't have to come crawling. She just has to come."

There isn't any questioning the fact that some people
enter your life at the exact point of need, want or desire.
Nikki Rowe

CHAPTER 56

When Lady Ashworth arrived at North Audley Street, Mr. Grey, St. John's butler, felt relief. Here was someone who might enlighten the staff on their missing master. So when he opened the door and she walked past him into the house, he didn't try to stop her. He didn't say, "But the master isn't in, ma'am," or, "But, my lady, Mr. St. John isn't home. He hasn't been home for two days, and left no word as to where he's gone, or when he'll return."

Her Ladyship, upon handing Grey her things, said, "Bring tea, Grey, to the library." She preferred the library to the parlour, perhaps because it was St. John's favourite room, aside from his study. "And I must speak to you," she added.

"Thank you, my lady," said the servant. He moved smartly to order the tea, along with a tray of biscuits and seed cake. Her Ladyship always did enjoy a little repast when she called. Joining the marchioness shortly, he found her just as she picked up a letter that sat on a side table against the wall. Grey had seen the letter there, but dared not read it himself. He wondered if it held the answer to the riddle of where the master had gone. Lady Ashworth put it back and moved to a wing chair near the fire.

After the butler settled the tray and poured tea for Her Ladyship—not something he did often, but was nevertheless graceful in the doing—she said, "Tell me, Grey. Where is your master?"

Grey frowned. "My lady, I rather hoped you would enlighten me on his whereabouts."

Lady Ashworth put a hand over her heart. "Do you mean, you don't know?"

Grey shook his head. "I am sorry, ma'am."

She cleared her throat and looked at him squarely. "Did he take a gig or a coach?" Julian's love of racing might be the simple answer to his disappearance, she thought. He oftentimes drove to Brighton in hopes of beating Mr. Selby's record of eight hours, there and back. Perhaps he had gone and was still with the Prince Regent at Brighton Pavilion.

Grey licked his lips and looked at her plaintively. "That's just it, ma'am. All the equipages are in the mews, accounted for."

She stared at him. "And the horses? He does love a good gallop."

"All here, ma'am." Grey looked as troubled as Her Ladyship.

Lady Ashworth studied the carpet, in thought. "Have a seat, Grey, please."

But the servant shook his head. "If you please, ma'am, I'd rather not." Grey wouldn't be comfortable sitting in the presence of the marchioness.

She surveyed him. "So it's true, then, what I've heard. That he's—missing?"

Grey nodded, looking down.

Her Ladyship sniffed. "Does he often leave without a word?"

"No, ma'am."

"Has he never gone off on a lark to Brighton, racing the Regent or some other whip, without sending word?"

"He has gone off, indeed, ma'am, on many an occasion, either to Brighton, or some estate, or simply stayed on the town overlong—but he has always sent word, ma'am."

"Well," she said, in an optimistic tone, "I daresay he is too deep in his cups somewhere. We are certain to hear, shortly." She didn't believe this, but she hoped to sound convincing. She didn't want Grey to know how deeply worried she was.

The butler nodded, but the look on his face said he, too, thought this unlikely.

Lady Ashworth studied him. "You've known him since he was a boy. What is your worst fear?"

"My lady?"

"What do you think has happened to your master?" she asked

softly, as though the subject was sacred and could only be spoken in solemn tones.

The butler met her eyes. His were grey, like his name—and, at the moment, haunted. "I—I hesitate to speak of it, ma'am."

"Come, Grey, I'm sure you've an idea."

He licked his lips and swallowed. "I fear, ma'am, that he has suffered a coaching accident. The master, as you know, can never resist the call of the road. If another gentleman dared him to a race—"

"I see," Lady Ashworth said, nodding. "That was my thought, exactly." But she looked up in a moment. "But surely had there been an accident, we would have had word from someone, or read a notice in the paper!"

"I take comfort in that thought, ma'am." He cleared his throat. He looked at her rather questioningly.

"You wish to ask me something?" she said. "Go on, sir."

"Ma'am—is Miss Channing—that is, if Miss Channing might be consulted on the matter. Perhaps she might know something of it?"

Lady Ashworth's face became guarded. But then she saw what he meant. "You're wondering if your master eloped with my granddaughter, but no, no, I'm afraid she has no more idea of his whereabouts than either of us." But suddenly her face lit with a thought. "Thank you, Grey, for your time."

"Your servant, ma'am."

"Send Fletch to me, please."

"The valet, ma'am?"

"Yes." She smiled. "'Tis an unrelated matter, but he may be of help." Grey bowed and left the room. Fletch appeared in minutes, a wiry man, straightening his waistcoat, and with eyes full of curiosity. He came and bowed before Her Ladyship.

"Your servant, ma'am."

"Fletch, I wonder if you can help me. You see, Miss Channing left a shawl here, a very particular shawl that she favoured." The valet immediately wore a knowing look.

"You know the item I'm referring to?" she asked eagerly.

"I do, ma'am." He frowned. "There's no sign of it here. The

master asked me for it—right before we lost him, wouldn't you know."

Lady Ashworth's eyes widened. "What do you mean, right before you lost him?"

"Well, ma'am, Mr. Grey and I like to keep abreast of his whereabouts; he often takes me with him, you know, when he goes about town or travelling. So I consider it my part to know where he is, ma'am." He raised honest, brown eyes to hers.

Lady Ashworth nodded. "Yes, good man."

"Thank you, ma'am, but here's the thing, ma'am." He looked rightly serious and shook his head. "After he ast me for that shawl"— he looked up earnestly—"the piece Miss Andrews didn't cart off after she got her claws in't and ripped it right in two, that is—!" His face wore all the disapproval that anyone charged with the care of textiles, like Fletch, would understand. "He disappeared, ma'am."

"What do you mean?" she asked.

"He grabbed the shawl and hurried off, like." He looked at her squarely. "And that's the last any of us laid eyes on 'im, ma'am."

Shuffling one foot uncomfortably, he said, "It was my surmise he took it to Miss Channing; give 'er back what belonged to 'er, I thinks." He looked at her questioningly.

"Not a bad thought, sir," she said, "but no such thing, I assure you."

The valet's face fell, and he shook his head again. "Well, that leaves us neither here nor there."

"I'm afraid so," she agreed. She emptied her teacup. "Thank you, Fletch. I'll go now." She rose and then stopped to say, "If you hear anything of your master, please—" She stopped and looked at him feelingly.

"O'course, ma'am." The servant bowed and left the room.

Lady Ashworth stopped to examine the letter that lay on the table. This time she unfolded it, hoping she wasn't overstepping her bounds, but her concern for St. John fueled her resolve. It was the one Clarissa had tried to bamboozle him with! She pocketed it, looking troubled. It was lies, spurious lies, all of it. She thought of Clarissa using the shawl, and her heart throbbed with grief. Only Claire should have use of it! And Julian—oh! He was never meant to use the tallit she was sure! He shouldn't have been able to! She could only hope and pray he would find his way back, and that somehow, some way, Claire would, too.

The pull of past and future is so strong
that the present is crushed by it.
Jeanette Winterson

CHAPTER 57

Claire found an empty parking lot and turned in. It was large and surprisingly well lit—a perfect place to let Julian drive. Had the black Trailblazer been at their heels, she wouldn't consider it, but they'd seen no sign of Clarissa and her mysterious henchman since they'd gone for dinner. And Julian loved anything on wheels. It would be a thrill for him to drive, not unlike the excitement some feel on roller coasters, she thought.

She spent minutes going over the dashboard, but Julian had read the car owner's manual and apparently memorized what each gauge and dial was for. Same for the gas and brake pedals. So when they changed places, and he turned the key in the ignition—his face brimming with boyish anticipation—she was hardly surprised when he put the car into gear properly and gently started them off with barely a jerk or stop.

"Fabulous!" he said. She loved the intensity on his features and the smile as the car obeyed his will. He went to the perimeter of the lot and started circling. He practiced using the brakes, starting off to different speeds and then braking. Claire didn't mind, even when he braked too sharply and her belt tightened.

She marveled at how well he drove. What had he once told her? *I was born for speed.* She had to agree. After a full half hour of traversing the parking lot in all directions, a police cruiser entered, moving slowly. It came to a stop, keeping its headlights on. Claire didn't want trouble with the law. Imagine if they asked St. John for ID! So she insisted on taking back the wheel, making him change places with her without getting out of the vehicle.

He slid toward her, lifted her onto his lap—and kept her there for a warm, sloppy, delicious kiss. "This is what teenagers do," she said with a smile, when she could speak. But his brows furrowed. "Mere youths? Alone together in cars at night? That's a recipe for disaster! Does society keep no check on its youth?"

"Not enough, I think," she said soberly.

She started the car and drove quietly from the lot, thankful that the cruiser didn't stop or follow them. It was pitch-black when they arrived at the cottage except for two weak solar lights at the foot of the porch. As their eyes adjusted, Claire was infinitely relieved to see no sign of Clarissa's truck. Somehow she had half expected to find the black Trailblazer in the driveway. And Clarissa would be on the porch, wild-eyed, with a gun or something, declaring to Julian, "If I can't have you, no one can!"

But hadn't she left a light on inside? A nervous shiver ran down her spine, for the house was dark. She was glad to be with Julian— she thought of his muscular build and remembered how easily he'd carried her in his arms. But she took a flashlight from the car's trunk and turned it on. As soon as Julian saw it, he asked for it. "A handy, enclosed lantern," he said.

She let him light their way inside.

When she flicked on the light switch, nothing happened. Julian turned the beam this way and that, and they went through the house checking each room for an intruder—for Clarissa and her driver, really—but there was no one.

"There's a generator that will power a few things," Claire said. "But it's in the cellar, and we'll have to turn it on." She had ventured downstairs only once on a quick explore when she'd first moved in. The washer and dryer were on the main level, so she'd had no need to return to the old, danky basement.

At the cellar door, he took the lead, and she followed him down a rickety wooden flight of steps into the cold, dense, dark, which seemed to increase as they descended. For some reason Claire felt positively spooked. She didn't get jumpy often, but it felt as though at any moment she might feel a bony hand upon her arm, or hear a witchy cackle of laughter. Julian's strong grasp of her hand was reassuring.

She led him to where the breakers were and found the power switch for the generator—fortunately clearly marked. After she flicked it on, they heard the faint rumble as it came to life outside.

She kept a tight hold on Julian's hand as he led them back up.

The kitchen light was on. "Can you start the fire?" she asked, while heading to the kitchen and her cell phone to check for messages. To her surprise there were three. She hoped to find a message from her agent. All three, however, were from Adam—of course. To Claire's consternation, she saw they were from two days earlier. Somehow she'd missed them.

"Hey, uh, Claire," Adam's message began, "Just thought I'd give fair warning that your electricity is about to be shut off." So that explained it. "We own the property now, so we were able to go ahead and do that. Um, it had to be done in order to schedule the demolition." His voice perked up. "But the good news is, we're paying last month's bill for ya." As if that would impress her?

"And even better" his voice message continued, "your suite here at the lodge is all ready for you." The message shut off at that point, but Adam called back and left another. "If you come to our mixer tomorrow night, I'll show it to you. You're gonna love it."

The mixer would have been last night, then. Guess Adam realized by now that she'd not be taking them up on the offer of a suite. No problem there, for even if she couldn't return with Julian, Claire still wouldn't stay at the lodge. The Winthrops were causing the destruction of the cottage—she'd never stay with them.

Adam's third message was more of the same. "Hey," he said. "Even if you don't need our suite, you ought to take it. People pay big bucks for it. It includes a daily buffet breakfast. *Ciao*."

"Thoroughly poor form to oust a woman from her home," Julian said, coming from the other room.

Claire smiled as she took his coat. "Even if said woman is about to disappear into the past?"

"Adam doesn't know that." His eyes had lighted upon her laptop, and before she'd even hung up their coats, Julian was seated before it. He powered it up and entered her password. She surveyed

him in his Brooks Brothers duds and could not find one little thing
to dislike in the view. She'd thought it was his Regency attire that
lent him his air of dignity and manliness, but from his thick black
hair and sideburns with their distinguished hint of grey, all the way
down to his loafer-clad feet, Julian looked wonderful.

Claire felt suddenly awkward being alone with him. When he
hadn't remembered her, it was like sharing space with a stranger.
Now that he loved her, she'd have to keep her distance. Julian
disliked loose women—but it was going to be like ignoring the pull
of a magnet—a very handsome, incredibly sexy magnet.

When she joined him, sitting beside him in order to share the
screen, he said, "I had a thought. Before we return—"

"Yes?"

"I should like to drive a car once more."

Of course—he hadn't had a chance to get moving with any real
speed. But parking lots didn't offer such opportunities. And being on
the road was too risky. She looked at him apologetically. "I'm sorry,
you can't."

"Why not?" He turned to her. A smile played on his lips and his
gaze swept over her face and fell to her mouth. Uh-oh. He felt it too,
the pull of the magnet. She pushed her chair back a few inches, and
then looked at him earnestly. "Because you need a birth certificate
and another form of ID. Something to prove your identity in case
you're stopped. Not to mention, a learner's permit."

"To prove my identity? I *have* an identity," he scoffed. "Why is
that not enough?" His eyes narrowed at her. "Why did you move
away?" With one arm, he drew her chair back to where it had been,
and they studied each other, practically nose to nose. Claire took a
deep breath. And pushed her chair back again.

He put his head back with surprise. "Are you afraid of me?"

Claire stared at him, not wanting to say that yes, she was very
afraid. She was afraid because, until now, she'd never felt the least
interest in knowing a man sexually, in her life. And now it seemed as
if it was all she could think—or rather, try not to think—about.

His gaze softened. "I've given my word, Miss Channing." He

smiled. "To behave."

"I'm not afraid of you misbehaving," she said miserably. "I think I'm afraid you won't!" He suppressed a smile, but took her hands. Gazing at him, she said softly, "You are the most beautiful man I've ever known. The most wonderful human being—except for when you weren't reformed," she added quickly.

He grinned.

She paused and swallowed, and looking miserable, added, "Please understand! I've never been involved deeply; and I've certainly never been in love before—" She glanced around at the cottage. "And here we are, alone! I trust you, utterly, but I don't trust me." She tore her hands from his and shot to her feet, but St. John clasped her and brought her to his lap.

Smiling gently, he grazed her cheek with a finger and moved a stray curl behind her ear. "I understand you," he said.

She had to chuckle at that, for his words brought back the terrible scene when he had said exactly the same thing and then kissed her passionately, though he meant nothing by it.

He placed his forehead against hers. "I had hoped to stay longer only to get behind the helm, er, the wheel of a car. But come back with me now, and I'll take you to Scotland. We can be married in less than twenty-four hours."

"That soon?"

"'Twill take time to reach Gretna Green, but we'll be married as soon as we do." He kissed her nose and her forehead. "And no one," he added softly, "can drive you there faster than me. Not in 1816, that is. Not even the mail coach."

She looked up and smiled. "The mail coach—it is the fastest in your day, isn't it?"

He kissed the side of her face. "Not faster than me."

She smiled and nestled her face against his. He said, "After we're married and settled, we'll come back. And then I'll get behind the wheel again." Claire's heart sank. He enveloped her in his arms, but she pushed against him.

"The cottage won't be here. We won't be able to come back."

"The shawl is what brought me; it worked from my town house."

"And brought you to the cottage. It's tied to this place, though I don't understand how."

He reflected on that. "Miss Andrews wasn't brought to the cottage."

Claire stared at him, realizing he was right. "But she was evidently brought somewhere nearby. Grandmamma told me the shawl and the cottage only work together."

He said, "Ah. Her Ladyship." And gave a breath of a laugh. "I gave her quite the set-down when she told me she came from the future."

"She told you?" Claire was surprised but delighted, for some reason.

"I gave her grief, unfortunately. I was desperate to know what had become of you."

"Were you?" Claire's heart swelled. She threw her arms around his neck and he clasped her up against him. He kissed the side of her face and then found her mouth. It was a warm and wonderful kiss. She drew apart and rested her head against one strong shoulder, and he settled his arms around her.

"Come," he whispered into her hair. "Let us return. We'll go to Gretna, by Jove. And begin our lives together." She looked up at him with shining eyes, and he said, "You are indeed beautiful, Miss Channing. In every way." He kissed her again. "You'll be even more so as Mrs. St. John."

Claire left to retrieve the shawl but with a heart pounding strangely. She was either about to leave her present life for good, or discover that she was stuck in it. She was ready to leave it—if the tallit would work for both of them. Her career, her books, the cottage, the pesky Winthrops—the life she'd known—it would all be behind her. And that was okay. She'd have Julian! She'd be his wife! It really did seem like a fairy tale.

She gathered Grandmamma's jewelry. She wasn't dressed for diamonds and sapphires, but she put on the set. Still her heart pounded, thumping like a bass drum in her ears. Whatever happened, whether she was able to return or not, at least Julian would be safe in the past, safe from Clarissa, and where he belonged. If only that thought would calm her frayed nerves!

When she returned with the shawl, St. John's eyes roamed over her. "Those are fancy baubles," he said.

Claire smiled. "They're Lady Ashworth's. I told her I'd bring them back with me if I could." He nodded. Looking back at the laptop, he ran a hand along it.

"Do you think—" he started to say, but Claire shook her head. "It would be useless. It only holds what I've downloaded, that is, copied onto the hard drive, er, the memory. Everything else it can do here won't exist, and the battery will run out in hours."

"I would yet have hours to read information?"

"Only what I've saved, and if it came through unscathed." She turned troubled blue eyes to him. "I'm concerned that we won't both make it with only half the shawl. Much less a laptop."

He nodded. "Let's find out."

Holding the torn piece, Claire put her arms carefully around Julian's neck. He entwined his arms around her and couldn't help planting a small kiss on her mouth. Looking up to meet his gaze, she smiled. A beautiful sense of anticipation filled her, and her fears floated away—she was going to her new home, to 1816! It was a vastly different world, but one to which now she would belong. She thought of Grandmamma and how happy that lady would be when they were back.

Seconds passed, and still they stood with the tallit in Claire's hand, but nothing happened.

"When I left the past," he said, "'twas against my chest."

"Of course," Claire said. It had only worked that way for her too, from the present to the past. She put the shawl against his crisp Brooks Brothers checkered shirt and then twined her arms back around his neck. "Hold tight," he said. She felt him stiffen, as if he'd had an important thought.

"What is it?" Claire asked.

But it wasn't an important thought, it was time travel. And just like that, Claire fell forward and landed flat on her face on the floor. Julian had vanished.

There's not a joy the world can give like that it takes away.
Byron

CHAPTER 58

Claire's worst fear had happened! Half the tallit wasn't enough for both of them! She picked herself up, rubbing her head where it hit the floor. She went and took the chair Julian had so recently occupied and stared off into space. She wouldn't panic—not yet. Julian still had the shawl; the cottage was still standing; he could return. And he would. Of course he would.

But she shook her head. It wasn't supposed to happen like this. They were meant to be together—she'd dressed and spoken properly for life in the Regency—the tallit had somehow made that possible. So why hadn't it been smart enough to transport them both?

As minutes ticked past and he didn't return, Claire tried to squelch a growing sense of despair. She was again stuck in the present without him!

To keep herself occupied—and in order not to get frantic with worry—she boxed up anything that she wouldn't want demolished come morning. What else was there to do? And Adam said they'd empty the house first of anything worth saving. But her heart was only with Julian. Please, come back! Once more!

She ought not to wish him back. With Clarissa in the present, he was safer in the past. But he had to come back. They still had one more night before the cottage would be razed. One more night to be together. He could leave safely the following day—so long as Miss Andrews remained, she couldn't cause a coaching accident in 1816.

And then it hit her. Two people *could* time travel. Clarissa had come to the present with the other half of the tallit. That was Claire's ticket home! All she had to do was get it.

Oh dear.

Sometimes, you have to manufacture your own history.
Give fate a push, so to speak.
Sarah Dessen

CHAPTER 59

Julian found himself in his library—the very room he had vanished from when he left for the future—but Claire wasn't with him. This was no good. He couldn't possibly stay without her. The shawl had fallen to the floor, so he picked it up. At that moment, a maid walked in with a coal scuttle. She saw St. John and stopped dead in her tracks, her eyes wide as saucers.

"Oh, sir! I beg yer pardon, sir!" she said, in the hoarse tone of one seeing a ghost. She dropped the coal scuttle to curtsey. St. John put his hands behind his back, still holding the cottony shawl.

"That's all right," he said. He motioned with his head at the grate. "Go on." She obediently picked up the coal scuttle and shuffled to the grate to stir and add to the fire, which had been kept going at Mr. Grey's order. But she took a sideways look at him as she passed as if she couldn't credit her sight.

St. John, meanwhile, realizing the shawl hadn't brought Claire, figured he'd be spending more time in the future until they found a solution to get her back as well. He'd best take a quick peek in his study to see if anything needing attention had landed on his desk. As he hurried along the corridor, the quietness of his house enveloped him like a warm blanket, and he couldn't deny a sense of elation at having returned. The future had gadgets—and cars—but his home was here.

When the maid saw him leave, she dropped what she was doing and ran pell-mell to the servants' quarters to find the butler. When she found him just leaving his room, turning the key in the lock, she gasped, "Mr. Grey! He's back! I just saw him, sir!"

Grey looked thunderstruck. "What, the master?"

"Aye, sir! 'Twas him, right an' tight!"

Grey moved swiftly down the corridor. "Where is he?"

"He was in the library sir, but he left. I can't say as where he went." Grey gave her a concerned look and then strode quickly on. He checked the library just in case, then hurried on toward the master's study. If he didn't find him there, he'd check his bedchamber. At the study door, he hesitated and gave a small knock, holding his breath.

"Come in," St. John said. When the door opened, he only glanced at Grey and then went back to a letter upon his desk. "Yes?" he said.

When Grey was silent, he looked up, this time with more attention. "Grey?"

"Sir!" he managed, almost choking on the word. He swallowed. "If I might say, sir—on behalf of all the staff—how happy we are to have you back." He was blinking rapidly and looked away. Finally he dared to meet his master's eyes. "Have you been home long, sir?"

St. John's eyes softened. "I'm sorry, old boy. Didn't mean to worry you. I took a rather…unexpected trip, I'm afraid."

The butler still looked troubled. "All of your equipages were here, sir. None of your horses missing…" He looked pained.

St. John said, "Ah, yes. I..er…took passage on a different vehicle. I'd describe it to you, Grey, but…" He hesitated. "'Twas beyond description," he finished with a sparkle in his eye.

Grey stared at him. "Beyond description, sir?"

"Another time, perhaps, I'll explain it to you. I owe you that." He folded the letter and put it down. "All you need know now is that I shan't be staying. I'm very likely to take another such trip tonight. In fact, I depend upon it." He gave the servant a bracing look. "Hold the fort for me, sir," he said.

"The fire in the library, sir?"

"Keep it going. I won't be gone for long."

"Lady Ashworth was concerned about you, sir. She called yesterday."

"Send a message," he said, coming to his feet. "Tell her I'm endeavouring to arrange a wedding with her granddaughter. That will satisfy her, I daresay." He wore a small smile as he met the butler's eyes as he strode past.

The servant gazed affectionately at him. "May I offer congratulations, sir, on behalf of the staff?" His eyes smiled. Grey understood, now, what was what. The master must have been away to see Miss Channing's family. He was now off to cement the arrangement with them and marry his bride. A fortuitous event! All that worry for nothing—thank God, for nothing! And the master, to have a wife!

He returned to his room with nearly a bounce in his step, to pen that note to Lady Ashworth. Then he'd make an announcement to the staff—first, of Mr. St. John's safe return, and then of the impending nuptials. Imagine it—they'd feared the loss of their master, and now they not only had him back, but would have a mistress in the house! Smiling at the thought, his mind soared ahead, envisioning little miss and master St. John's running about the house. Grey held no dislike of children. Wouldn't it be grand!

St. John returned to the library. For some reason, he felt positively superstitious about going back; it had to be from the same room. He wanted to end up in the same place—Claire's cottage—so why not leave from the room that had brought him there? He made his way to the room, looked around, and took a deep breath. He took the shawl from his pocket and held it up against his chest. And vanished.

Love recognizes no barriers. It jumps hurdles, leaps fences,
penetrates walls to arrive at its destination full of hope.
Maya Angelou

CHAPTER 60

Julian was on Claire's front porch. Why he ended up outdoors
was a question perhaps worthy of contemplation, but at the moment it
paled next to the need to get to Claire. The door was locked so he
knocked rapidly. Soon the curtain to the window overlooking the
porch was moved aside while Claire peered out cautiously.

In seconds she was shutting the door behind him. She threw
herself into his arms. "That was frightening!"

"I had no doubt of returning."

They came apart. "You changed clothing!" she chided. "I thought
you liked your new clothes."

"I didn't change!" he said, innocently. "I appeared at home
dressed like this."

Claire's lips pursed. "I'd like to know what the tallit did with
nearly $2,000 of Brooks Brothers clothing." But she smiled and
patted his chest. "I do like your usual style."

He studied her. "We must try again. I'll carry you in my arms. If I
hold you closer this time, perhaps we'll both go back."

Claire frowned. Suddenly it seemed absurdly obvious: their only
recourse was to get the other half from Clarissa. Leaving it with her
meant she could follow and plague Julian, and perhaps still incite him
to a fatal chase. She'd still be a threat. Even if Claire could get back
with him, Clarissa could plague them like she'd done that very day on
the highway.

"My dear sir," she said. "I've just realized we must get the shawl
from Clarissa. If we return together without it, she could follow and
still plague us."

"It matters not." He kissed her forehead. "My only concern is
making you my wife. She cannot stop that." He scooped her into his

arms and looked into her eyes. "Ready?"

She swallowed. "No. When you vanished before, I fell on my face. If I don't go with you, I'll be dropped again."

He glanced down at the floor. He frowned.

"Now are you ready?" Julian smiled into her eyes. He was standing rather unsteadily, upon Claire's queen-size bed with her in his arms.

"Hold me as tight as you can!" she said. He shifted to do so, wobbling on the mattress.

"Watch it!" Claire cried. "Or we'll—"

They crashed to the mattress.

"Fall." She made a move to get up, but St. John tightened his arm around her. He gave her a husky look.

"Oh dear," said Claire.

He pulled her in for a soulful kiss. Claire was immediately immersed in the delicious warmth of him, and overcome with only one thought: to stay in Julian's arms forever. But she could not forget his danger! The demolition crew would show up in the morning and start their destruction. And Miss Andrews was still a threat. No, even if she could not go back with him, Julian must return before it was too late.

Claire forced herself to draw apart from his intoxicating embrace. "We must try again."

He blinked. And sat up. "Right. Once more then." She started to rise, but he said, "Let's try it from where we are." He circled her in his arms, and Claire laid the shawl this time against her breast, after which he drew her up against him as tightly as possible. Half a minute passed and nothing happened.

"What could be wrong?" Claire asked, into his ear. She drew apart from him just enough to meet his gaze. Somehow the shawl had transferred from her chest to his, though she didn't realize it. "Why isn't it working?" she asked.

"I don't know," he said. And then he was gone.

Claire hardly felt the small drop from where his lap had been to the mattress. She stretched out on the bed and sighed. It was no use. Getting Clarissa's half of the shawl wasn't optional. Without it, Claire could never return.

A minute later she heard the door open and rushed out to meet him.

"We must get the other half from Miss Andrews," he said.

Claire studied him. "I must get it. You have to go back."

He raised a brow. "Leave you at Miss Andrews's mercy? Perish the thought! I've more honour than that."

"You do, of course; I'm sorry. But I can manage her."

He looked at her affectionately. "Let me send you back, and I'll stay and get the shawl."

Claire grimaced. "Absolutely not! You're forgetting—you could be stuck here for good when they raze this place tomorrow!"

His lips compressed. "Then we must get the shawl before that happens. But we'll do it together."

Claire sighed. A part of her loved that he didn't want to leave her. If only the rest of her wasn't worried. She said, "You have to go while you can. We don't even know where she's staying. What if we can't find her?" Her clear blue eyes clouded with worry.

"Not to fear," he said. "If I know Clarissa, she will find us."

"But it might be too late!" Claire cried. "Tomorrow—"

He put a finger lightly on her lips. "Don't fret. Even demolitions take time. They may arrive in the morning, but they won't begin wrecking the place until afternoon."

Claire hoped he was right, but sleep evaded her that night. She and Julian never did share a glass of champagne before the fire as the atmosphere was fraught, for her at least, with fears of the morrow. Julian was impressively calm, glued to the laptop. He was determined to learn everything he could about car tires and engines, for his idea was to speed up the advancement of the carriage when he returned home. He'd emerged from the spare bedroom dressed in the extra Brooks Brothers clothing she'd bought. He wore his Regency-fitted trousers and boots, but had on the shirt and argyle sweater from the mall. He had that five-o'clock shadow, which somehow she hadn't noticed earlier—her heart gave an extra beat at the sight of him.

But Claire couldn't stop worrying. What if Clarissa wouldn't give up the shawl? Only one other person could return with it. If Claire got the shawl, then Clarissa would be sentenced to life in the here and now. If Claire didn't get the shawl, Clarissa could return after Julian and still manage to get him killed. And if they didn't return before the cottage was razed, they'd all three be stuck in the present! Oh! What to do!

She really had to convince Julian to return without her. Then, assuming she could find Clarissa and keep her here for the day, he'd be safe. She and Clarissa would both be stuck in the present, but Julian could go on to live a long life. She sighed.

If she could convince Clarissa to give up the shawl before the cottage was demolished, even better. But it was taking a huge risk to count on that. Why would Clarissa want to stay? Claire continued tossing and turning, filled with unrest. She got up, grabbed her robe, and went out to where Julian was seated at the laptop.

He didn't hear her coming in her soft slippers. Claire leaned over and saw he was reading about the Prince Regent. But his hand slipped out and took one of hers—he had heard her.

"Cannot you sleep?" he asked.

"You shouldn't be reading this," she said, her face creased in worry.

He met her gaze. "Why not?"

"It's spying on people."

He raised his brows at her, while she pulled out a chair and sat. "How could I possibly spy on people who lived more than two hundred years ago?" he asked, innocently.

"Because you're one of them."

He turned back to the screen, repressing a grin.

"What have you learned about the Prince Regent that you didn't already know?"

"That he will try to divorce his wife and fail; that he will be cruel and bar Caroline from the coronation; and that she will die shortly afterward, conceivably from a broken heart."

"You know too much." Claire tried to shut the laptop, but he put a hand over hers and stopped her. She gazed at him with full eyes. "Don't you see? You still have to live through this. It will be terrible when you already know how things turn out!"

"Terrible? I call that providential." He smiled roguishly at her.

"Seriously, you shouldn't be doing this."

He took a breath and sat back. He pushed his chair out a foot and motioned for her to come to him. "In all honesty, there are so many things I wish to know more about that I don't think I could sleep at all if I lived in this time and had this at my service." When she stood up, he took her by the waist and drew her onto his lap. He stroked the side of her face.

She said, "Promise me you won't look up anyone else."

He studied her. "Ah. You are afraid I will look up myself."

"No, not that," she said, hoping he'd believe her. "I don't think it's healthy." But he took her chin in one hand and studied her face. "You're a terrible liar."

Claire frowned. "All right. I don't want you looking up yourself." She stared into his grey-blue beautiful eyes. "Stick to car engines, and I won't say a word."

He kissed her. "Go back to sleep."

"I wasn't able to sleep, that's why I'm here." She paused. "And what about you? If you don't sleep, I won't let you drive tomorrow."

His eyes narrowed. "I only have tonight," he said, and glanced at the laptop. "With this. I can catch up on my sleep when we're back home."

"You have to be fully alert to drive. Cars are dangerous, Julian."

"Of course; in the wrong hands." He gently stroked her face with his thumbs. "I was born for speed, I assure you." A smile played at his lips as he added, "Look how fast I got here, to your time. In the blink of an eye."

Claire frowned. "If getting the shawl allows me to return with you, we'll be leaving Clarissa here—for good."

He nodded. "I've had that thought. We'll have to deduce a way for all of us to go back."

Claire's pulse jumped in her throat. "But she mustn't return the same day as you! Not tomorrow!"

Julian bit his lip and gently pushed a tress of hair behind her ear. "I do believe you are jealous," he said softly. "I can assure you—"

"Yes, I'm jealous," Claire said, glad to let him believe that was her motive. Her real intention—of keeping Clarissa from causing his death—must be kept from him. It was the only thing she'd ever been able to keep from him, she realized.

"You needn't be. But we must endeavour to find a means of getting all of us back, unless Clarissa wishes to stay here."

Claire's eyes lit with a thought. "Remember the publishing contract I told you about? All that money is guaranteed me." He nodded, so she continued. "Clarissa looks just like me—I've always wondered about it. If she did wish to stay, she wouldn't be penniless."

He added, "And she is well able to look out for herself."

"Precisely. All she need do is assume my identity. She'll be famous enough after the book's released." Claire's eyes grew large as she warmed to the idea of how easily Clarissa could transition to modern life due to their mirror images. "And because she's actually *from* the Regency, she'll be able to write better books than mine!" She drew back and smiled at him. "I think she may well be happy here."

"You are still the most beguiling woman I've ever known," he said, smiling gently. "You almost convince me. But I wonder if Miss Andrews would agree with your assessment?" His eyes lit with a thought. "I'll look her up and see what her fate is."

Claire grasped his arm and cried, "No, do not!"

He surveyed her calmly. "There is something you do not wish me to know."

She averted her gaze instantly, assuring him that he was correct. She said, speaking slowly, "I know this: that any information you can find from that"—she motioned at the laptop—can change." She looked back at him. "It happened for Grandmamma. After she fell in love with the marquess, she looked up his family line—and there was her own name, listed as his wife, Charlotte Grandison."

He gazed off into the distance, thinking it over. "Let us see if your name appears as my wife." His hand moved toward the keyboard, but Claire stopped him, looking rather tragical. He directed a patient look at her.

"Do not," she said softly. "I couldn't bear it. If my name doesn't show." She gazed at him sadly. "Please—stick to car engines, or your Regent, if you like. But leave us and our fate to God." With earnest eyes searching his, she added, "You are a man of your word. If you give me your word that you won't look up yourself—I'll believe you."

He looked at her thoughtfully. "I have a better idea. I'll look up your books."

She chuckled and said, "No! Don't." But he'd already entered her name in the search bar. When various images of Claire came up, all of them the old Claire, with long bangs covering her face and eyes, he turned to her with a smile. "I cannot credit my sight! How on earth did you manage to hide your beauty so well?" He looked back and shook his head. "I must say, 1816 was good for you. It brought out the real you."

She leaned up and kissed the side of his face and said softly, "It did more than that. It brought me to the real you." It seemed ludicrous to her now that she'd ever thought St. John was a figment of her imagination—a mere fictional character. Thank God, he was not!

Before he could respond, they heard the sound of vehicles approaching the cottage. It sounded like heavy trucks or equipment. They went to the window. It was still dark, but sure enough a parade of headlights was coming slowly up the drive.

Claire hurried for her coat and boots. Was the machinery here already? And not even dawn, yet? She'd have something to say about that. And they were blocking her way—she wouldn't even have room for her car to leave if she didn't stop them.

If it be now, 'tis not to come.
If it be not to come, it will be now.
If it be not now, yet it will come—the readiness is all.
William Shakespeare

CHAPTER 61

Omar and Clarissa had searched the mall for another half hour before conceding defeat. They returned to the Trailblazer.

"Use that tracking device," she said. "We can't leave yet, if they're here."

But instead of doing as she asked, Omar turned thoughtful eyes upon Clarissa. "Let me understand something," he said. "Are we tracking this guy because he ripped you off? Or because you're jealous?"

Clarissa studied him cautiously. She wasn't sure what he meant by "ripped you off." As she considered how to answer, he continued, "He didn't really do what you told me before, did he? Pilfer your money? Or take advantage of you?"

Clarissa looked away. "I told you I needed to follow and harass him, and I'm paying you for it. You don't need to know why."

He leaned over toward her. "But you haven't paid me yet."

She looked at him nervously. "You said you would wait until I get that first installment of the advance from…from that publisher."

He raised a brow at her. "Did you forget the name of your publisher?" He stared out the windshield a moment, thinking. "There's a lot you're not telling me. Something weird's going on with you."

Clarissa took a deep breath. "I don't want that woman to have him."

"I thought so," he replied. "How come three people said they saw you with him in the mall?"

"She looks like me."

"Is she your sister?"

"No!"

Omar gave her a dubious look, but started the engine. "Methinks the lady doth protest too much. Why are they staying in the cottage? If it's your place, and you hate her and don't want them together, why are you letting them stay?"

"I'm done with the cottage. I've moved into the lodge," Clarissa replied.

He looked over at her with a smile. "They don't know, do they?" He shook his head, smiling. "You're a devious bit of devilry, aren't you?"

Clarissa didn't know what he meant. "Why do you say that?"

"Because!" he said, backing out of the space. He headed toward the lot's exit. "They don't know the cottage is getting razed tomorrow, do they? You didn't tell them!"

Clarissa stared ahead, her mind buzzing with this new revelation. Even the amazingly bright lights of the stores and streetlights at night—like a magical fairyland in contrast to the dull lighting she was used to—failed to get her attention. So the cottage was about to be destroyed? She remembered Adam's reassurance. *You can stay here as long as you want. Be with me. I'll make sure you have everything you need.*

No wonder!

"Okay—you don't have to answer," said Omar, turning smoothly onto the main road. "But I'm beginning to understand you, Miss Channing."

This got her to turn to him in annoyance. "Call me Clarissa."

He glanced at her with a raised eyebrow and a smirk. "I'll call you whatever you like, your beautifulness." He turned his attention back to the road, but said, "But if you want my advice, save your money and give it up. Whatever you think you'll gain by trailing that guy—it won't be worth it. Let them get thrown out of the cottage tomorrow—and let it rest."

"I don't want your advice!" she fumed. "I only want your help. And I will pay you."

"Fine. Where do I take you? To the lodge?"

"No. Find them. Or let us wait by the cottage until they get back."

"What's the point in that?" He was scowling.

Clarissa stared miserably ahead into the darkness, and didn't answer.

"Look," Omar said, turning the car onto a highway, "I've been with you since this morning on a wild-goose chase for a guy you have the hots for. That doesn't excite me, see? You're not paying me enough for 24/7 surveillance, and frankly, the job no longer interests me."

She stared at him in consternation.

Omar shrugged. "I thought we were after a bad guy; what you told me before, that he stole from you. And I get it, you know, the wrath of a woman scorned, and all that. But I'm done, here. I'm taking you back to the lodge."

Clarissa frowned. She looked large-eyed at him.

He felt her gaze and wouldn't look at her.

"Omar," she said softly. "I understand. But what if I were to pay you more?"

He shook his head, still refusing to look at her. "I'm going home," he said. "I'll drop you and then I'm going home. I'm done here."

"But—but—I thought you would do any work for hire." She stared at him in consternation. He said nothing, just kept that intense face on the road. Clarissa had an insight.

"Take me with you," she said softly. "Take me home with you again. I don't want to go to the lodge. I don't want Adam."

He glanced at her, a mixture of interest and wariness on his features. "I know you don't. You want that St. John guy."

"No," she said. Her face hardened. "I only want to give him grief. I want to hire you for one more day just to give him grief. Then, you can forget about me. Or—or—take me home with you again." She paused, letting him digest her offer. "If you'll help me, I will forget about St. John, I promise you."

He looked over at her again, his lips pursed, thinking. "I don't know," he said. "I don't know about you."

"Can you stop the car?" she asked.

He looked ahead and saw a wide shoulder, but asked, "What for?"

"Please. Just stop the car!"

Omar pulled onto the shoulder. He turned off the engine, and then, frowning, turned to Clarissa. She had already unbuckled her seat belt. She slid over to Omar and put her arms around his neck. She remembered that kiss from Adam and knew exactly what to do. "Here's all you need to know about me," she said. She twined her arms around him like a boa constrictor. And pulled him in for the kiss.

CHAPTER 62

Claire and Julian watched from the front porch while various vehicles pulled up to the house, coming to a halt in a line on the driveway. A police car made its way alongside them, just able to squeeze past the large vehicles and slowly sidle up to the house. Claire was sorry she'd paid to have the area cleared of snow.

Sheriff Levin got out and came forward. "I'm sorry, Miss Channing," he said. "But I have a warrant here. I'm afraid you'll have to leave the premises." He glanced at Julian. "That means both of you."

Julian looked him over. "Are you a military man?"

"Huh?" said the sheriff, squinting in the light of the porch to get a better look at him.

"He's police," Claire explained. "Like a Bow Street Runner, only institutionalized and paid by the government."

"A public servant, in other words," Julian said, eyeing him with disdain. "Not a landlord." He was about to continue, but Claire took his arm and then shook her head when he looked down at her. She turned to the sheriff. "It's all right, I understand. But it isn't dawn, yet. Surely you can call off these men until we've had a chance to eat breakfast."

Sheriff Levin pushed his hat back. "Well—I guess they can start the unloading. We've got a POD here in this lineup. You understand, of course, anything still remaining now belongs to the Winthrops—unless you're hauling it out when you go."

Julian moved as if to object, but Claire tugged on his arm and shook her head again when he glanced at her. "I understand," she said. "But they can't start until we've eaten. And we'll need a path to get out. They've completely blocked the drive."

The sheriff took a deep breath. "They're already here, ma'am," he said. "It's gonna be a big deal to get them to back out."

"It's a big deal already, Sheriff," she replied.

"Tell you what," he said. "When you're ready to go, I'll back my car out. You can get out the way I came in."

Suddenly Adam was there. "Clarissa!" he said, looking curiously at Julian. To their surprised faces he added, "Er, Claire. Her real name's Clarissa," he explained to Julian, as if he had insider information. He turned to the sheriff. "It's all right, Sam, Clarissa's already moved out. She's staying with us at the lodge."

Julian and Claire exchanged surprised glances.

Adam turned back to Claire. With a sideways glance at Julian, he slipped an arm about her waist and leaned in to kiss her on the mouth. Claire leaned back in horror, but suddenly Julian pounced like a lion on its prey. Adam went flying off the porch, landing on his rear-end on the hard, packed snow of the drive. St. John looked ready to jump down after him, but Sheriff Levin instantly put his big bulk in front of him.

"Stop right there!" he cried.

Julian gazed at him with narrowed eyes, while the sheriff stared at him belligerently.

"It's all right," Adam said, getting himself up. He looked at Julian. "I guess that makes us even, now." He brushed snow off his pants and looked plaintively up at Claire. She turned to Julian and whispered, "He thinks I'm Clarissa."

"I comprehend that. But if he thinks—"

"Please," she said, putting a hand upon his arm. "Go back to the analytical engine. We have very little time. Let me talk to Adam and the sheriff."

He scowled. "Leave you to the wolves? No gentleman could countenance such a thing."

She let out a breath. "Please. I promise you, I can manage. This isn't—" She hesitated and lowered her voice even more. "This isn't 1816. I can do this. I need you inside. And it's your last chance to—" She didn't complete the thought. She knew the pull of the laptop and its magical "compressed library" was strong bait for him.

"Call me if they give you"—he stopped and glared at the men—"the merest hint of trouble."

Meanwhile, Adam and the sheriff had been talking, but now Sheriff Levin walked away. Adam climbed the steps to Claire, looking wary. "I wondered where you went," he said. "You are coming back, aren't you?"

"Why wouldn't I?" asked Claire. "But you'll give us time for a decent breakfast, right? My last meal in my grandmother's home," she added wistfully.

Adam checked the windows as if searching for Julian. No stern face appeared but he kept his distance from Claire. "The suite is only for you," he said, in a lowered voice.

"He won't be with me," she replied.

Adam's gaze swept over her face. His eyes softened. "I don't know what it is about you, Clarissa," he said. "But ever since I first saw you—"

"Give us two hours before these men begin," she said.

"Two hours?" He looked back at the line of trucks, their lights blinking. The sky was still black. "Fine." He looked at his watch, and then thumbed on its backlight. "The clock's on."

"Thank you, Adam."

He nodded. "There's a lot I'd do for you," he said softly.

She blinked, surprised. Clarissa had evidently given Adam encouragement—far more than Claire ever would have. And he'd fallen for her charms. If only Clarissa would be satisfied with having this man who so wanted her! Adam turned and approached the closest long-bed truck, going around to the driver's side to inform the driver of the delay. Claire hurried back inside the cottage.

Julian wasn't at the laptop, but it was open. She remembered that he never had given his word not to look himself up. She pulled down the history tab. She saw a series of sites leading to information about car engines—so far so good. She kept looking; she'd go back as far as the search he'd done on her name so she wouldn't miss anything.

She saw a page about the Prince Regent, then one about his doomed wife, Caroline of Brunswick. After that more pages on car engines. And then—her heart sank. There it was—St. John's name in a URL. Claire clicked through. She cursed her own curiosity for she saw he'd gone directly to the page of the newspaper story about his coaching accident. If she hadn't dug for two hours to find it, he'd never have been able to come across it so soon. Blast computer memory!

She sat back in despondency, staring at the page. Her grandmother's name had appeared as the wife of the marquess after they fell in love. She didn't say whether they were married before it changed. Why hadn't St. John's death notice changed? Here he was in the present—he couldn't possibly die on the road to Wembley in England in 1816! Today was the day he would have died—or would die—if he returned to the past. If only the newspaper had included the time of day, Claire could hold off his return until after that hour.

But once the demolition began, who knew when the tallit would cease to be a portal?

She heard Julian approaching and closed the page with the old clipping.

"I suppose I understand now, what you were trying to keep from me?" he asked, as he approached.

"I suppose you do," she said quietly. "My thought was to keep you here in the present until the day was past, but with the demolition crew at our door, we have no choice but to return you while we can."

He came over and kissed the top of her head. "And I thought you were jealous," he said.

Claire smiled sadly. "I am jealous. Of anyone and everyone who lives in 1816 and knows you and will get to know you and live out their lives near you—especially if I cannot."

His jaw hardened. "You must." He paused. "Coming here and knowing you, my dear Miss Channing, has apparently saved my neck. I owe you thanks."

"Don't thank me until I get you home again safe and sound," she said, with another sad smile.

"Until we both get home."

Her eyes watered at the thought of not getting back with him. He kissed her. "Do not despair. The shawl in Miss Andrews's possession belongs to you. She never had a right to it, and it must be returned to its rightful owner, wouldn't you agree?"

"I entirely agree," she said. She sniffled and tried to smile up at him.

"Clarissa has taken residence at the lodge, according to Adam," he continued. "Let us hope she likes it there." He looked around. "Is there aught in this place she will need if she stays?"

Claire said, "I've put my important documents in a safety deposit box—er, a safe," she explained. "All she needs from here is my copy of the contract." And it was true—Claire's legal identity amounted to a stack of papers in that box. She owned an appalling lack of personal mementoes, but those things wouldn't matter to Clarissa anyway.

But Claire couldn't erase a feeling of doom. It seemed so unfair that Julian would have to leave because of the Winthrops and their darned lodge. If only they'd had more time!

He took her arms to look deeply into her eyes. "We will get home. Together."

She loved it when he said home. And together! The very thought filled her with longing. But what if she couldn't get back? What if Clarissa wouldn't give up the shawl? Claire would be trapped two hundred years away from Julian! Why, why, was her fate dependent upon that woman?

Julian grabbed her hand and led her toward her bedroom. Claire looked at him curiously. He stopped at the bathroom door. "Give me that shaving equipment. I'll manage for myself."

She frowned. "We have so little time! Must you shave? I like that shadow, for your information." She ran a hand along the line of his jaw.

He squinted at her. "A gentleman does not leave the house unshaven. The equipment, if you please."

Claire pursed her lips, but said, "Not on your life. That chin is all mine."

An hour and 15 minutes later—the length of time needed for Julian's shave and their breakfast, as well as packing a few more boxes of things into Claire's car—she backed the Capri out of the garage, giving a last, long look at the cottage. The quaint dwelling with its red metal roof was really appealing. Why couldn't the Winthrops keep it? Why did they insist upon destroying it? She saw Adam's gaze settle jealously upon Julian as they backed out. As they slowly went past him, Claire stopped and lowered her window. He came over with eager strides and leaned his hands upon the door.

"You'll be emptying out the furniture and other things, right? Before starting the demolition?"

He hesitated. "Only the big stuff. I tried to tell you to put in storage anything that was important." His lips compressed. "Do you want to show me what you'd like to keep? We did bring a POD for that stuff." Claire thought of the contents of the cottage. There was nothing other than what she'd already packed in the trunk and back seat of her car that was truly important. If she never returned to the past, she'd miss the cottage, not what it held. But there were perfectly good things in it. She said, "You ought to save the flat-screen TV and Bluetooth speakers. And the other appliances."

"Sure, sure," he said, nodding. "We'll do that." He gave her a searching look. "I'll even store it for you in case you ever want it." He paused. "But you won't need any of your old stuff. Not if you stay with me." His heart was in his eyes.

Claire almost felt sorry for him. She bit her lip. "Thank you," she said. "But it will take a few hours, won't it? Emptying the furniture? Before you start razing the building?"

He nodded. "Oh, yeah. There's preliminary stuff they have to do. Make sure the electricity's unhooked, and the gas lines are empty and all that."

She glanced at Julian. "That's good. We've got a few hours, yet."

Adam's brows furrowed. "You can't go back in there; you know that, right? Even if the wrecking doesn't start for hours yet, you won't be able to go back."

Claire stared at Adam. His words, *You can't go back*, were like a

haunting chorus, echoing her biggest fear. She nodded. "I know."
And raised her window.

AGAMEMNON: Oh immovable law of heaven!
Oh my anguish, my relentless fate!
CLYTEMNESTRA: Yours? Mine. Hers. No relenting for any of us."
Euripides

CHAPTER 63

When they hit the road, Claire was downright disappointed not to find the black Trailblazer behind them. Had Clarissa given up the chase? Worse, could she have returned to the Regency? If so, Claire's shawl would have gone with her. She had visions of Julian going back to retrieve it. He'd chase Clarissa's coach—and still die in a crash! That could be why the old news clipping hadn't changed.

He turned to her, pulling her from her thoughts. "I should enjoy above all things having another go at that." He nodded at the steering wheel.

Claire glanced at him and then turned back to the road. She remembered how well he'd driven on his first attempt, and how much he'd enjoyed it. Also, this was his last chance to experience such a thing. They passed an intersection. As they went by Claire got a split-second glance at the vehicle sitting at the stop sign: a black Trailblazer. Her pulse picked up as it turned onto the road behind them. It gained on them swiftly.

"I believe we will have opportunity to get your shawl," Julian said, as he gazed into his side-view mirror. He pulled down the rearview and met Clarissa's eyes. She offered a cold, insolent look. "We must be making some progress with Clarissa," he said. "This is the first time she didn't offer me a brazen smile. Perhaps she realizes I am a lost cause? We can only hope," he added.

Claire began slowing, and, when a wide shoulder appeared, she pulled over. The pines lining the road with mountains in the distance made a pretty sight. When the Trailblazer duly parked behind them, Claire said, "Let me try first." She got out and walked to the passenger side of the truck. Clarissa looked at Omar, who lowered the window for her.

"Well, well," she said, when Claire appeared at her window. "Come to negotiate terms with the winning party? Unless you're offering surrender, I have no interest in it."

Claire stared at Miss Andrews in surprise. She spoke like an American! It was disconcerting. It had to mean something—but Claire had no time to consider what it was. Gathering herself, she said, "Surrender what? Do you mean, Julian?"

Clarissa looked at her driver. "I no longer want Julian." She turned back to Claire. "In fact, I haven't the faintest idea what made you come speak to me."

Claire glanced at the man at the wheel—he was staring at her in surprise. She guessed he'd no idea that Clarissa had a lookalike. She took a breath. "I've come to make you a proposal." Glancing again at the mean looking man she added, "But I need to talk to you privately." She opened Clarissa's door. "If you would?"

Clarissa pursed her lips; for a moment Claire thought she wouldn't cooperate. She started to get out but the man said, "You said she looked like you—not that you were twins."

"She's not my twin; she's not my sister," Clarissa muttered. She got out of the car, frowning. Claire moved out of the man's earshot.

"What is it you're talking about?" Clarissa asked.

"Just as I said. I propose to offer you a new life. Here in the future."

"With Julian? Tired of him already?" She glanced at Claire's car to where Julian sat in the passenger seat.

"Not that." Claire's lips compressed. "Adam Winthrop believes you are Miss Channing the author. And if you take that identity, you have just won a contract for $100,000. You will also get royalties." When Clarissa did not look impressed, she added, "It's a great deal of money."

"I know all about that," Clarissa said, with an impatient shake of the head.

"You'll be famous. And you can write more books that will be even more lucrative," Claire said evenly. "You'll have Adam at your beck and call—he already worships you."

Clarissa couldn't help cracking a small smile. But her animosity returned. In an acid tongue, she said, "I, write more books? How do you see that working, when I've never written a book in my life?"

"You can hire the help you need. Just ask Nigel, he's my agent—your agent, now. He'll get you an editor, a book doctor, a ghostwriter, whatever you need. But with your firsthand experience from your life in the past"—Claire leaned in—"you will be unsurpassed as an author of historical fiction in this day and time. You'll be world famous. And rich; far richer than you could have been with St. John, had you captured his interest."

Clarissa stared at her a moment, considering. "I won't know any of your friends or relations."

Claire gave a bitter laugh. "No worries there. I've been reclusive for years; my own mother only speaks to me twice a year, and no one knows me well enough to ever suspect that you are not me."

Clarissa crossed her arms, surveying Claire. "And you, I suppose, will return to the past with Julian and live happily ever after?"

"The moment we disappear to the past, as far as you're concerned, we're long dead. While you will be very much alive."

Clarissa took a slow, long breath. She thought of her life in 1816 and of everything Claire had said. You'll be world famous…incomparable as an author…far richer than you'd ever be in the past… Last night's experience with Omar had taught her that people were far less concerned with scrutiny and manners, not to mention, morals. She could enjoy that, for sure. She had already envisioned herself playing both men—Omar and Adam—to her heart's desire. And having a great deal of fun in the process.

She looked back at Claire. "I already have your identity. I don't need your permission or help. No one can tell us apart. So what do you have to offer?"

"You look like me, but that isn't enough. There are things you need to pull it off that I alone can give you," Claire said. "For instance, a birth certificate; and you'll need my driver's license—"

Clarissa's eyes lit up. "You mean to drive a modern carriage, er, car?"

"Yes. You must have someone teach you how, but I'll give you my license. And my college-degree certificate, my old photos— Clarissa just blinked at her—and all the paperwork I have to prove I am me. Finally, I will give you bank account access, or the money will be useless to you."

Clarissa now looked almost vulnerable. "And in return—what do you want from me? What can I possibly have that you require?"

"I want my shawl back. The piece you—you stole."

Enlightenment dawned upon Clarissa's features. She looked thoughtfully at Claire and her eyes narrowed. "You cannot return, can you?" Slowly, she smiled. "You can't go back with Julian without it!"

"And you can't have my life unless you part with it," Claire returned.

The women stood there facing each other. Behind her, Claire heard a car door open, and then another. Julian had climbed out of the Capri, and Clarissa's driver quickly followed suit. But as Julian approached the ladies, he glanced into the Trailblazer—and stopped short. As Omar rounded the front of the vehicle, Julian lunged for the door to open it, but Omar clicked his remote and it locked.

"What are you after?" he growled, coming to stand abreast of Julian. Both men were tall and muscular. Both gazed at each other with suspicion and dislike.

"Miss Andrews has something that does not belong to her," he said. "I saw it." He nodded at the passenger seat. "In there."

Omar's brows furrowed. "Miss Andrews? Who is Miss Andrews?"

Clarissa heard this and came toward them, looking faintly alarmed. "Miss Channing is my...er, pen name," she said.

Omar raised his brows. "Oh." He paused, studying Julian. "He says you've got something that doesn't belong to you."

Clarissa's face took on a shade of caution. "And they have documents that belong to me," she returned. "Which is what I've just been explaining to Miss—er, to this lady." She turned to Claire. "I'm perfectly willing to make a proper exchange."

Claire's heart lifted. "Perfect. Follow me. I have some of my documents." She glanced at the driver and hurriedly amended, "Er, some of *your* documents, here in the car."

Clarissa frowned. "Some? Not all of them?"

Claire turned back to her. "The rest are in a safety deposit box. I'll give you the key."

Omar nudged Clarissa. "Don't give up anything until you get everything you need. Let them open the box and prove what's in it, first."

Claire frowned. Looking at Omar she said, "You know perfectly well that what's in a safety deposit box is safe."

Omar said. "I don't know what's in the box. I don't know if anything's in the box." He looked at Clarissa. "What is it you need from these people?"

Clarissa swallowed. "It's a long story. But I can handle it." She paused. "Can you wait in the carr—er, the car?"

Omar gave her a silent long look. "Yeah. I'll wait in the truck." He gave a pensive stare to Julian and Claire and then returned to the Trailblazer.

Claire took out a file holding a copy of the contract. She was about to hand it to Clarissa, but Julian put out a hand and stopped her.

"Wait," he said. "She can come with us to see that everything else is in the box. And when she gives up the shawl, we'll give up the documents and the key."

Julian was right. Besides, what if it was too late to go back at all? What if the cottage, even now, was being razed and neither she nor Julian could get back? She would need her contract and all her IDs if they were stuck in the present. She hung on to the file. Clarissa tried to take it forcefully, but Julian took it from both women.

Clarissa pursed her lips.

"After we've gone, it's all yours," Julian said.

Claire turned to Julian. "Let me call Adam and see how far they've gotten with the demolition. I don't want to wait too long for you to return, whatever happens with me!"

"What difference does that make?" asked Clarissa irritably.

"All the difference in the world," said Claire. "The shawl only works in tandem with the cottage. It must remain standing."

Clarissa looked duly impressed with that response and said nothing. Then her face blanched and she said, "Do you mean to say the three of us could be stranded here?" She glared at Claire. "Living here is no advantage to me if you remain!"

At that moment she noticed Clarissa's driver had returned, and wore a look on his face that said he'd heard more than he should have. More than he understood. Clarissa turned to him with a look of trepidation. All he said was, "This is getting really interesting. I knew there was something strange going on with you."

She pressed her lips together but said nothing.

Claire's cell phone was to her ear, as she waited for Adam to pick up. "Adam!" she said now. "Have they started the demolition yet?" Her face fell. "How far along?" A pause. "Oh. So they haven't done any *wrecking*, yet." She gave Julian a look of reassurance. "No, no, I'm not hoping they won't. No, I'm not," she said again.

But her face lit with a thought. "Adam. I have a key to a safety deposit box that belonged to my grandmother. Can you hold off the wrecking ball—or whatever it is you use—until I check it for a deed to the property?" She held the phone away and hissed to Julian, "I wish I'd checked it before! I looked in it once, but I was distracted. It was when I couldn't get back to you. But there could be a deed in that box!"

"Your grandmother?" Clarissa asked, with a look of amazement. "Do you mean Lady Ashworth? She lived here?"

But Claire was listening to Adam, her brows furrowed. She said, turning away so the others might not hear her, "I know I'm asking a lot. I promise you—anything. No, I don't—I don't want to keep living there, even if there is a deed. I just don't want you to destroy it." Claire didn't care so much that the cottage was never destroyed, as much as that it wouldn't be destroyed too soon. They needed time to get to the box and show Clarissa its contents. Then, she'd give them the shawl, and they could be off for the past—for good.

Adam said, "What does that mean, you'll do anything?"

Claire didn't know what to say.

In a softer tone, Adam said, "Tell me you'll stay with me. We'll get married. I'll stop this. I'll stop it right now. I'll save your cottage. But you have to have a deed, or my father will still destroy it."

"But you'll stop the work while I check the box?"

"If you say it. If you agree to be mine."

Claire glanced uneasily back at Clarissa. "Do I have your word? You won't let a board of that cottage be removed? Until I get back to you?"

"You have my word—if I have yours."

Swallowing the pangs of her conscience, she whispered, "I will. I'll be yours. You have my word." When she'd clicked the phone shut, she turned back to the others. "Okay. Let's check the box and get on with this." Looking to Clarissa she added, "If there's a deed to the cottage in that box, you'll get to keep it."

Clarissa said, "I don't care about the cottage as long as you—" She glanced nervously at her driver. "Give me my things and go where you said you would."

"Everything's in the box," said Claire. "So follow us—you're good at that."

"We'll be right behind you," Clarissa said icily. She took Omar's arm and turned back toward the Trailblazer.

Julian watched them go and then gazed at Claire curiously. "The demolition—?"

"Stopped for now," she said. She paused uncomfortably, struggling with her conscience. "Clarissa merely had to agree to be engaged—" She cleared her throat. "To Adam."

He gave her a look of amazement. "You mean, she's betrothed?"

Claire nodded. He turned to look ahead of them. She started up the engine, wondering if he thought her awful for making such an arrangement for Clarissa. Adam would no doubt be furious when the lady failed to honor it. But as the Capri eased onto the road, the sound of laughter from the front passenger seat trailed into the atmosphere.

————————⚜————————

As they drove toward the credit union that held the safety deposit box, Claire said, "I hope there's a deed in the box. I hate the thought of the cottage being razed."

He gazed at her. She felt his eyes even though she kept hers on the road. "You wish to keep the cottage standing," he said softly, "to hold on to this life."

"No!" Claire cried. "I long to go back with you."

"But there will always be a part of you here," he insisted, still in that soft tone. "Unless the cottage is destroyed—or the shawls."

She looked at him in consternation. "That's not it. I wasn't thinking of that, really I wasn't."

He looked at her thoughtfully, and they drove on in silence. Claire searched her heart, but all she wanted was to marry him. She said, "There may always be a part of me here. Just as there is always a part of us that remains a child. I lived here. I found you by living here. I can't erase that."

"Nor would I ask you to," he said.

She glanced over and saw a look of affection in his eyes that made her tingle with pleasure. Soon, soon, they would get the tallit and return to the past and be married! It was all turning out too wonderful for words! As long as Clarissa kept her side of the bargain. The only thing Claire would linger in the present for, was to give Julian another chance at the wheel. He adored driving; how could she deny him a last opportunity?

When they pulled into the parking lot at the credit union, the black Trailblazer pulled in to their left. Claire looked over and found that awful man with Clarissa gazing intently at her. He certainly didn't have the face of a nice person, she thought with a shudder. Perhaps she'd saved Clarissa from him by promising her hand to Adam! Clarissa was speaking earnestly to him, even as he watched her and Julian. Claire wondered what story she'd given him, and how much he knew—or didn't know.

The four of them walked into the building. A clerk asked to see the key before leading them to a room lined with steel drawers—the boxes. He unlocked Claire's box and left it for them to inspect.

Beneath Claire's portfolio of documents, she discovered the piece of the diamond and sapphire set, a beautiful brooch, that she'd left behind. Clarissa snatched for it—and was stopped from taking it only by Julian's quick hand.

"The documents are yours," he said. "But that's all."

"But you don't know if you can take it with you!" she cried, derisively.

"Where are they going?" Omar asked, curiously. "Where can't they take jewelry?"

Clarissa gave him a guarded look. "I only meant, they shouldn't take it. Travellers are notoriously held up by highwaymen."

"Highwaymen?" Omar looked at her, thinking hard. "What planet were you raised on? I sometimes get the feeling you're from another *century*."

Clarissa tossed her head. "That's because...because...I'm an author. I do a lot of research." She looked at Julian. "It's safer to leave it here in the box," she said, barely hiding a smirk. Claire had to hand it to Clarissa. She was moving into her new identity seamlessly. But she did not return the brooch to the box.

She pulled out the old love letters and other papers. She hadn't been able to read them or look through all the papers the last time she came. They went through one after another, finding stock certificates, a marriage certificate, and some old photos. One envelope held German and Italian currency, probably from World War II. Finally only one folded sheet of aged paper remained. The ink was bleeding through. Claire carefully unfolded it. The deed!

"The deed, indeed," quipped Julian.

Claire turned a smile up to him. "I knew it! Somehow I knew it!" She handed it to Clarissa. "Why should the Winthrops get the property when it really did belong to my—um, your grandparents?"

Omar's eyes narrowed.

Clarissa took the paper and then held out her hand. "And now, the rest of my documents, if you please."

"If you please," repeated Omar, shaking his head. "You know, there's only one other person I've met who speaks as strangely as you." He pointed at Julian. "Him."

Clarissa said, "Not now, Omar." She turned back to Claire. "Well?"

"The shawl," said Julian. "It belongs to Claire."

"Claire?" Omar's head went back. "Her name's Claire? Wait a minute." He looked at Clarissa. "I thought Claire was your pen name."

"It is," Clarissa said.

Omar's jaw hardened. "All right. What's going on here?" he asked. "What's really going on?" The clerk came back to the room.

"All finished here?" he asked. "I need to lock up."

The foursome hesitated. But Claire grabbed all the papers, shoved them into the leather portfolio, and headed out. "Yes, we're done, thank you."

Outside, Clarissa dug in her purse. "Here is your shawl. Give me your documents."

Omar said, beneath his breath, "I thought they were your documents."

She held out the shawl. Claire took it, while handing her the portfolio. Clarissa started rifling through it. "That license is here? To drive the, er, car?"

Omar shook his head with silent anger. Clarissa must think him a fool if she expected him to buy all this at face value.

Claire said, "You have everything else. I still need the license for...a little while longer."

Clarissa's lips compressed. She would have snatched back the shawl but it was out of sight, tucked already in one of Julian's pockets. "What could you possibly need it for?" she asked with disbelief.

Claire looked at Julian. Perhaps Clarissa was right. Perhaps she didn't need it. They had both pieces of the shawl. They could return to 1816 at will. She took a wallet out of her purse, hesitated, then put it back and gave the whole thing to Clarissa. She felt there was something wrong about doing so—but a deal was a deal.

Clarissa took it and turned on her heel. She motioned to Omar who immediately kept stride with her, but she stopped and looked back at Claire and Julian. "Give my regards to Margaret," she said. Turning back, though no one but Omar heard her, she added, "Even though she is a lack wit."

Omar nodded as if he finally understood something.

It is madness for sheep to talk peace with a wolf.
Thomas Fuller

CHAPTER 64

When they were back in the Trailblazer, Omar sat staring out the windshield, but didn't start up the engine. Clarissa was going through the fascinating assortment of documents. A college degree! Amazing.

Meanwhile, Omar turned to her with new eyes, a knowing, wizened look. She glanced at him and shut the portfolio, putting it between the console and her seat.

"I know you have questions," she said.

"You better believe I have questions!" His eyes blazed at her. Beginning with this one. "Who are you, and where are you from?"

Clarissa paled. She licked her lips. "Can we not return to your apartment and talk there?" She winced at her own words. Though she still had an American accent, her speech was more and more betraying her Regency roots.

"Can we not?" he repeated, his brows raised. He paused, staring at her. "Where are you from?"

"I'm from England," she said. "Is it a crime to be British?"

"You don't sound British."

"I've worked hard not to," she lied. "Anyway, what difference does it make?"

Omar watched while the clerk who had been in the credit union went out to his car, got in, and drove off. It was lunchtime. The Capri was slowly circling the parking lot for some reason, but he ignored it. He looked back at Clarissa. "Here's the difference it makes," he said. He leaned over so that he was too close, his face in hers. "Nobody makes a fool out of me. If you were a man…" he said.

Omar's mean face had become almost invisible to Clarissa as he'd been more gallant than expected, even kind. She'd grown fond of him. But now the meanness of his features seemed to encapsulate the real Omar. This Omar. She'd not seen it before.

He moved away but kept a wary eye on her. "I think you ought to get out of this truck. We're done."

Alarmed, Clarissa looked around, then back at him. "Why?"

"Because you haven't leveled with me." He shook his head. "I wanted it to work out with you, sweetheart," he said. "I liked you. But you haven't once leveled with me."

Clarissa stared at him. She didn't want to lose him. "What is it you want me to tell you?"

He took a breath. "I want the whole story. Who you are, who those people are to you, and what you've all got to do with each other. I want to know why you're taking over Claire's identity."

Clarissa felt a stab of alarm. Omar was smarter than she'd thought.

"And I want to know what the fuss is about a shawl—a torn shawl, a piece of junk."

Clarissa took a deep breath and turned in her seat to face him. "Very well. If I tell you, will you still be done with me?"

He reached over and took her hand. "No. I don't want to be done with you." He released her hand and sat back. "Let's have it. From the beginning."

You're playing with Pandora's box. Sometimes it's better not to open it.
Sometimes, it's better not to know.
Tatiana de Rosnay

CHAPTER 65

Julian sat behind the wheel of the Capri, carefully turning it to circle the perimeter of the parking lot. He turned to Claire. "We've circled four times. I think I may safely take us elsewhere."

"Not yet," Claire said, with an indulgent smile. "People generally practice for days or weeks before getting proficient with a car."

"But wouldn't you prefer to be away from them?" He motioned with his head at the Trailblazer, which hadn't moved.

Claire shrugged. "Who cares about them?"

He looked over at her wistfully. "You realize, I must try this on a road," he said, inching towards the lot's exit. "I need to pick up speed," he said.

"You could be arrested for driving without a license," she said, smiling. But she had to admit that already Julian was turning smoothly, and had only moved in small starts during the first lap of the lot. He was amazingly adept for a newbie.

"They'll have to arrest me in 1816," he replied. "For the moment they try, we shall take our shawls and vanish."

"Once more around the lot," Claire said. "Then we can try a small spin on the road. But remember to stay on the right side!" She gazed at her handsome companion and felt amazingly at peace. How wonderful to know that with both pieces of the shawl they could return together and soon start their lives as man and wife!

He came to a stop and then went into reverse. To Claire's questioning look, he said, "I had to try that. Getting a horse to move backward is much trickier, you know. This thing"—he nodded at the wheel—"turns on a shilling!" Claire suppressed a smile. If only they could let him drive a really smooth car! But knowing Julian, that sublime experience would make him never want to go home.

"One last time," she announced, as they came around the lot yet again. He gave her a patient, amused look, but did as she said.

Omar stared at Clarissa as if dumbstruck. He sat forward, his eyes narrowed. "Are you telling me—that shawl—that it really brought you here, from 1816?"

She nodded. "It's the truth."

He could tell she wasn't lying. Everything about her told him she wasn't. Her mannerisms, her speech—even her naïveté in the bedroom. He stared out the windshield. Across the parking lot, the Capri went by again, moving faster now. Suddenly, it seeped across his brain that the shawl—the unbelievable shawl, an item that would be worth millions, maybe billions—was right there in that car. People would pay big bucks to take a trip to the past. He came to attention as the Capri suddenly veered toward the lot's exit.

He sat up and started the engine, hurriedly finding the buckle with his left hand. "Get buckled," he ordered. Clarissa did so, wearing a look of alarm. Omar took off in pursuit of the Capri.

"What are we doing?" Clarissa asked.

Omar didn't turn his head. Keeping his eyes on the silver car ahead, he said, "We're getting that shawl back."

Where wolf's ears are, wolf's teeth are near
Volsunga Songa (Viking)

CHAPTER 66

Julian slid the car onto the road, centered it in the lane, and stifled a sense of glee. Claire swallowed, wondering whether it was wise to let him drive. He seemed so proficient in the parking lot—but that was with no traffic or obstacles to speak of. So far, he was keeping to the lane well. He picked up speed.

"Don't forget to use the rearview mirror," Claire said. "You have to learn to take quick peeks while you still pay attention to what's ahead of you."

He flicked his eyes at the mirror. His brows furrowed and he stepped on the gas.

"Whoa," Claire said. "You're doing fifty-five. That's fast enough for this road. This isn't a highway."

"We have a tailgater," he said, almost as if he enjoyed the fact.

Claire looked in her side mirror and her eyes widened at the sight of the Trailblazer. "You'd think, now that we made a mutually agreeable transaction, that she'd at least be polite. Why would she still want to harass us?"

Julian shook his head. "I haven't a notion." He came to attention as the road widened, and signs indicated they would soon have opportunity to take Route 1—Maine Turnpike, either north or south. As they approached the north entrance ramp, Julian continued straight ahead. But just as they would have passed it, he veered suddenly onto it, making Claire hold to her seat. To her consternation, the truck swerved to take the ramp after them, even though they had to cross a section of unplowed snow, jostling and bumping, to do it!

"Well, he's obviously got four-wheel drive," Claire said.

Julian glanced her way. "Do we not have four-wheel drive? Are we not in a car with four wheels?"

She was about to explain when, watching the Trailblazer's progress, the words froze on her tongue. That driver was crazy—the black truck was gaining on them with wicked speed, coming on as though it had the road to itself.

"Change lanes!" she cried.

He glanced in his side mirror and moved them smoothly across the turnpike to the left lane. But he said calmly, "Don't worry"—even as the black truck moved right behind them and continued to approach. When it was only inches away, he hit the gas and the car sprinted ahead. But the truck quickly matched speed. It seemed they were trying to nip their heels—while doing 75.

"They're crazy!" Claire cried. "I can't believe a sane man would do this for her." Clarissa certainly had an iron grip on that driver, she thought, to make him behave so dangerously. What was wrong with that woman? And then an awful thought struck Claire. This was the day, in 1816, when Julian would have died in a coaching accident! *This was the day.* And now, though he was on a different road, driving a car and not a coach, Clarissa was again on his heels—just like in the past! Claire hadn't saved him from anything! With sickening clarity, it dawned on her that Julian was still going to die—and her along with him!

Why had she let him get behind the wheel on *this* day? Why hadn't she realized the danger? Just then the Trailblazer bumped them from behind, sending Claire and Julian jerking forward. Julian's foot never wavered from the gas pedal, and he pressed it now.

"If he sets off our airbags, we'll crash," Claire warned.

Julian glanced in the rearview and his lips compressed. "Let's see how fast this can go," he murmured. But Claire cried, "It's too dangerous!" With alarm, she added, "You're a new driver, Julian!"

He turned toward her for a split second and then resumed watching the road. "On the contrary, I've been handling equipages since I was twelve. My father's groom was indulgent toward me."

"That—that was nothing like this! You're new at this. Please—"

She was surprised to see a small smile on the handsome face. "Dearest, you must know—really, you must realize—I've told you before. I was *born* for speed."

He had accelerated to 90mph. He was handling the car beautifully, but it did nothing to calm Claire's fears. And the truck was still on their tail. "You said once you would never drive at top speed if I was with you, for it would endanger me." She paused, glancing at the beautiful, serene landscape whizzing by. "We are in a great deal of danger at these speeds."

"I have no wish to endanger you," he said softly. "The thing is, I feel as though I've been issued a challenge." He paused. "A gentleman never turns down a challenge. 'Tis a matter of honour."

"And please recall where that got you two hundred years ago on this very day."

He glanced over. He took a breath.

"We need to get off the turnpike," Claire said. "Start changing lanes, please." Suddenly Omar swerved to the right and now came abreast of them.

"He's boxing us in," Claire said. "Slow down and move to the right; we'll get behind him." But she took a searching look at the occupants of the truck, now so close to them. To her shock, Clarissa's face was distraught, and she met Claire's eyes with an apologetic look. Her driver, however, glanced at her, and she saw something entirely different. He looked mean as before, but there was more in those dark eyes. They were lit with a fire of some sort. He meant business. Whatever was making him drive recklessly, it was no accident. No accident, *yet!*

The Trailblazer suddenly edged into their lane. She cried, "Watch out!"

Julian moved into the left shoulder, then took his foot off the gas and hit the brake, letting the Trailblazer dart ahead into their lane. He quickly moved across the road to the right, crossing two lanes, and slowed even more, for now the truck had also slowed down.

"Pull over!" Claire cried. "Let them keep going!"

Just as she spoke, a police cruiser came along. Neither they nor the truck were speeding now. "If only he'd seen their last move! He's trying to cause a crash!" Claire cried. They had slowed to forty miles per hour now, as the Trailblazer kept decreasing speed. The police car was already well past them.

Her heart pounded in her ears as she reached for her cell phone. Why hadn't she thought to call the police? She'd report the truck! But no sooner than she grabbed her phone and brandished it, than the Trailblazer suddenly came at them from the left—the vehicles were again side by side. Omar swerved in their direction—he wanted to cause a crash! The cell phone flew out of Claire's hand. Julian hit the gas and darted ahead.

"Catch up to the police!" Claire cried.

With the Trailblazer at their rear, they sped forward. Claire felt sick.

Do you ever wonder why things have to turn out the way they do?
Nicholas Sparks

CHAPTER 67

As the Trailblazer careened toward the smaller Capri, Clarissa clutched Omar's arm. "Omar—"

"What?" He didn't turn his head.

"We ought to leave them be." Her face was a picture of sad thought. "They fell in love," she said, almost to herself as much as him. As she said the words, their truth—that St. John had fallen in love with Miss Channing—was suddenly quite real to her. She'd never given it a thought before that St. John might truly care for this woman. She'd been single-minded. She'd been determined. She couldn't understand why he hadn't cared for her, Clarissa. So many other men were interested.

As they came up to the rear of the Capri, she said again, "They fell in love!"

Omar scowled. "Who cares? They can love each other all they want. After I get a piece of that shawl."

"They need both pieces," Clarissa returned. Her eyes widened and then closed in horrified anticipation of the impact as the truck spurted forward and bumped the Capri. She gulped and clung to her seat.

"I don't care what they need," Omar said. "Do you realize what one piece of that shawl is worth? We could cut it up and sell lots of pieces. We could be the richest people in the world! No one's ever been able to time travel before!"

"Yes, they have," Clarissa said, thinking of her great aunt Lady Ashworth. "You just didn't know it."

"Me and the rest of the world," he said. His eyes narrowed in concentration. "This Julian knows how to handle a car." He paused and glanced her way. "But I've got more engine power. Sooner or later, I'm gonna make them stop."

"Just follow them! You needn't threaten them on the road like this."

He frowned. "You think they're gonna give up that shawl just for the asking? Not! I have to waylay them and take it."

Clarissa started blinking hard. To her surprise, tears filled her eyes. She couldn't remember the last time she'd actually shed tears! But she was overcome with a sadness that seemed almost unaccountable. Except that she had just secured a lovely future which Omar's driving was threatening to destroy. And he might mean to harm St. John and Miss Channing. That had never been her plan. She'd done risky things concerning Julian, but never considered there was any real danger in them. This was different. This high-speed chase was terrifying, and could only end, she was sure, in their demise.

Finally she saw that she'd been remorseless in her pursuit of St. John for too, too long. Had she given it up sooner, this hair-raising chase wouldn't be happening.

The truck came alongside the Capri. Clarissa met Claire's eyes and looked apologetically at her. She gasped as Omar swerved at the car, but the Capri suddenly fell back. Instead of ramming them, the truck took the left lane. The car, behind them now, crossed the turnpike.

Omar swore, and let up on the gas. Clarissa turned in her seat to watch the Capri, which had continued to slow, and was falling farther behind. Omar hit the brake, keeping his eyes in the rearview. Clarissa tried another tactic.

"If you cut that shawl again, it might not work," she said. And then she remembered what Claire told her, and added, "It won't work at all if anything happens to the cottage."

Omar was already scowling, but his frown deepened. "What's the cottage got to do with it?"

"Claire told me they only work together. The cottage and the shawl. And the Winthrops are razing it today!"

He grimaced, dug in his pocket with one hand while keeping an eye on the Capri in the mirror, and then tossed his cell phone at her.

"Call Adam. We've got the deed! He's gotta call off the wrecking crew."

Clarissa looked blankly at the metallic item in her hand.

"Call him!" Omar barked. "If he gives you grief, tell him we'll sue if they touch a board of that place."

"I don't know how," she said, brandishing the cell phone in the air.

Omar's lips compressed. "You don't know how to use— Oh, you *don't* know how," he realized. "Of course not. You're from the past," he said, as if reminding himself.

"Look, tap it. I'll tell you what to enter."

Clarissa tapped it, but said, "Enter? How does something enter this?" Before he could answer, his attention veered to the Capri, which had found a shoulder and pulled to the side of the road. Omar scanned the road behind him and saw the turnpike was empty for at least half a mile, maybe more.

"Hold on," he said. He put the truck into reverse and turned to watch the road behind him, hitting the gas hard. The truck was swerving as he raced toward the car, but he didn't care. He'd straighten up when he got close. And ram into them.

"Omar!" Clarissa cried. "Do you know what you're doing?"

"I certainly do," he said. "I'm becoming a billionaire."

It's always just when a fellow is feeling particularly braced with things
in general that Fate sneaks up behind him with the bit of lead piping.
P. G. Wodehouse

CHAPTER 68

Claire had hoped to switch places with Julian when they pulled
off the road, but when Omar started backing toward them—on a
turnpike!—she knew they'd have no time. "Give me the shawl! And
get yours!" she cried. "We can disappear right now and put an end to
this madness!"

Julian reached into his coat pocket and quickly passed Claire the
piece they'd gotten from Clarissa. "Where's yours?" she asked. But
the Trailblazer was careening backward toward them, swerving
crazily. Julian stiffened. "He's aiming for us," he said. He hit the gas,
taking off in a sharp left to avoid the truck. A semi was coming up
behind them and hit its deep bass horn as the Capri crossed the
turnpike, missing it by seconds.

As the blaring horn moved ahead, Claire cried, "That was close!"
Julian said, "My apologies. I saw the Trailblazer coming at us and
could only think to get out of its path."

"We need to use our shawls," Claire said, gritting her teeth. "The
cottage should be safe, but we can't stay here! That man with Clarissa
is after us for some reason."

"The driver? You mean, Clarissa."

"No. I saw her face. She's not behind this, I'm sure of it." She
paused. "Or perhaps she regrets our deal? I don't know, but she
looked sad. I've never seen her looking sad before."

"Nor have I," he said, glancing at the rearview. "Hold tight!"

Claire turned to look behind them just as the black truck rammed
them; but Julian had hit the gas—the vehicles barely touched. She
swayed forward and back, clutching the seat.

"Where's your half?" she asked. "This is insane! He's going to get us all killed!"

"In my trouser pocket."

Claire blinked. "I thought men's trousers of your day didn't have pockets!"

"I have my tailor sew them in."

"Can you get it?" The Trailblazer nudged them again, causing Julian to give another burst of speed to the Capri, putting them at 90 again. The turnpike had slowly been gaining traffic, most of which was large semis. A truck driver saw what happened and beeped at the Trailblazer. He waved and nodded at Claire. She hoped he would get on his CB and somehow raise the alarm about Clarissa's vehicle. The semi swerved suddenly—toward Omar's truck! Omar refused to slow down and let it in, but the truck driver, for some reason, had decided to interfere. It continued to veer toward the Trailblazer. Claire turned in her seat to watch.

Poor Clarissa had covered her face with her hands.

Julian found an opening, hit the gas—taking the car to 95—and darted in front of the semi. With the huge truck behind the Capri, Omar must have realized he couldn't squeeze in, for he came up on their left. A second semi pulled behind Omar, and the next few seconds passed like slow motion.

"Get the shawl!" Claire screamed. Julian's hand went for his pocket.

Omar swerved to get back behind the Capri, but the other truck was too close. The Trailblazer hit it and spun completely around, then got rammed by the other semi. Julian must have let up on the gas momentarily, for the Capri got rammed by the semi that Omar hit, for the driver, looking in horror at the Trailblazer's fate in his side mirror, wasn't watching ahead. Claire and Julian's car went flying and spinning, and careening ahead for a couple hundred feet until it came to a precipitate stop on the turnpike. More huge trucks hit their brakes behind the collision, but ended up ramming into each other. The turnpike was a huge mass of trucks and cars folded into each other, and with some that had tried to veer out of danger, now sitting at odd angles where they'd been forced to stop by the wreckage.

Claire's last thought before the car folded up like an accordion was that she ought to have been smarter, smart enough to never get on the road with Julian. Not on the day of his death. She tried to pull up the shawl at the last second—then the air bag hit her hard. And everything went black.

Where you go, I shall go; where you die, I shall die,
and there will I be buried."
Rosamund Hodge

CHAPTER 69

The Trailblazer landed on its side, on the median between the north and south tributaries of the turnpike, facing the wrong way. Omar was bleeding but he blinked and looked around. Clarissa didn't have a scratch that he could see, but she was out cold.

The Capri was farther down the turnpike—or at least he thought it was, for all he could see were huge semis, engines smoking, laying at odd angles across the road. He felt a pang of conscience for causing such a mess, but some things were worth making messes for. Time travel was one of them.

The windshield was shattered, and Omar could feel his face was bleeding. But he'd have to get over to that car and grab the shawls before those two had a chance to stop him. Except when he tried to move, he realized he was stuck. He couldn't feel his legs. Uh-oh.

He took another look ahead. Truck drivers were now standing outside their vehicles, assessing the situation. Two of them were on cell phones. There—ahead of the first truck—it was the Capri! Just as he spied it, it burst into flames. *No! No!* He fought to move himself out of the vehicle but couldn't budge. The door was smashed in.

Clarissa moaned and blinked. She came to, slowly sat up and got her bearings. Her body ached. Her head ached. Men appeared outside the car, opened her door and helped her get out on shaky legs. She seemed, miraculously, to be mostly unharmed.

"Hey!" Omar called. "You okay?"

She looked in at him, grimaced, and turned away. She never wanted to see Omar again. She'd never even speak to him again.

The wicked is snared in the work of his own hands.
Psalm9:16b

CHAPTER 70

Claire opened her eyes and saw St. John gazing at her lovingly. *She wasn't dead! Julian wasn't dead!* She gasped and sat up. They were in his house! On the settee in the library!

"We're here!" she cried. "We're really here and in one piece!"

He kissed her forehead.

She threw herself into his arms, blinking back tears of relief. "I thought I'd lost you! I thought we were both done for!" She moved apart from him. "You realize it's the same day, the day that you—that you—might have—"

"Shhh," he said. "I know. But I'm here."

"But the shawl was in your pocket," she said. "How did you get it to your chest?"

"I managed to get it in hand, that's all I know. And you had yours, and here we are." He drew her upon his lap. She fell against him again as they both took in the enormity of their close call, and how they had managed to escape the spectre of death. Claire's heart still pounded at the image of the semi ahead of them as they went careening toward it—thanks to Clarissa's driver, who'd apparently gone bonkers! She snuggled her face into Julian's chest gratefully.

"Thank God that's over!" she murmured. "No more worries about Clarissa chasing you on the road!"

To show his agreement, he lifted her face and kissed her. Then he said, "We'll send for Lady Ashworth, and she'll come to collect you. Tomorrow, the day after I might have—you know—we'll leave for Gretna." He gave her a searching look. "Unless you prefer to wait and have a traditional ceremony? I comprehend these things may matter to a bride."

Claire gazed up into the handsome face she loved so well. The blue-grey beautiful eyes were intently upon her. She circled his neck tighter with her arms and leaned up so their faces almost touched. "Prefer to wait? Mr. St. John, I assure you." She smiled impishly. "I was born for speed." She kissed him with her whole heart.

EPILOGUE

A year later

Officer Jones and his partner, the policemen watching cars whiz past from a cruiser on Maine Turnpike, came to attention when their radar detector beeped. Jones started the engine as a green Jaguar darted past in the left lane. This would be a reckless endangerment ticket—good income for the township.

He switched on the siren, setting off the lights simultaneously. It was early for a speeder, and fortunately the road was mostly empty. He crossed the highway.

Hearing a siren, Claire glanced at her side-view mirror and saw the lights of the oncoming cruiser. She took a breath. "You'd better slow down and pull over."

Julian glanced into the rear-view and sighed. "Already? We've hardly been out."

"We've been out fifty minutes," she said with a glance at the dashboard. "We've gone almost a hundred miles."

He raised a brow. "One of these days I won't slow. I'll outrun them."

"You'll do no such thing," Claire said. "It's too dangerous."

Julian crossed the highway and came to a stop at a shoulder. The police cruiser pulled up behind them.

He turned to her. "If I had ID I'd take the ticket and be done with it."

"I doubt it. They'd confiscate your license at these speeds—if you had one," Claire grinned. Looking in the rearview she said, "Here he comes. Are you ready for this?"

He turned and kissed her forehead. "Clarissa won't like it."

"No, but she'll get the car back after they impound it. She always does."

He nodded. "It helps having a world-famous author beholden to one, does it not?" He watched as Claire put a brand new shiny silver guinea under the floor mat.

"One who adores cashing in perfect, antique coins for ready money," Claire agreed.

"Perhaps next time we should leave her 50 pounds sterling. She'll get a fortune for it on today's market."

Claire smiled. "Whatever you like; though if you would stay nearer the speed limit, we wouldn't have to go through this again. And neither would she."

"Keep nearer the speed limit?" He gave a roguish grin. "My dear Mrs. St. John—surely you know by now—I was *born* for speed."

———⚓———

After checking the car's plates in the database, Officer Jones was about to leave the car when his partner said, "Let's just keep going. Forget this one."

Jones said, "Forget it? Why? We got him clocked at 100."

His partner, a black, middle-aged paunchy man named Curtis, shook his head. "I've stopped this car twice before. I got the license plate memorized. Every time I get to the window, there's no one inside."

Jones raised a brow and looked ahead at the vehicle. "There's two in there, now."

Curtis nodded. "Yup. They won't be there when you reach the window."

Jones stared at Curtis. "Come with me. Don't let 'em run."

Curtis shook his head. "They don't run. They vanish."

Jones stared at Curtis, who raised his hands and said, "I know, I know it sounds crazy. I'm telling you, man, they disappear! I looked into this car. Some big wig writer by name of Clarissa Winthrop owns it. Maybe she's a magician, too, I don't know. But the car is on record for being impounded at least five times for being parked illegally like this on the side of a highway. But not a single speeding ticket's been issued."

Jones was growing annoyed. "Look, there could be lots of explanations for that. I don't care about the owner or the history of the car, okay? I can see two people in there—" he stopped and peered ahead to double check—"and I'm gonna give 'em a citation."

Curtis folded his arms across his chest. "You do that." He leveled his gaze on the shadowy forms of the two figures in the Jaguar.

Jones gave his partner a strange look, got out of the cruiser, tightened his belt and approached the car. Curtis was usually level-headed, so he didn't know what to make of this. Looking ahead, he saw the two figures in the front seats and relaxed. If Curtis was right and somehow they'd escaped the scene in the past, they wouldn't get away this time; not on his watch. He'd give the driver an earful about endangering their lives, not to mention innocent motorists, and issue the ticket.

At the door to the vehicle, he squinted and blinked. Wait a minute! He'd seen two people only seconds ago! He tried the door, and finding it unlocked, threw it open, and searched the front and back. Empty! He looked around the car, at the highway, and saw no one. Feeling foolish, he nevertheless looked under the car. Nothing. He glanced at the trunk and opened it. Empty. He scratched his head. It was impossible—but the driver and passenger had vanished!

Curtis was chuckling when he climbed back into the cruiser.

"I told you, man. I told you," he said. "Don't write it up. We'll get it towed; that's all we can do."

The mystery of how the driver kept escaping the law remained a mystery.

And probably, to this day, it still is.

Julian and Claire were back in the library of their townhouse, on the settee from which they'd shared their first kiss. It seemed like ages ago.

"You realize I'm ruined for carriage racing?" he asked, as he nuzzled her face with his nose.

"I do," she said smiling. She kissed him and wrapped her arms about his neck. "Good thing, too, for now you must die of old age; it's what your obituary says." Clarissa had told them this, to Claire's great relief. It was the only reason she agreed to visit the future with him on occasion so Julian could get in some recreational driving. Happily, Grandmamma's claim that the return path had dried up for her turned out to be not quite true. What had really happened was that the tallit had simply disappeared on her once she married the marquess. Fortunately for Claire, it had returned to the cottage for her to find.

But the two halves of the shawl hadn't disappeared on Claire. She'd even stitched the edges of them nicely, painstakingly copying the embroidery so they no longer looked torn and ragged, but complete and pretty.

Trips to the future were such fun. It was somehow comforting that the world she'd grown up in was still there, even as she and Julian continued to live in the past. And Clarissa was so amiable now! Marrying Adam seemed to transform her. She had moved into her new career with nary a bump, did book signings all over the world, and continued to publish Regency romances which Claire edited for her, to great success.

There was a story going around, started by the wheelchair bound Omar Rashid, that she was a time-traveller come from the past.

Of course, he was laughed to scorn.

Other Books by
LINORE ROSE BURKARD

Before the Season Ends

Inspirational Regency Romance sparkling with heartwarming humor in the vein of Georgette Heyer.

The House in Grosvenor Square

*Mystery, perils and romance beset Miss Ariana Forsythe, our lovable heroine from **Before the Season Ends** in this award-winning sequel!*

The Country House Courtship

What are wealthy sisters for, if not to help younger sisters marry well? Beatrice Forsythe is ready for a romance of her own!